All the Places I'v

By Colette

Also by Colette Coen:

Five a Day

The Chocolate Refuge

Dedication

To Gerry, Tony, Helen and Liam with much love

All the Places I've Ever Been

1985

April: Glasgow Apollo

No one waited for Maggie. The school bell rang at the end of the day and kids packed their bags and formed groups to make their slow way home. They knew Maggie wouldn't be coming to hang about the streets or cadge fags off old drunks. They knew she wasn't interested in hearing about their latest crushes, and they had already given her their requests for next week's autographs, so no one waited. Maggie put her school books in strict order — tonight, tomorrow, next week. Then she checked the bag's inner pocket, as she had started to do since her sixteenth birthday, to see the blue and gold, an identity you could always prove.

Miss Gillespie stepped in front of her. 'Did you get a chance to look at the prospectuses, Maggie?' she asked.

'I'm sorry, Miss, I really can't hang about.'

'You need to consider your options. It's not too early to start making decisions, you know.' The teacher took off her glasses, folded them carefully and lay them on Maggie's desk ready for a big conversation, but Maggie just gave a half smile, put on her jacket and lifted her bag.

'Yes, Miss — I'll think about it,' Maggie said, as she started to walk towards the door. It made sense to spend time on her, she was clever, she got that, but Miss Gillespie really was nuts if she thought for a minute that Maggie was heading for college. *'There are grants, you know,'* she had said in a guidance lesson and they all laughed. '*Uni, get real.*' But the thought had lingered with Maggie, and it made her sad to think how little Miss Gillespie really knew.

She went out the gates, ignored the older boys hanging about and started her walk into town for her job. Since she had no brothers or sisters, or cousins on the corner to look out for her, she had devised a strategy early on. She waved at the right people as she went by their closes, said hello or nodded with respect. She never forgot a name; asked after relatives; did the odd message when she had time. Old Isa chapped on her window as Maggie passed by. Some days she would pull open the window and pass out 50p and a shopping list written on scraps of envelopes, but on other days she'd just give Maggie a lopsided smile. She kept herself just visible enough for people to remember her; just anonymous enough to be left alone.

Firecrackers landed in the gutter next to her and though she flinched she only whispered 'wee buggers' as the boys ran on, screeching and chucking more mini-bombs into the road.

The cold dark evenings of winter had gone but the Southern Necropolis' high black wall meant that little warmth reached the pavement. She hated passing the gates the most, peeking in as she did at the elaborate headstones from another era, and checking out if any glue sniffers or alkies were close enough to be a nuisance. Caledonia Road — the corner pubs that once nestled among tenements stood exposed on derelict land. She didn't ever see anyone enter or leave, but the pubs' continued existence suggested constant trade. As she passed The Citizens and the new Mosque, her teacher's words reverberated in her brain. Was it possible that someone like her could go to uni? But as she crossed the swollen river and came into the town she knew that the people were in the shops, not watching plays or praying. And shops meant money, and money meant work – she made up her mind to talk to Tam.

To begin with she had just helped her mum with the cleaning and setting up at the Apollo, but from fourteen she was allowed to sell tickets, and as long as she hid if the licensing board appeared, she could work the bar too, pocketing tips to squirrel into her bank account, or buy some decent food.

She did her trigonometry homework in the circle while the band went through their sound check, then she filled the fridges behind the bar, and helped Tam with the beer delivery. She felt the thump, thump through the walls as she pulled pints for the sweaty hordes. And listened as the cheers gradually subsided and the place emptied while she wiped down the counters and swept the floors.

When she was finished she knocked on the open door of Tam's office. 'Have you seen ma mammy?' she asked. Tam threw a bundle of notes into the large gun-metal safe and locked it with a huge key before he swivelled round on his chair, pushed back from his columns of figures and shrugged.

'Think she left with the band, pet,' he said pulling a Capstan from the packet in his shirt pocket and lighting up. 'They're staying at the Albany if you want her. She said she'd get their autographs for you, mind.'

Maggie had forged enough signatures not to be impressed, but she said 'Thanks,' as Tam reached into a box below his desk and threw a bag of Tudor crisps over.

'Come on now Maggie, you know what Val's like.'

Yeah, she knew what she was like alright — ready to bugger off at the first chance and leave her to do all the work. She slumped against the doorframe, pulled open her crisps and let the prawn cocktail melt onto her tongue.

'Do you want me to go out with the posters tonight, Tam?' she asked.

'It's alright Maggie, it'll wait,' he said. 'You and Val can do it tomorrow.'

'She'll not do it tomorrow either — you know she hates fly posting.'

Tam shrugged, 'Well, I suppose it's not raining.'

Maggie finished her crisps and tipped the crumbs into her mouth. 'Where are they then?' she asked.

Tam pointed to over to the rolls in the corner, but pulled himself out of his chair and blocked her way before she got to them. 'Have you got your pepper with you?' She nodded. 'And your whistle?'

Maggie patted her pocket. 'Never leave the house without them.'

Tam stepped back, but she stopped, coiled her plait under her fisherman's hat and zipped her bomber jacket before she took the paste and the Style Council posters.

'See before I go, Tam,' she said as casually as she could even though her heart had decided to beat faster.

'Uh huh?'

'I was thinking about what I'll do when I leave the school in summer,' she paused and swallowed hard. 'Can I get more hours here, do you think?'

Tam lit a cigarette and took a long draw before he answered. 'A smart girl like you shouldnae be hanging around here,' he said, 'and besides, yur here when it's busy, that's enough.'

'Can you think about it? Maybe train me up for something?' But Tam lowered his eyes to his figures. 'I'll see you tomorrow then. Is it this lot back again?'

'Aye, at least we don't have to change the signs,' Tam said and he looked up and gave her a friendly wink, 'See you later pet.'

The lifts were broken again, so Maggie started the paced climb up the ten flights. Too fast at the start and she would have to stop for breath on *Seven*. Too slow and she might never make it. She watched her feet, noted what stairs had been washed; what ones only swept. The new folk on *One* just seemed to be emptying a bottle of

Domestos at the top and sloshing a bucket of water down the stairs, so they were streaky and reeked of bleach. Between *Two* and *Three* the feud was still going on about whose turn it was, and on *Four* someone had tried to scour out the CODY graffiti and more lurid suggestions that decorated the walls. The top of her legs began to ache. On *Five,* the wind jagged through the broken pane of reinforced glass on the stair-head window. She pulled her jacket tighter. She paused on *Eight*, looked out through the grime, to the lights across the river. *Tinsel Town in the Rain.* The song ran through her head, taking her thoughts far away. *Tinsel Town.* If only she could believe it. *Ten.*

She pushed the fire door slamming it outwards into the corridor. The flap to the chute was stuck again, letting the stench of rubbish back up. *Was she the only one who ever sorted it?* She used both hands and shoved it shut, the metallic bang preferable to the stink. Then her own mustard front door, the bell melted by a lighter, the Sellotape on their name, brittle and brown. She reached inside her jeans for the key, careful not to snag it and let herself in.

There were outsiders in the bread bin but the milk was turning, so she washed a plate, made herself a piece and jam, and forced it down with a glass of water.

She took her school uniform out of her bag and laid it over a chair to air for the morning. She ran a bath. Her hands were grazed, dried blood under her nails. She brushed and spat Colgate into the sink, watched as the ring of confidence dribbled down into the plughole. She stripped, checked the temperature with her toes and lowered herself into the bath. The Raddox crystals scratched like Vim, filling the room with noxious pine as they started their slow disintegration. The finger marks on her arms and thighs were still visible, so she scrubbed with the back brush until her whole body was red raw. Then she sat.

Normally she looked at the ever-changing damp patch on the ceiling to find shapes and images she could weave into a story. Normally she would shield her eyes from the avocado fern leaves on the fake tiles and imagine herself somewhere else. Normally she would top up the bath, stick her toe into the tap, and pull it out with a satisfying pop as the water gushed out.

Tonight she sat. The water went cold. The world outside the Venetian blinds turned off its lights and went to sleep.

When she got out of the bath she threw her clothes in. Watched as the blood and dirt seeped out from them and turned the water a muddy brown. Stood naked on the linoleum until she shook with cold, but the shaking subsided and she stared into the bath a little longer, rocking gently.

When she arrived at the Apollo the next afternoon, her mum was hoovering the engrained carpet in the foyer. Maggie knocked until Val lifted her head and came to unlock the door.

'You look pale, hen,' Val said, 'I hope there's not something hanging on you.'

Maggie shrugged. 'It was with all that battering at the door. I'm fine, but. What do you want me to do?'

Her mum pointed to a bucket at the bottom of the stairs. 'Will you wipe down that banister? You know I can't handle the gob that's on it.'

She changed out of her school clothes, lifted the bucket up to the landing, took the cloth out of the tepid water, wrung it slowly and started to clean. If she kept her eyes on the posters on the opposite wall she could close her mind and just about manage the banister without gagging. *Why could she not just say no?*

'You've not asked me about last night,' her mum said when she was back in range.

'What?' Maggie said.

Val laughed, 'You were away with the fairies there. I'm trying to tell you about last night.' Val must have picked up something in Maggie's expression, 'Aye, sorry I went off without telling you,' Maggie lifted one shoulder to acknowledge the apology as Val continued, 'but that Mac guy is seriously hot, and he really fancied me Maggie. Could've had younger lassies — but these guys like a bit of experience, you know what I mean.' Val did what she must have thought was a sexy dance, but it made Maggie cringe. Tam appeared from the office, applauded Val and called Maggie. As she walked over she tried to read in his face if he'd any phone calls, or if he'd want to know why she hadn't returned the paste bucket and brush.

‘Mon and help wi the merchandising pet,’ Tam said. ‘I don’t know where that new-start has got to. I might have known he’d bugger off, bloody workshy.’

Maggie let out a sigh she hadn’t realised she’d been holding all day. ‘Aye, sure.’ It was Maggie’s favourite job and not just because you could legitimately help yourself to a T-shirt. It also required a bit of thought; what items did you want close to hand; how could you make the display look nice; where should you put things so they were visible but wouldn’t be nicked? It was just what she needed instead of slopping out the Gents and having her mind free to wander. She pulled a small white T-shirt over her black polo neck. It had the band’s brain logo on the sleeve and the album cover for DirtyMind printed in red and black on the front. She helped herself to a badge too, and slipped a key ring into the pocket of her denims, even though it had no sharp edges. Then she got the trolley and moved the programmes to the usher points in the hall.

The new-start had left the place in a mess, so she kept herself busy rearranging the products, throwing out the packaging and stamping on the empty boxes he had left lying, which normally gave her more satisfaction. Around six, Tam appeared again. ‘Maggie pet, gonnae go and get some coke for the band. Git yourself a wee somehin too,’ he said as he handed her a fiver.

The drizzle of the last few days had finally gone and it was a bright sunny evening, so Maggie walked around the block a couple of times, conjugating her French verbs before she went into the chippie. She bought fish suppers for her mum and Tam, and chips and Irn Bru for herself, then paid for the coke out of Tam's fiver, making sure to get a receipt. She noticed bruises starting to form along her knuckles.

The light never got into the side lane, and there were always puddles of water and vomit to avoid, but tonight she noticed the doorways and the bin bags too. Places to hide. She looked both ways as she walked towards the stage door, and checked behind her before she let herself in.

She emptied the ashtray, shoved crisp packets into the metal bin and gave the stained coffee table in the dank staff room a wipe before she put the food down. Then she shouted down the stairs for her mum and Tam before she went along the corridor to the band's dressing room. It was her policy to bang on doors before entering, shouting out as she went, and keeping her eyes to the floor. She knocked.

'Yeah, come in.' The voice was deep, Australian.

'I've brought your ginger,' she said coming into the room with the blue plastic bag lifted slightly in front of her.

'I don't think I asked for ginger.' The Australian looked puzzled, and Maggie replied with a similar look.

'Tam said you wanted ginger. Here it is.' She took the glass bottle of cola out of the bag.

'You said *ginger*?'

'Aye, ginger.'

'Well Ginger, I'm Kyle.' He put out his hand and Maggie placed the bottle in it. He laughed, and while it didn't sound unkind it made her uneasy. He put the bottle down and held out his hand again.

'I'm Kyle.'

'You said.' She looked at his hand and realised with a flush that she was meant to shake it. She had never done that, except at mass with the school at the sign of peace bit, but she put her hand in his and he moved it.

Maggie looked at him; working her way down his tight trousers then up from his red-laced, black leather baseball boots to his studded belt and loose white shirt. Blonde surfer curls eased over his shoulders —*just the right side of Bon Jovi* — to a square jaw and the brightest blue eyes she had ever seen.

She usually snuck about the place without paying these guys much notice, without being noticed herself. She was rarely spoken to, and if she was it would be a command for water, a towel or a blow job. Even when the girls at school were begging for information, she could hardly remember who the band were, never mind judge '*if their eyes really are as sparkily as they looked on Top of the Pops*', or '*if they looked like they would be a good kisser'*.

She cocked her head to read the title of the book he had just put down *What They Don't Teach You at Harvard Business School.* It looked like he'd been writing notes and drawing diagrams in a foolscap pad too. *This guy was weird*, but his bright blue eyes *were* sparkly and his lips *were* moist.

'I'm,' she hesitated, as if she couldn't remember her name. Maggie was a girl who cleaned spit off banisters; who walked about the city late at night asking for trouble; who went to school and only had friends who wanted something.

'I'm Meg,' she said.

'Cool name. I like it.'

A voice shouted from the corridor. 'Maggie, your tea's getting cold.' Then Maggie's mum appeared in the doorway. 'Sorry,' Val said to Kyle, giving him the once-over, 'she's not meant to be in here.' She signalled for Maggie to leave, but smirked as she did.

'Don't,' Maggie mouthed.

'I didn't realise anyone wiz here,' Val said as she looked around. 'Is Mac about? I met him at the party last night.' She held Kyle's eyes with her last comment, and Maggie watched as they tried to get the measure of each other.

'Yeah, I remember. You met me too.' He replied with a flatness in his voice that Maggie hadn't notice earlier. 'The others aren't here yet. I came down early to run through a couple of songs, but if you guys are having a cuppa maybe I could join you?'

Despite a double wrapping of newspaper the food was fairly cold by the time they got along to the staff room, but Val shared her fish with Kyle and even persuaded Tam to give him a couple of chips.

'So what do I need to know about Glasgow?' Kyle asked.

Maggie had only ever heard her mum refer to the place as '*a pile of shite,'* so she was surprised when she came out with a sanitised, tourist board-approved spiel about the Salvador Dali and the Burrell. '*Glasgow's Miles Better*, you know. They even based

Mr Happy on Tam here.' Val laughed in her outrageous way and when Kyle caught Maggie's eye they joined in. Tam was certainly small, round and fairly yellow, but didn't look very happy.

'Whereabouts are you from?' Maggie asked when the laughter died down and Tam had decided he had better things to do than listen to their nonsense.

'Sydney,' Kyle said, and then in case they were stupid, added, 'Australia.'

'Right, like *Sons and Daughters?'* Val said, as she pulled a packet of cigarettes out of her pocket and offered one to Kyle.

He shook his head, 'I can't say I've really seen it,' he said.

'Aye, I find it a bit arsy myself,' Val lied. She was always nipping away to turn on the telly, 'but she likes it.'

Maggie rolled her eyes and Kyle crinkled his in a conspiratorial way, 'Meg looks to me like she'd prefer, what is it? *Brookside*? That's what they were all talking about in Manchester?'

'Liverpool,' Maggie corrected, but quickly wished she hadn't needed to be such a smart arse.

'Anyway girls,' Kyle said, standing up, 'I've got things to do, but how about I treat you to dinner tonight? The hotel has a nice carvery.'

Maggie and her mum exchanged a glance — they had been offered many things in their time, but never a carvery.

'Sounds perfect,' Val said as she brushed little bits of plastic chair off Kyle's trousers. 'Sorry, this place is falling apart.'

'God, Mum, did you have to grope him?' Maggie said as Kyle left.

'What? Are you jealous? He certainly is a looker. You should see the singer though. Some mover on the stage and off.'

'Aw, enough. Don't make me boak.'

By the time the concert had ended, and Maggie had packed away the unsold merchandise, her mum and MindSet had disappeared. Her stomach growled as she handed the boxes over the counter to the roadies.

'That reminds me,' one of them said, 'if you're Meg, Kyle said you've to go to the hotel. He left money for the taxi. Oh, and the cleaner said I'd to give you these.' He winked and held out a three-pack of Durex. 'If you can't find Kyle, I'm in 822.' The roadies looked at each other and laughed.

'Get your own bloody boxes,' she said, dropping a carton of T-shirts to the floor, an inch from his foot. She grabbed her bag and jacket from their hiding place and stormed out.

Tam stood out the back, minding the gear while he smoked a cigar. 'Do you think you could come in early tomorrow Maggie?' he asked as she started to leave. 'I need you in the box office.'

Here we go again, she thought, one of the pretty girls would have batted her eyelashes and given Tam some drivel about a dying auntie or a bunion that needed emergency surgery. She nearly kept walking but it was Friday night, and he owed her.

'Wages, Tam?'

‘Please?’ he said flicking his cigar into the night.

‘Come on Tam, I’m knackered.’ She felt it more now she had said it, the aches in her bones suddenly crying out as though they were riddled with arthritis. ‘Can I get my wages, please Tam?’

‘Your mammy’s taken them already pet. She said she’d gee you them.’

Maggie closed her eyes and took a deep breath, quelling an urge to stamp her foot and scream. ‘Shit, Tam, you know I’ll not be able to make the rent now.’

Tam shrugged, but he punched the roadie who suggested she might find a fiver in his trousers if she looked hard enough.

‘You do tomorrow then?’ he asked again ‘Promise I’ll give you the cash.’ He rubbed his knuckles and nodded for her.

Meg had only been in a taxi once before, for her granny’s funeral, and she wondered for a minute if it was worth it. But there was no cloud cover and the night made her edgy again, so when she saw a yellow light she hailed it. For a minute she considered just going home, but she knew there was no food there and Kyle was a distraction, one that had made her a bit tingly since she’d met him, so she gave the name of the hotel and held onto the grab handle. The taxi bumped and swerved its way through the town as the driver monologued over late night radio. Meg ignored him and looked out the window instead, at the shuttered shops and courting couples making their way to the bus stops.

'And now the news at midnight: A man is in a serious condition in Glasgow Royal Infirmary after being found badly beaten in the Cook Street area. It appears he suffered a sustained attack and police are appealing for witnesses, particularly a young man dressed in dark clothes who was thought to be fly-posting at the time.'

She said it to herself a couple of times until it seemed real *young man, young man,* then she paid the driver and got out of the taxi. *Not dead then.* In front of the entrance she let the night air prick at her skin. There were a few MindSet fans huddled together in the T-shirts she had sold them under expensive jackets. A guy wearing a get up from *Upstairs Downstairs* watched them closely. She had seen him clock her too as she got out of the taxi but as she walked towards him, he signalled the way in. Whatever it was, she didn't look like one of them.

The lobby was warm and bright, with staff and visitors milling about, and a gentle chatter in the background. Another uniformed man approached her, but she had been trained from a young age to set her chin against authority and summon up confidence she didn't feel.

'I'm meeting someone in the carvery,' she said using the word she had heard for the first time earlier.

He gave a forced bow. 'This way, Miss.' *Miss*, it never failed.

The restaurant was only half full, and she easily spotted Kyle's table among the lounge suits and shoulder pads. He broke off from his conversation and smiled as she approached. She recognised the dark tattooed guy as the guitarist and she had seen the two blonde women chatting backstage earlier, one as tall as the other was short. They hadn't looked at her then and gave no glimmer of recognition in their casual smiles now. The wee, dumpy one had a slightly pox-marked face beneath heavy make-up and wore the same black biker jacket as the guitarist. Her short peroxide hair was cut in an asymmetric style which she had the attitude to pull off. The tall, skinny one had razor sharp cheek bones; tousled sun-kissed locks straight out of a Timotei advert; a Bondi tan and wore a lime green vest-top and braces which emphasized the fact that she was almost as flat-chested as Meg.

'I'd given you up for lost. Your mum's here already,' Kyle said, despite there being no sign of Val. 'Well, she's, with Mac.' He used his eyes to point upwards, but Meg already knew where Val would be. 'We've started without you, I'm afraid,' Kyle said. 'Grab a plate and get some food.'

The carvery reminded her of the school dinner queue with its heating lamps and metal trays, but when the aroma hit and she looked at the array of meats, she realised the similarity ended there. The large silver platters which lined the counter, showed the remnants of a feast. Scrappy but succulent slices of beef, ham and chicken lay in some of them, while others shone with the kitchen porter's labour. She chose chicken legs and some thin slices of beef, with roast potatoes and what was left of the vegetables. The closest they ever got to cooking greens was a tin of mushy peas, so she nodded as the chef pointed to the carrots, garden peas and green beans, letting him empty his terrines onto her plate.

'Wow, you've certainly got an appetite for a slim one,' the peroxide blonde said with a nasally Australian accent. Meg blushed — she hated it when people commented on her appetite, as if they knew she was worried about when her next meal would be.

'I stole her chips earlier,' Kyle explained, patting her hand as though he could read her mind, 'so I had to make it up to her. Suzie, Zed,' he nodded introducing them, 'and Clare.' He squeezed Clare's knee, who looked straight at Meg and giggled, making sure Meg knew he was off-limits. *Of course he was*. 'And this,' Kyle said, as he stretched his arm out like a showman, 'is Meg.'

As he spoke a waiter came across with an extra seat, and Kyle and Zed scrapped their chairs along to make some space. Then the waiter waited. 'Jacket?' he said.

'You're alright,' Meg said as she shook her head, put her jacket over the back of her chair and sat down. She'd saved up for ages and wasn't going risk some cloakroom where her jacket would be mysteriously lost when she asked for it back.

'So how come you work at the Apollo, Meg?' Suzie asked as Meg began to eat. 'Should you not still be at school?'

'I'm older than I look,' she lied. 'And you know what it's like — you've got to muck in.'

‘Well good for you,’ Kyle said, ‘you’re doing the right thing, finding out about the business from the bottom up.’

Yeah, she thought, *that’s why I’m cleaning shit off walls, so that I can learn the business.* But she decided to go with it. ‘I like the way you’ve got your logo on everything,’ Meg said between mouthfuls of food. ‘It’s cool.’ She pulled at her T-shirt and continued, ‘but the quality could be a bit better — you’re asking £4 for these and they’re quite thin, they’ll not last.’

‘Sounds like us,’ Zed said laughing, but Kyle had been visibly taken aback by what she said. When they had met earlier Kyle’s smell had been polluted by a thousand stars, but now as he leaned towards her, she detected a crisp fragrance that didn’t claw in her throat like cheap aftershave. He fished a small notebook out of his back pocket, almost touching her in the process, wrote the word QUALITY, underlined it three times and said ‘Tell me more?’

Meg talked for a while, letting her nervousness at the surroundings fuel her conversation. She surprised herself at how much she’d noticed— bands with too many hangers on bleeding them dry; managers that wanted a cut of everything; mixing desks with the backing singers louder than the main mike. Then the talk moved on, and she listened as Zed and Kyle talked about the gig and sound quality.

‘That’s some shit-high stage you’ve got back there,’ Zed said, almost accusing her of building it herself. ‘My God, I had vertigo at one point. Everything went really swirly.’

‘That wasn’t the stage, Zed.’ Suzie said.

'It's best not to look down,' Meg said.

'So what are your plans for after it closes?' Kyle asked.

Meg put her fork down. 'What do you mean?'

'Todd, our manager, said it was closing soon, didn't he Zed?' Zed nodded, 'and we had to relish the experience 'cause we wouldn't get it again.'

'It's not closing,' Meg said.

Kyle nodded and frowned. 'Everyone's talking about it: *the legendary Glasgow Apollo and its thirteen foot stage going to the dogs.* You must know about it?'

Meg looked at her empty plate. 'I didn't…' Half-heard conversations started to come back to her, and make sense. 'I mean, I know the council have been in a few times and they've been talking about essential repairs and things, but Tam's never said anything about it closing.'

'Sorry to break it to you, Meg, but I suppose these things happen.' He wiped his mouth with his napkin. It certainly explained why Tam hadn't asked her to do the cuttings recently — he obviously wanted to keep her away from the papers. *Shit —both of them out of work.*

Clare dabbed the corners of her mouth and stood up. 'Are you coming to bed babe?' It sounded to Meg more like a command than a question and she was surprised when Kyle immediately signalled the waiter and signed for the food. She thought he had been enjoying himself, and it was early yet, not even midnight.

'Will you be able to get home okay?' Kyle asked as they walked out of the restaurant.

Meg looked towards the windows which the black night had turned into mirrors reflecting the comfort of this new world. 'I'll be fine,' she said, but she didn't argue when he pressed a twenty into her hand. Suzie and Zed both kissed her on the cheek and walked off entwined towards the lift. Clare smiled a goodbye and as Kyle brushed her cheek with his lips she had a thought. *To Hell with Tam and his shitty Apollo. To Hell with Val. To Hell with this city.*

'What time are you leaving in the morning?' she asked.

'We're meeting in the lobby at 10 a.m. Why?' Kyle asked. 'Are you coming?'

'Do you think I could? If I'm going to be out of a job then maybe I could cadge a lift down to London? I'll work my fare,' she said, forming a plan as she spoke.

Kyle put his hands on her shoulders and turned her around to read the tour dates on her back.

'We've got two weeks before London,' he said, 'but I'm sure there's room on the coach for a little one.'

Clare shook her head, her long hair rearranging itself to sit perfectly again. 'I don't think so Kyle,' she said. 'You can't keep doing this.'

But Meg ignored her and smiled, 'I'll see you in the morning then.'

Edinburgh Playhouse

'OK, strange little Scottish girl, what am I meant to do with you?' Todd asked once he had handed out the keys at the Old Waverley Hotel and set Mac up with his first interview of the day. 'Do you sing?'

Meg shrugged, *God, it was like being with one of those wanky careers advisors who just told all the girls to become nurses, even Sandra who passed out at the mention of blood. In the music business it was — why don't you become a backing singer?* 'I've not got much of a voice.'

'Who are you going to sleep with then?' he asked casually as he looked through his messages. 'I think Wayne is lonely.'

'What?' If Meg only knew one thing, it was that she wasn't going to repeat her mum's mistakes. But she couldn't waste the little money she had on a bus back to Glasgow.

'I'm only kidding mate, I'm not that cruel,' he slapped her back, and let out a roaring laugh that didn't suit his rather buttoned-up demeanour. 'Kyle says you're our new mascot, although I didn't know we had an old one.' He laughed again, and Meg answered with a smile. 'I'll need you to work, though. We can't have too many free-loaders.'

'Sure, of course. I'll do whatever,' Meg said, letting herself breathe again.

'Well, I'm not looking for an over-anxious puppy so we'll need to think of something else,' he said as he handed her a key. 'You could always find us somewhere to party after tonight's gig, and maybe provide translation services. That journo wants Mac in a skirt or some shit for a photograph. Sort that out.'

She sorted it out by telling the photographer that on no account would Mac be seen in tartan, citing the Bay City Rollers. The photographer understood, but Mac watched them and nodded in inappropriate places like he didn't understand English.

'Just put him on the couch, that's checked at least?'

'Can he hold a scarf?'

'For God's sake, he's not in Ally's tartan army.'

'Oh, alright.'

Meg turned to speak to Mac for the first time, 'Are you happy with that?'

'Sorry, Mate' Mac said, looking genuinely confused, 'but who are you?'

Meg raised her eyebrows to the photographer suggesting it was Mac and not Meg who had drifted into a parallel universe.

'Great,' Meg said 'I'll leave you to it then.'

She took the lift to her room on the third floor. It was the first time she had been in one that was carpeted and smelled of vanilla sponge rather than piss. She glanced at herself in the mirror, another first for a lift, and noticed the graze just under her eye and the slits in her lips where she had bitten too hard. She ran her fingers over them, cracked and peeling, pulled at a loose flake until it bled, whispered

You're Meg now, Maggie's gone, then turned back to the door and waited for it to open.

The corridor carpet was a similar loud pattern to the one at the Apollo but this one didn't have beer and puke stains adding to the golds and blues, and she couldn't see any threadbare bits.

She closed the room door behind her, dropped her haversack onto the floor and put the oversized key ring on top. The bed had a pale blue spread on it which was thrumbed and pulled, but beneath it were the whitest sheets she had even seen – a boil wash maybe. There wasn't a time when she hadn't shared a room with her mum, and although Val frequently spent the night elsewhere, her Charlie lingered. Finally, she had a room of her own, but it was unlike any room from her dreams. There seemed to be a disproportionate number of switches to the number of lights and too many lights for the size of the room. There was a phone, a TV, a desk, a strange strappy seat thing that wasn't strong enough to take her weight, a cupboard, and a spotless bathroom with clean white towels. She ran her hand along the desk — *dusted too* — and pulled back the net curtains to look out at tiered lawns. The place was bustling with people going about their business or casually stopping to point their cameras up to the castle or along at the huge stone buildings which punctuated the greenery. She breathed deeply, letting her eyes luxuriate in the scene. Then she pulled herself away and made a cup of tea using a tiny kettle and a teabag with a string attached. She took her tea and sat on the end of the bed, breathing slowly she tried to work out her next move.

The phone rang and brought her thoughts to an abrupt end. She recognised the blocked-nose tones of Suzie at once. 'We want to see the castle before the sound check. Will you take us?'

Meg agreed, but it was only as she put the phone down that she realised she was expected to be the tour guide. She'd never been in Edinburgh in her life, never been out of Glasgow in fact, but the castle loomed over their hotel, so it wouldn't be too difficult to figure out how to get there.

Suzie had said five minutes. *Was she allowed to use the phone in the room*? She wanted to phone her mum, make sure Val didn't do anything stupid. *What the hell.* She picked up the handset and dialled, remembering the 041. Nothing happened. She tried again — just a buzz. Then she noticed a list of numbers on the phone, 0 for the switchboard.

'Hello, could you put me through?' Meg gave the number but it rang out and when she gave the operator Tam's number at the Apollo it was engaged. *He was always leaving the phone off the hook.* Hopefully her mum had been back to the flat and found her note. She would just have to try again later.

By the time she got down to the reception, MindSet had gathered, conspicuous among the tourists and the Edinburgh ladies who lunch. She saw the concierge give Kyle a map as she walked towards them, and he was ready to lead off as soon as she caught up. Suzie took her by the arm, introduced her to Wayne, the bassist, who had sandy coloured hair and a sandy coloured face, and Mac.

'We've met before.' Meg said.

'In Glasgow?' Mac asked, screwing up his eyes as if he needed her to come into focus. 'Did we…?'

'That was ma mammy, sorry, my mum.' Val loved it when people mistook them, but Meg was less impressed to be confused for a 32 year old, 'this morning, with the photographer.'

'Right,' Mac said, clearly none the wiser.

The group crossed Princes Street, took in the black spikes of the Scott Monument and the open topped buses which lined the Waverley Bridge. Meg looked down to where she expected the river to be, but saw instead a railway station — *weird.* She practically had to run to keep up with their long strides, but they slowed as they began to wind their way up Cockburn Street, stopping at the shops, looking in the windows before going in to buy T-shirts and leather accessories. They turned on to the Royal Mile to be met with a babble of nationalities: Japanese with big video cameras chained to their arms; Italians in their diamond padded jackets; Americans, loud and profuse. Meg followed as the Australians wandered from quality purveyors of traditional tartans to souvenir shops. She touched the clothes they had on rails on the pavement but she stayed outside, reading the names of the dark alleys and staircases that stretched back down the hill they had just climbed — Anchor Close, Fleshmarket Close, Geddes Entry. At the International Newsagent Kyle went in to buy an Australian paper, but Meg's eyes focused on the *Glasgow Herald*:

MAN LEFT FOR DEAD

Meg felt someone at her side and snapped around.

'Here you go,' Kyle said placing a book in Meg's hand — *The Origins of the Burns Family and their place in history.* 'I think my tartan's a bit funkier than yours,' Kyle said, holding up a similar book with *Watt* instead of *Burns*.

'God, I didn't even know there was brown tartan, that's minging,' Meg said, looking enviously at Kyle's book with its red, yellow and green cover.

'At least you've got Robbie,' Kyle said as he started back into the shop, 'I'm just going to get a clan pin for my mum.'

This place felt so alien to Meg, with its over-the-top Scottishness and its well-dressed tourists, but Glasgow was still only forty miles away. Not far enough.

Eventually they made it up to the esplanade. The castle walls were thick and strong, guarded by knights and cannons, and if that failed a now-dry moat. But times had changed and for the price of an entrance ticket, all strangers were welcomed in.

Clare hung onto Kyle as she wobbled her way through the cobbled streets of the castle complex. *Imagine wearing stupid bloody shoes like that when you're going for a walk.* 'This castle is so old,' Clare said, glancing at a leaflet for her facts, 'It's older than Australia.'

The Australians marvelled at this, and Meg thought better than to question whether they were right. They took their time going in and out of the castle buildings —the armoury, the kitchens — then made their way to the ramparts. At one o'clock precisely, Clare and Suzie squealed as the gun went off while Meg tensed her body, half-expecting blood. Then Wayne handed Meg his disc camera and she lined up them up and took some snaps at Mons Meg, using Edinburgh as a backdrop. It really was a beautiful city, older, more monumental than Glasgow. After a few shots, she suggested that Suzie and Clare step out of the picture, 'Just with the band,' she said. Meg thought their look was a bit orchestrated, as if someone had decided how to keep all the fans happy: Zed, the dangerous one — black leather and tattoos; Mac wild, yet with an air of artiness about him; Kyle just drop-dead gorgeous; and Wayne, safe — for girls who would only fancy a blander version of themselves, his face almost totally flat, as though his nose couldn't be bothered to make the effort to form an angle.

'You can use it in your next programme,' Meg said when she finished the disc, 'MindSet at large.'

'MindSet? MindSet?' A couple of teenagers started to look around. Someone had said a magic word, and they became alert.

'Shut up Meg.' Suzie began to pull her along after MindSet who had immediately moved and began to try and merge into the crowd. 'Let's go, people have spotted us. You never say their names when we are out like this. Never.'

'I'm sorry.' *Shit, one day and I've blown it.*

Clare slowed down to let them catch up, but it wasn't to keep them company, it was to berate Meg as well. 'Idiot,' she said. 'We were having a nice day out and you've ruined it. Now they'll just want to go to the venue and I'll not get the cashmere Kyle promised me.'

'I'm really sorry,' Meg said again, but she realised that none of the guys seemed that bothered, in fact they had been stopped by a different group of girls on a school trip and were happily posing for photographs and pecking cheeks. The girls peeled off their blazers and asked for autographs on their white school blouses. Their teachers frowned when they pointed to their breasts and signalled for them to give the more modest canvas of their backs for signing. Then the teachers giggled at Mac's flirty comments and posed for photos too, letting him move their hair from over their eyes and adjust their bodies so that they were angled to perfection. Meg took one camera after another, winding them on and clicking before passing them back to their owners. The girls thanked the band over and over and Meg could see a joy in their faces which she tried to imitate, then even Suzie got in on the action, chatting to the girls, asking them about themselves and shaking hands. But Clare stood apart with her air of untouchability.

'See you tonight then girls.' Mac said in his sultry tones, managing to look each of them in the eye in turn, and make them visibly melt. 'We'll be listening for your screams.' The girls gave a practice scream — *why could I not scream like that?* — which drew even more attention to the guys, so Meg decided to ignore the looks from both Clare and the castle guards and brazen it out.

'MindSet, tonight at The Playhouse. DirtyMind Tour. One night only,' she shouted. Suzie smiled, slapped her back and joined in.

Birmingham, UK

It wasn't until Birmingham a week later that Meg got another chance to phone home. She had already accompanied the band to the morning show at BBC West Midlands and it was still a couple of hours before she had to round them up for the sound check. She hoped that her mum would be at home, grabbing some lunch before her next shift, so she went to the phone booth in the hotel foyer, dialled and pushed in a 10p when she heard her mum's voice.

'Mammy, it's Meg. I mean Maggie.'

'Maggie, oh thank God. Where the hell are you?' Her mum sounded concerned, which freaked Meg a bit.

'I'm okay. Did you get my note? I left it on the kitchen table, on top of a tenner.'

'Yes, I got it. But what on earth are you playing at?'

The pips went, and although Meg didn't think she had to justify herself, she fed in some more coins. 'I had to get away. You always said I should, and well…'

'I didn't mean you should run after some stupid band. Your French teacher's been on the phone and everything, wanting to know where you are and if you'll be back for your exams. You can't just disappear like that.'

You always did, Meg thought as she pulled at her thumb cuticle. 'Make something up. If I can get a job in London I'm gonnae stay,' she said, 'even if it's just for a while.'

'I've already lied to the school, Maggie. Said that you were poorly so they wouldn't come round. You know I hate lying.'

Meg snorted. 'What about the Apollo? You lied about that.'

She could almost hear her mum thinking. 'Tam says it'll be alright,' Val said. 'Anyway, you're meant to be gettin an office job after your exams. You shouldnae be worrying about the Apollo.'

'That's not the point — it's our living, you should have told me.' Val didn't answer and took a minute before she went on. 'Maggie, love, what about that mess you left? Your clothes were in an awful state. Did something happen?' Meg closed her eyes and tried to push Maggie's past away.

'I'll phone you from London.'

'Just don't do anything stupid,' Val said as the pips began to go again. 'Git yourself on the pill, Maggie, do you hear me?' Meg hung up and sat for a moment visualising her mum at home and wondering how Val would cope without her. *I bet she hasn't even opened the curtains.*

BANG. A sudden rap on the window made her jump and a large red face mouthed at the window, 'Hurry up.'

'All right, I'm finished.' She was barely out of the booth when the fat businessman squeezed in, pulling his BO with him.

Meg wandered back towards the lift but instead of pressing the button she detoured into the bar area to get a coke. She chewed on her nails, still feeling like a fraud as she charged the drink to her room, then turned from the bar and looked around the place. Zed sat in the corner absorbed with writing in a large book, his dark hair veiling his eyes. Todd had told her that the band liked their own space, so she took her drink to an armchair facing out into the lobby. She sipped slowly, letting the sugar and the caffeine take effect. *God,* that guy had given her a fright with his banging. *Arsehole*. Now here he was again, out of the phone booth and into the bar. Meg was aware of him trying to engage the barman in small talk without much success, and then *shit*, he was coming to her table with two drinks.

'Just wanted to apologise for my impatience,' he said sitting down without waiting to be asked. 'I had a very important business call to make and you seemed to be finished.'

'Yes, sorry. I hadn't realised you were waiting.' She gave a small smile to acknowledge the drink he had put in front of her, but kept with the one she had in her hand.

'So can I take it a young girl like you is here to work,' he said.

'Yes,' Meg said, and since he didn't look like he would have heard of MindSet, she didn't elaborate.

'So?' he said.

'So?'

'Shall we?'

'Shall we what?' Meg said.

'Go to work.' He put his hand on her thigh and squeezed hard, digging his nails into her skin through the cheap denim of her jeans.

'What the fuck?' Meg jumped up and stared down at the man. 'Fuck off.' Meg's heart began to pound but her feet wouldn't run. 'Pervert.'

She heard Zed coming across the room behind her. 'You okay, Meg?' he asked.

The man stared at Zed and addressed him sharply. 'You'd better get your girl in check here. I thought we had a deal, now she's causing a scene.' Meg looked between the men, as they focused on their fight.

'Well you thought wrong mate. What sort of a paedo are you? She's just a kid.'

'She said she was working.'

'Not that sort of work, shithead,' Zed said as he pushed the man with measured force. For a moment the man looked like he was going to retaliate, but instead, he just laughed, like it was all just a big joke and backed off.

Zed took Meg's hand and led her over to his table, nodding that everything was cool to the barman. 'You're shaking,' he said as they sat down. Meg stretched out a hand in front of her and was surprised to see he was right.

'Sorry. He just took me a bit off-guard. Things like that don't normally get to me.'

'It's happened before?'

Meg shrugged. 'When you wander about on your own it happens every now and again. It's no big deal. Shit. Sorry.' She shook her head and tried to rid herself of the thoughts coming to the surface. *His face screaming at her; the pressure on her legs; the feelings of shock and helplessness.* 'What are you up to, anyway?' she said. If she knew nothing else, it was that people never probed too deeply if you could turn the attention back to them. 'Are you writing a new song?'

'Good God no, I leave lyrics to Mac. I only do the music and look, no guitar.' For a second Meg imagined that he might conjure a guitar out of thin air, and prove that the past couple of weeks weren't real, but instead he carried on talking. 'I think Kyle's scratched in some writing time after Europe and before America. A couple of weeks might mean a song or two,'

'I thought Todd organised stuff like that?' Meg said, welcoming the chance to find out more about the inner workings without having to pry.

'No. Todd just does the day- to-day things, keeps the wheels turning and the money coming in. Kyle's in charge of everything else — just don't tell the others.' Zed said, a broad smile coming across his usually sombre face.

'Have they never noticed?'

'Do they seem the most observant pair?'

Meg laughed. 'I suppose only when it comes to eyeing up girls.'

'Well, you're right there, Meg. Now observations, that's where this comes in,' he tapped the book in front of him, 'so I'll remember all this.'

'Do you think you could ever forget it?' Meg asked. 'I know I never will.'

'You'd be surprised. We've been to the UK before. Didn't make it to Glasgow though, but we have definitely been in Birmingham and it's only when I read what was in here that it came back.'

'What did you write?'

'Now, now Meg,' he said shaking his finger, and pulling the book to his chest, 'diaries aren't for public consumption.'

'Just don't write about what happened with that tosser,' she said pointing over to the bar where her would-be punter sat cradling a whisky.

'Are you kidding — that's my heroic deed of the day, it's got to go in.'

Meg gave a playful scowl and shook her head.

Coming in at No 6, all the way from Australia to the Top of the Pops studio,

let's hear it for MindSet with Take your Time.

May: Dover to Calais

'I thought you were getting left in London,' Clare said as they queued at Passport Control, making her sound like a piece of lost luggage.

'Change of plan,' Meg replied as confidently as she could, although she still wasn't sure what the new plan was. She had walked passed a cop in London and as his radio crackled she felt panicked again. Leaving the country was a huge risk, with officials all around her, but if she could get across the Channel she was pretty sure she'd be safe, even if he died. She took a deep breath, *just act normal, like you're right and they're wrong.*

'Can I have a drum roll please Kyle?' Meg asked, forcing cheeriness. 'It's the first time I've used this.' She held up her navy blue passport with a trembling hand. 'I've never been as excited in my whole life'.

Kyle frisked himself, 'I'm afraid I don't have a drum on me right now, but I could get a beat going on that guy's counter if he'll let me.' They both looked over at the official's doughy face as he dealt with Todd's copious paperwork.

'He doesn't look like he'd appreciate it,' Meg said.

'Kyle,' Clare said, cutting across their laughter, and drawing him back to her, 'would you be a honey and take my vanity case? My neck is starting to hurt again.'

Meg had never known anyone so physically inadequate when it came to anything other than looking pretty, she wouldn't last a day if she had to do any real work. *'My feet hurt, my head hurts, boo hoo, poor me.'*

They were called forward and the Australians were questioned, but Meg was waved through with little more than a glance at her passport. *Made it.* She caught up with them and they left the terminal building together and went across the tarmac to the ferry. The wind was beginning to whip up and horizontal rain smeared their eyes. Waves crashed over the quay wall, and they had to bend and push forward through it. Meg watched as the ferry rose and fell, causing the gangplank to float in mid-air then crash down into the entrance doorway. For a second she hesitated, wondering if it was her fate to be lost at sea, but the torrent ahead seemed preferable to the one she was leaving behind, so she gripped onto the handrail and pulled herself up and on board.

MindSet immediately went to find the bar but Todd took Meg to check that the truck drivers and their cargo had made it safely on-board. The rocking wasn't too bad on the lower deck, but the engine noise increased and a klaxon sounded, indicating they had to leave and move upstairs. They made their way slowly onto the passenger deck, being bumped and tossed as they went.

'So the agreement was that you were coming as far as London,' Todd said as the boat made its way out to the Channel and they finally sat down in the bar with some drinks. Meg sipped through her straw and tried to find the words to explain herself, but when she glanced up it was amusement that she read on Todd's face, along with a veneer of cold sweat. 'I speak French?' She said tentatively. 'I thought maybe I'd try Paris instead of London. Is that okay?'

'I bought your ticket,' he shrugged, 'I just get the feeling that next week you're going to tell me that you're fluent in Italian too, and that maybe you'll stick with us until Rome.' He was teasing her, she was almost sure of it.

'Is it a problem, Todd?' The boat took a lurch to the right and Todd gripped onto the table, a look of fear suddenly coming into his eyes. Meg reached out and caught their glasses before they slid off the table.

'Well, I suppose you can juggle too,' he said, but without any humour in his voice. The boat suddenly dipped, 'Oh, oh God.' He fixed one hand over his mouth and waved her off with the other before he headed for the Gents. It was comical to watch him — one minute struggling to climb up the deck, the next running down it. He finally staggered through the toilet door leaving Meg to consider the scene in front of her. People slumped onto the floor or clung onto railings as though their lives depended on it. A big fall even got to Meg's stomach, making her suddenly conscious of the smell of vomit and the increasing sound of moaning. So she lifted Todd's files, squeezed them into her bag and picked her way outside.

The waves crashed over the rails, spraying salt water into her face and she immediately felt better. It didn't seem to have the same effect on the crowd gathered to the left of her at the stern, jostling for places as they tried to steady themselves against the horizon. Meg watched seagulls beat against the wind, circling for regurgitated offerings. Then she turned the other way and saw Kyle a few paces along the port side from her. He waved and shouted something but the combined roar of the engines and the elements made it impossible for her to hear. She eased her way towards him as they dipped again.

'Are we the last men standing?' Kyle asked.

'I don't know. The roadies went off to their cabins and I know Todd isn't enjoying the sail — last seen at the bog.' A wave came over the side again and drenched them. They shook it off and laughed.

'Wow, this is incredible,' Kyle said.

'It's like being at the shows,' she said, 'on a big rollercoaster.'

'I love the way you talk, *the shows,* you mean carnival, right?' Kyle smiled.

Patronise was one of the first big words Meg remembered Val using '*Don't you patronize me, pal.'* She was older when she looked it up in the school dictionary *—condescension, but also support.* She certainly felt the first when Suzie said she sounded cute, but with Kyle she felt more like he was trying to teach her, to rid her of the tell-tale signs of her past.

Kyle cut into her thoughts. 'I'll give it to you poms — you certainly do dramatic weather. Are you sure it's spring?''

‘Maybe France will be warmer. Can you believe we’re nearly there?’

‘Have you never been?’ he asked.

She shook her head, not adding that before she met Kyle, she had never been to Edinburgh, or Newcastle or any of the dozen other stops they had made.

‘Really? It’s so close. Mind you, compared to Australia everywhere is close.’

Meg saw another wave coming and ducked, letting the full force hit Kyle. He didn’t laugh this time and she apologised, as if she had summonsed Poseidon herself.

‘Exhilarating, but getting a bit tiresome,’ he said. ‘Will we go in and get dried?’

When they got back inside, Meg pulled a hotel towel out of her bag and offered it to Kyle.

‘Ladies first,’ he said. She dried her face, and wrung out her ponytail, the water splashing onto the floor, before she offered the towel to Kyle again. He waved his hand in a small gesture of refusal and watched as she rolled it and popped it into a plastic bag then into her haversack.

‘You seem to have everything in there.’

‘Well, you should always know where your towel is — *Hitchhikers’ Guide to the Galaxy*.’ She pulled on the cord and clipped the fasteners.

‘Meg, I don’t want to seem rude, but is that all the luggage you’ve got?’

‘I’m fine. I don’t need much.’ Meg looked at her feet, but a sudden jolt made her grab out and clasp onto his arm, which tensed to take the strain. A month ago it had been her schoolbag, and she was always saying ‘*It’s fine*.’ Now it was a portable office and a carrier for her spare knickers and T-shirts.

‘Surely you need more stuff,’ he said, and Meg was aware that he was scanning her face for a reaction. ‘Has Todd paid you yet? He can be a bugger at remembering things like that.’ he said, as he put his hand on her back to steady himself.

‘I’ve got bed and board — that’s enough.’ Meg said, ‘I don’t really need anything else.’

‘Well, that’s very noble and all, but it’s not on. You seem to be chief goffer now that Pam’s left. I’ll sort it with Todd. Listen, I’d better go and check on Clare now. You look after yourself.’

Meg nodded; people said it like it was the easiest thing in the world. ‘*Look after yourself.*’ She had no other option, but it would be nice if someone else would look after her the way Kyle looked after Clare. She watched as Kyle walked away. He took off his sodden jacket to reveal a drenched shirt which clung to his back though his leather trousers still looked dry — *God, what a tight arse. Clare was a lucky bitch.* He disappeared around a corner and Meg suddenly became aware of her own soaked denims and freezing legs, so she pushed through the mayhem, into the Ladies and under the hand drier.

The coach journey to Paris was the most subdued Meg had experienced. Everyone was either still delicate after the sail or so drunk that they had fallen asleep the minute the coach pulled out of the dock. Clare rested her head on Kyle's shoulder but Meg stopped glancing back when he started to kiss her head and pull her closer, nuzzling her under a blanket.

Soon only Meg and the driver were awake. The storm gave way to rain and then to drizzle and when the driver finally turned off his wipers Meg was able to scan the dusky view unimpeded. She kept alert to the possibility of Paris and gasped when she finally saw it: Le Tour Eiffel. Paris — no longer just a concept in a reading comprehension or a weekend destination on *Wish You Were Here.* It *did* exist and she was really here. Meg in Paris — she felt it with each pounding. The lights of the city reflected in puddles and as she saw the girls loitering on corners, *Roxanne* came into her head. Girls could always make money, but she was on the inside now, looking out. She felt the tears come, but no one witnessed as she let them run unchecked down her face.

Paris – La Cigale

Meg stood at the foot of the stairs with a bundle of towels to give out as the band came off stage. Riggers and venue staff moved all around her, but she stayed in her spot, ready for the end of *Things to Come.* She had been in Paris for twenty-four hours but other than the elevated Sacre Coeur and the Eiffel Tower, she had seen little of the city. The light seemed different, though, and the air too, and she wondered if it would be a good place to live. She could get a job in a café in a tourist area where her English would be an asset, but somewhere to stay meant a deposit, and money was one thing she didn't have. When she was in London she had been amazed to see young people bedding down on cardboard and huddling into shop doorways at night. In Glasgow it was only down and outs that slept rough, and while she instinctively fought to keep a roof over her head, it had been years since she thought that she might end up on the streets. She wasn't clear what she'd actually agreed with Todd on the boat, yes, he'd got her here but she had learned that there was a fluency in arrangements, as people drifted on and off the tour, maybe it was her turn to leave. She kept still, listened to the drumbeat and waited. She'd cope.

Her day had started with a phone call at 6 a.m. from Todd. He couldn't find Mac for his early morning radio interview and needed Meg to placate the presenter while he conducted a search. '*Could she get to it right away?*' Then at 10 a.m. a bell hop arrived with boxes of promotional material to be mixed into press packs for the European leg. At 2 p.m. she managed to grab a pastry from the coffee lounge and at 4 p.m. she calmed down the concierge who had been dealing with fans trying to sneak into the lobby. After a quick dinner she counted everyone onto the tour bus, and counted them all off again at the venue. Todd kept her busy with various requests while the support act were on, and between his phone calls he put down a marker to talk to her later.

During the gig Meg checked in on the First Aid area where the passed out girls were being fanned and re-hydrated; and tidied the dressing room, making sure it was ready for the band to make a quick getaway.

From where she stood she could see nothing more than the changing colours of the spots and just the occasional flash of Zed moving in the way Keith Richards had taught all guitarists to do. So she waited, ready for the big finish. The thoughts came back, maybe she should write them down, all the jobs she had done for Todd to show how much he needed her, but she had no paper and Kyle had hit the final beat and the band were off stage.

'You right Meg? You look worried. Were we shit?' Kyle asked, peeling off his top and drying the sweat from his chest, arms and head.

'No, not at all. Great gig,' she said, still slightly taken off-guard by his casual strip. 'Your clean top's in the dressing room.'

'Boss. Five star service.'

Wayne took the last towel off her outstretched arm and grunted, in way of thanks.

They always tried to leave the gig before the fans could get out of the hall and block their way, so Meg hurried everyone along and jumped on the coach after them. As she negotiated the legs and feet that sprawled out across the aisle she realised Todd was already asleep, hands flat on the trousers of his 60s retro suit, jacket still buttoned, as though at any minute he might need to press down hard on his legs, stand up and deal with a new problem. But his breathing was deep and she was relieved that her fate wouldn't be decided just yet.

She had a restless night, not able to settle in the bed she feared might be her most comfortable for a while. The traffic noise began to pick up and influence her dreams, until an insistent car horn woke her around seven. She pulled on a jumper, opened the window to the tiny balcony and leaned over the railings, taking in the sights and sounds of the street below. Paris at dawn was just how she imagined it — a peachy light softened the stone buildings, air waited to be stirred, and the faint smell of buttery goods baking. She watched women walk by in their shift dresses and kitten heels until the balcony creaked and she pulled back. *What sort of jobs did they have, that they could go to work like that? What sort of lives that let them walk with such confidence?*

Then the wrought-iron filigree brought her focus back onto the balcony and she marvelled at the artistry of metalwork leaves entwined with creeping ivy. Her grandfather had been a welder in the shipyards, though she never knew him, and didn't know anything else about him other than he was a drinker who they were all better off without. She popped her head back into the room and grabbed the Canon T70 Kyle had given her in Newcastle so she could document the tour. '*It'll give you a purpose,'* he'd said, not realising that Todd was managing to fill most of her day. But she received it graciously, opening the case to reveal the camera, flash gun and half a dozen yellow boxes of film. *How could you love something so much that you didn't even know you wanted?* She had lifted the camera out from its padding, turning it in her hands; fingering the metal grooves that mirrored those on the flash; wondering at the rows of numbers on the lens. *'It's meant to be really easy to use,'* Kyle had said, although Meg had doubted it at the time, '*the manual's in there.'* She held the camera to her eye, but everything was black until Kyle reached forward and removed the lens cap. *'Say cheese.'* Kyle smiled and she clicked the shutter before he said, *'Film might be useful too.'* She laughed, *'Good point,'* and she gave him a thank-you peck on the cheek, feeling a shudder of appreciation.

A powdery green-grey dust sat on top of the black painted leaves, so thick in places that it looked like a real leaf was trying to break through. She zoomed in. The little split circle in the centre of the picture wobbled and the focus blurred, so she lay down on the cold stone of the balcony and steadied her elbows in front of her. Then she slowed her breathing, felt an inner stillness move through her like gel, making her blood thicker, slowing her pulse, steadying her hand. With a slight twist to the lens she made the circle whole again and began to play. Sharp, close images of the leaves. Then she used the stalks to frame the architecture of the buildings opposite, stole shots of the people below. When she was finished she went to the bed, pulled the covers over her and removed the film, writing on the spool *Paris Balcony 1985*. She didn't know how she would explain that one.

The day passed more peacefully than the previous one, but Meg didn't dare wander far in case she was needed. Instead she spent the day laying low, dozing and flicking through a couple of books that had been left on the bus. She didn't deliberately avoid Todd, but she didn't she seek him out either. When they got to the venue she spent some time front-of-house ingratiating herself with the theatre manager in case he would come in useful.

She checked her watch, another half an hour before things would get going, so she grabbed a sandwich from the catering table. 'Right Meg,' Todd said as he slammed through the door, strode across the room and began shredding a slice of parma ham and popping tiny pieces into his mouth, 'let's cut to the chase. Dave used to help with some of the band stuff, but the rigs are getting bigger and he's got more men to look after, so he can't give me a hand now. I'm getting really good vibes from the record company and I think I'm going to need you to stick with us. That suit you? Bit more than running errands now — we'll call you an assistant, PA-come-PR, that sort of thing?' He struggled with a cork and poured himself a large Chablis. 'The next single isn't out in the States until next week and we've already added more dates, so that should be really jumping, and we're moving up the charts here and in Germany.

Okay? Count yourself official.' He patted her back and she allowed herself a little smile. 'Great,' she said but in the same instant reminded herself that Tam always said that he couldn't live without her either and then was ready to shaft her without so much as a bye-your-leave. She chomped on a mouthful of food. 'Of course I'd like to stay on, but, I hate to ask you this,' she said swallowing, 'but what about money?'

Todd looked puzzled, as if no one had ever asked to be paid before.

'Yeah, Kyle mentioned that you were worried about that. I think there's been a breakdown in communication somewhere along the line. I called your mum when we were in the UK for your documents — didn't know you were only 16, Meg,' he said in a slightly accusatory way, but carried on, 'she gave me your bank details then.'

Meg didn't understand and her face clearly showed it, so Todd continued as he dabbed at some mayonnaise which had dripped onto his lapel. 'She didn't tell you? The money should have gone into your bank sometime around London. I've ordered a company Amex for your tour expenses and we can work out the rest of the details when we get it. But if you're having problems getting your money I can give you some cash for now.' He pulled out a bundle of francs and crushed a couple of notes into Meg's hand, then Mac shouted for him and their conversation ended. She looked at the notes he had so casually dispensed and folded them into her back pocket. She lifted a can of Sprite and hurried back along the corridor to find an empty dressing room. She opened her can and took a couple of sips before she picked up the wall-mounted phone and dialled most of Val's number. But she hung up and growled, took a couple of deep breaths and tried again.

'Hello,' Val answered.

'I've found out about the bank account,' Meg said. 'You really are despicable, you know that?' Val said nothing for a few moments which Meg took as an admission. 'Did you think I wouldn't find out that you were stealing from me? I'm out here in some God-forsaken place and you're living off my wages. I don't know why I'm even surprised — you've been doing it for years.'

'I'll thank you not to talk to me like that my girl,' Val said sharply. 'And what are you going on about? What bank account? And where the hell are you? I haven't heard from you for days.' Her mum always did this, tried to wriggle out of awkward situations by changing the subject. 'I was getting worried,' Val continued. 'Oh, wait a minute; I know what you're talking about now — that Aussie guy? He wanted to start paying money into your account — I gave him the details, what's the big deal?'

'What details?'

'From that TSB book you had hidden under the bed, the one your granny set up that I wasn't meant to know about — the money's in there.'

She'd forgotten all about that book, and had only grabbed her secret stash of cash in her rush to pack.

‘So don’t dare say that I’ve been at it,’ Val continued. ‘I haven’t touched a penny. Tam’s set me up cleaning for his mate at Fury Murray’s, so I don’t need any of your money thank you very much. You’ve got a bloody cheek Maggie.’

Meg had never had to apologise to her mum before, but this time she did, and she meant it. ‘Sorry Mum. This whole thing’s just a bit crazy. They’ve said I can keep working for them — go to America and everything. Isn’t that mental?’ She didn’t give her mum time to reply. ‘But listen, I need to get myself some new clothes. I can’t keep wearing MindSet T-shirts. Do you think you can ask the bank how to get some money to me? I’ll write and tell you where we’re staying for the next couple of weeks. See how much I’ve got and send over a bit.’

‘Aye sure,’ Val said.

‘And Mum, take something for the rent too if there’s enough.’

‘Okay love,’ Val sounded like she had moved the mouthpiece closer to her, and began to talk in a distorted whisper. ‘I’ve had the polis here love.’

Meg pressed her palm against the painted white brick wall and closed her eyes. ‘What did they want?’

‘They’re investigating an attack. Said they thought it might be self-defence. The guy who was attacked had form you know, for hurting girls.’

‘Is he dead?’

'No, be better if he was. The polis say he wants to pursue an assault charge. They think it's to put them off looking into other stuff he's been up to.'

Meg picked a flake of paint. 'Do they want to question me?'

'They want to know where you ur. They're tracking down anyone who might have been fly posting. Although I don't know what nosey bugger told them about you?'

'You didn't give them my clothes did you? I tried to wash them, but I don't know if I got all of the blood out. I was going to wash them again, but I never got the chance. I didn't mean it, mum, honest. He just came at me, and,' she closed her eyes tight, trying to stop herself from seeing it and clenched her fist, 'when, when I got my chance, I picked up a stone and…Oh God.'

Meg heard someone move behind her and turned to see the door close. She dropped the phone and ran to the door, but the corridor was empty.

'Maggie, are you there? Are you listening? Did he hurt you?'

'I'm okay,' she said, but her heart was pounding.

'It's only us know what happened, love, and that's how we'll keep it. Tam isn't going to let on — he's in enough bother without that. I binned the clothes after you'd left, so don't worry, there's no evidence. Okay? Just put it behind you.' Meg nodded at the phone, and made a little noise of agreement, then Val continued, 'I'll get the money sorted in the morning.'

'Thanks mum. Do you think it's going to be okay?'

'I just wished you'd telt me. Oh, I don't know — maybe you were right to scarper.'

'I hope so,' Meg said and she finished the phone call and sat down on a grey plastic chair. *Who had been in the room?* She tried to replay the conversation she had just had. *Would her side be enough for a listener make sense of?* Maybe she should just go into the concert crowd and meld into it. But then what? If she could ride her luck for a few days then her money would be through and she would have enough cash in her pocket if she needed to run.

Nimes

The gig had been fantastic, one of those nights when everything went to plan — no one in a strop and the crowd wild. Meg accompanied a couple of competition winners into the hall and decided that she deserved to stay and watch the show with them. Tonight she would just be a fan. Suzie came up behind her and squeezed her waist. 'They're awesome tonight,' Suzie shouted in her ear.

Meg nodded and as Zed hit the first chords of *Transvaal Avenue,* Suzie started to sway Meg's hips. 'My God, Meg,' she said, 'I've never seen anyone so stiff at a gig before. Loosen up, babe.'

'Sorry,' Meg said, but she was suddenly back at home with Val. She could almost hear her mum's voice as she would lift Meg out of bed and onto the blankets in the corner. '*Ssh, don't move okay?*' and then the music, AC/DC or Status Quo. Meg would burrow under, knowing that in the morning she would get a bacon roll from the café down the road, paid for by the notes left at the side of the bed by the men she had to hide from. All she had to do was keep completely still, so music became syrup to dose her. But now, with Suzie and the screaming teenagers to encourage her, she let a more natural response to music emerge, a twitching of the muscles that yearned to become a dance. She smiled, let it in. She even managed to convince herself that whoever had heard her on the phone in Paris couldn't have understood what she was talking to Val about— maybe they didn't even speak English. With every beat she felt her burden lighten and the distance between here and home finally started to mean something.

But now there was something else, tension had been replaced by a growing niggle that didn't feel like fear. About half way through the gig, Mac slowed everything down, and sat on the ledge beneath the drum kit to sing *Remembrances,* his one ballad, and she realised what it was. Mac was irritating her. All through the show he strutted across the stage; unbuttoned his shirt just to make the girls scream; threw his hair and hips about the place and generally drew attention to himself with his gesturing and posturing — he got in the way. Now that he was sitting down, she had an uninterrupted view of what she been unaware she was straining to see — left arm, boom, right arm, boom, boom, head, nod, nod, high hat, pow, pow. Toms. Snare. Bass. Kyle.

No one notices the drummer, even gorgeous ones like Larry Mullen, Jon Farris or either of the Roger Taylors, tend to go unnoticed by the casual observer. But Meg could see that Kyle eclipsed even Mac in sexiness. He had no need to strut his stuff for the screaming crowd, it was enough that they clapped and jumped to his dictated rhythm. She watched him in action and felt the beat deep within her. She couldn't make out his features from this distance, but she superimposed the look of concentration that she saw at sound checks, and held him in her mind. His brow slightly furrowed as each part of his body moved at a different speed, creating sound waves that rippled across the audience making them dance in time.

Back at the hotel Meg found herself in the lift with Suzie, Zed, Kyle and Clare. She kept her gaze at waist height, not daring to look anyone in the eye after the feelings of arousal she had felt at the concert. But even with her eyes down she could see Kyle's arm loosely slung around Clare.

'We're going to give it a miss tonight, Suz,' Kyle said as the lift doors opened. 'Catch you tomorrow.'

Clare looked up demurely and Meg found she had to quash an urge to hit her. *Why did Meg always get the feeling that Clare called the shots, even when Kyle did the talking.*

'How about you, Meg?' Suzie asked, 'Are you coming to the party?' Meg watched as Kyle opened his bedroom door, and felt her key heavy in her hand. *Another night of CNN and trying to follow a French soap or hanging out with Suzie and the others*? It shouldn't be that hard a decision, but it was crossing a line and she knew it.

Suzie pushed through a small crowd that had gathered at the bedroom door, unlocked it and welcomed them in. There were a couple of guys she'd seen at the venue and some Australian tourists who had managed to claim enough of a connection to get an invite. Other than that, it was just Mac and Wayne and a couple of blondes that Dave had picked out of the crowd for them.

Meg felt a slight pressure on her lower back as Zed pushed her into the room. 'Come on girl, you're holding up the traffic here.' In Meg's room the dressing table was piled with folders and notebooks, but the identical one here was lined with bottles of spirits and beers. Her mum used to describe scenes like this and now it was in front of her — Bombay gin, clear in its blue bottle, Tequila in amber glass, Black label Smirnoff, pure spirit, Glenmorangie, nectar coloured and smooth. Then the beer — Grolsh, loved as much for the intriguing bottle top, as for the taste, and some local brew or something to remind them of home — yes, there it was — XXXX.

'This is all very organised, ' Meg said as Suzie took her hand and pulled her into the party.

'Well, I like things to be nice,' Suzie replied, as she adjusted a tray of nibbles that had been put down slightly off centre. 'It's good you came, Meg, and looking very smart. Are you actually going to let your hair down tonight?'

Meg instinctively touched her ponytail, but couldn't manage more than a shake of it. 'I just felt like a bit of company tonight, and you know how crap French TV is.'

'Well, enjoy yourself,' Suzie said and danced off to turn up the music. For the first time Meg felt conspicuous in the inner sanctum of the band. No matter how often she had banged on doors to waken them, or pushed schedules underneath, she had never been in one of their rooms. She knelt down and busied herself with her new leather satchel, feeling its softness then checking she had everything in place. Suzie had taken her on a shopping spree that morning, trying to persuade her out of black jeans and into long straight skirts like Suzie's and when that didn't work helping her pick out more practical chinos, leggings and 501s. Meg even made a concession that her Docs were too heavy for the heat and let Suzie buy her sandals and brogues. While Suzie paid for them, Meg's eye was caught by the bags at the back of the shop, but Suzie steered her away.

'You need quality, and we'll not get that here, come on.' Suzie led her through the narrow Roman streets of Nimes and onto the broad Boulevard Gambetta, dense and shaded with trees. Suzie stopped occasionally to look in shop windows and check out styles, while Meg marvelled at the outside kiosks selling newspapers and magazines from across the globe. *'The papers would turn to papier-mâché if you did that at home,'* Meg said, and immediately looked again to check there was no photo of her underneath *Wanted*. But then what could they use? There were no pictures of her, unless you counted a class photo from her first year at school, and she was hardly more than a dot in that. Not something she could be identified from. On almost every corner they saw tourist signs trying to entice them to the Amphitheatre or the Maison Carree, maybe they could visit one of them, and take a couple of snaps, but Suzie would not be swayed.

'We'll be back here one day and have time to see the sights then. For now, we shop.' But she obviously picked up on Meg's growing boredom, so when they came to the next leather shop Suzie said it would have to do. The smell of new leather hit them the minute they entered, as if it had been sprayed out of a can, and they were immediately greeted by an assistant, dressed in a sharp suit and thin tie. He seemed to pick up immediately that they did not speak French so welcomed them with a cautious *Hello*. Meg looked around. Even without doing the conversions, there seemed to be too many zeros on the price tags, but Suzie wouldn't be stopped.

'How do I say *that one*?' Suzie asked her, pointing to one bag after another, getting the assistant to lift them off the shelf for inspection without waiting for the translation. 'You really need something better than that daypack.'

Meg squeezed the tattered canvas bag with her feet. 'How much is this?' Meg asked, holding a haversack of patchwork leather.

'1000 francs Miss,' he replied in his best English. The words acted like an electric current which shot through Meg's hands and caused the bag to lift a little in the air. 'That's £100,' she whispered to Suzie.

'No wait. This one's better.' Suzie took the haversack from her and put a satchel diagonally across Meg's body. 'That's definitely better, more sophisticated and feminine. We'll take it.'

'It's not big enough.'

'And the red *Samsonite*. Perfect.'

It was perfect. When she got back to her hotel room she had spent ages unwrapping the tissue paper from her blouses, imagining that Christmas must be like this. She snipped the labels off the clothes and dropped them in the bin before laying her new clothes carefully in the suitcase. The tissue paper with its raised monograms looked so delicate and classy that she couldn't throw it out. Her granny's thrift drawer was long gone so she folded it with sharp creases and popped it into the back of her desk diary. She could see it nestled there now.

When she had finished unpacking her booty, she changed into chinos, tucking a chocolate coloured satiny blouse into them and rolling up the trouser legs. It was a bit of a departure from her usual black, but it had felt fresh. Mind you, that was hours ago, and the grime of the concert hall had taken the new look off the cream cotton. She looked around at the room which was filling up. Girls, outnumbering the men, danced in cropped tops and harem pants daring everyone to watch them. Meg felt acutely aware of how different she was to them.

Her hand strayed again into the bag and touched her camera. The hard plastic against her fingers instantly made her feel safe. She lifted it out, took off the lens cap and started to photograph the party. Zed sitting cross-legged on the bed rolling a joint for Suzie, both nodding in time to the Beastie Boys; Wayne crouched in front of the TV watching *EuroSport*, ignoring the desperate hand working its way up his leg. Meg felt she had a purpose now — Mac sitting on the chair, snap, tousling blonde hair up and over a nameless shoulder, snap, then brushing a breast, so gentle, whispering in an ear, standing up, leaning against the groupie, putting a guiding hand on an arse. She felt the erotic charge but none of the jealousy that had risen with the floors in the lift. She took a final frame of a closing door to conclude the sequence.

'Did you just take a photo of a door?'

Meg took the camera down from her eye 'It tells a story,' she said, trying not to blush as Kyle had materialised from her thoughts and was now standing in front of her.

He raised an eyebrow.

'*Mac's Seduction*,' Meg said, 'I know he's a rock star and all that, but he seems to enchant them. It's weird.'

Kyle shrugged, 'Just practice — he knows what works. Personally I couldn't be bothered with all that — one woman is more than enough for me.'

'You know he does exactly the same thing with every girl,' she said ignoring the reference to Clare. 'The way he looks at them, touches them, whispers to them. I've watched him,' then she laughed realising that she was sounding a bit pervy, 'well, up to a point.'

'Yeah, that would be a whole other type of photo.' Kyle pushed back the wire on his *Grolsh* and popped the ceramic stopper. 'So have you been taking secret photos of me too?'

Meg felt her face blanch under his scrutiny and she looked down and shrugged. 'How could I?' she said. 'You've just got here?'

'Yeah, I know. Clare had a bit of headache but she's asleep now, so I thought I'd come along and here I am at a momentous event — Meg's first party.' He smiled and raised his beer bottle to her can of coke. 'Cheers.'

Meg squeezed the can in her hand and suddenly felt the need to explain herself. 'I just didn't think I would settle tonight, and Suzie said it would be okay.'

'Oh, you should have told me earlier — I know my roadie is dying to help you settle down at night,' he said nudging her. 'He keeps going on about you, Meg this, Meg that.'

Meg made a half-hearted attempt to place the roadie, but could only think of the guy who had weaselled his way into the crew in London and gave her the creeps with his greasy hair and coffee breath. 'I don't think I know who you mean.'

'It's no biggie, he can catch up with you another night.'

Meg gave a half-smile, and made a mental note to steer clear of the roadie. She decided to change the subject. She didn't want to be set up, especially by Kyle.

'It's a bit crazy I suppose,' she said, 'but I watched the gig tonight and now I feel all jumpy.'

'That's the adrenaline for you. Do you not normally watch?' Kyle asked.

Meg shook her head.

'Charming. We're bursting our balls trying to entertain you and you don't even watch.' He took another drink, waved to a couple of people Meg vaguely recognised from TV and continued. 'Did you have your camera with you at the gig tonight? I thought I saw you taking some photos.'

'Yeah,' Meg said, 'I thought it would be fun.'

'I'll need to see them when they're printed. I want to think about what the crowd sees — make sure the balance on stage is right.' Meg didn't think he could possibly have noticed her in the crowd, but was pleased he pretended he could.

'I don't think they'll be that great,' Meg said, 'but I was thinking I could talk to Todd about taking some on the stage. If I wore black and crawled about I'm sure I wouldn't get in the way. I think performance photos would look really cool.' Kyle nodded, so she went on, 'You don't want to get a reputation of just being pretty boys. Action shots would be good.'

He snorted and pretended to be insulted. 'I thought our music did that.'

'Well, the press just see good looking guys like Mac, and you of course,' she tried to do that head down, eyes up thing that Clare did, but felt daft, so finished the move with lifting a pretend lash from her eye. Yeah, they see you appeal to girls so it's harder to have any credibility.'

'Have we not got credibility?' He sat down on the floor with his back against the wall and signalled for her to join him. She noticed the Celtic thumb ring he had bought on the Royal Mile and felt a pang for home, before she realised that she hadn't seen anything Celtic before that day in Edinburgh.

'You're selling shed loads of records, so I wouldn't worry. Credibility, I'm not sure?'

'You know Meg — you're the only one who ever dares say stuff like that.'

'I'm sorry,' she said, wondering why he was even paying attention to her drivel. 'I used to watch the bands at The Apollo, look at what they wore, check out the fans' reactions and then do the review clippings the next day. You start to notice things.'

'Is that why you're never impressed by what we do? You've seen it all before?'

She had seen it all before. The nose powdering; the vomit and beer; the punches and shags; the fights and the tantrums. She had seen women faint, called ambulances and told lies; screened phone calls and barred doors. She knew when to be stroppy and when to act dumb. This lot weren't meant to be any different. 'I am impressed by what you do' she said, flattering him. 'You take it seriously. You don't let people down.'

'Well then, I'm honoured,' he said. *No, I'm honoured,* she thought, *you are different — you know my name.*

Clare came through the door and looked around the room, frowning when she saw Kyle and Meg on the floor together. Kyle stood up as she approached and offered his hand to Meg, but she got up without it, fearing that Clare's look might kill her if she dared to touch him.

'I've got a few frames left,' Meg said stepping back to a respectful distance. 'Why don't I take a couple of pictures of you guys?' And she hid her face behind her camera and snapped photos that would show none of Clare's famed softness, but all of Kyle's fire.

June: Juan les Pins

Suzie knocked on Meg's door after breakfast and told her to get ready for the beach. The price of giving in to Suzie about the shopping trip and party seemed to be that she would no longer take excuses from Meg. 'It's toasty out there — and before you say you don't have a cossy, I bought you this.' Suzie tossed a little blue and white dotty bikini over to her with a matching sarong. 'Now go get changed.'

Meg went into the loo and quickly popped the bikini on, but the wrap defeated her, so she put her shorts and t-shirt back on over it. 'I don't want to intrude,' Meg said as she opened the door. 'I was just going to hang about here today. I'll be fine by myself —I've got stuff to read.'

'Nonsense,' Suzie said very deliberately. 'I know you can look after yourself, but the beach has got to be more fun.' She picked up the book of Cartier-Bresson photos, had a quick flick then dropped it on to the bed again. 'Come on Meg, otherwise I'll have to talk to Clare all day.'

Meg traipsed down the burning sand after Suzie. The band and their entourage had colonised the sun beds near the water, forcing other sunbathers to stay clear by sheer force of numbers. Despite their vampiric life, Meg was surprised to see how brown everyone was.

‘Come on, Meg, let’s soak up some rays,’ Suzie said as she undid her sarong. Meg stepped out of her shorts then sat down and turned her back to the crowd before she pulled off her top and adjusted her bikini. The minute her flesh was exposed, Suzie started to rub sun cream on her back, then plopped the cold bottle between her thighs for her to do the rest. ‘Slip, slap, slop, my girl’.

Meg looked around, she hadn’t really spoken to Kyle since the night of the party, but she had gone over the conversation in her head practically every night since then. *Why on earth did I say they didn’t have credibility? He’s going to hate me now.* But Kyle hadn’t noticed her arrival and as she watched his chest rise and fall she wondered if he was even awake. She tried to settle herself on a sun lounger which had been brought over by a beach boy who waited for Suzie to find the appropriate payment. She lay on her back, but after a few minutes she found it too uncomfortable and blinding even with sunglasses on, so flipped over onto her stomach where she could at least take in the view. It was a mystery to Meg how the girls were able to sunbathe without sand sticking to them or sweat dribbling down between their breasts. There was only the slightest breeze bringing a chill off the sea, but every time it blew it sprayed a fine film of sand over her. She tried to ignore the gym-toned bodies and skimpy bikinis of the models who had hooked up with Mac, Wayne and the roadies. She tried to avert her eyes from the tanned muscles of the near-naked band. *How could they be so brown when it was only May? May, wow, she should be doing her English exam right now.* She really tried not to look at Kyle, but allowed her eyes to linger just long enough to fuel a little daydream where she was as confident and pretty as the other girls and Kyle, well, he would find her irresistible. He stirred and she moved quickly and turned over so that he wouldn't catch her watching him, which would be a total beamer.

Her arms and hands had got enough sun in the short bursts in outdoor cafes or walks to the shops to start a tan, but her legs were resolutely white, almost luminous next to the coconut oil brigade. Her stomach was as blue-white as her legs but it pleased her to see that her ribs only poked out now when she raised her arms to shield her eyes. She lifted her head slightly and pretended to look out to the Med, but she was actually admiring the little breasts which were beginning to emerge now that she wasn't using up every calorie she consumed. Clare and the other models weren't much heavier, with Suzie being the only one with *Big Mama Boob*s as Zed liked to call them. Meg finally lay back and relaxed, letting the sun warm her skin, the sea rock her mind into restful bliss and the gentle conversations ease her.

'Right, who's for paragliding?' Kyle broke her daze as he jumped into her eye line and began to rally the troops.

'Now Kyle, we're meant to be here chilling out,' Clare said. 'It's your first day off in ages — you need to take it easy.'

'No, I'm done relaxing. Come on. Who's with me?'

'I'm with you,' said Zed.

'I'm with you,' said Mac.

‘Yo,’ said Wayne.

‘My God it’s like Spartacus,’ Suzie said as the band members all leapt up one by one, joined hands in a star and whooped.

‘Any more?’ Kyle asked, hamming up the role of ring master. Meg started to shift, but Suzie’s hand stilled her. ‘Just for the boys, I think.’

‘Oh don’t worry — you wouldn’t get me doing that, even at knifepoint. I was just making myself comfortable.’

‘Too comfortable if you ask me,’ Clare said as she moved onto the bed next to Suzie.

‘What *is* your problem?’ Suzie asked the question that Meg daren’t.

‘I don’t know who she thinks she is. She said something to Kyle at the party, and now he’s working harder than ever. He’s shattered.’ The girls looked towards Kyle who was running along the beach to the water sports cabin, he didn’t look shattered to Meg; he looked invigorated. ‘And she’s here with us.’ She turned to Meg for the first time. ‘You should be over there with the crew.’

‘Now come on Clare,’ Suzie said. ‘Everyone’s working hard and we just all need some downtime. You wouldn’t leave her to the mercy of the roadies, would you?’

Clare gave a *like I care* look while Suzie kept talking. ‘The guys are loving every minute of this — the venues getting bigger, the album sales racking up. It’s incredible, just enjoy it.’ Clare didn’t look convinced, so Suzie continued. ‘Remember when we were travelling round the pubs in Australia, hardly making enough to cover the diesel, now that was hard work. This is a breeze.'

Meg sat up, lifted her book, her towel and bottle of Evian, and slid her feet into her flip flops. She felt the same apprehension around Clare that felt around the popular girls at school — at any moment they could turn their attention back to you and you'd be toast. It was safer to leave while Suzie was still reminiscing. 'I think I'm going to get some shade — I don't want to burn.'

Suzie eyed the red parches beginning to appear on her pale skin and didn't argue, and Clare gave her a look that suggested she thought she'd won — chasing her away like a dog. Meg padded up the beach but turned again when she heard squeals and laughter. Wayne was frantically running, his parachute puckering and deflating, lifting him up, then dumping him back onto the sand before finally catching enough air to lift him high over the water. 'Woo man.' *Bassists — two strings short of a guitarist.* She laughed and waved before walking back to the hotel.

She found a shaded seat under a tree in the hotel gardens, ordered some ice tea and picked up her book. Todd and Dave wandered by, but didn't go beyond pleasantries, which was a relief to Meg, as Todd was in speedos, while Dave's red-raw belly spilled over the top of his shorts. As they walked away she breathed deeply, grateful not to have to live up or down to any expectations, and felt peaceful. But soon she began to wonder what she had done to irritate Clare so much? And what Clare had done to irritate her so much? Suzie was so much easier — she just accepted Meg for who she was and what she did. Suzie didn't mind that Todd had taken her under his wing, or that the band seemed happy having her around. Clare on the other hand resented every breath that she took. She couldn't walk into a room without Clare acting as if she'd brought a bad smell with her. *'She doesn't like you, 'cause you're younger and prettier,'* Suzie had said one day, although only the first bit of that was true. And she visibly bristled whenever Meg talked to Kyle, '*Will you leave him alone, Meg.'* Suzie didn't do that when she talked to Zed, but then maybe she talked to Zed differently, without blushing or hyperventilating. She closed her eyes and visualised her conversations with Kyle, his smile, his sea-blue eyes that seemed to penetrate her soul, the blonde downy hairs on the hard muscles of his arms, those deep, deep tones. She heard his voice, warming her to the core, felt his breath on her cheek and smiled. If she reached out her hand just now, ran her fingers round the waistband of his swim-shorts.

'Hey sleepy head, I've been looking for you.'

Meg woke with a start to find Kyle was actually leaning over her and not just starring in her dreams.

'We're going for lunch just now and we didn't want you to starve. You want to catch up with the others?'

Meg blinked a couple of times to check she had really wakened, then nodded and wiped the dribble from her mouth as discreetly as she could. 'Do you think we should get Todd and Dave?' she said, trying to clear her fantasy from her mind. 'They're over at the pool.' She took one step towards them but Kyle held her arm and stopped her. She felt the pressure ease before she could process the feeling.

'No leave them; they'll just talk business if they come.'

'And I won't?' she said as she threw her stuff into her beach bag. *Come on, Meg, business head.* 'I've just been told I work you too hard, I should say sorry.'

Kyle laughed. 'You just lead us where we want to go. It's good to have a bit of honesty, so don't beat yourself up.'

Meg smiled. 'I'll try not to.'

As they walked along the street she felt happy that Kyle hadn't forgotten about her. Passing faces flickered with recognition or just admired how good Kyle looked, and Meg felt the same smugness she'd had for the two weeks when she'd gone out with Sean McCargill. Captain of the football team, good-looking, in a schoolboy way, she'd even let him touch her up. But then he dumped her the day after she'd sneaked him into the Big Country gig, and she'd never been conned again.

It wasn't hard to find the rest of MindSet — they just followed the crowd. Mac's voice was preaching to a collection of beach babes who swarmed round the café, while harassed waiters tried to figure out who was ordering and who was just there for the show. Meg burrowed through and let Kyle follow in the gap she made, but the minute she came under the canopy she realised she'd been wrong to accept Kyle's invitation.

‘We’ve been waiting to order,’ Clare said to Kyle, her voice harsher than Meg had ever heard it.

‘I told you not to,’ he said lifting up the menu and acting oblivious to her bad mood. ‘So, what’s on offer?’

Suzie signalled to Meg to sit with her and Zed, while Clare pulled Kyle down forcefully onto the seat she had kept for him.

‘Shit,’ Suzie whispered to her ‘I think Kyle is using you as a weapon in his war against Clare. She was really pissed when he went off to get you.’

‘Why are they at war?’ Her disappointment that his lunch invitation was tarnished was coupled with curiosity that their relationship might not be as perfect as it looked.

‘Zed thinks it fuels the passion, don’t you babe?’ Zed didn’t give more of an answer than a shrug, ‘but personally I think it’s a bit of a drag. Still, Clare is being left in Milan so we might have peace for a while. Seriously Meg, you don’t have to look quite so pleased about it.’

She hadn’t even realised she was smiling, ‘Sorry,’ she said, but she was pleased. ‘What is she doing in Milan?’

‘She’s going back to work. She’s only ever tours with us for a few weeks, then she leaves and Kyle mopes about the place for a while.’

‘How long have they been together?’ Meg asked as casually as she could.

‘Since the *Peace of Mind* tour I think,’ Suzie said. ‘Am I right Zed? Yes, it must have been. They met at the photo shoot for the cover.’

Zed suddenly became animated. ‘Yeah, I don’t think Mac ever got over the fact that she went for Kyle instead of him, but Kyle made sure it was his face her arse was in. Do you remember Kyle?’ he asked, expanding the conversation, ‘That cover shoot, when you two met?’ Kyle and Clare both nodded and their polite laugh turned genuine and the argument they were having was postponed for a while.

‘And don’t you forget,
The people that we’ve met
Are all I’ve got to remember you.’

A cheer went up as Mac finished his song and as he turned to his lunch, the crowd took their last photos and returned to their own lives.

Rome

Although Meg had dreamed about visiting Paris for years, it was Rome that she couldn't leave unexplored. She had arranged for the band to be photographed outside some of Rome's most famous buildings and she said would accompany them, something she would never have had the confidence to do the previous month. When breakfast was finished she shook hands with Gio Valetti and Antonio Angelini, the photographer and journalist from Io Donna magazine, and they set off.

MindSet were photographed on the Spanish steps; wandering passed the shops of Via del Tritone; and throwing coins into the Trevi fountain, hoping to return. Mac had been in a strange mood since they hit Italy, asking more questions than he answered, taking his time when they had places to be, wandering off to be on his own. She was worried about what he might say to the journalist, so cut over him. '*Yes, the people of Rome were definitely the most stylish he had ever seen.*' '*Yes, he was amazed by the beauty of the place.*' '*Of course he could find inspiration here for lyrics.*'

They stopped for lunch at a café in the Piazza Navona, finding seats in the shade next to the Fountain of the Four Rivers. Mac waited until everyone was seated then took a table by himself, opened his sketch book. He looked cultivated in crumbled linen, posed as tortured artist, smudging the charcoal with the edge of his thumb as drew the muscular figures on the fountain while he waited to be served.

It had been cool in the morning, so Meg had put on a sweatshirt and chinos, but the sun had broken through the haze and at each stop there was an increase in temperature which the Scot still couldn't quite believe. She would need to take Suzie's advice about layering more seriously. For the moment she was just glad to be able to sit down with a drink that was more ice than coke.

'So how long is Clare going to be in Milan?' She asked as she crunched on a cube.

'I don't know,' Kyle said with a shrug. 'She's got a bit of work lined up and then it'll depend on how her castings go.' Kyle shook the sugar canister, listening hard as the granules rearranged.

'I suppose it's tricky with both of you having careers that mean so much travelling.' She could feel his knees nudge the table in a nervous, insistent beat, and wondered how it would feel if they accidently hit hers. She stretched her legs a fraction.

'Well, we try to work around each other's schedules, but apparently I'm holding her back.' He glanced at the journalist who was laughing with Zed then leaned in towards Meg and lowered his voice. 'Who knows? We'll see how she gets on in Milan, maybe she's not the hotshot she thinks she is.'

For a moment Meg felt sorry for Clare. But then folk like her always wanted you to feel sorry for them — as if it wasn't enough that they had money and beauty; everyone had to like them as well. But Kyle's brooding wasn't particularly attractive; in fact it was draining her energy as quickly as the heat was, she had to stop torturing herself about Clare and changed the subject.

'I finally got my photos developed,' she said, beginning to rake in her bag. 'You know the ones I took a couple of weeks ago at the concert in Nimes, they're really cool.'

'Yeah?'

She opened the envelope and started to show him, but it was the magazine photographer who leaned across the table and picked them up.

'You need widen your aperture and this is all wrong,' he said as he flicked through the photographs, discarding some on the table, and drawing squares with his fingers to improve the framing on others. 'I would shoot less from under and more side. It's better. More movement too, in these, yes,' he said quickly flicking a photo out of the pack before choosing another. 'What speed you shoot at for this?'

'I don't know,' Meg cringed, 'I just used the automatic settings.' Kyle nudged Wayne. 'Swap places will you. I want to hear what this guy's saying.' Gio came and sat next to Kyle and they critiqued Meg's photos as she ate in silence. She couldn't even see what picture they were talking about, as Kyle questioned Gio on atmospherics and optimum exposure. She tried to follow, but the vocabulary was getting more complex and attempting to memorize key terms meant that she began to lose the thread of the conversation.

‘We were talking about refreshing the programme for the US,’ Kyle said. ‘Are you up for shooting the gig tonight?’

For a moment Meg felt a rush of excitement, but the Italian nodded. ‘It’s cool,’ he said, pulling a black leather Filofax from his camera bag. ‘I’ve time.’

‘Meg will get Todd to sort out a contract for you. It’ll be great.’

Kyle crumbled his napkin, threw it into the centre of the table and walked with Gio into the centre of the square, leaving Meg to pay the bill. He’d bought her the camera and encouraged her to experiment so it wasn’t fair that Kyle was trampling all over her dreams. She collected her photos from the puddle of condensation which had dribbled off the San Pellegrino, shook them, and decided she needed to give herself a shake too.

At the Monument to Victor Emmanuel and despite the sun needling its way into her eyes and pricking at her shoulders, Meg paid closer attention to Gio.

‘Move,’ he said between moaning about the lack of time and the incompetence of his assistants. She asked about the lighting set up, but he ignored her the way only Europeans could. Maybe later, when they had finished she could buy him a coffee and get him to explain some of the things he had talked about at lunch. But by the time her taxi had honked its way through the city to the Colosseum he had already taken his photos and packed up for the day.

Meg slammed the door of the taxi as she climbed in with Mac and Kyle. Her constant frown and the overwhelming heat had given her a headache and she lacked the will to suppress her irritation. 'I thought you were going to use my on-stage photos,' she said the minute they started to move. 'Why did you arrange for that guy to do it?'

Kyle leaned forward, then turned his head back to look at her, apparently surprised that she was upset. 'Well I got a good vibe,' he said, 'and let's face it, they need to be done professionally. I thought that was obvious.'

Of course it was obvious, but it didn't stop it hurting like hell. The driver pressed on his horn, and gesticulated as a school group crossed in front of him. One of the girls replied by flicking her skirt to show her silky brown thigh. Did Kyle think of her as a stupid school girl? Was that all she was to him? Mind you he wasn't much older than some of the student teachers they used to get, neither was Mac, so why did she let them treat her like a child. Instead of crying she turned her frustration on Mac. 'And what was that crap about the lost souls of the Tiber calling out to you and infusing you with the spirits of the masters? That journalist must have thought you were on an acid trip or something. It sounded really wanky.'

'Gee thanks Meg, you know, I am an artist,' he said without a glimmer of pretension. 'I've earned the right to talk like that, so don't dare change my words into some anodyne drivel again. Just because you're pissed about your snaps, don't take it out on me.'

The taxi stopped at a junction and Mac slapped Kyle on the knee and signalled to look at some girls walking by.

Horns blasted out across the city, interspersed with sirens and alarms. She closed her eyes, but it only seemed to amplify the noise, so she watched two guys try to bump cars along the street to make room for them to park. *What is it with guys and space?* Mac kept stretching, bringing his hands up like he was trying to take the off the roof, and Kyle splayed out his legs, squashing her into the door. But as she felt his legs against hers, she began to wonder why she felt so bad tempered; it wasn't all about the photos. And maybe she'd misinterpreted his gift as an instruction to be their photographer when really he was just being kind. She had been desperate for Clare to leave the tour, thinking that all her anxieties were tied up with how inadequate Clare made her feel. But Milan was three days ago, and if anything she felt more tense. In some weird way she knew where she was when Clare was about. Now the boundaries had shifted, but instead of Kyle being more accessible, he seemed to have drifted further away. The taxi took an unexpected sharp left, and Meg fell into Kyle's shoulders, and had to push against his thigh to steady herself.

'Sorry,' Meg said instinctively as she righted herself, then she carried on with more meaningful apologies. 'I'm sorry. I shouldn't have spoken like that. I'm just having a really bad day, my head's pounding, and I'm roasting. I'm really sorry.' She turned from them again. If she was any other girl Mac would have told her to strip off and cool down and they wouldn't peek, ha, ha. But they would never see her like that — not one of those girls, and she couldn't stand the thought of just being one of the boys. She looked out of the window but the passing sites of Rome had lost their shine.

'No worries kiddo,' Mac said as he leaned across to pat her knee. 'No hard feelings, eh?' And Kyle nudged her leg, ever so slightly making the nerves tingle all the way up her spine. Maybe he wasn't so distant after all.

Things to Come	*No 1 —Finland, Sweden and Belgium.*
	No 2 – Germany, Italy, UK and Holland
	No 5 – France
Dirty Mind LP	*No 1 album in Spain, Holland, Sweden*
	No 2 album in UK, Ireland, Belgium

August: New York

The thrill of her first flight made it impossible for Meg to sleep. The airport had been crazy — Suzie alone had seven cases over her allowance, and when Todd remonstrated, Zed gave him a look of *indulge her.* Then Wayne misplaced his passport and it was only after a ten minute search, that Meg found it stuck in a plant pot. Throughout their check-in, until they made it to the relative calm of the VIP lounge, there were autographs and photographs. Meg realised that even people who didn't know who MindSet were, would see a kerfuffle and want to join in. *'Is it Men at Work?' 'No!'*

Todd let her have the window seat and she sat staring out of it as the concertina walkway separated from the plane. Her stomach knotted with excitement as she watched tiny trucks push enormous planes, and saw passengers spill down stairs and onto buses to be transferred back to the terminal building. The tail fins of Swiss Air, KLM, Singapore Airlines with their Singapore Girls, Qantas, Iberia, presenting a whole world of possibilities.

She examined her emergency exit laminate and watched intently as the air hostess went through her routine. No one else paid any attention even though it seemed to be fairly vital stuff. Then the engines started to roar and Meg gripped the arms of her seat and gulped hard trying to equalise the pressure in her ears until the aisle came level again. The monopoly houses and patch-worked fields got smaller until all Meg could see was grey mist and then finally pure blue, like she had reached heaven. With no point of reference she wasn't sure if they were even moving. She waited for the plane to start to drop, *surely it couldn't stay in the air if it wasn't moving forward*, but they didn't fall and mass panic didn't break out, so she settled to watch *The Breakfast Club*. When the film was finished, the air hostesses came round with dinner. As she ate the sky darkened until her window reflected her new life — Business Class. Five months ago she was studying for exams she never took and slopping out pint glasses that the punters had pissed in. By now the result envelopes would have dropped onto doormats, yet here she was, without a qualification to her name, flying across the Atlantic, with America just hours away. Her face had changed too, even with the strange double image she could see it was no longer gaunt or perpetually worried; she could almost pass for normal.

During *View to a Kill* she took out her earphones, snuggled down under her blanket, punched her pillow into the nape of her neck, and tried to settle her jumpy legs. It wasn't as if she couldn't use some sleep. The last few weeks had been a frantic dash across Germany, Belgium and Holland; a touch-down in Manchester for *The Tube* and few hours in London for *Live Aid* where Clare had joined with them again. She had considered giving her mum a call, asking her to get the overnight bus down to London, but spending time with Val meant looking after her. She couldn't remember when she first realised their relationship was upside down — maybe when her granny made her promise not to write any more stories in her news jotter about mummy being drunk; or the first time she dialled 999.

With the lights dimmed Meg found herself distracted with the next week's itinerary, checking off to-do lists in her head and worrying about decisions she wasn't sure were hers to make. She had hoped to check some things with Todd during the flight, but he and Dave settled down before take-off and were now snorting and snoring next to her. She smiled, wondering if uber-controlled Todd knew how noisy he was when he slept. She sat forward on her seat to stretch her back and saw across the aisle Wayne gooseberried next to Kyle and Clare. Clare relaxed into the innocent look she cultivated for her magazine work; while Kyle's face looked alert even though his breathing spoke of deep sleep. It was only when she realised Wayne was watching her that she gave a half-smile to disguise her unease and picked up the *Cosmo* Suzie had given her earlier.

Shortly before touch down the cabin crew started to move around again, turning on lights and handing out warm soft cloths. Meg watched the others and followed suit, laying the cloth over her face, then wiping her hands and wrists with it. *How could such a small thing feel so amazing?* The level of activity increased around her as the band turned Business Class into a changing room, stripping off their jumpers and pulling on jackets, gelling hair, popping wake up pills and getting sunglasses ready for the glare of the airport. Clare and Suzie both changed in the loo and did full make-up before the seatbelt lights came on; while Meg managed to run a brush through her hair and add another layer of blue eyeliner.

The plane touched down at JFK after midnight but that didn't deter the fans or photographers who had gathered at Arrivals to witness MindSet's entrance into the USA. Todd grabbed Meg's arm and pulled her in front of the band as they made their way through to customs. 'Get ready,' he said.

'For what?' Meg asked.

'America. Just stay cool and keep everyone moving. Okay?'

'Okay,' Meg said, but she wasn't sure it was. Police and security officers stood ready to greet them, their hands resting on long batons and for a moment Meg worried they'd all be arrested for whatever they had stowed away. But the officers nodded, and led them on through the glass doors into the arrival hall and *flash click.*

'Coming through.' *Flash click. Blink.*

'Keep walking.' *Flash click, flash click.*

'No autographs.' *Flash click, flash click, flash click, flash click, flash click.* 'MindSet coming through.'

'AAAAAAAHHHHHH.'

Flash MAC, *flash* MAC, *flash click click. Blink.*

'We want MAC.' *Flash.*

'I love you Kyle.' *Blink.*

Flash 'Wayne will you marry me?' *Flash click. Crush.*

'Coach on the left hand side as we exit.'

'AAAAAHHHHH.'

'Zed, Zed, come to my bed.'

'I can't see.' *Blink blink.*

'Quick. Don't let anyone on the coach you don't know.'

Flash. Click. Blink.

As soon as Meg had shoved the last girl away from the door, a policeman signalled to the driver and the bus pulled away. Meg fell forward against the windscreen before Todd pulled her back and into a seat.

'Welcome to America,' he said.

'What the hell was that?'

'That was you doing your job. Remember I told you to send a press release with our flight times. Well, that's what happens.'

'You wanted that?' Meg asked as she tried to catch her breath and blink the floaters from her eyes.

'Of course we did; that's what it's all about.'

'I can't believe there were so many people, I mean, what time is it?' She looked at her watch, but she hadn't changed it and her brain wasn't up to the calculation.

'1.30 a.m.,' Todd said, 'Eastern Daylight. I told you things were looking up.'

'It's incredible.'

'We tour Europe for the panache and America for the cash. If things carry on like this we're made. This place is going to be awesome.'

Meg looked up the bus and saw no reason to disagree. The guys were really buzzing as they compared their hauls of teddy bears and roses. Mac had a pair of lacy knickers on his head and Wayne was mesmerised by an Empire State snow globe. Zed regaled the coach with his experience of the airport walk-through, as though he was the only one who had been there and Kyle caught Meg's eye.

'Congratulations,' she mouthed.

He nodded and gave a long satisfied smile.

After the interview at *Drumming Monthly*, Kyle and Meg jumped in a yellow taxi for the journey back to the hotel. The windows were down; the sticky heat and overpowering fumes preferable to the background mixture of cheap aftershave and onions in the cab. Kyle looked out of the window, craning his neck to see the architecture then scanning the pavements. Meg watched him, more interested in his reactions to the world outside than to forming her own.

'Why do you always squirm when they ask why you chose the drums?' She said after a while, bringing Kyle's focus back into the cab.

'Do I?' He paused, 'do you think they notice?'

Meg shrugged, 'Maybe they're not looking for you to be evasive. It's a fairly straightforward question after all, and they're expecting an honest answer so that's what they hear.'

'And it's not what you hear?'

Meg wondered for a minute, she wasn't even sure why she had brought it up — it wasn't as if she was going to phone round every journalist he had ever spoken to and set the record straight. But it was a rare opportunity to talk to Kyle with no one else around, and she did want to know. She had always found it useful to know what motivated people, but this time she wanted more of Kyle. He turned his body to face her.

'You know that my Mum and Dad were both musicians, right? Of course you know — it comes up in every bloody article that's written about me. They all talk about how I turned away from classical music and got into rock. It gets so clichéd, but it doesn't explain half of it.' The cab screeched at a red light, and Kyle had to steady himself, but he went on without prompting. 'You see, when I was younger, every time I picked up an instrument, and I mean every time, mum felt she had to instruct me. It didn't matter if it was a toy keyboard or a trumpet, I was told how to position my fingers properly, or how to breathe or whatever. Drums were different — she didn't even see them as a proper instrument, just something you hit. She hated it when I said drums were my instrument, didn't understand that controlling the rhythm was all that mattered. She's come round bit, I suppose, now I'm making some money.'

'What about your dad?'

'He died, Meg.' Kyle said, in a way that made her feel cut-off.

'Sorry I didn't know,' Meg said, and felt her hand slide off her lap and move to rest on top of Kyle's. He twitched at the contact and pulled away.

'You should know,' he said, irritation filling his voice. 'That's what you're paid for.' He banged his hand against the screen separating them from the driver. 'Let us out here, will you mate? I need some air.'

The driver stopped and started to rant about the shortened journey and how he had to make a living, but Kyle dismissively threw enough money at him to stop the tirade. Meg climbed out and ran to catch up with Kyle as he strode along the street. There was less fresh air outside than there was inside the cab, the pollution getting up Meg's nose and into her lungs, her legs feeling heavy from the plane journey but the buzz of the street made her nostalgic for home. How could she not have known his father had died? It was a stupid error — no wonder he was annoyed with her. What else didn't she know? He seemed lost in his thoughts, no longer looking about him, but only directly ahead. She was wished she could share her excitement at seeing the Twin Towers or nudge him and make him laugh at the women wearing business suits with trainers. *It must be sad to lose someone who was there for you*, she thought, but her sympathy was coupled with sadness that she never had the luxury of caring parents who actually wanted to spend time with her. All Val had taught Meg was how to pull a pint, and that was only so she could nip out for a quick fag.

When they stopped at the end of a block to wait for the *Walk* sign, Meg could see that Kyle's shoulders had relaxed a bit, and his face seemed less set, so she tried again to get answers to the questions niggling at her. 'So, the drums?' she said, and when he didn't wince, she continued, 'sounds like you took them up to spite your parents?'

'It wasn't so much about spite,' he said slowly, as though he was thinking about it for the first time, 'at least I don't think it was. I just wanted freedom to find the music myself. I didn't want the fun trained out of me. I used to feel sorry for the guys training for the

State swim team who never had the energy to mess about at the beach. I didn't want music to be like that.'

'But you're so focused Kyle,' Meg said looking up at him. 'You're always practising — the others just seem to turn up and play, but you stay after the sound check and keep going.'

'Well, it's my life — and anyway the others can practise in their rooms, or play on the bus. Drums aren't so portable.'

Meg nodded — she hadn't really thought that the strumming and humming that constantly accompanied them counted as work. 'It must be nice to feel so passionate about something,' she said.

'It is. You need to find your passion too — I thought photography would work since you're always taking everything in— but I've not seen you with your camera for a while.'

Meg felt guilty — he had been good enough to buy it for her. 'I don't know,' she said, suddenly conscious of the weight of it in her bag, and the iconic streets around her, 'I got a bit put off in Rome, I suppose,' she said, waiting for Kyle to remember, 'with that Gio guy.'

'If it is your passion nothing should put you off. Okay, you're not as good as him yet? So practice, get better.' Someone else might have said it with a smile on their face, but with Kyle there was the air of expectation, and Meg wasn't sure what would happen to her if she let him down.

'I will,' Meg said. He was right — she was an observer— trained to be alert to the possibility of trouble. It would be good to have a dream, even if she wasn't sure it was hers.

They walked on in silence and when they finally made it back to the air conditioning of the hotel Kyle said a quick goodbye and Meg had to go straight into introducing Mac to a *Rolling Stone* journalist.

She apologized for her lateness; set up her Dictaphone next to the journalist's and took a chair nearby so that she could discreetly listen to the interview. The chair was well upholstered, padding her legs and hugging her back. She felt heavy, sinking, as though the seat was pulling her down into its upholstery. But Mac called over a few times to ask for confirmation of facts, making her snap back into consciousness, sometimes having to consult her notes, but more often just knowing the answers. When the appointed time was up and Meg's little travel alarm rang in her pocket, she stood and eased the journalist away with the promise of a little more time before the gig.

Mac yawned. 'Any more, Meg?' he asked, 'I'm stiffening up here and you look like you're about to drop off.'

'Sorry, the jet lag just hit me. We need to get to the radio station' She checked her diary. 'WRXP — 2pm. I hope they've got some food, I'm starving.'

Meg negotiated a night off and was in bed by 8pm, sleeping soundly until she woke with a start at 4am, and couldn't get back to sleep. The nightmares had more or less stopped, but the early hours made her feel vulnerable and hyper alert to every noise. To calm her mind she went over the events of the day but kept coming back to the conversation she had had with Kyle. Changing it slightly each time she returned to the beginning. In the first version he opened up to her about his father, but by the seventh or eighth retelling as she drifted back to sleep, he was sobbing in her arms and she was holding him tight, whispering comfort in his ears.

When she came down for breakfast Kyle was already on his way out. He passed her with barely a nod, and looked tired, like he had also spent a restless night. She hoped the blush she felt wasn't too noticeable.

She looked around the breakfast room while she waited in the queue at the buffet table. Couples on sightseeing trips; businessmen catching a bite before their second meeting; families trying hard to have a great time; only the cities changed. She saw Todd sitting alone near a window, surrounded by the review pages of half a dozen newspapers, so after she had exchanged good mornings with Zed and Suzie, she took the opportunity to sit with him.

'I need to ask you something, Todd.' She stopped and took a deep breath before continuing, 'now that you're sending me out on more interviews I want to know if there are any topics I should be aware of.' Todd didn't respond, so Meg took a slug of lukewarm tea then rephrased. 'Anything I should guide the journalists away from?'

Todd took off his glasses and folded them on top of the *New York Times*. 'Just don't let them talk about drugs or underage girls,' he said, 'no matter how funny they think the story is. This country seems to disapprove of everything but guns and poverty.' Meg nodded; she didn't need to take a note of that.

'What about more personal stuff?' She asked, as she spooned some cereal into her mouth.

'Just so long as no one knows that Mac and Wayne sometimes share, then everything's fine.' Meg almost choked on her breakfast and didn't ask what exactly they shared. Instead she inched towards the information she really wanted.

'What about the others?'

'Well everything seems rosy in the garden of Suzie and Zed,' he said looking at them like a proud father. 'As for Kyle and Clare — well you'd know more about that —looks like you're his new project.' Meg pulled her napkin to her mouth and gave it an unnecessary wipe.

She'd been a project before and she wasn't sure she liked the invasion that came with it. *'Here's a jacket my daughter's grown out of, do you think you'd like it Maggie?'*

'The janitor found these shoes in lost property, are they yours?'

'How is your mother doing Maggie? She wasn't looking too well the last time I saw her.'

She'd never told Val, although she must have noticed. The teachers, the other parents who gave her little parcels, even the creepy old man on the corner who would give her a piece and jam if she scratched his back. Val would think it was charity. And you never accept charity, except if it comes from a boyfriend — then it's different.

'What if anyone asks about Kyle's parents?' Meg asked Todd. 'He got a bit tetchy yesterday when I mentioned his dad.'

'I can imagine,' Todd said, but reassured her with, 'No one will ask here, and in Australia it's an old story. Now let's look at this schedule.'

Dirty Mind 1985 - North America

Beacon Theater	New York, NY	2—5 Aug
Paradise	Boston, MA	6 & 7 Aug
Spectrum,	Montreal, Quebec	8 Aug
Concert Hall	Toronto, Ontario	9 & 10 Aug
	REST DAY	
Mann Music Centre	Philadelphia, PA	12—14 Aug
Pier 6 Concert Pavilion	Baltimore	15 Aug
The Bayou	Washington DC	16 Aug
Kings Dominion	Richmond, VA	17 Aug
	2 x REST DAY	
Riverbend Music Theater	Cincinnati, OH	20 Aug
Clowes Hall	Indianapolis, IN	21 Aug
Orpheum	Minneapolis, MI	22 & 23 Aug
Uptown Theater	Kansas City, MO	24 Aug
	5 x REST DAY	
Ogden Theater	Denver, CO	29 Aug

Queen Elizabeth Theatre	Vancouver, British Columbia	30 & 31 Aug
Paramount Theatre	Seattle, WA	1 – 3 Sept
Hollywood Palace	Los Angeles, CA	4 – 6 Sept
Kabuki	San Francisco, CA	7 – 9 Sept

BREAK

After Boston and Canada they began their slow crawl on America's freeways. When Meg climbed onto the tour bus each day she felt a wave of despondency hit her with the smell of boiled feet. As they hurtled through Europe, she had been filled with adrenaline, even making a list of the places she'd like to see again, like that was a possibility. She'd ticked off world-famous sites and compared the styles of people, architecture and even farming, sending postcards home to chart her travels as she went. South through France, where she had taken photos of the sunflower fields, to Spain, with old men on corners, widow women in lethal black and young men clicking their tongues as she walked by. Across to Italy, with its olive groves and villas; further south to lemons and coastlines that hair-pinned and plunged. Then northwards, through Austria and Germany and everywhere the towns and cities built around water: rivers, lakes and seas. Now across the ocean, the skyscraper canyons of New York gave way to long, straight roads, low-rise and Taco Bells. It struck her that, except in the very centre of cities, people were few and far between; locked inside buildings or cars — walking didn't appear to be a concept they were familiar with. So each stretch of road became identical to the last with hardly a bend to break the monotony.

The rising summer heat and close quarters were beginning to make the atmosphere inside the bus tedious too. There was no singing and larking about any more, now it was all snapping and fighting. One fart too noxious could start a riot. Even Suzie, who was rarely quiet, hadn't talked for a whole day after Zed forgot to buy her a Hershey bar at a truck stop. Todd had also discovered the joys of bourbon, so the crash course in music management, which he had been imparting to Meg, had been replaced by drunken snores or slurred thinking. So she was forced to amuse herself — catching up on sleep, daydreaming about non-specific blonde drummers, or reading to pass the endless hours. She picked up the poetry books Mac bought and always left behind in dressing rooms — a mixture of the classics and beat. She wasn't sure if he used them as inspiration or props, but there was an endless supply and their spines were rarely cracked. She could read a little then spend the next ten minutes trying to figure out what the poet was on about. Maybe she could take her English Higher next year at college. Occasionally, when she felt that her budget would allow it, she stocked up on photography and art books, trying hard to learn about being creative. An Ansel Adams book travelled in her suitcase to be savoured at night when she finally got a chance to flop on her bed. Its heavy board backing and glossy pages revealed a beauty in the landscape she found impossible to see through the coach windows, and she wondered if she had it in her to be anything more than a gopher.

Sometimes Suzie or a chancing-his-arm roadie would come and lean over Todd to pass the time of day with her, but before long Todd would shout '*Shut up*' and they would scuttle back to their seats. Dave, who had improved his title to Transportation and Logistics Executive, always sat across the aisle from Meg, but he never spoke to her unless it was absolutely necessary. She could tell she was an annoyance to him, a hanger-on who hadn't evaporated the way they usually did when their parents caught up with them or their lack of passport made it impossible to carry on. She had stayed put and if he didn't like it he could shove it up his arse.

Name: Maclean Marchmount
DOB: 22/04/63
Star Sign: Taurus
Loves: Beautiful women
The Beat Poets
Root beer
The Doors
Hates: Wasting time

Name: Kyle Watt
DOB: 25/10/63
Star Sign: Scorpio
Loves: My girlfriend Clare
Champagne
Jelly babies
The Stones
Hates: Rudeness

Name: Zed
DOB: 18/02/62
Star Sign: Aquarius
Loves: Suzie
Fender Stratocaster guitars
John Cale
Hates: Ugly buildings

Name: Wayne the bassist
DOB: 10/01/59
Star Sign: Capricorn
Loves: Practical jokes
Existentialism
John Cage
Hates: Gardening

When they arrived at the latest hotel, Meg would start on her tasks in order of importance. Within five minutes she would have tracked down the trendiest looking waitress and pumped her for information about which nightclub the band should be seen at after the show. Then she would use her fail-safe check by asking the concierge. If they agreed, she was in trouble, but normally he would either recoil in horror at her suggestion, or shrug his shoulders and say he'd never heard of the place — *result.*

A few phone calls later and the band's name would be on the guest list and local photographers lined up for the door. She could rely on lots of buzz too, as she hadn't met a waitress yet who didn't immediately share her recommendation with all her friends. '*It's like, they're here in the hotel, and I'm telling you they're going to be at Bar Lux tonight. I know. And I think the lead singer Mac fancies me — he keeps looking right at me and smiling, that way he does. He is sooooo hot. And you know, we could come back here later, yeah, I'm sure I could sneak you in. Oh my God! Can you imagine?*'

Once the after-show party was sorted she could leave the lobby and get settled in her room. The beds in America were bigger and so were the TVs but her routine remained the same: toiletries laid out; a quick shower; clean t-shirt and knickers; pyjamas on the bed; a reorganisation and check of her suitcase to see when the laundry was required. Only once she'd made herself at home would she start on the bundle of messages she had been handed at check-in; making arrangements for interviews and appearances; getting back to reviewers; passing figures to Todd for reports on coverage and impact for the record company; answering hand-delivered love letters with postcard-sized, pre-signed photos of the band. She kept a large diary, bulging with lists, tickets and post-it notes that she held together with elastic bands. She divided each page into uneven columns and used a different pen colour for each of the guys. Once she had firmed everything up she would transcribe individual schedules and post them under their doors, making sure that Wayne never realised that no one ever really wanted to talk to him.

Some days she would be able to catch up with a little sleep or call home and chat for a while, making sure her mum was okay, and reassuring her that everything was fine. On others, the phone would ring constantly for clarification about whether Hendricks or Tanqueray Gin was preferred for the rider, and would they mind if the vodka wasn't Russian — *'this State won't deal with the Soviets'*. Some days she didn't even bother closing her door, as the band checked plans or met up before interviews, and all the time there was food. '*Bring us up some sarnies and a couple of bottles of Krug.' 'Can I get two quarter-pounders? No make that three, what? Four? Four quarter-pounders and some fries.'* Occasionally she wanted to scream '*Get out of my room and leave me alone*,' but mainly it soothed her, particularly when they just came to hang out. Suzie sitting on the bed, painting Meg's nails turquoise while Zed conducted a phone interview. Kyle examining her files, adding his own notes, the tension falling away a little each time he dropped by. 'Do you think we should be adding products to merchandise?' Kyle would ask, or 'How many buttons have we sold?' or, 'Did Todd get things sorted with the Orpheum?' Why he didn't ask Todd himself, she didn't know, but she would answer his questions, pulling out the relevant statistics, feeling his heat as he bent over her.

The easy camaraderie reminded her of when she went to wakes with her granny, and folk would drink and tell stories and sing the occasional plaintive song. She was happy then.

'What do you think you'll do when the tour is over Meg?' he asked one day as he flicked through *Rolling Stone.*

'I've not given it much thought,' Meg replied, suddenly aware that her heart was palpitating at the mention of the tour coming to an end. Black nights and hidden lanes. 'I can't see me going back to Glasgow, whatever I do.'

'No?'

'There are better places,' she said.

'Do you think so?' Kyle asked. 'I always think it's what you make of the place that matters?'

Meg thought for a moment, went over to one of her suitcases, reached into the inner pocket and pulled out a scrapbook with the words *All the Places I've Ever Been* written in her best hand on the front. 'Look,' she said, handing the book to Kyle. He flicked through it, stopping every now and again to look more closely at a restaurant matchbook or a carefully cut out header from hotel notepaper.

'Why do you keep all these?' he asked.

'Do you think it's stupid?'

'No,' he shook his head and handed it back to her. She placed it on her knees and folded her hands on top of it. She had bought the scrapbook at a stationer in Venice, spent practically a whole day's wages on it, but the shop had been too tempting and once she was in, the smell of the ink had overwhelmed her. Leather bound books with marbled paper beat the Holly Hobby scrapbooks she had hankered after as a child. And now she didn't need angels with pastel wings sitting on clouds to fill the pages; she had real things from real places.

'It looks like you've spent a lot of time on it, Meg,' Kyle said gently nudging into her reflections.

'My granny had a jam jar full of sand from the beach at Magheraroarty and she used to take out a handful when she was feeling sad and run it through her fingers,' Meg said, miming her granny's actions. 'She always put back less than she took out, but she didn't care. She said dropping a few grains was worth it for the smell and the memories.' Meg got up from the chair and put the scrapbook away. She kept her back to Kyle as she remembered how she had mixed her gran's ashes with the sand before plopping the jar into the Clyde and hoping that the river would take her back to Donegal.

'My gran wanted to hold *home*,' Meg said wondering if her granny had made it, 'but I want to hold *away*.'

Kyle wriggled forward and put his hand into the front pocket of his jeans. 'I keep this with me,' Kyle said, opening his hand to show a small silver object. As he turned it in his hand, mother of pearl caught the light, showing a shimmer of colours to Meg.

'I like to have it close,' he said.

Meg opened her hand and Kyle placed it on her palm. She lifted it carefully between two fingers, her hand shaking slightly as she held it, feeling the give as the plainer side swivelled on a tiny hinge. 'What is it?' she asked.

'Cufflink.'

She nodded, even though the word had not given an adequate explanation.

'It was my dad's,' Kyle said as he took it back from her. 'He had a box full of them, with tiny compartments to keep each pair separate. I don't know what happened to this one's partner, but at least it meant it didn't go to the auction. Mum got rid of everything a few years back — she'd go nuts if she knew I'd kept this.'

Meg nodded. 'I never knew my father,' she said, and for the first time in her life she felt the loss of him.

'Did he die?' Kyle asked.

'Buggered off, more like. Mum never talked about him. I don't know if he even knew about me.'

'Sometimes even when they know they don't stay,' Kyle said.

But before Meg could ask for an explanation the phone rang, and Kyle popped the cufflink back into his pocket. Meg answered the phone and said '*yes*' when Suzie told her that she had booked a couple of lanes down at the local bowling, and did she want to come.

Minneapolis, MI

The bowling alley sat on the edge of the town between WalMart and Dunkin Donuts. Pickup trucks and battered Fords littered the car park — the only thing saving it from being an episode of *The Twilight Zone* was tumbleweed blowing across the tarmac. Gucci sandals and Doc Martens were swapped for two-tone bowling shoes and placed in pigeon-holes behind the counter next to cowboy boots and HiTech trainers. Meg tied her chewed laces while Todd sorted everyone into teams and she found herself in Kyle's team against Dave, Todd, and two of the road crew. She sat on the vinyl bench and watched as they ordered beers and punched their names into the scoreboard. *How come everyone else always knew what they were doing? Even Todd.* She watched them bowl and felt sweat form under her arms from the sticky atmosphere.

'Meg, come on, it's your turn,' Todd said, stirring her from her torpor.

She lifted the bowl awkwardly in two hands, surprised at how heavy it was and tried to figure out how she could possibly fit her fingers into the spaced out holes.

'Looks like you've picked the novice,' Dave gloated. 'We're two strikes up already — maybe it's time to concede.'

'Not likely,' Mac said, stretching out his arms to crack his fingers.

Meg dropped the bowl onto the alley and watched as it rolled straight into the gutter. 'Why does it look so easy when you guys do it?' She asked as her second bowl followed the first.

Clare moved forward without waiting for Meg get out of the way and positioned herself, bowl in hand, arse in air, ready to roll. No matter what she did; no matter how unflattering her footwear; she always looked graceful, Meg could give her that. But while Clare's bowl started straight it veered off at the end and dropped into the gutter too.

'Help me Kyle,' she said in a pathetic voice that made Meg's insides curdle.

Kyle moved forward and fitted in behind her, his left arm around her waist, his right hand pulling her arm back to aim. They bent in unison, swung through, let go and watched as the pins all fell.

'Yeah, go me,' she said.

Kyle lifted Clare and swung her round, then put her down and prepared for his own turn. But as he was about to bowl, Clare put her arm around his waist and made him release the bowl with so little momentum that it only hit one pin on the left hand side.

'For Christ's sake, Clare, what are you doing?'

'I was just trying to help,' she said, and Meg thought she could hear her eyelashes bat.

'Well don't. We're far enough behind without you handicapping me.' His next shot hit straight in the middle and brought down the other nine, but it didn't improve his mood. Mac bowled, then Meg again. This time Kyle and Mac coached from their seats and she managed to knock three pins down with her shots. She clapped at her success, but when she turned around for appreciation they had looked away. Mac was eyeing up girls in tight shorts a few lanes over and Kyle and Clare stared into their laps.

‘You’ll not miss me if I duck out for a few minutes,’ Meg said, and, since there was no reply, she reckoned they wouldn’t. She walked slowly along the alley towards the toilets. She had thought bowling was just meant to be a bit of a laugh but she saw the intensity in the faces of one bowler after another. *My God, they’re competitive.*

The whole building stank and the toilets suffered from the same lack of cleanliness, so she placed her handbag on the shelf in the cubicle and put a paper seat cover onto the pan. But she hadn’t even sat down when she heard the toilet door open and the familiar voices of Clare and Suzie.

‘He’s just being so horrible to me. I don’t know what to do,’ Clare whimpered.

‘Don’t worry, Clare — we’re all going a bit stir crazy and he’s pissed we’re not here for two nights. They’ve been getting crap about it all day.’

‘That still doesn’t give him the right to be so mean. He’s making a fool out of me. The more I tell him I love him, the more he moves away.’

‘He does love you, Clare — you can see it when he looks at you.’

'Yeah, but he's not looking anymore, is he? He's looking at that little runt.'

Meg gasped, *runt, I'll give her a bloody runt.* But instead of bursting out of the cubicle to confront her, she took the canny option and listened.

'Ever since she joined this tour he's been different. I don't know why he's so fascinated with her, but she's upsetting me and he doesn't seem to care.'

'You're overreacting, babe.'

Meg could picture Suzie's concerned look and maybe a comforting hand round her shoulders too.

'Don't. That's what Kyle says. "*It's all in your head, Clare. You're making too big a deal of it.*" But it's not in my head — he keeps sneaking off to her room for cosy chats and he won't tell me why. They think I'm too dim to see what's going on.'

Meg smiled, and wondered where Kyle was going, and why Clare thought he was with her. Okay, so he did drop by to quiz her on other bands she'd seen, but not as much as Clare was making out. *Maybe,* she tried to stop the thought before it could go any further, but it nagged, *maybe if he's going off her....*

'You're beautiful,' Suzie said, Meg clicked right back to reality, 'and there's no way Kyle's going to finish with you. Just think of those pictures you did for Rolex — my God, you're made for each other.'

'I don't know if that's enough anymore. I'm missing prime modelling time to be with him and he can't bear to look at me. And

I'm bored of all of this. I should be in Milan, or New York, not this bloody bush town with him screaming at me.'

'I know, babe, the guys don't get how hard it is for us. The first time I went on tour with Zed I went mad, waking up in the middle of the night with not a clue where I was. I'd walk into walls trying to find the loo and I'd forget room numbers and get lost in hotels. Total nightmare — so the next time I stayed home, but that's was even worse. I know Zed wouldn't be unfaithful, but your mind starts imagining things. That's why I packed in my job.'

'At least you've got something to do.' Meg heard her say.

'Well, cutting their hair is hardly a full-time job. You should ask Todd for something to do. Meg's job doesn't look too hard, and then you've solved two problems. Now dry your eyes and we'll grab a drink.'

Meg heard the door close, so she flushed the toilet and came out to the sinks, but Suzie was still standing at the mirror putting on her lipstick.

'Meg?' she said, cringing.

Meg started to wash her hands, carefully lathering them and rinsing while Suzie watched her in the mirror.

'Did you hear that?'

Meg looked straight into the reflection of Suzie's eyes. 'It's fine. Forget it.'

'I was just trying to cheer her up, Meg — she's feeling vulnerable just now. I didn't mean anything by it — Todd would never get rid of you.'

'Yeah?' Meg snorted, threw her paper towel into the bin and brushed by her. Suzie had been so nice to her, but now it looked like she was just the same as everyone else — ready to betray at the first chance. She thought Suzie understood that this was more than a job for Meg, it was survival. And the fact that she'd told Clare she was beautiful in the exact same tone she used with Meg — it made her want to spit. Suzie couldn't be friends with both of them, and it was obvious that Suzie would always be on Clare's side.

Meg went back to the lane, blinking her eyes hard to absorb the tears which were gathering there, lifted her bowl, focused on the pins and sent it straight down the centre of the alley. Then she turned to Kyle, 'You've to play for Clare,' she said, 'she's given up on the game.'

'And it looks like you've been taking lessons.'

'Well, you've just got to keep your eye on the target, don't you?'

'Very philosophical,' Kyle said, 'Just keep putting it into action; I've got a hundred bucks riding on this.'

They had an early start the next day with more long straight roads predicted and little more than dusty mountains in the distance to look at. While they waited for the luggage to be loaded Meg did her usual checks: making sure that Todd and Dave were happy; clocking how many groupies had been added; tactfully removing, with a firm hand on their elbows, any that were too young or too ugly. Kyle and Clare were last to get on, but instead of their usual seats, Kyle signalled for the groupie next to Mac to keep Clare company and he took the seat she vacated. The doors closed and as the bus juddered into action Meg took the seat behind them. She bent over some papers but gave her concentration to the words coming through the gap in the seats.

'Do you think you could pull together some lyrics in the next few days?' Kyle began, 'I want us to get back into the studio as soon as this tour's over.'

'Give it a rest,' Mac said, 'it's only 8.30 — I can't think about lyrics at this hour. My head's thumping man.' Mac rubbed his eyes, then his scalp and nose, each one apparently irritating him in a different way.

'We're just building up so much momentum — we need to capitalise on it. This is our time — I can feel it. I thought we could book Air Studios in Montserrat — it would be like a holiday.'

'Yeah, but it wouldn't be a holiday, would it? We'd never see daylight. I know what you're like man, and honestly Kyle, fuck off. It's too early.'

Kyle stretched to open the air vents above them, but wasn't put off. 'Come on, Mac. We're wasting our time sitting on this bloody bus. Zed said he'd work on some stuff; maybe the two of you could get together later.'

'I can't write to order. I need to be inspired,' Mac said. 'And look at this place. My God, it's so bleak.'

Meg looked out at the scrub planes before Mac continued his voice less aggressive now. 'I started scribbling some stuff in Europe but it's nowhere near ready. You need to give me time, and if you think I'm going straight into a studio after this, you're wrong man. I'm off to Whitsunday the minute I can.'

Mac bent down and pulled a Walkman out of his bag ending the conversation. Kyle stared at him for a few moments, but Mac seemed unmoved as he raked through cassettes, so Kyle poked his head through the gap to talk to Meg instead.

'Can you try to give him a break from all these interviews?' Kyle said. 'He needs to be fresher.'

Meg shrugged; they all looked like they needed to be fresher. Mac's interest in girls seemed to be slowing; Wayne's pallor was getting greyer; Zed was switching between stupor and frenzy; and even Kyle was losing some of his boundless energy. 'I'll try, Kyle, but they all want Mac — it's just how it is.'

'Okay,' he said, and untwisted back into his seat.

But it wasn't Mac they all wanted, some of them wanted Kyle. She wanted Kyle. Wanted to stretch out her hand and lose it in his curls; wanted to stroke the nape of his neck, have him turn again and smile; wanted to breathe in the very essence of him. She glanced down at her paperwork, but the thought kept coming back — maybe with Clare and him fighting, there was a chance for her after all.

Kansas City, MO

They walked along the Parkway, past a grand fountain and a Spanish looking tower and into the M&S Grill. After the glare and stifling heat of the midday sun, the yellowed hue from the ceiling lights was a relief. The maitre d' welcomed them and led them to a private dining room. Heads turned towards them, but Meg knew how to react as she smiled gently at no one in particular.

'Wow, this is very sophisticated, isn't it?' Meg said.

'Well, if you don't mind me saying, it's not very *sophisticated* to say how *sophisticated* things are. And Kansas City, are you kidding?' Clare said, ignoring the M&S staff.

'Back off, will you, Clare?' Kyle said, 'You're being infantile.'

'Well, her Hicksville act is getting old and it reflects badly on us.' Clare said to Kyle, although her voice was loud enough for everyone to hear.

'Well, this place is beautiful and she's excited by it,' Kyle said, slurring his words ever so slightly. *Had he been drinking already?* 'Maybe if you weren't always so cynical, you might be able to enjoy things once in a while.'

Meg moved away from their bickering, and let the maitre d' pull a seat out for her at the far side of the table. She didn't care if Clare thought she was naïve, she still got excited in nice restaurants, and didn't mind reminding them that they should feel lucky. She sat with a straight back while a waiter unfolded a napkin onto her lap and the others arranged themselves around her — Zed and Suzie on one side, Mac and Wayne on the other. Todd took the middle seat of the remaining three, forcing Kyle and Clare to either side of him.

'Will you calm down a bit, Kyle?' Todd spat a whisper. 'I don't want a scene every time you two go out in public. I've asked Meg to put out some nice pictures of you to the press, so don't ruin it.'

Looking through their photos had taken Meg longer than it should have — going off-task she tried to find one that would show an image of perfection, yet suggest, if looked at with hindsight, that something was amiss. Clare's slightly forced smile, or Kyle's hand placed reluctantly around her waist. She had examined Clare's face for almost as long as she spent on Kyle's, wondering what it was in its make-up that made it so beautiful. Suzie maintained that it was all down to attitude — *'If you think you're beautiful then you are,'* she had said, but Meg knew that wasn't true as she compared Claire with her own features. Blonde/ dark; tall/ short; gorgeous/ not ugly, no, she had seen ugly, but not beautiful either.

'Don't bother,' Kyle said. He looked at Todd but his comments were only for Clare. 'Her bookings go up when she's seen with me, but I don't get anything out of it.' Kyle raised his voice louder as Clare got up and made her way to the toilets. It was the first time she had ever seen Kyle lose control and it unsettled her, but to see Clare dismissed, well, that gave her a little thrill.

Kyle signalled to the waiter, 'Give us your best Chablis, when you're ready mate.'

The Grill did the best steaks in Missouri and they weren't disappointed. Everything in America was bigger than in Europe, but she couldn't imagine an animal large enough to produce their dinner. Blood oozed onto their plates and mingled with the porcini mushroom sauce, making Meg feel like she had died and gone to meat heaven. The guys heaped purple, green and orange vegetables onto their plate, bulking up for the concert ahead, while Clare picked at her side salad, and pushed her steak to the far side of her plate.

'You want some wine, Meg?' Zed asked, as the sommelier lingered.

'She's underage. Remember.' Clare spat.

'It's fine. I'll just have a coke.'

Clare thought she was scoring points, but it suited Meg to have a clear head when the rest of them got fuzzed with drink and drugs, if she needed to she could down a vodka later when the guys were on stage.

She ordered strawberry cheesecake for dessert and realised how used she was to this upside down life — three course meals at lunchtime, snacks for dinner and anything they could lay their hands on after the gig. She knew it would still be daylight when they left the restaurant and that the working day wouldn't kick up a gear until later, but for now she could sit back and listen to Todd and the band share stories of past times and plan for the future. She was part of that future now. She could feel it every time Kyle crinkled his eyes across at her and smiled so subtly only she could see.

MindSet – One Night Only
Uptown Theatre, Kansas City, MO

There was a loud rap on Meg's door around midnight. She popped the cleanser-drenched cotton wool into the bin and crossed to the peephole. She closed one eye and squinted through, took the chain off and opened the door. Kyle walked in and flopped onto the bed.

'Can I crash here?' He asked, picking up the TV remote.

'Would you not be better in with Mac or Wayne?' she said, still holding the door open.

'They've got company.'

'I thought they were alone when we got back here,' Meg said.

'What can I say?' He gave his shoulders a weary shrug. 'They move fast.'

'Kyle, I really don't think this is a good idea. Clare is permanently pissed off with me, and letting you stay here?' But she closed the door anyway.

'Just chill Meggie. Will you get me some vodka out of the minibar, there's a mate.'

She threw him a miniature, which landed on his stomach with an ooff, then picked up her key. He was too drunk for Meg to take any chances. 'If you're staying here, I'm not. I'm going to find somewhere else to sleep.'

Kyle responded by turning on the TV and grabbing a second vodka from the bar. She shook her head and left.

Out in the corridor she felt rather foolish, *he just wanted to sleep*, or maybe she'd wished so hard she'd made it come true. Even so, the thought of Kyle actually in her room terrified her. She thought about knocking on Suzie's door but her list of room numbers was on her desk, and she couldn't chance knocking on random doors. She took the lift down to the foyer, but the hotel was slipping into night mode, with lights dimmed and bars closed until morning. The concierge looked up as she walked by, but she didn't know how he could help her, so she took a seat in the lobby. It wasn't meant to be like this — when Kyle had asked her for dinner all those months ago in Glasgow she just saw his generosity as a way to escape. Fancying him was just for fun, but she knew that her feelings had been growing stronger and now he was in her room. Val would tell her to get back up there, but she wasn't like Val, in fact she had tried all her life to be the exact opposite. But if she didn't go back, where she could go? Kyle wouldn't hurt her. She said it to herself, closed her eyes, and breathed deeply. *And if he does?* For once in her life she had to trust. She went back up to her floor.

As she walked along the corridor a door opened and Clare's head poked out. Even in the dim light her face looked puffy. 'Have you seen Kyle?' she asked, sadness seeping from her voice.

Meg shook her head. 'Not recently,' she said and continued on to her own room.

The American football obviously hadn't captured Kyle's attention and he lay snoring on the bed, empty vodka bottles lying on his chest. His blonde hair flopped over one eye and her heart lurched. He definitely wouldn't hurt her. She knew this tiff with Clare would blow over like they always did, but in the meantime he was in her bed. Well *on* her bed. She changed and slipped under the covers.

'Goodnight Kyle.'

'Goodnight,' he said and he turned over and kissed her gently on the lips. 'Goodnight.'

Meg lay on one elbow, her fingers pressed to her lips where he had touched her. She watched him sleep for a while, frightened that he would wake up; frightened that he wouldn't. She looked at his eyelashes, the way they intertwined; at the slightly reddish stubble that began to emerge on his chin; at his parted lips; at his stomach, taut from the exertions of drumming, exposed when she lifted his t-shirt. She turned out the lamps and settled down, comforted by the sound of another person breathing beside her. But when her alarm-call came at 9 a.m. he had gone, leaving only the smell of musk and stale alcohol behind him.

The hotel had cordoned off a section at the back of the dining room for their late breakfast, and by the time Meg got there the place was filled with the increasing number of people needed to keep the tour going. Meg reminded Mac they had to leave for a remote interview with MTV at 10.30 a.m., then sat between Todd and Suzie, passing Todd the day's schedule as she did.

Clare and Kyle sat opposite, Kyle guzzling waffles and bacon, while Clare picked a croissant apart. 'I see you found your runaway,' Meg said — the previous night having made her bold.

Clare looked up with hate in her eyes, 'You should get your eyes tested Meg, you said you hadn't seen him and it turns out he was in your bed all along.'

'On the bed,' Meg and Kyle said together in an attempt to clarify, but their giggle made them sound even more conspiratorial.

'Maybe in future you could send Kyle back when he goes wandering,' Clare said.

'Maybe,' Meg replied as Kyle raised his eyebrows, lifted the maple syrup and drizzled more over his breakfast.

'Listen guys,' said Suzie, breaking into the tension, 'I've got a bit of a hangover with all of that champagne last night, so could we get through breakfast in peace. Please.'

'Well, if you don't mind me saying, I think someone should remember she is just a hired hand.'

Meg thought hard for a retort, but her mind was still reeling with the memory of Kyle's scent on her pillow and the feeling that she didn't care anymore if she had got above herself.

‘That’s enough Clare,’ Kyle said, spitting out each word.

‘Meg,’ Todd said as he prodded her elbow, ‘We need to go over this schedule —let’s get some space.’

Meg picked up her toast and grapefruit juice and moved to an empty table with Todd.

‘I don’t know why you annoy her so much Meg. I really don’t,’ Todd said once they were settled. ‘OK, so Kyle slept in your room last night.’

‘Nothing happened,’ Meg said earnestly, suddenly feeling it was very important that Todd knew.

‘Well, yeah,’ Todd said and he laughed just a little too much. ‘But will you try to not to wind Clare up so much? If she’s happy, Kyle’s happy, and if Kyle’s happy we’re all happy.’

All the Words I Never Knew

Carvery
Sommelier
Concierge
Maitre d'
Canapé
Cufflinks
Jealousy
Love

After breakfast Meg couldn't bring herself to go back to her room in case the maid had already smoothed away the imprint of Kyle, so she took her coffee out to a shaded area by the pool and tried to proof-read a press release. But no matter how hard she tried to focus, the words kept swirling around the page and she couldn't figure out how she should spell *centre*.

'I'm not disturbing you, am I?' Suzie said as she sat down on one of the wicker chairs. 'Are you still upset about what Clare said at breakfast, babe?' She asked. 'You know you should just ignore her. You're more than a *hired hand* — you're one of us now.'

Meg put down her paperwork and stretched her hands out over it. 'It's not what Clare said that upset me — I know she hates me. It was Todd.'

'Why, what did he say?' Suzie asked pulling her chair closer, 'Do you want me to have a word?'

Meg shook her head, signalled for a waiter and ordered a couple of mineral waters before she answered. 'He laughed when I told him that nothing happened last night with Kyle.'

'Well of course he laughed. We all know that nothing is going on, it would be ridiculous.'

Meg slipped off her sandals and put her feet on the cool shaded tiles under the table.

'But why is it so ridiculous? I know I'm not some 6 foot anorexic model, and it's not even as if I fancy him, but why is it such a joke?'

Suzie sat back in her chair and looked at Meg's anxious face. 'You're just a kid Meg,' she said with real kindness in her voice, 'and Kyle and Clare, well, they've been together for years. She's part of who we are.'

'It doesn't feel like she's part of it,' Meg said. 'And I don't think Kyle…' But she realised that she sounded like a petulant teenager, so didn't she finish what she was going to say.

Zed appeared from inside the hotel and gestured for Suzie to join him.

'I need to go now, babe. Just don't put yourself between them. You're not indispensable and you shouldn't risk losing all this over someone like Kyle. I know he's a looker, but trust me, he's not worth the agro. Just watch how you go, will you?' Suzie bent over her and kissed both cheeks, 'You right?'

'Yeah, I'm alright.' She drained her drink and went up to her room.

For the rest of the morning she put together press packs, spreading the components on the floor and working methodically. It was a job that required no thought and normally Meg found it calming, but her mind still wouldn't settle. A different thought attached itself to each item: she knew Suzie was right (t-shirt); she didn't even fancy Kyle (programme); she was too young for him (baseball cap); he was with Clare (key ring, badge); he had spent the night in her room (fact sheet). When she was finished she changed into her bikini and found Suzie back at the poolside.

Meg sat down next to her and dangled her feet into the water, feeling the coolness work its way up through her body, lowering her temperature. Suzie described the delights of the Country Club Plaza and how great the shopping had been, and Meg listened dutifully. Then Zed came up behind them, and as they squinted their hellos, he put a hand on each back and gently pushed them into the pool.

Gasping at the cold Meg went down, eyes clenching tight, the water nipping in. Feet battering something hard, pushing against it. Arms flapping, gasping again. Air. She punched, she kicked but the water wouldn't support her. *Oh my God, Oh my God.* Water crushing in, pushing, forcing, holding. *Help.* The back of her eyelids flashed blood red and she opened her mouth, tried to fill her lungs with something that wasn't icy and blue. Down again. She felt her heart expand to twice its size as it tried to escape through her chest. Take me with you. Swelling, breaking, oozing. Her arms swung wildly, her hands grasped to find something solid, but water ran through them. Dulled noises tried to break into her mind but she could only process the sounds of her own body. Heart, pound, pound. Eyes, blinking so loudly that she could hear each drop of water as it separated from the lash. Sloshing feet and hands. She opened her eyes to an oscillating blue. *Oh my God, Oh my God.* Legs kicking, running, fighting. She gulped down a mouthful of water and drowned her scream. *Help, someone please help.* Then a force under her arms pulling upwards; a sudden change in pressure bringing her back to life and she was on her side, tiles warm beneath her skin, sun caressing her back and a sea of feet in front of her.

A hand beneath her elbow and she sat up slowly, coughing and clearing water from her eyes. Fingers adjusting the cup of her bikini, bringing it back over her breast as she coughed some more. People on either side guiding her to a chair, sitting her down, placing a towel over her shoulders, giving her a cup of sweet tea, stilling her hand as the cup rattled in its saucer.

'I'm sorry Meg. I'm so sorry. I didn't realise you couldn't swim.' Zed was excluded from the circle around her but she could hear his voice.

'Are you okay? My God, you're shaking.'

Meg nodded at Kyle, at Suzie, at Todd as embarrassment began to replace shock. 'I feel so stupid,' she said as she wiped the water from her face and tasted salt and chlorine.

'You're fine.' Kyle knelt in front of her, held her hand. 'Take your time.'

She sipped her tea and Todd retreated cursing Zed while Suzie stayed by her, arm around her shoulder, smoothing her hair, whispering calm words in her ear. 'We'll look after you. You're safe now.'

At 6.30 p.m. Meg stood on the pavement outside the hotel, waiting for everyone who needed to be on the coaches to get their arses in gear and actually get on them. *Why did it have to be like this every single night?* The lower down in the pecking order, the more likely they were to be on the bus. Roadies could always be replaced, so they were first on; then the sound and lighting guys, but only if they had actually made it back after the sound check; then the session guys, who came and went depending on how souped-up the gigs were meant to be at any one time; then Todd. Only after he had taken his seat would the band plus ones, minus one, appear, deep in conversation about the night ahead, then, after another quick call to his room, Mac. By 7.00 p.m. they were ready to leave, due at the venue just in time to see Dave whip the support act onto the stage.

Meg walked up the bus to double-check her numbers, while a new dark-haired girl from Seattle performed the same task on the next bus. 'No Clare tonight?' she asked when she saw Kyle and Wayne sitting together. Wayne picked at his nails while Kyle shook his head slowly. She held on to the top of his seat as the bus pulled out.

'How come you can't swim Meg?' Kyle asked before she had a chance to move on.

'I never learned,' she said, conscious for the first time of the nap of the velour seat.

'Not even at school?'

She shrugged. 'The roof of the pool collapsed, and Mum couldn't be bothered taking me to the local baths. She can swim though. She used to talk about how she loved going with her dad. But it messed her hair too much and I suppose it was just too much hassle. It never really mattered until today.' The thought of the water pulling her down made her stomach feel bloated and sick again, and she clenched the seat back even tighter, making sure she had something to anchor her.

'I'll teach you,' Kyle said.

'No,' she said. 'Just leave it,' and before he could argue she spotted Suzie signalling for her. 'It's fine.'

'I thought Todd would have given you the night off,' Suzie said once Meg had plopped onto her seat.

'He did. But I didn't want to be on my own.' She wondered if she should add that it was her birthday, but it sounded too pathetic for words, and besides, Val never went in for celebrating Meg's birthday much.

'I would have stayed with you. I'm still raging at Zed.'

'Don't blame him,' Meg said, 'he wasn't to know I couldn't swim and I feel such a fool. But listen,' she said, pausing, 'who pulled me out?'

'What? Out of the pool? It was Kyle. I hadn't even realised what was going on, babe. I'd swum to the other side and I saw him leap out of his chair. My God, he got to you before I had a chance to react.'

‘It felt like I was under for hours.’

Suzie looked around to check they weren’t being overheard and then moved closer. ‘Now Clare’s even angrier with you, and with Kyle. When he was checking you were alright, she was whining and pulling at him. I hate to say this, but I think she would have been happier if he’d left you.’

‘Oh God, really. I just didn’t know what was happening, it’s weird, it’s still all a bit fuzzy,’ Meg said, but a weird recollection drifted back, ‘other than a pair of black shoes stinking of polish among all the bare feet.’

‘Yeah that was the hotel manager — he gave Zed such a bollocking. Zed’s devastated, you know.’ Then she whispered, ‘He froze — brought back nasty memories.’

‘Of what?’ Meg asked, but Zed was making his way to them, and Suzie shushed her. Zed squeezed Meg’s shoulder and said *‘sorry’* with such contrition that Meg thought she might cry again, so Suzie changed the subject for everyone’s benefit.

‘Clare’s leaving,’ she said with a gossipy grin. ‘She’ll be away by the time we get back. Kyle’s making out like it’s no big deal — saying she’s got a booking in New York, but it’s very convenient if you ask me.’

It was stupid, but Meg thought Kyle would be happier with Clare gone and that he would seek her out; persuade her to let him teach her to swim; come by for more late night chats; sleep in her bed again. But instead he moped: he was always first to the check-in desk asking for messages; first to pick up the phone the minute they stopped for a comfort break. He became tetchier, shouting at anyone and everyone who got in his way; answering interview questions with the minimum amount of words; partying less, then partying more. There was a darkness under his eyes and a hollowing of his cheeks, but it pained Meg that he was still in love with a woman who wouldn't have cared if she drowned.

Name: Mac (the Knife)
DOB: 22/04/63
Star Sign:Tauus
Loves: Meaningless Sex
Bondage
Cocaine
Himself
Hates: Commitment

Name: Kyle Watt
DOB: 25/10/63
Star Sign:Scorpio
Loves: Jelly babies
Drumming
Velvet Underground
Meg Burns
Hates: Rudeness
Bimbo models with nae boobs
and bitchy mouths

Name: Suzie's Zed
DOB: The day he met Suzie
Star Sign: Gemini
Loves: Suzie
Hash
More hash
Pills
Uppers/Downers
Hates: Himself

Name: Wayne the bassist
DOB: Arrived from Mars
Star Sign: Thog
Loves: Good conversation
Cheese-making
Origami
Pils
Hates: Gardening
Cheese

San Francisco

The tour took a break after the dates in San Francisco and the band and crew scattered. Suzie and Zed headed to Vegas to lose money and get married; Mac moved down to LA with a young actress to cultivate contacts with movie producers; Wayne set off on a pilgrimage to Memphis; and Kyle mentioned Hawaii and Clare.

No one asked Meg where she was going. She supposed, if they gave it a moment's thought, they might imagine her going home, but she wasn't inclined to blow what little savings she had on moving backwards. Instead she moved to a smaller hotel where she could pay her own bill, and tried to relax. She thought it would be nice to do nothing for a while, but there was no pool to lounge beside, and the public areas consisted of a dining room which was locked after breakfast and a faded winged armchair in the hallway. You could sit there long enough to look through a leaflet, but even that attracted the attention of the owner who would come into the hallway with a '*Can I help you mam?*'

She tried to use her time constructively, clearing out her growing number of suitcases. As her new hotel only provided her with a used bar of soap, she lined up her impressive array of hoarded toiletries on the vanity unit — the tiny bottles representing everywhere she had ever been; lavender and pink rose; honeysuckle and amber; *Hiltons, Hyatts*, and the rest.

She wet some toilet paper and rubbed off the chalked hieroglyphs that decorated her *Samsonites*, but left the airline stickers. Then she cleaned out the elasticated inside pockets, amazed at how many rolls of film she had amassed; emptied the detritus into the bin; poked around the bottom of her satchel and parcelled up all the souvenirs and books she wanted to keep, *Fed-exing* them back to her mum.

She stacked most of her clothes in the corner to leave as a fairly rubbish treat for Sarita, the Mexican who cleaned her room, but binned all her bras and knickers, greyed from too many laundrettes. The jumpers she had bought to deal with desert nights were kept for the San Francisco damp and the worrying prospect of home, but everything else went. Then she shopped for new clothes — cropped tops to team with denim shorts; slogan T-shirts to wear over black leggings; espadrilles and ethnic print cotton; mish-mashing styles to find her own. She bought primary-coloured chunky jewellery and hung it from her ears, wrists and neck; bought Arab scarves and felt hats; bought fake ID and bottles of beer; bought canvas bags and notebooks of every size; bought another suitcase.

The Bay at Fisherman's Wharf changed in shape and colour as the mist and the fog rolled in and out. Meg took photos at different times of the day and snapped tourists as they took their own photos. She stopped for coffee in the middle of the day, answered every casual '*how are you*?' and revelled in no one calling her name. Her walk usually took her to the Beach Street galleries, and she would stand and stare at the abstracts and landscapes; the line drawings and photographs of the Golden Gate, Alcatraz and the cable cars. A huge print entitled *Chambered Nautilus* drew her eye each time and she would stop, transfixed by its beauty.

'Do you like it?' A small woman with a pierced nose and short spiky pink hair popped her head around the door.

'It's amazing,' Meg replied.

'I've seen you look at it all week, are you interested in buying?' The woman asked, moving beside Meg, inviting her to look more critically.

'I like the texture,' Meg said, a little flustered at the proposition, 'it's really cool being blown up so much.' Meg looked at the photograph again, then back to the woman. 'I love taking close-ups, but they never turn out the way I imagine them. This one's amazing.'

'You maybe need to tweek your processing.'

'I don't…' Meg said a little ashamed, 'I occasionally slip in one of my own when I'm getting work stuff processed properly, but normally it's just chemists', sorry, drugstores' one-hour service. I've got loads of canisters just lying around — cause I'm fed up getting ruined negatives back.'

'That's a pity,' the woman said, 'you've got a decent camera there, but so much is in the developing. You need to be in charge of it if you want anything worthy.'

Meg heard a phone ring inside the gallery and saw it as a chance to leave, but when the woman said, 'Come in,' Meg had no reason not to.

She stood awkwardly while the woman consulted her diary and laughed down the phone, making arrangements for what sounded like a full life, but as soon as she hung up she turned her attention back to Meg. 'So, your ruined negatives,' she said, 'what do you think has gone wrong?'

Meg shook her head. 'I don't really know that side of things. I just see something I like and try to capture it.'

The woman laughed. 'C*apture it,'* she said in a Scottie from Star Trek voice and made a grasping swipe at the air.

Meg laughed and hoped this wasn't all part of the sales pitch, there was no way she could afford the $200 for the picture in the window.

'I'm Cerise,' the woman said putting out her hand.

'Meg,' Meg said, smiling as she shook it.

'Well Meg, if you're interested, I run a little side-line in photography lessons here.' When Meg was non-committal, she continued. 'I only charge for the chemicals.'

'Yeah,' Meg said, 'why not?' It would give her something to do.

'Well come on Meg, no time like the present.'

Despite there being '*no time like the present'* Cerise first showed Meg around: one white wall was filled with photographs of more huge shells, sponges and sea urchins with tiny labels at the side giving their Latin names.

'Do you dive?' Cerise asked.

'God, no!'

'You should, it's wonderful. A whole different world under the ocean.'

'I've still not seen all of this one,' Meg said.

The back wall housed a collection of images that Meg recognised were from the hippy quarter of San Francisco, with their hemp leaf and peace symbols; and on the wall behind the pink Perspex counter were smaller, more affordable prints, and a wire stand of postcards and greetings cards.

'These are how I make my money,' Cerise said, as Meg chose and bought two 8'x10's and a card for Kyle's birthday. Then Cerise left her to wander around again before reappearing with some coffee. 'You said you take photos for your job?' she said handing Meg a mug with Andy Warhol's Marilyn on it.

'Yeah, I work in PR,' Meg said, not wanting to be too specific. 'I take candid shots that are cropped and edited by someone else.'

Cerise put her hand on Meg's arm, as though she needed some support. 'Don't ever hand over your work like that,' she said with real horror in her voice. 'You need to be in control. Always'

Meg would have agreed with that for most things, but said, 'It's just part of my job. I can't be too precious about it. I kind of fell into this job and I suppose I'm still half-waiting to get found out.

Meg took a gulp of her coffee. It tasted like crude oil and she had to suppress an urge to splutter.

'So what are you working on now?' Cerise asked as she offered Meg a biscuit that looked like it was made of Trill. 'I've seen you stare at my window all week and you've never come in to say hello?'

Meg looked at her, *why would she have come in*, yet here she was. 'I'm just really hanging about just now,' said Meg with a weak smile. 'To tell you the truth I think I've been forgotten.'

Cerise smiled. 'This is beginning to sound interesting.' She led Meg to some large white cubes in the centre of the gallery which acted as chairs.

Meg realised she hadn't had a proper conversation in over a fortnight, so she saw no harm in giving in to the temptation to divulge. 'I work with this band, you see, and they're having a bit of a break. We had a big party on the last night and when I got up the next morning they had all either gone or were heading for the airport.'

'And they left you behind? Oh that's got to hurt.' Cerise grimaced, contorting her face and her body to illustrate the point.

Meg laughed and felt her shoulders relax. 'A bit. The tour starts again in a few weeks and I've left messages, so they know where I am. I just need to wait and see what happens. Feels like there are worse places to be stranded.'

Cerise looked over at the window where a couple of men stood looking in. She gave them a broad smile, but they just waved and walked on. 'I don't like wait and sees. I wasted half my life with them. No, Meg,' she said, looking straight into Meg's eyes, 'I'll introduce you to some people — get you some work.'

'But you don't even know me,' Meg said.

'You're a thirteen year old Brit who likes my shells. What else is there to know?'

Cerise smiled at her for a little too long before Meg broke the spell. 'Do I really look like a thirteen year old?'

'Maybe fourteen?' Cerise said with a shrug.

'God, no wonder I got left behind. I'm seventeen, you know.' Meg stared into her coffee, watching the milk make greasy patterns on top.

'What a fabulous age.' Cerise said with such enthusiasm that Meg looked up and immediately stopped feeling sorry for herself. 'Use youth to your advantage — grab life by the balls when you still have the strength, although saying you're eighteen might get you further. Now come on, let's get some chilli and we can take some photographs worth printing.'

Cerise shut early and they took a cable car to Haight-Ashbury which stank of patchouli and hash and grooved to the sounds of The Grateful Dead. Meg tried not to show too much contempt for a neighbourhood whose rebelliousness seemed to have ended with Nixon and whose inhabitants looked like they planned to smoke away the Reagan years.

'A bit wild?' Cerise said.

'Yeah,' she said unimpressed, 'just a bit.'

‘Do you have hippies in the UK?’ Cerise asked.

‘Aye, but they keep themselves hidden.’ Gays kept themselves hidden at home too, other than Bronski Beat and Frankie, but here she saw guys holding hands in the street and no one stopped for a second look.

They had a coke and some chilli and at Cerise’s insistence Meg took out her camera and ran through the features, proving that she knew about f-stops and depth of field. Cerise wasn’t impressed that she only had one lens, so when they finished eating she took her to a photography store and chose a wide angled and a zoom. Cerise asked for developers, fixers and packs of paper, building up a pile that Meg was shocked to find was all for her. The assistant rang up the items, added tax and presented the number to Meg. San Francisco was eating up a lot of cash, but as she opened her purse she decided this was a legitimate business expense and charged it to MindSet. *Maybe a credit card bill will remind Todd of my existence?*

As day turned into night they took a cab away from the fug of marijuana and into a seedier part of town. Cinemas as large as the Odeon displayed posters for their xxx movies and bondage shops pulled up their shutters for another night’s business. Cerise told the driver to stop outside a shop called Gimp and helped Meg and her bags out of the cab. Cerise brazened through the shop and started to climb the stairs, following an arrow that pointed to Shock. Meg watched her go, but walked slower. A few hours ago she didn’t even know Cerise, now she’d followed her to a dodgy shop. Some of the stuff reminded her of punk — the studded dog collars and chained up trousers; but the whips and the masks made her want to weep — *Is life not hard enough?* She stood next to the dildos and considered whether it was wise to follow her new friend. But Cerise had one of her bags, and if nothing else she wanted it back.

There were two black painted doors in the corridor at the top of the stairs, one with a logo painted in silver with a lightning bolt through it; the other unlabelled. Nightmares didn't come with harder choices, but at least she could prepare herself for Shock. Knowing instinctively that the handle would be sticky, she pushed the door open with her elbow. Cerise leant on a glass-topped counter chatting to a girl with a short green Mohican.

'Here she is.' Cerise said, as she held out her hand and invited Meg to walk towards her. The walls and ceiling, like the shop downstairs, were black, and small lamps barely illuminated the reception area, but behind it was a more comforting scene of wash basins, hairdryers and people draped in cloaks. *Heart of Glass* blared above the thrum of the driers and Cerise had to raise her voice to make herself heard. 'She's looking for a change of image. Pol said she could fit her in.'

The junior nodded, led them through to the back area and held out a black gown with Shock on the breast for Meg to slip on.

'Pol's the best in the business. Go for a signature colour the way I've done.' Cerise said, 'People won't forget you after that. Blue would go with your eyes. Iris is a good name. Yes,' she said decisively, 'only wear blue.'

Meg humoured her with a smile, but she had just bought a whole load of clothes and couldn't afford to throw out any that didn't conform to the new brief.

Pol and Cerise chatted behind Meg's head but above the sound of the driers and the thump of the music it was hard to make out everything they said. But Meg kept her eyes on Pol's mouth. Every few seconds something appeared that didn't seem right, giving her the lisp Meg had heard earlier. Cerise caught her looking and nudged Pol, who satisfied Meg's curiosity by sticking out her tongue. A black pearl-like stud was perfectly centred. Meg recoiled slightly and the girls laughed.

'It adds a little something,' Cerise said, knowingly.

'I think it would make me gag,' Meg said.

Pol brought her mouth right next to Meg's ear and whispered, 'You get used to it. We do it here if you're interested. Cerise would like it.'

Meg shook her head, not sure what Cerise had to do with this. 'Maybe another couple of holes in my ear; but not my tongue.' She screwed up her face to emphasize the point.

'One on the rim and two on the lobe would look good on you, Cerise said, pulling at the blue feather dangling from her left ear.'

Meg nodded. 'Yeah, let's do that once you've finished with my hair.'

Cerise lent over and kissed her on one cheek, then the next, her braless breasts dangling down in front of her. 'I'll catch up with you tomorrow, yeah?'

'Ok,' Meg said and she took a deep breath and let Pol do what she did best.

Val used to chop off her split ends with the kitchen scissors, but there was one time when she'd got to go to the hairdressers. She'd had to give a horseshoe to one of Val's friends at her wedding and hadn't to show Val up. The smell of the hairspray had made her cough, but she loved watching the old ladies getting shampooed and set. She'd got her hair cut into a pageboy that day. Val kept repeating, '*pageboy, for a wedding*.' She hadn't got the joke then, and didn't find it particularly funny now, but it had made her feel good, a proper haircut. Every bath night after that, as Val's sharp nails scratched her scalp, she dreamed of the gentle way the woman had washed her hair. She'd even put conditioner on without charging the extra 10p, since it was for a special occasion.

She closed her eyes now, and enjoyed the massage, as the apple scented shampoo lathered up. She breathed in deeply, letting herself concentrate on the sensations before she was led through the half-light to a spot-lit mirror. It reminded her of some of the better dressing rooms, and she tried to imagine herself a star. But with her wet hair combed straight she thought again about her pageboy days. The style hadn't lasted long — Val reckoned it was too much hassle to always be trimming her fringe and within weeks she was back to clasps, trying to contain the awkward length.

Pol ran the comb through her hair one more time, getting rid of the last of the knots, then began to fold Meg's hair up, trying out different lengths for her.

'What about a Louise Brook? It would suit the shape of your face.'

'What's that? Meg asked, so Pol pointed to a photo on the wall.

'Who, not what. She was a silent star, one of the best, but poor Louise, she never made it to the talkies. She's my favourite.'

Meg considered the sharp bob, black like hers, just curving to brush her cheek. 'You think it would look okay?' She asked.

'Sure. Unless you want to go short and spiky like me?' It wasn't that Pol didn't suit her hair, but Meg wasn't ready to lose all her cover — a bob would be a good starting place.

Jacqueline McBride had once invited Meg up to her house and told her that she had read in *Just17* that you had to spend at least five minutes every day looking at yourself in the mirror before you even started to apply make-up. '*That way,*' she said, '*you got used to the arc of your eyebrows, the bow-ness of your lips and could create the perfect face. After a week you'd be able to put your make-up on in the dark.*'

Meg wasn't sure at the time why you might need this skill, and while she had listened to the girl who was trying to be her friend, she found the whole thing too difficult. She couldn't concentrate on her eyebrows, which Jacqueline said she'd pluck for her, nor could she stand to look at her lips while trying to draw them in the handy frame the magazine had left blank for the purpose. Instead, she'd looked into her own eyes, the colour of chilled fingers, and she didn't like what she saw.

Now, five years later, as Pol first chopped her hair then pulled strands through a holed-cap and pasted them with dye, she was forced to confront her reflection again. Pol worked quickly, quietly, set alarm clocks to ring, left her alone, and checked back in. Meg drank coffee and flicked through magazines, but at every page turn she looked up and saw a girl trying not to be lost, looking back.

'You've got a pretty smile there Meg,' Pol said as she held the mirror to let Meg see the back of her head once the final trim was done. Meg caught herself from a different angle and had to agree.

Meg woke from a great night's sleep, her body finally adjusted to daylight hours. The hotel had been converted from a family house and still retained many of the feelings Meg always imagined a home would have. The proprietor kept the small vase of flowers fresh on her dresser, and the towels weren't stitched with the name of the hotel. The furniture looked like it had been collected over years, all a bit mismatched and worn, but it was comforting to think that the next bedroom along would have an entirely different look. Not pale blue wallpaper, dappled with clouds, but maybe lemon and daisies, or pink with red poppies.

She stretched out her body, pointed her toes against the tight white sheets; snagged her nail on a mend; cracked her knuckles and opened her eyes. The room felt a bit stuffy, but Meg couldn't relax lying below the juddery ceiling fan, so she didn't reach for the pull cord. San Francisco felt different from the rest of America, more like home with its compact terraces, steep hills and the feeling of rain just moments away. If time had to stop, she was glad it had stopped here.

She ran her hand up through the stubble on the back of her neck and realised she wasn't afraid anymore. America did seem ridiculously optimistic to her, but she was glad that some of was rubbing off. She thought of Cerise and her absolute belief that anything was possible. Green cards were a luxury she assured Meg she could live without and she could find work and a place to stay. But then she thought of Kyle; pictured him sleeping on her bed; felt every casual touch again, and every deliberate one; remembered his smell pre-concert and post; thought of his smile; let her hands caress her skin. She threw back the covers and jumped out of bed. *Don't be an idiot.*

She had arranged to meet Cerise in a deli near the gallery and had to hurry to be on time. As it was, Cerise beat her there and was already eating French toast when she arrived.

'I'm liking the hair, girl,' Cerise said as she sat down. She raised her coffee cup, 'here's to the reinvention of the unforgettable Miss…,' she paused.

'Burns,' Meg said, filling in the gap. 'Do you think my hair's okay? I'm not sure. I kept catching glimpses of myself in windows and not realising it was me.'

'You look beautiful,' Cerise said, leaning across the table to tease the bob. 'It frames your face; it's beautiful.' Cerise touched the fuzz on the nape of Meg's neck, moving her hand slowly through it. 'Cool,' she said, bringing her hand onto Meg's cheek and stretching to kiss her — just a quick, medium pressure, test-the-water kind of a kiss. It made Meg pull back slightly, but she held Cerise's gaze.

'Am I wrong?' Cerise asked.

Meg hesitated. 'I don't know.' This time it was Meg who moved forward, touching Cerise's pink lips with her fingers. 'I don't know.'

Best Band nominee in Smash Hits awards —1985

Best Album nominee in Smash Hits awards — 1985

Grammy for best song — Remembrance.

One month ended, and then another. *Entertainment Tonight* reported that Mac had gone into hospital to have nodules removed from his throat, and that he might never sing again. Christmas came and went with only a bottle of fake Poison from Val; a framed photograph of the moon above the Golden Gate from Cerise and a printed Christmas card '*from MindSet'*. Meg cried when she opened it, panicked because it should have been her job to send it. But true to her word Cerise had spoken to her friends, and as Winter turned to Spring, Meg filled her days temping around the city. In the evenings she would pick up some Thai food and make her way to the gallery to process and print the photographs she had taken of crumbled paper in office trash cans or women in industrial laundries, their faces as wrinkled as bed sheets. They worked comfortably together in the red light of the darkroom until it was time to head out to a bar, or back to Cerise's place to bed. She was always gentle; taking things at Meg's pace; making sure she didn't feel threatened or anxious. But Meg could feel her getting more irritated when she replied to Cerise's probing questions with vague answers.

'I still feel like you don't trust me, Meg.' Cerise had said one morning as they lay in bed waiting for the rain to stop.

'I do,' Meg said without any conviction. Once or twice she had tried to explain how difficult it was for her, that intimacy was a skill she had never learned. If anything, she trusted Cerise more than anyone she had ever known. But she held back her secrets: told her she had been raped; but not the extent to which she had fought back. Told her about the band; but always made sure she gave each of the guys equal weighting. Told her about Val; but not the extent of the neglect. '*If you tell folk your mammy's not here they'll take you away, Maggie, and who'll run my messages then?*' Cerise knew there were things she wasn't telling, and Meg knew that she knew, but they kept the pretence of honesty as best they could for as long as they could.

Then one evening, Cerise headed for a party without her. 'I need a bit of time with my friends, Meg,' she said as she put on her mascara. 'You need to find people your own age.'

Meg could rationalise Cerise's actions, she wasn't even surprised or hurt by them. People got fed up with you and then they left, everyone did it, her dad, Kyle, even her gran didn't put up much of a fight when her final illness came. Now Meg was being dropped in the same gentle way that Cerise did everything.

She headed back up the steep incline to the hotel she called home, she would miss the way Cerise held her and stroked her hair, but she'd get over it. As she turned the key to her bedroom she noticed two pieces of paper stuck under the door. Both said *Call Todd:* one dated three days ago; the other only a couple of hours before. A few weeks earlier she would have sprinted downstairs to call back, but she paused. Everyone was an outsider in San Francisco and it suited her. She had been offered a house-share by one of the Shock girls and was seriously considering it, but every time she went to say *yes,* she felt a drum beat inside her heart.

'Meg, there's a call for you downstairs.'

She didn't go back to the gallery to collect her things — just left a message on Cerise's answer machine. 'Hi, Cerise, listen, sorry I didn't catch you, but I'm off on my travels again. I'll give you a call. Bye.'

1986

April: Chicago

Meet us at 6 in hotel bar.

Todd

5.30 p.m. — arrived at the hotel; dumped bags; quick freshen up; black fisherman's jumper, stinking of oil, over 501s; gel-covered fingers through hair. Make-up — gone the school girl's pale pink lipstick and blue eyeliner to be replaced by scarlet and kohl. She smiled at her reflection, checking her teeth for smudges, before she lifted her key and went down to the bar.

She heard them before she saw them; the exaggerated voices and raucous laughter. As she approached, she strained to differentiate between the voices; felt her heart quicken, and her mouth dry. They turned to look when she entered, and she heard a murmur of approval.

'My God, look at you,' Suzie said as she approached and gave Meg a warm hug. 'What have the Americans done to you? Ponytail gone and everything.'

Meg smiled, she'd had two haircuts since and the scrutiny no longer made her self-conscious. 'You look well.'

'Married life obviously suits me,' Suzie said, thrusting her left hand forward to show off an extravagant diamond band. 'Elvis did it. In Vegas,' she said, as if Elvis married people anywhere else. 'You know, Meg, it was really tacky and really special at the same time. I can't believe it, I'm Mrs Zed.' She threw her arms around Meg again, and spun her around. Suzie filled her in on the details of the wedding, showed her the intertwined initials tattoo she'd got on her back and Meg listened intently while nodding *hellos* to various members of the crew as they joined the throng. But she also took in the changes that had affected Kyle since she last saw him. His blue eyes shone out from his tanned face and his long blonde hair, which darkened after months on tour, was now bleached almost white and cropped in tight, leaving only a few curls at the front. His face looked more relaxed, as though a frown had been rubbed off.

'Clare's not here,' Suzie said, following Meg's gaze. 'Kyle's not saying much, but I think their holiday wasn't quite as idyllic as they had hoped.'

'So, is it over between them?' Meg asked, barely able to contain the glee she felt.

'I think so,' Suzie said. Kyle looked over at them, as if he realised he was being talked about, and when he smiled across, even Suzie blushed at his sensuality. 'He's looking good on it though.'

'Isn't he,' Meg replied, but she had been here before — excited that Clare was out of the way, only for her to reappear and for Kyle to fall for her all over again. 'So how's Zed?' Meg asked as she looked round for him.

'Good, yeah,' Suzie said, but when Meg saw him sitting down when everyone else stood, she wondered. His eyes looked even darker than usual, black rimmed and shadowed, and he had lost weight.

‘Are you sure?’

Suzie took Meg’s hand and led her away from the crowd. ‘He’ll be fine. He’s just going through a bit of a bad patch.’ Suzie struggled to pull together the words. ‘He gets bored when his not gigging, he needs to relax. You nearly drowning brought back some bad memories for him. He’s not been himself since then.’

‘I’m sorry,’ Meg said, ‘I hadn’t realised.’

Kyle’s laugh suddenly filled the room. Meg looked over and watched for a moment as he spread his arms and continued the story which was amusing the group clustered around him. His haircut changed him too, and she could see his strong chin and whiter than white teeth without his curls obscuring them.

‘He shouldn’t have pushed you,’ Suzie went on, ‘now he’s punishing himself all over again.’

Meg pulled her focus to Zed and then back to Suzie. ‘I’ll speak to him,’ she said, and went over before Suzie could object.

Zed sat with his head almost on his knees, but as she approached Meg realised that he was writing in his diary. ‘Hey Zed,’ she said, but when he looked up there was nothing in his eyes that said he even recognised her. ‘What you up to?’ She asked, trying to be cheery, but she felt a chill that came from deep in her past. Zed didn’t respond, and when she glanced down at his journal all she could see were random words and scribbles that fell off the lines.

‘Zed?’ She said, touching her hand on his knee. ‘Zed?’

Zed continued to retrace a skull he’d drawn.

'Is that going to be your next tattoo?' She asked. She brushed his black curls away from his face, 'Zed?' closed her eyes. *Greeting for a wee bobbie, to buy mare Coulter's candy.* God, she hadn't thought of that song for years, but here it was at the front of her mind again. *Here's wee Jeannie she's looking awfy thin, a bag o bones tied oer wi skin.* Val used to put Maggie's name in or her own instead of Jeannie's, but when it was Meg's turn to sooth she preferred to stick to the words her granny had taught her. *Noo she's gitting a wee double chin, for eating Coulter's candy.*

'What's he using?' Meg asked when she got back to Suzie.

'He'll be fine, Meg,' Suzie said, knocking back a shot of tequila. 'Just leave it.'

'He needs help.'

'What do you know about it, Meg? You're just a kid.'

'I'm not a kid Suzie,' Meg said, annoyed at Suzie's dismissiveness, 'I've never been a kid, and I'll tell you why,' she swallowed hard saying the words she had never dared utter before, 'my mum was a junkie.'

'Zed's not a junkie,' Suzie said, breathing heavily through her nose, 'he's fine.' She turned and tried to walk away but Meg caught her arm and pulled her in.

'If you love him you'll help him.'

'Let go of me,' Suzie said, loud enough for everyone to hear, even though nobody reacted. She wrenched her arm free. 'You've already split up one relationship. Don't meddle in another.'

Meg watched speechless as Suzie dragged Zed to his feet and led him through the crowded bar and out into the body of the hotel. She let out a deep sigh. And jumped when she felt her arm touched.

'Hey,' Kyle said. 'You okay?'

'It's not me I'm worried about.'

'He's a big boy, he can look after himself.'

'Are you really not concerned? He's totally out of it.'

'Meg, honestly, it's just rock 'n' roll.'

She wanted to tell him that it honestly wasn't, but he was smiling, asking her if she wanted a drink.

She hadn't seen the guys for months, and she'd wasted too much of her life worrying about junkies. 'I'll take a Bud,' she said, tilting her head to him the way she had seen so many other girls do before. 'So, how's it hanging with you?' She was determined to have some fun.

There was often a lull around lunchtime, when the morning interviews were over and the gig still hours away. Todd had employed more people who were willing to move boxes and pick up cleaning, so Meg took an hour away to wander around the city. A few blocks from the hotel, in one corner of a modern mall, she found a bookshop furnished to look Dickensian with sconces fixed to the side of the shelves giving just enough light to illuminate the titles. Calligraphy marked the sections of each display and classical music just about covered the thrum of the heating. Meg felt as though the air was pumped with a synthetic bookshop smell, but she didn't care about the lack of authenticity.

It had only been a couple of days since she had met up with the band and already her brain was filling with lists again. In the bookshop, people made slow progress passed the shelves, as though choosing the right book was the most important decision of their life. It reminded her of how she felt in Cerise's gallery, that she could pause, and breathe, and live. She took off her watch and slipped it into her pocket. Cerise talked incessantly about Diane Arbus, but Meg had never even looked for the fabulous book she had mentioned. Now it was her only goal. 'Hi there, I was wondering if you could help.'

She stopped browsing when her bundle of books got so big she worried she might need a cab, and headed out of the mall and back along the street. She paused outside a deli to readjust the weight in her bags and saw Kyle sitting inside with his back to the window. She recognised his frame at once. She had planned to go back to the hotel, phone Cerise and tell her she'd been thinking about her, that she had bought the Arbus, but instead she stood in the roar of the traffic and decided on a different path.

'Mind if I join you?' She said.

Kyle looked up from his newspaper and smiled, 'Sure.' There was something welcoming in his smile that provoked a crinkling of her eyes and a grin back. The waitress came over and tapped her pencil while Meg quickly scanned the menu.

'You should try the BLT — they say it's the best in the city,' Kyle said, nodding to the waitress to write it down.

'I wonder if anyone ever admits to being second best in the city,' Meg said. 'It would still be pretty good.'

Kyle shrugged. 'I guess it's like being No.2 in the charts, why would you bother?'

'You used to get excited about being No. 2.'

'Don't let me again. No. 1 or bust from here on in.' She'd heard him say it before, but there was more fun in his voice today, less desperation that it would all end in disappointment. Maybe since Todd had got rid of the forty-four-seater budget bus and replaced it with leather seats and bunks and talk of a private jet, he felt he could relax more. Now, Meg thought, as she sat opposite him and let her knees gently rest against his, he was more like the man she created in the lonely nights before she met Cerise and more like the man she dreamed about when Cerise touched her.

'I hope you don't mind me asking, Kyle,' Meg said when there was a lull in the conversation.

'Clare?' Kyle said, obviously expecting the question.

Meg nodded. 'I know it's none of my business, but…'

'It is your business,' Kyle said, and she immediate felt glad she had dared to ask. Even so, it took a minute before Kyle continued. 'We just didn't want the same things anymore.'

She'd read similar phrases a hundred times in magazines, and could almost see the copy she would give to any journal that enquired. But she knew it didn't explain half of it, so she gave him the space he needed to go on.

'She said that I wasn't giving her the attention she needed, but that was all I did. I made up charts for her about what castings to attend — made her change her agency. I couldn't have done more. And she just threw it all back in my face.'

'I took your advice,' Meg said as the waitress laid down her sandwich, and when he looked blank she continued, 'I got some photography lessons.'

'Oh right, it's always good to learn I suppose.' Kyle nodded in an approving way that warmed her, then leaned over and stole a chip. 'Did you go home?'

'No, I stayed in San Francisco.'

'I hope you didn't get up to any mischief. Not kill anyone or anything?' Kyle asked, with a cheeky grin on his face.

'What?' Meg said, more shocked than she should have been at his teasing.

'It's just Zed's got you pegged as an international assassin,' Kyle explained. 'He reckons you're using us as cover for all your evil deeds.'

Meg gave a half-laugh. 'Maybe it's Zed who needs watching rather than me,' she said.

'He'll be right,' Kyle said, 'but honestly, you should hear him, he's got this whole routine about Meg the Enforcer. "*She might look small, but she can take a man out at fifty paces.*"'

The sandwich felt dry in Meg's mouth and she took some coke to help it down. *How could Zed know?* It had been so long since she worried about what happened her last night in Glasgow, and her overheard conversation. She had figured it was just some lackey who had left the tour; or a staffer from the venue who didn't speak English. Now Zed was the most likely candidate. 'It's cold in here,' Meg said, pulling her scarf back around her neck and playing for time. Zed being wasted would make him a less reliable witness, but it might also loosen his tongue if he was questioned. *God, I thought this was all done with.* She would have to be careful. 'You were right about the sandwich,' Meg said. 'It's good.'

'You've got…' Kyle reached across the table and wiped some mayo off the corner of her lips, 'got it.' She smiled. Clare was gone, and she had to make sure she was more than just a runaway in Kyle's eyes.

After the gig, people began to disperse into smaller groups to go to different nightclubs and bars. Meg showed her fake id to the bouncers and walked with confidence into the throb of the club. Within minutes girls began to attach themselves to the fringes of the group, and Meg watched anxiously as Kyle chatted to a couple of Bangles-styled blondes. A few bottles of champagne arrived at the table courtesy of the management, and Meg helped herself to a glass.

'I thought you didn't drink,' Suzie said, squeezing in close between Meg and Zed.

‘Things change,’ Meg replied, and she wondered whether she would tell Suzie her tales from San Francisco or if she would even be asked.

The gentle bubbles of the champagne massaged Meg’s brain, letting her ease down her alert settings. Zed was high after the concert, maybe it was just adrenaline, and joked around with them, calling her and Suzie *my girls.* Suzie seemed to have forgotten their argument, and Meg began to reassure herself that no matter what Zed knew he wasn’t the kind of guy to deliberately hurt her

Some guy, whose girlfriend was desperately trying to be seduced by Mac, asked Meg to dance. She danced to *What You Need,* feeling powerful and free but before she could sit down at their table again, Kyle came out from the booth, took her hand and led her back to the dance floor. His hands felt rougher than she had imagined — calloused and dry. She set her lips tight together, trying not to let the excitement of his touch bubble over.

His white shirt turned blue in the strobe lights, and the flashes mesmerised her. She looked about at the other clubbers; felt the floor move with the bass; matched each beat with an underplayed movement. She could feel his eyes on her, and the eyes of the nightclub on him. She hardly dared look at him, but a smile emerged when the music changed. He put his hand on her arm and whispered ‘*Drink*’ into her ear. His breath made its way down her ear canal, tingling each hair and nerve as it went. The tones dispersed through her body before she nodded and let herself be guided towards the bar. But Kyle stopped suddenly, took her hand and manoeuvred her against a pillar.

He mouthed something she couldn't make out over *True Blue*, but she thought maybe there was something about the Californian sun and that she looked fantastic. She looked into his eyes, felt his arms encircle her, and kissed him hard. When they stopped for air, Kyle wrinkled an eyebrow, checking he could go on, and kissed her again. It was all Meg could do to stay on her feet, not let her knees buckle and collapse into a heap, like she had seen so many front-rowers do. She felt his tongue roll round the back of her teeth; felt every inch of her body connected to his; tasted the champagne on his lips and on his breath. *Savour this.* Music pounded their bodies, whistles punctuated the beat, people bumped into them and they pushed against each other to keep their balance and the lights flashed red and blue and green and all that she could think was *Kyle, Kyle, Kyle.*

'Thanks,' she said when they separated.

Kyle laughed, 'Why do women always thank me, like I'm doing them a favour or something?'

She looked straight at him, hoping that he wouldn't destroy her. *He wasn't doing her a favour was he?* But he smiled. 'You know your new look has been making me feel horny all night.' He finished his sentence with another long kiss, his tongue darting deeper than before. Meg ignored the ghostly feelings of Cerise's hand as Kyle's fingers swept over her neck. This wasn't going to be difficult at all.

‘Come on guys — time to split.’ Mac’s head was suddenly between them, Suzie pulling Meg away, handing her her bag and jacket, taking her by the arm, pushing the men in front for the paparazzi assault.

‘What the hell are you doing Meg?’ Suzie asked. Meg had expected her to be excited, but Suzie teetered on anger.

‘It’s nothing, just a winch in a nightclub,’ she said, not believing it herself, ‘it doesn’t mean anything.’

‘He always gets back with Clare, you know that, right?’

‘He’s says it’s definitely over,’ Meg said more firmly.

‘It’s never over.’

Meg shrugged and followed up with a huge smile.

‘I’m serious babe, when things go wrong you’ll lose your job and I won’t have anyone to talk to. Plus you don’t want the reputation of a girl who’ll sleep with the drummer. You’ll never work again.’

Meg stumbled on a raised paving stone, and regained her balance against Suzie.

‘Just don’t get hurt,’ Suzie warned.

It would take more than that, she thought but she watched with growing concern the scene on the pavement in front of her. Todd had Kyle by the arm and by the looks of it they were having an identical conversation to the girls. ‘Todd doesn’t look happy. If you leave he’ll have to start working again.’ Suzie said.

‘Todd can go to hell,’ Meg said with more force than she meant. She was fed up being treated like the band’s pet. ‘I’m good at my job, and that's all anyone should care about. I've got this band on the front of more magazines than Todd knew existed, so he can stick his displeasure where the sun don't shine.'

Suzie stopped dead in the street. 'What's happened to you?' she said, but a smile was finally beginning to tickle around her mouth. 'I think you've grown balls since we left you.'

'I've always had balls Suz. I just kept them well hidden.'

It was 02.08 by the time Meg got back to her hotel room. Todd had grabbed the first taxi and shoved the boys into it, and it had been ages before another one appeared. Using only the light from the street she found her way to the bed and switched on a chrome lamp. A red dot flashed on the phone — message waiting. She sat down, took off her shoes and pulled her feet under her while she listened.

'Hi, it's Kyle. Sorry we got separated. Call me when you get in.'

She picked up her list of room numbers and ran her finger over the names to Kyle. She pressed the buttons — 641 — and waited.

'Hi, it's me.'

'Hey. What you doing?'

'Nothing. I just got in.'

'Can I come and hang?'

'Sure.' Her heart pounded. She found the remote and switched on the TV to give some background chatter, cleared space on the armchair, bundling her papers into her satchel. *Can I come* *and hang? S*he downed a miniature of vodka and resisted the temptation to turn on more lights. She ran a brush through her hair, smeared red across her lips and *breathe, breathe,* before she answered the door to his gentle tap. His hair was damp, fresh from a shower, making Meg acutely aware of the smoke and sweat that still clung to her from the club.

'Hi,' she said, letting him in.

'What you watching?' Kyle asked looking at the TV as CNN tickertape ran across the screen, giving more reactions to the explosion of a nuclear power station in the USSR. Meg shrugged — she wasn't interested in tragedies that didn't touch her. He sat on the bed, his back against the headboard, flicked through the channels and settled on MTV playing Prince. Meg hovered, unsure where to put herself.

'Do you want a drink or something?' she asked.

'Yeah, is there a beer in there?' he said, pointing to the mini bar.

Meg crouched down, 'Miller or Bud?'

He took his beer with one hand and her free hand with the other. Her eyes flicked across his face, looking for clues, before she joined him on the bed.

They sat together for a moment, watching *Kiss* end and *Rock me Amadeus* begin. Kyle casually put his hand on her thigh, sipped his beer and tapped in time with the music. Above it, Meg could hear each gulp he took; saw his Adam's apple out of the corner of her eye; felt him as he turned towards her. He leaned over her, took another sip of beer, put his can down on the bedside table and brought his lips to hers. She opened her mouth slightly, letting the liquid, then his tongue in. He smelled of soap and shampoo; tasted of peppermint and beer; felt hard and strong and gentle.

The ridges of their jeans pushed into her flesh as they moved. She wanted this — she wanted him. He pushed down harder on top of her, smothered her with his mouth. Claustrophobic, panicked, she stiffened, pushed him with the heel of her hand, but he was bigger, stronger.

'You want to go on top?' he said, as he rolled them both over.

She nodded, finding she could breathe more easily. *It's Kyle, Kyle, Kyle won't hurt me.* Her fingers worked their way under his shirt, up his back, over his shoulder blades, down his spine. It was fine, more than fine. She ran her hands across his back, fingered his neck, gently bit his lip. His fingers danced on her waistband then moved up over her body, squeezed her breasts. *He'll stop if I tell him,* she was sure of it, but she didn't want him to stop. Instead she felt her neck bend back, elongating with pleasure, her arms lifting as he eased her t-shirt over her head, pulled down the cups of her bra and licked her nipples. She whispered, 'what about Clare?' *What about Cerise?* But her hands were unzipping and he was quietly shushing.

He kissed her shoulder after he came, nibbled her earlobe and asked 'You right?'

She nodded.

'You were a bit,' he seemed to struggle to find the right word, 'anxious to begin with.' He kissed her nose and pulled back a little to look her in the eye. 'I'm not your first, am I?' he asked.

'Kind of,' she said.

He kissed her again, then jumped out of the bed and walked to the toilet. She watched the muscles and sinews of his legs and arse, pulling and stretching; his broad back, straight and strong. He closed the door and she immediately sobered up, alternately smiling and frowning. It had been great, better than she dared to imagine. Cerise had helped her feel ownership of her body, now she happily gave it away. *'If things go wrong you could lose your job.'* She heard the gush of water and reached for her top. Suzie was wrong, Kyle would look after her. She wouldn't get left behind again.

'Oh, it's cold in there,' Kyle said as he did an exaggerated shiver and strode back to the bed. 'You need to heat me up.' He got back in and held her tightly in his arms as she exhaled — safe.

July: Houston, TX – Boston, MA

Meg pressed for Ground in the lift at the Magnolia Hotel and was putting her key card into her purse when a hand appeared in the gap of the closing doors and forced them to reverse. Dave came in, wearing his Black Sabbath t-shirt and smelling like he'd been shovelling shit. Despite the fact he now had fifty roadies under him, rather than five, he hadn't changed from being the same arse that Tam flattened outside the Apollo. He still viewed Meg with unconcealed contempt so she did a very quick half-smile then looked at her feet.

'How's Kyle?' he asked.

'Fine,' she replied. It was the first time he'd spoken to her in weeks and she wasn't going to get into a conversation now.

'Just, I normally get the cast-offs.' He moved closer to her. 'Should I be getting myself ready?' He grabbed her hand, thrust it against his crotch and squeezed.

'Don't be an arse Dave,' she said, pulling her hand back and bracing her body.

'You know the hierarchy — after the drummer it's the roadie, although most of you chicks start higher.'

'Piss off.' She knocked his hand off her shoulder.

'What's left, the bassist gets,' he snorted a laugh.

'Very funny,' she said. *Prick.*

The door pinged and opened on the ground floor, but Dave covered the exit undefeated. 'They all say that before they come running. You're not the first stray to warm his bed, and you won't be the last.'

The doors closed, and although Meg pressed insistently on the key pad, the lift ascended again. It stopped at *3* and Zed got in, pushing one suitcase, pulling another, and pressing G with his elbow. As the lift started to move he lurched towards Meg. She saw him coming and raised her hands to stop him falling against her. He did a mock cower and said, 'Don't hit me,' then he stroked her cheek as though she had turned up in a dream and he needed to check she was real. Meg winced, *why did they all keep touching her?* She backed away, but Zed had already turned to Dave and was hugging like a long lost friend, holding on tight, thumping his back with '*Mate*' thrown in.

'We're not leaving today man,' Dave said, squirming out of his grasp, 'What's with the cases?' Zed looked down at his luggage, then at Meg as though she was to blame.

'Where am I going, Meg? Where's Suzie?'

The lift doors opened and Meg pushed the men aside finally getting into the purified air of the lobby.

In the hours between interviews and gigs, Kyle and Meg snatched lunches together; played pool and pinball; lay side-by-side as aromatic oils were rubbed into their bodies, then continued the sensuous experience when they were alone. Meg had never appreciated how amazing it felt just to lie together in silence, hands and limbs entwined, not sure where one body ended and the other began. With Cerise she had felt comfort, but not completion.

In Detroit Kyle decided to teach Meg to swim, but she froze at the side of the pool and refused to be coaxed into the water.

'Why won't you let me teach you?' he asked when they got back to their room, 'it's like you don't trust me or something.' Meg considered for a minute — everyone told her not to trust him. Val warned of the fickleness of men in every phone call, dripping in tales Meg already knew of how she had been let down.

'I'm just having a bit of fun, Mum, that's all.'

'He'll break your heart, and then where will you be?'

And Suzie suggested that she shouldn't get too comfortable, mentioning Clare and how great she looked in her new ads. She pushed the thoughts to one side.

'I do trust you. It's not that. I just can't do it.'

'It doesn't make any sense Meg. You need to learn. It's stupid not to.'

'I can't.' She knew he didn't understand — it wasn't the water that terrified her. She had grown up on red alert, always on the look-out for problems; working out how to keep the rent man from throwing them out; or how to stop one of Val's many friends from going too far. Now twice within the year she had fought for her life, had ran, had been rescued. Her luck was running out and she didn't fell like chancing it again.

'You shouldn't be frightened of new challenges, Meg,' he said.

She lifted the phone and dialled for room service, trying to deflect what was coming next, but Kyle started again. 'It's only by confronting our fears that we become stronger. You have the same look in your eyes when I talk about swimming as when I talk about your life plan. The tour will be finished before you know it, and you still haven't said what you're going to do — you can't just float about in San Francisco again.'

'I liked floating about in San Francisco.'

'But did it move you on as a person?'

Meg smirked. 'Yeah. And even if it didn't, I had fun.'

'Fun only goes so far, Meg. Then you need to get serious.'

The words formed in her head *I've been serious all my life,* but something stopped her from saying them. It was nice that he cared, but maybe his constant nagging was what caused his fights with Clare. 'I could always take some courses in photography, get good at it,' she said without conviction.

'You're beyond that. You need to learn by doing now. I thought that woman taught you about developing, surely that's enough? You just need to work towards your goals — it's straightforward from where I see it.' He sounded like one of the business gurus he was always watching on TV, and she wanted to tease him but he was totally earnest, making furrows in his brows to show his displeasure. 'It's like trying to tour without a map,' he said, 'it just can't be done. I sat down years ago and charted this out, every bit of it — how long we'd play the pubs; when we'd approach the record companies; when we'd take time out to write new material. The dates have changed a bit, but you've got to know where you're aiming at or you won't know when you've arrived?'

'Maybe when you've got tens of thousands of fans screaming at you?' she said, trying to get him to lighten up.

'If that's what you count as success. But it's just the start. Now we need to think about how it will last? You've got to be in control or someone else will be.'

Meg didn't like to say how much she was enjoying being out of control, of allowing herself be carried along in Kyle's wake. As for the future, she felt inclined to leave that to chance, even though the mental calculations she did each day, 34 days, 35…40,41… made her worry that her fate was already decided.

Exclusive: Supermodel Clare Driscoll talks about her traumatic break-up from MindSet's hot drummer Kyle Watt.'His rejection made me focus on my career — now I'm on the cover of Elle.'

August: New York

It had been a late night, travelling through the early hours and arriving in New York just before dawn. Rest days had become more frequent since Mac's throat problems, and she was increasingly glad for them. As she woke up, Meg instinctively rolled over to curl into Kyle's back, only to find his side empty. She got up and peed, and, since it was only 10.30, went back into bed. She knew she should plug the hotel phone back in, but she was knackered and the messages could wait. Kyle was no doubt doing fifty lengths or in the gym, lifting weights to tighten his already tight abs. *Mmm, tight abs*. She sank into the huge goose feather pillows and let the comforter swaddle her as she drifted back to sleep.

She woke again at noon, and this time hunger propelled her to move. She dialled for room service and went to shower. She lathered her body with the complimentary Clarins products, and let the power shower massage her bones. There was a noise in the room and she realised she hadn't checked the door chain. She quickly turned off the water and grabbed a fluffy bathrobe from the door. She opened the door just enough to see Kyle empty bags of clothes onto the bed, one bellhop lay out her food, while another arranged vases of red roses.

'Don't these look cool?' Kyle asked when she came through the door. He held a pair of dark brown leather trousers against his legs. 'And this?'

She smiled, nodding as he held up garish shirt after outrageous jacket. 'Work clothes?' she asked tentatively.

'Play clothes. I bought another dozen black vests for work. And I got you this.' He lifted a black lycra dress and held it against her body. 'You like?'

'Very *Addicted to Love*,' she said with a silent wish that he wouldn't choose clothes for her. 'Do you want to eat? I'm ravenous.'

'Let's go out. I've booked a table at the Windows on the World. Put the dress on and we're good to go.'

'I need breakfast first.'

He made no comment about how it was more like lunchtime, but she detected and ignored the disapproval as she lifted the cloche from her plate and began to devour her fry. Kyle went back to unpacking his purchases, then was behind her, kissing her neck and whispering in her ear.

'I bought you something else,' he said, and as he spoke he clasped a chain around her neck and eased a solitaire into her cleavage, 'Happy Birthday Babe.'

'Kyle. My God! What is this?' She touched the stone, turned it so that light caught the diamond sending rainbows through it. 'It's so beautiful. I don't, you really shouldn't.'

'I thought my girl needed some sparkle,' he said leading her to the mirror so she could fully appreciate it.

'It's the most beautiful thing I've ever seen in my life. Thank you, thank you,' she whispered.

Meg's new dress looked awful; pulling tight over her body and riding up. Kyle couldn't hide his disappointment and Meg had no option but to change. She pulled on black ski pants and a red shirt then picked a thick black belt off her chair and fixed it round her hips. 'Will I do?' she said as she tried to ignore her waist band digging in to her.

'I'm not sure,' Kyle said running a critical eye over her, 'but we'll miss our reservation if we don't leave now. I suppose you'll just have to.'

The maitre d' escorted them to the more casual bar in the World Trade Centre, where Kyle's lack of tie wouldn't be a problem, and his mood softened as they looked out over Manhattan to the rivers and islands. 'This is amazing, Kyle, it really is. The most amazing birthday ever.'

'I did a sky-dive when I turned 18,' Kyle said, the gin and tonic helping him chill a bit. 'Such a buzz you wouldn't believe.'

'Oh God, that does not sound like my idea of fun.'

'You want to go out to the Statue of Liberty later?' he asked.

'As long as you don't push me off,' she said, and they laughed for the first time in a while. Recently their lazy afternoons had turned into business seminars and his visible irritation whenever Clare appeared on a billboard at the side of the road was beginning to get her down. She needed him to forget about Clare and focus on her, not her career. He didn't seem to have noticed that she had become obsessed with getting enough sleep rather than with the meetings he set up for her at photography galleries. She didn't want him to control her; she wanted him to take care of her.

'I need you to talk to Zed,' Kyle said as they crunched through their Caesar salad.

'What?' Meg tried to grab back Kyle's previous sentences as they floated through the air away from them.

'Zed — I need you to have a word with him. He's out of control.' Kyle snapped his bread apart. 'I've tried, but he won't listen. He's in danger of screwing things up.'

'Do we really need to talk about work on my birthday?' she asked, but Kyle didn't want to change the subject. 'Suzie says he fine. She'll not let him do anything stupid,' Meg said.

'Do you believe that?' he asked.

'Maybe Todd should speak to him. He won't listen to me.'

'He will — he's got a soft spot for you, Meg.'

'I've never noticed.'

'That's because he gets Suzie to look out for you.'

'I didn't know anyone was looking out for me.'

'We're all are, Meg. We always have been.'

She smiled, and she really wished he meant it. Suzie was always in her face, that was for sure, but recently she thought that Kyle's focus had been elsewhere.

'Have you enjoyed your day?' Kyle asked as they snuggled together in the taxi to take them back to the hotel.

'Of course.'

They had sailed to Liberty and Ellis Islands, had refuelled at the Russian Tea Room and wandered around Central Park. Kyle couldn't have laid on a more perfect day, but she felt a tinge of sadness as she had been unable to find the words she needed.

'I've got one more present for you back at the hotel,' Kyle said.

Meg yawned, 'I just want to go to bed. Or is that the present?' she asked, squeezing his arm a little tighter.

'Come on, the night is young.' Kyle paid the driver, and they went into the hotel.

Instead of taking her up to their room, he led her to the Kennedy Suite and a surprise party. Everyone who worked on the tour was there and even people she didn't know came up to kiss her on the cheek and wish her Happy Birthday. *Happy 21st* balloons floated above the tables as waiters presented canapés or topped up glasses. 'We told them you were twenty-one so we wouldn't have a problem with the booze,' Kyle said.

'Looks like you've thought of everything,' she said and as Kyle nodded her eye was drawn to movement across at the bar, and she saw Val hurry towards her.

'Mum!' Meg shrieked and threw her arms around her mum. She felt her mum hold her tightly and she began to cry.

'Hey, what's all this? Are you not happy to see me?' Meg was aware that people were looking, but she couldn't stop the overflow of emotions.

'I can't believe you're here. Oh, this is so fantastic.'

‘I couldn’t miss you’re 21st,’ Val said with a conspiratorial wink. ‘Or your 18th,’ she whispered in her ear. ‘Kyle sent me a ticket, but I’ve been sworn to secrecy. I was bursting to tell you as well.’ Val wiped her eyes, and then Meg’s cheeks with her hankie. ‘This is a bit fancier than a pint at The Blarney Stone, eh?’

‘Just a bit,’ Meg said, ‘changed days.’

Val stroked her cheek again and looked around at the party before turning back to Meg. ‘Look at the change in you. My baby girl — all grown up.’ Meg blushed, feeling younger under her mum’s eyes than she had in months. Val pushed her away slightly so she could get a good look at her. ‘I can’t believe the change in you — finally got some meat on your bones, eh? And the hair — very swish.’

‘You look great Mum. Have you been okay?’ Meg asked — glad to see that the tell-tale rings which blackened Zed’s eyes hadn’t re-appeared on her mum’s.

‘Oh, I’m grand. I’m looking for a job in an office now that my reading’s better. I’ve had enough of cleaning.’

‘Brilliant,’ Meg said, and for the first time she understood the sacrifices Val had made for her. All her life Meg had to be the grown-up, writing letters and sorting out bills, but now she realised how hard it must have been for her mum — pregnant at fourteen; kicked out at fifteen; it was no wonder she never finished school.

Then, as if she was following Meg’s thoughts, Val said, ‘Just be careful, though,’ she pointed at Mac, ‘I mean, I slept with him and he doesn’t even recognise me. These guys will use you and then let you go. Make sure you don't get hurt. Mind you, I hadn't realised just how hot Kyle is. Here's me and my obsessions with the singers and there's you squirreling away, catching the good ones at the back.'

Meg hugged her mum again, squeezing tight, wishing she could push out all that was brewing within her, or at least share it. But her news would devastate Val, so she kept quiet until Suzie came over to break them apart. Meg wiped away the last of her tears, introduced Suzie to Val and showed off her new necklace.

'I suppose you could always get it made into a ring,' Suzie said as she cupped the diamond in her palm.

'She's too young for all that nonsense, aren't you hen? Time to enjoy yourself.' Val said.

'Don't spoil it,' Meg said to Suzie. 'Isn't it beautiful? From Tiffany's and everything.'

'Well, good on you,' Suzie said, but she turned round and met Kyle's eyes. 'I was just saying to Meg…'

Meg nudged her, 'Don't Suzie.'

'She could do with some earrings to go with that.'

'I'm sure you were saying more than that, Suzie,' Kyle said and he smiled at Meg more warmly than she'd seen all day, 'What was she saying Meg, do you need a ring?'

She felt a flutter. 'Just ignore her.' But it had been said, and even though Kyle put his arm around her shoulders she felt a change in his touch, as though Suzie had broken the fragile spell. She moved away slightly from the women and turned to Kyle. 'I love the necklace. You know that? It's perfect.'

'I know,' he said, but when he kissed her it was on the forehead then he went back to the rest of MindSet. Meg looked at Suzie and Val as they chatted together, clucking and laughing like mother hens.

'This lady is so cool Meg. Why did you never say? Do you know she's met everyone?' Suzie said.

Meg had to admit it — her mum's stories were great, that was if you omitted the bits about the baby lying in the cot while you took a hit; or the school girl having to pull fag ends from the sink before she could wash her knickers. Suzie pulled her back to the present.

'So what's legal today that you couldn't do yesterday?'

Meg thought for a minute, she had considered the same question earlier.

'Well,' Meg said, accepting another glass of champagne from a passing waiter. 'Drinking,' she whispered, 'at least in the UK and I think I can have sex in more of the states where it's not compulsory at fourteen.'

'Are you coming home soon?' Val asked suddenly through the girls' laughter.

Meg instinctively put her hand over her stomach.

'Everything's fine at home, you know,' Val said earnestly. 'There's nothing to worry about. You can come back.' But before Meg could answer, Kyle grabbed a mike.

Ask me, ask me, ask me. 'Right, so we're here, yeah?'

'God Meg, he's shaking, do you think this is it? The grand proposal.'

'Shut up will you?' But there was a quiver in his voice, a hesitancy, making him seem vulnerable.

'Right we're here for Meg's birthday, so, song, cake party…Happy Birthday to you.'

Meg forced a smile as a huge cake in the shape of a suitcase was wheeled in, but all she could think was, *Was that it? Was that a speech? Oh, eh, Happy Birthday. No "I love you." No "to my best girl." Just "Happy Birthday." Bugger it.* She downed another glass of champagne, stabbed the knife into the cake, licked the creamy frosting off her fingers then grabbed Kyle's hand. She didn't need a proposal. 'Come on, let's dance.'

Todd let Meg have another couple of days off and she played the tourist again with her mum, managing to keep up a frenetic pace before falling into bed after dinner. Suzie took Val to the gigs, and didn't question Meg's dipping energy until Val was dispatched at the airport.

'So should we stop at a drugstore for a test?' Suzie asked as the taxi drove them back into Manhattan. Meg didn't answer. 'Did you tell your mum?' Suzie asked. Meg shook her head, and a single tear rolled down her cheek. 'It'll be okay,' Suzie continued, 'I'll look after you.'

'How long have you known?' Meg asked.

‘I know what that worried look means, so I kept an eye on your waistband. The baggy shirts aren’t fooling me — I doubt they’re fooling anyone. I thought I’d better come with you today in case you jumped on the plane with your mum.’

‘You know the last thing she said to me, before she left? “*Just don’t do anything stupid.*” Like she did, she means and I’m the stupid bloody mistake. I’ll never let this kid feel like that.’

The taxi driver turned up his bhangra music, and lit another cigarette.

‘So what’s Kyle saying about it? Was that what the necklace was all about?’ Meg thought for a moment, and had to confront the other fact she had been trying to avoid —there was no way Kyle hadn’t noticed. What she couldn’t understand was why he hadn’t said anything or even made it easy for her to tell him. He’d even bought that stupid tight dress and was annoyed when it clung to the swelling in her womb. Suzie waited for an answer. Maybe the diamond was his way of saying he knew, and that he cared. She hoped it was, at least.

‘You need to tell him Meg,’ Suzie said, but then she stopped and turned to Meg, lifting her hand into hers before she continued, ‘Unless? I could stay here with you, get things sorted?’

‘No,’ Meg said. She was certain of that. Val had never given her anything, except the biggest thing of all. The taxi pulled up outside their hotel and Suzie went into her purse to pay.

‘I just need a bit of time,’ Meg said as Suzie counted out dollars. ‘And Suzie, please don’t tell Zed. I don’t want anyone else to know.’

Suzie stiffened at the mention of Zed. ‘He’s not really himself, just now Meg. I don’t think he would remember, even if I did say to him.’

‘Will he be alright?’ Meg asked, remembering that she was meant to be checking for Kyle, but Suzie didn’t answer and they parted to pack for the next leg of the journey with their worries unresolved.

September: New Orleans

The limos dropped them at the Royal Sonesta Hotel at 1pm. The hotel's marble lobby was designed to be airy but the heat in New Orleans was different — clawing, humid, constricting. They checked-in in near silence: Zed had made an arse of his big riff the previous night; Mac had forgotten his words half way through *Drums in the Distance;* Wayne had puked on the jet; and Kyle had been pestered for a comment on the new improved Clare. The band kept as much space between each other as they could, even Meg and Suzie didn't dare to break the deadlock with their usual chatter.

Meg fanned herself with a magazine in the lift and ordered ice tea from room service the minute she got into their room, but the heat was unabating. She undid the buttons on her trousers and lay down on top of the bed. 'How do you think the gig will go tonight?' Meg asked, but Kyle ignored her question, opened the shutters letting in too much light and noise.

'Isn't this place amazing?' Kyle said from the veranda. 'The whole place seems so alive.'

Meg covered her eyes and groaned from the bed.

'I'm going to have a quick wash and we can have a look around,' Kyle said.

Meg said *Yes* even though she meant *No*. They'd hardly had a minute together since New York, and it would be fun to explore a place neither of them had been before.

They left the air conditioning of the lobby and walked into a wall of heat as they joined the hubbub of Bourbon St. After the uniformity of Mid-West towns New Orleans sparked. Young black boys, with cardboard trays in front of them, tap danced for change; tourists sauntered to the easy beat; while transvestites shopped for new feather boas at the seedier end of the street. Kyle dragged Meg into a fetish shop where she stood impassive while he held up waistcoats, gloves and hats for her approval. 'They would look good on stage,' he said. She pulled a face and said she wanted to get moving again.

Back on the street Meg had to marshal him by other shops and curiosities and tried to insist they stop for a drink. But he wasn't listening and they walked further and didn't stop until they reached Café du Monde on Jackson Square.

'What's wrong with you today?' Kyle asked the minute the waiter had left. 'You're cranky as hell. I thought you'd love it here.'

'I'm as cranky as hell. You should listen to yourself. I thought you were going to hit that guy that bumped into you.'

'He didn't bump into me — he crashed his beer keg into my leg. It bloody hurt. I've got to look after my body you know. It's my livelihood.'

Meg sighed. It had looked sore.

'Why are you not photographing this place?' Kyle said suddenly. 'Surely it's a great opportunity to add something to your portfolio.'

'It's too hot.'

'It's like you don't even get what an amazing place this is!' He waved his arm around.

'I get it,' Meg said, wishing he would shut up, 'I've left my camera in the hotel. And I don't know — I'm not in the mood. I'm feeling a bit of sensory overload today.'

'You say that like it's a bad thing? God Meg, can you not just buck up and enjoy it? Now where has our waiter gone?' Kyle said, as he twisted round and tapped his watch at the waiter.

'We've just ordered — give the guy a break?'

'And what's with acting like a bloody prude in that shop. It was embarrassing.'

Meg took a bite out of the beignet which had been laid before her by an apologetic waiter. *She was embarrassing? He was the one being a prick.* She felt like shouting out there and then, *I'm pregnant*, but something other than the beignet made it stick in her throat. She gazed out over the square and saw Mac among the tourists, looking at artwork which was tied to the railings. He was talking and laughing with the artist, pointing to different paintings, before choosing a couple and shaking hands on the deal. Wayne was out there too, giving his attention to a range of crystals on a trestle table covered in crushed red velvet. A toddler lay asleep in her buggy behind the stall and for a second Meg felt the enormity of what was happening inside her, but then her gaze was broken by two girls giggling behind Wayne, obviously trying to find the courage to ask him for an autograph. Mac saw their predicament and immediately went to them. He could still be charming with the fans, despite being an arse to everyone else, Meg thought as she listened to their squeals above the chatter of their café.

'Look at him,' Kyle said, as he too looked out to the square, 'You'd think he get tired of all that, try to keep a lower profile.'

'Just as well he doesn't,' Meg said, ignoring Kyle's derision. 'His smile is worth a fortune.'

'It won't be worth anything if he can't write some new songs. You need to push him on that.'

'You know Kyle,' Meg said, looking him in the eye, 'you keep telling me to sort Zed out and now Mac, well Todd's your manager. I'm doing enough.'

Kyle gulped down the end of his coffee and called for the bill. 'Just do it Meg. Okay?' And he was on his feet before Meg had a chance to respond to the sharp command. 'Now come on, there's a great place I need to see before we go back.' Kyle took off, leaving his purchases from the fetish shop under the table. Meg bent down, *Sod it,* and left them, before she hurried down the street after him.

There were no favours at Preservation Hall. *If you want it, you got to wait like everyone else.* Condensed sweat ran down the nicotine-stained wall of the holding pen, as body parts crushed together. The muted sound of swinging jazz seeped through the walls, with intermittent whoops and claps. Sepia photographs lined the walls, and Meg and Kyle listened as a man behind them treated his companion to a roll call: Sweet Emma Barrett, Willie and Percy Humphrey, Jelly Roll Morton. Louis Armstrong was the only one

Meg knew, from old films on the telly, but she admired the photos. 'There's a man who enjoys his work,' Meg said pointing to Armstrong's grinning face.

'That's a man enjoying life,' Kyle replied, and despite the jostling, she felt happy now he wasn't snapping anymore. He was right — you could see it in the way the musicians held their instruments, as if they were married to them, each depending on the other. She looked up at Kyle and saw the same expression in his face, music and life interconnected, sometimes to the exclusion of everything else. But Kyle must have picked up Meg's vibe and bent to kiss her gently, easing away the earlier tension. 'You'll love this.'

Although the place was full, a shout to move crushed more people inside. Meg kept one arm crossed over her stomach. She fanned herself with the other hand but the air barely stirred. Finally a door opened in front of them. She hooked her index finger through Kyle's belt loop and held on tightly as they squeezed into the back of the Hall. Anticipation rose like steam to the ceiling. People craned to watch as the old men adjusted their seats and whetted and blew quietly into their instruments — there wasn't one who looked under seventy.

'I didn't know you liked jazz,' Meg shouted up to Kyle, making him glare at her. Her face flushed hot.

'Of course I do. Besides, you can't come to New Orleans and not come here.' They had been to Paris and not entered Notre Dame; to Rome and not even glimpsed the Vatican, but this place seemed to hold a different resonance. 'I hope I'm still playing at their age,'

Kyle said with a look of reverence which Meg had never seen before.

She peeked through shoulders to get a better view of the band. Despite their decrepit looks, when they started to play, they were vibrant and smooth. Meg's neck hurt with straining, so she contented herself with watching the people around her. It looked like some were in the grip of a religious experience and even Meg felt something deep inside her swell and rise.

The first set finished and when the clapping subsided, a door opened to let the front third of the Hall out. Everyone who remained shuffled nearer the band, and more people squeezed in from the back. Meg and Kyle separated for a moment but then Kyle's hand appeared through the crowd and pulled Meg forward and in front of him. This time she could see as the musicians took turns to stand and lead the melody. Kyle tapped and swayed, his hands on her hips making her move in time with the rhythm. She could feel happiness run through his hands into her body and the humidity and crush didn't matter anymore. She closed her eyes, felt V*elvet* whispered in her ear. The clarinet's plaintive rise and fall; the trumpet's resolute soar; the singer's hoarse telling of *The Saint James Infirmary Blues*. Her face felt wet, so she brushed away the moisture and ran her hankie round her neck to mop up the sweat.

The heat suddenly seemed to press around her, crushing down from above like a giant hand wanting to concertina her into the floor. She let out a gasp and suddenly felt very light. The crowd surged forward again and hot blood rushed up from her feet. Fuzz filled her ears. Her stomach dropped, knees buckled and everything turned red then faded to black.

Something flickered and for the first time in this city, she felt a slight breeze.

'What happened?'

A black hand stopped fanning her and helped her into a sitting position on the pavement.

'Kyle?'

'You fainted,' the man said.

'Oh?'

'You okay?'

'I don't know,' she said. She was sure that was Kyle's voice, but the sun blinded her and it took a few moments to focus on the figures silhouetted in front of her.

'Take it easy ma'am,' the Louisiana voice said.

She pulled on his outstretched hand and he helped her up. Kyle stood, arms by his side, looking at the passing traffic, until he saw what he was looking for and shouted '*Taxi.*' He went over to the driver and opened the door for Meg.

'Are you okay to get back to the hotel yourself?' he said, his attention briefly on her. Meg nodded. 'It's just I've dreamt half my life of Preservation Hall and I really want to hear the end of the set. Yeah?' He turned to the other man. 'I can get back in? Right, mate?'

'Are you not seeing the lady home?' the man asked incredulously.

Kyle looked at Meg and she knew that he wanted her to absolve him. 'I'm fine — it was just too hot. Go back in.' She climbed into the cab and turned to wave, but Kyle and the stranger had already disappeared.

She sat slumped in the cab finally waking up to the fact that things weren't fine. She had been kidding herself. Kyle hadn't commented on her pregnancy because he didn't want to know. Today had made that perfectly clear, rushing her from one unpleasant experience to the next. All the excuses she had made for him, about the problems with the band and the pressures of being on the road, disintegrated. If he didn't want to know now, he never would. Meg thought back to a conversation she had had with Suzie a few days before. She and Zed had made an agreement not to have kids. It would just be the two of them, now and forever. Nothing and no one would get in the way of their relationship. Meg realised that she had never had that sort of conversation with Kyle — nothing about relationships, certainly nothing about kids, yet she'd let herself get into this situation, and so, for that matter, had he. Suzie had hinted about a clinic again, ready to help should the need arise, but Meg had detected a slight condescension in her voice and remained resolute. She didn't know how, but she would cope, no matter how shit-scared she felt.

The bedroom was cool when she got in. Someone had closed the blinds, put the air conditioning on full and turned down the bed. *How many hotel rooms*? Meg wondered. *How many maids turning down how many beds?* She poured herself glass of mineral water, and held it to her forehead before sipping it gently. She should have told her mum about the baby; she should have told Kyle, but she hadn't and she couldn't leave it any longer. But her head was woolly, so she turned on the TV for something mindless and found Clare.

'In today's programme we welcome Clare Driscoll. Hello Clare. Clare has become the poster girl for how to deal with break-ups. After dating MindSet drummer Kyle Watt for four years, she brushed herself down, got on her glad rags and took the modelling world by storm. Look what you're missing now, Kyle. So tell us your story Clare.'

'Well, thank you. You're so kind. Well, you see I met Kyle when I was very young, and I thought he was trying to do the best for me.'

'But then you realised that wasn't the case?'

'He liked the fact that I was a model, of course, but he didn't actually like me doing any modelling. Kyle likes weak women, you see, and I afraid that's what I let myself become.'

'Some men can manipulate you like that.'

'Yes, you're right, but I saw a pattern emerging when he gave a job to a homeless girl, and started to favour her over me. He just wants us to be grateful to him, so that we stay with him, but really he's clipping our wings. I realise that now, and I've grown stronger because of it. But

I don't want you to get the wrong impression — I do still love him, very deeply. I think I always will.'

'Thank you Clare. We all think you are a strong woman, Clare. Strong enough to stand up for yourself and move on from a relationship that was draining your soul. Isn't Clare is an inspiration to us all?'

October: Miami

By the time the tour bus started back to the hotel Meg's energy levels had hit zero and she was feeling really unwell. The book on pregnancy, which she kept hidden in her satchel, talked about sickness in the first couple of months, but she was 16 weeks now, and this was the first time she'd felt nauseous. She tried to go through everything she had eaten in case it was food poisoning, but it was too difficult to concentrate or remember. She had never eaten as much in her life — shoving potato chips, frankfurters and waffles down her throat at every opportunity. Now the bus seemed to stop at every traffic light with the driver slamming his feet between brakes and gas, causing her stomach to lurch and regurgitate.

Thankfully the gig had been flawless, the crowd pumping and after weeks of tension at lacklustre performances, the atmosphere on the bus relaxed again. Mac and Todd had chosen two of the most glamorous girls to sit beside them, and there were other models and groupies scattered throughout the bus. Meg recognised some of them from the fashion magazines she flicked through at the airports, but mainly she concentrated on not being sick.

Kyle bounced and tapped on the seat beside her like a hyperactive schoolboy, still full of adrenaline. 'I was so worried we were going to be shit again tonight. It scares me how precarious the balance is — fantastic or forget it. But we're back on track, I can feel it.' He squeezed her thigh, and she hoped he meant they were back on track too. 'Come on, Meg, we really need to party.'

'I can't Kyle, I feel like death.' She closed her eyes and waited for his agreement, but instead she felt him get up and walk up the bus.

'Who's for a party?' he said and the whole bus cheered. Suzie came and sat beside her, touching her arm until she opened her eyes.

'Don't worry — we'll have the party in our room. You look like shit.'

Meg felt herself swamped with emotion, but she managed to whisper, 'I feel like shit. I haven't had a minute today — every time I tried to get a break, something else needed sorting.'

'Have you told Kyle yet?'

'Ssh. He's been a bit stressed about the band recently and he didn't need me adding to it. But he's really happy again tonight, I definitely going to tell him when we get back.' Suzie turned to look up the aisle of the bus. 'Who's he with?' Meg asked, frightened to move her head.

'No one, it's fine.' But Meg could hear him, his voice punctuated with the giggling of bimbos. At least Clare hadn't had the nerve to get on the bus, although she'd been at the gig, and was worried that she was the reason for the improvement in Kyle's mood. Suzie squeezed her arm again, as though she had read her mind, so Meg put her head on Suzie's shoulder and drifted off for a while.

Suzie nudged her as the bus pulled up at the front of the hotel, then ran to the door, announced her room number and jumped off to get the key so she could lead the way to the party.

Meg sat, trying to become fully conscious before she dared move. But Kyle didn't wait, and by the time the bus had emptied and she got her bag from the overhead shelf, the hotel lobby had cleared. She had looked forward to being in Miami and all the Art Deco she had seen in the tourist adverts, but her surroundings barely registered as she asked for her key and put in an alarm call for an hour's time. She would sleep for a while and then join the party.

She had hoped that Kyle would be in their room when she got there, but only found the same chaos they had left. She shoved her paperwork off the bed and threw their discarded clothes into their open cases. Then she pulled back the covers and eased herself into bed. In what seemed like the next minute, the phone rang with her automated alarm call. The sleep had made her feel even worse, her eyeballs throbbed, there was a low ache in her back and the buzz in her ears seemed more pronounced than usual. She sat on the side of the bed for five minutes before she tried to stand. Her head felt ready to float away while her feet pulled with ten times gravity towards the floor. But she knew with every instinct in her body that she had to get to the party. There was no doubt that Clare would be there, *'I'll always love him',* so she forced herself to the bathroom and her make-up bag.

A couple of roadies stood arguing at one end of the corridor but Meg ignored them and turned the other way to where some strays hung about an open door. As she approached she could hear loud music and assumed she'd found Suzie and Zed's suite. The fug of smoke hit her eyes and the back of her throat simultaneously and made her retch. There were people sprawled everywhere, on the bed, on the sofas, leaning against walls, sitting in circles passing joints or squatting in front of the coffee table with rolled up dollars waiting for a hit. She scanned round the room: Todd and Dave having a conversation while topless girls lap-danced for them; Wayne getting a blow job next to the TV; while Suzie and Zed were curled up together on a large armchair etching lines into each other's skin with a blade. On another night Meg might have pulled out her camera to start documenting, calling the collection *Bacchanalian Nightmare*. As she stepped over bodies she remembered that Suzie had told her all about Bacchus — how he liked to party; how they thought about using it as a name, but Kyle had dismissed it, deciding that MindSet encompassed more of what they should aspire to. So MindSet they were, except they weren't all here.

'I was wondering where you'd got to. Didn't I just say "*I wonder where Meg has got to*"?' Suzie said to Zed.

'Yeah,' Zed replied, dozily, slowly dragging from the joint between his fingers.

'I thought I'd better make an appearance.' Meg looked around again, checking out each face in the hope that she would make a match with Kyle. 'But it looks like I'm too late. No Kyle and no Clare either.' For the first time since she had known her, Suzie couldn't meet Meg's eye.

'I think he went to organise more booze,' Suzie said. 'He'll be back in a minute.'

But Meg backed away. She always knew that Clare would come back and claim Kyle, Suzie had reminded her of it often enough. If only Kyle had kept beside her on the bus. If only he had been in their room. If only she had been able to find the right words.

'I've been so stupid,' Meg said. She'd let herself hope that the baby would make a difference but she realised now that she hadn't told him because she worried it wouldn't.

Suzie reached out to grab her, 'Meg, wait.'

Meg avoided her grasp and turned too quickly, causing the whole room to spin. She steadied herself on a nearby arm, found her balance and picked her way out of the room.

Her walk along the corridor was slow and difficult. Spots dashed in front of her eyes, lights like a Ferris wheel spinning in her line of vision. She staggered as though she was drunk. *Where is he?* When she reached her room she needed to rest her head against the door so she didn't overbalance while she picked her key card out of her pocket. And as she slipped it into the door and waited for the click she could hear muted laughter and the occasional raised voice, but zoning it all out she imagined she could hear Kyle.

Meg had never appreciated just how quiet airports could be. She was used to travelling in a pack that came with excess luggage, fragile egos and problems for just about every member of staff. But now the cavernous spaces echoed with the clangs of trolleys.

The logistics had been too easy. After a couple of hours of lonely sleep she woke, threw some leggings and baggy tops into her suitcase, took a taxi to the airport, went to the BA window and booked a seat through Dulles and London to Glasgow. All she had to do was watch for the Departures board to dispatch the flights above hers, and move her from *Wait in lounge* to *Proceed to gate*. It was too early for breakfast to be on offer, but Meg's stomach began to cramp. She rooted in her handbag and found a few squares of chocolate which had melted and reformed. Any other day she would have chucked them in the nearest bin, but she craved sugar. It didn't help, in fact, the pain multiplied and the creaminess of the chocolate seemed to lodge halfway down her throat. She bought a bottle of water from a vending machine, took some aspirin and settled across a couple of chairs. She dozed for a while but woke with a sharp pain in her stomach and a damp feeling, as though she'd wet herself. She looked around, eased herself off her seat and followed the signs to the toilets. In a cubicle another spasm doubled her in two. She knelt, fell forward onto all fours, and put her head into the pan in case she was sick. She was being ripped apart, struggling to stay conscious.

Gradually the pain eased a little and she sat back on her heels for a little while before she could finally clamber onto the toilet. She steadied herself against the walls and pulled down her trousers, gasping at the sticky clots on her knickers. She took them off, streaking blood down her legs. She folded them, threw them into the cubicle bin, and wiped her thighs. She bent down and found a clean pair of knickers in her hand luggage then dabbed the crotch of her black trousers with toilet paper, as though it mattered, turning it red. Her stomach cramped again. She felt clammy and sick, so she rested the side of her head against the flimsy partition until the feeling began to pass. Another contraction. Another spasm. The pain subsided. She closed her eyes and the lid and flushed. Waited and flushed again.

She fed money into the machine, and returned to her cubicle with pads. Then she sat for ten minutes or more trying to process what had happened. She had just spent most of her savings on a flight she wasn't sure she was fit enough to get on. But not leaving wasn't an option. Kyle was back with Clare. *Think.* Her medical insurance was tied up with the band, so maybe she should stay and get checked out. But she didn't work with the band anymore. She couldn't. Her head spun. *Kyle and Clare. Stupid, stupid bitch.* But if the baby was gone, she didn't need to go home. Outside, planes were lined up to take passengers to anywhere they wanted to go, but for Meg there seemed no way forward or back.

The bleeding didn't seem to be getting any worse and when she heard the cleaner making her way along the cubicles, banging open each door and slopping a mop around, she took it as her cue to move. She stood up carefully, washed her hands, making sure every bit of blood was gone and made her way gingerly to the nearest café.

She hadn't realised she was crying, but she saw Kyle walking towards her, and found herself sobbing in his arms.

'I'm sorry Meg. I'm so sorry. Suzie told me about the baby. I was so stupid. I should have realised,' he said, as he held her tightly.

Meg sobbed even louder, not caring that people would be looking at them. She clung to him even harder when he tried to pull back to make talking easier.

'Come on. Let's go back to the hotel and talk. I'm not letting you leave me. You know I can't cope without you.'

She nodded, relieved that a decision had been made, not really understanding what that decision was, but her body shook and he had to put his arm around her waist and half-carried her across the concourse.

'I've checked my bags in already,' she said, as she momentarily connected with her surroundings, but then, 'Stop. I need to sit down.'

She sat at the end of a row of seats and Kyle crouched in front of her, holding onto her hands. He looked at her as though waiting for an explanation, but she just concentrated on staying upright. There was a flash and giggles around them but pain shot across her stomach again. She squeezed Kyle's hands making him grimace.

'What is it? God Meg, what's wrong? You're sweating —,' he said putting his hand on her brow, 'have you taken something?'

'I think I need a doctor,' she whispered.

Kyle took her to the Emergency Room and sat beside her as she gave her details to the airport doctor. *Date of birth: 25/8/1968; date of last period: 16/6/86; estimated length of pregnancy: 16 weeks.* The doctor couldn't have been much older than Kyle, but he had a supercilious air that put Meg immediately on her guard. The room smelled of antiseptic, had peppermint green walls, the paint old, fading, a forgotten place in an over-designed city. A washed-out anatomical drawing curled on the wall next to a drug-suppliers calendar and Meg wished she was anywhere but here.

'Have all the products of the pregnancy been expelled?' The doctor asked. His red socks matched his tie, chosen with the care of a thoughtless man.

'I don't know,' she said, and wondered if she would have known if she had looked. She answered the rest of his questions as best she could but kept her focus on the side of the table where the veneer had started to crack and a piece had been picked off. She quelled the desired to pick at it too, kept her hands flat on her lap. Kyle's eyes were on her, she could feel them, but she didn't dare meet them. She was shrunken, just a daft wee lassie, wee Maggie Burns, who been seduced by a stranger's smile, not Meg, lynchpin and organiser.

The doctor pulled out some paper sheeting and signalled for Meg to lie on the bed. She wanted Kyle to take her hand but when she looked over he was fiddling with his shoelace. The doctor pressed on her belly. *Why did he come after me?*

'Is this the father?' The doctor asked, cutting into her thoughts.

'No,' she said without flinching. Out of the corner of her eye she could see Kyle stiffen, but her face remained impassive. The doctor's next statement convinced her she'd said the right thing. He looked at his notes, checking his facts.

'You conceived this child when you were seventeen,' he looked at Kyle. 'You know the age of consent in Florida is eighteen?'

'I didn't conceive in this state,' Meg said quickly across Kyle's attempt at forming words.

'Well, it looks like that's a moot point anyway,' he said as he began to scribble a note on headed paper. 'I'll send you over for a sonogram to see if you need a vacuum aspiration, but I think the pregnancy has spontaneously aborted.'

Meg sat on peach plastic upholstery in the waiting room while Kyle filled out the insurance paperwork. A couple of times he left the desk to use a payphone on the wall, and each time he returned to the clipboard he looked more ashen. It was maybe the harsh light of the hospital, or the remnants of a long night, but his cheeks were sunken with stubble pushing through and she thought how much older than twenty-two he looked.

She asked Kyle to wait while she was led off by a young nurse who said nothing to Meg after calling her name. She closed her eyes as they plopped the cold gel onto her stomach and pushed the probe around. A girl at school, who'd got pregnant at the end of 3rd year, had brought in her ultrasound picture for everyone to see, proudly showing off the grainy blob. Meg had met her the next year, pushing a pram in the rain, miserable and no longer enthralled by the life she had been able to grow inside her. Meg wondered if she would have fared any better. Maybe if she had seen a doctor in New York she would at least have a picture to hold and know that it was real. Maybe if she had acknowledged what was happening she wouldn't be here.

A large nurse with unnaturally red hair came to discharge her and gently explain about counselling but when Meg asked about flying she said, 'Don't rush things honey, you need to let your body recover.'

Meg nodded and whispered 'Thanks', not able to acknowledge the kindness in her voice. If she didn't look at anyone, she could get through this.

Kyle put his arm around her without exerting any pressure on her back as they left the hospital. He didn't say a word to her until they were in a taxi heading back to the hotel. She heard his gulp then he said, 'It was my baby, right?'

Tears starting again, running uncontrollably down her face. 'Of course it was yours. But you could have been arrested for statutory rape.'

'For God's sake Meg, how do you even know these things?'

'It's my job to know. I keep you guys out of trouble, remember.'

'And what about you?' Kyle said as he shook his head. 'I'm so sorry. I've really let you down.'

Meg turned her face into the folds of his jacket and closed her eyes.

He put her into bed, climbed in beside her and held her until she fell asleep, but when she woke up he was gone. She knew by the clock that they would be well into their set by now —— *Concrete Jungle* or *Alibi*. She could almost hear them; see them; watch Kyle holding the band together from the back. '*My beat is what makes the audience jump — makes them clap — pumps their blood.*'

Meg turned over in bed and her heart broke.

Kyle was already at the table by the window eating breakfast when Meg woke again. His side of the room was cleared of his belongings, his jacket lying on top of his packed suitcase. Her cases were there too, somehow returned from the airport while she slept. 'Hey, how are you feeling?' he asked.

Meg assessed her body, and reckoned that if she ignored the aches in her stomach and her heart, she was alright.

'Suzie's going to stay with you for a few days. When you're better you can catch up with us, it'll be fine.'

She wanted to believe that, but her mind was filled with so many uncertainties. 'What did Todd say?' she asked, her voice croaky as though she had an infection. 'Is he really pissed off?'

'He's just worried about you, Meg, we all are. He'll manage, but he asked me to get your diary and your files.'

Meg pointed over to the satchel she was never without. 'It's in there. Just don't take my personal stuff. The blue notebook's mine and be careful with my camera.'

He sifted through the bag, lifting out items for inspection and putting them in one bundle or another. At the bottom was her aqua Tiffany's box.

'Do you need to keep this?' he asked. 'You've always got your necklace on.'

Meg stretched out her hand. 'I like the box,' she said. She turned it over in her hand. It was too heavy to be empty, he must have felt that. She wanted to open it, show him that inside was a sterling silver dummy, a stupid thing to buy, but all she had. *Open it and we can mourn together.* She ran her fingernail along the slit, *just a little more pressure and he will be able to see.* But instead, she put it down next to the bed, 'One day I'm going to have a jewellery box and I can sit this inside. Until then it stays with me.'

The porter knocked on the door and came in to collect Kyle's luggage bringing their conversation to a close.

'I'll miss you,' Kyle said sitting down on the bed and giving her a gentle hug. 'I'll phone every day and I'll see you really soon.'

'I know,' Meg said, 'really soon.'

Suzie stayed in the background of Meg's grief for a couple of days, only popping her head around the bedroom door of the suite they shared to make sure she was eating and not bleeding too much. Then on the Wednesday she knocked briskly and entered the room less cautiously than before. She opened the curtains to reveal the bright aqua of the sea and took the remote off the bed to mute the news of an earthquake in South America.

'I think we should go down to the restaurant tonight. You've been in here long enough.' It was safe in bed: she could sleep; eat; watch TV; have the maids clean around her; she didn't even have to think. But the pale Miami colours of the room, which had initially soothed her, were beginning to infuriate her — like someone being too kind. Suzie sounded like she was acting on orders and since she didn't look like she would leave without agreement, Meg did the easiest thing.

'I don't want to go far,' Meg said, 'I'm still a bit wobbly.'

'I know,' Suzie said, sitting down on the chair at the bottom of the bed. 'But it's time to move on.'

Meg nodded. Her stomach still pulled every now and again, but she felt as though she had done her penance. She breathed deeply. 'Can you do me a favour?'

'Sure.'

'Can you get rid of those lilies?' Meg pointed over to a huge funereal arrangement that sat on the table opposite. 'The smell's too pungent.'

'I'll move them into the lounge if you like, put them next to the window,' Suzie said as she lifted the vase, and left the unopened card from Kyle on the table. 'I would have moved them before if you had said.'

'I couldn't be bothered. But could you get them thrown out? They're overpowering.'

The sommelier politely asked Meg for ID in the restaurant, forcing her to order a soda rather than adding to the alcohol she had drunk while she got ready. Meg tried to pay attention to what Suzie was saying, but found she just focused on Suzie's moving lips rather than on any sound they were making. She blinked and tried harder to concentrate as Suzie retold Zed's tales of Japanese toilets with their dozen options for a flush and the over-zealous fans that seemed to take obsession to a new level. She left enough pauses for Meg to join in if she had wanted, but it was obvious Suzie didn't want to ask about the baby. Meg wasn't sure if she wanted to talk about it anyway, frightened that if she opened her mouth, too much would come out.

Once they had finished eating they let the waiter take their coffee to the outside lounge area and sat under an up-lit palm tree. The air was still warm but Meg pulled her cardigan around her shoulders, feeling a chill from within.

'When's your mum coming out?' Suzie asked.

'She's not,' Meg said.

'Oh,' Suzie said. 'I thought she was going to take over from me. I'm meant to be meeting up with Zed again at the weekend.'

‘I don’t need a babysitter,’ she said very definitely then she deflated, as the force of her words echoed back to her.

‘You need company.’

‘I’ll be all right.’ Meg gazed out over the swimming pool and tried to convince herself that she would be. ‘People have lost babies before. I just need to get my strength back. I don’t need my mum to do that.’

‘Does Kyle know?’

Meg shook her head. ‘He wouldn’t understand. He thinks people can just drop everything and fly to the other side of the world with no consequences. She’s just started a new job, she can’t come again. I’ve just got to pull myself together and get on with it.’

‘Did Val say that?’

Meg shrugged, ‘Well, it’s true. I’ll catch up with you in a few weeks if Todd hasn’t already sacked me.’

Suzie shook her head ‘Of course he hasn’t.’ Then she ordered a double Remy Martin from a passing waiter. When it arrived, she leaned over for Meg’s empty coffee cup, put the glass and cup under the table and transferred half the brandy. ‘Cheers.’

‘You’re not really worried about Todd are you? My God, he would fall apart if it weren’t for you,’ Suzie said leaning in across the table.

‘Do you remember that night when Kyle and I first got together and you warned me off him?’ Suzie nodded. ‘Well I should have listened. I’ve put my job in danger because of what has happened.’

‘But what has happened? Kyle came after you. He got you back.’

Meg downed her brandy and indicated for the waiter again. ‘I don’t know why he bothered. It would have been better if I’d gone home. At least there wouldn’t be any need for this pretence.’

‘What do you mean? Kyle loves you, Meg, you know that, right?’

‘Do you think?’ Meg asked, but she answered her own question. ‘He’s hardly spoken about the baby.’

‘He’s just trying to protect you.’

‘I don’t need protection. I need love.’ Meg sat quietly for a minute then continued. ‘You know, I’ve worked out why I couldn’t bring myself to tell him I was pregnant.’

Suzie raised her eyebrows and waited for the answer. Meg gulped and said quickly, ‘He would have wanted me to get rid of it.’

‘You’re wrong,’ Suzie said forcefully. ‘He was so upset when I told him you’d left.’

‘That’s just because I’d mucked up his great plan for me to be this world famous photographer. You know what he’s like.’

‘His plans are bogus,’ Suzie said with a dismissive wave. ‘Whenever Clare showed any initiative he would shut her down. He would act all happy that she had got a modelling deal and then go all moody when she had to leave.’ Meg winced at the mention of Clare’s name, but Suzie continued. ‘He likes to think he’s helping you — that’s why he picked you both up, to give you an opportunity he saw you deserved. It was the same with Zed, he knew he’d skills

Kyle could only dream of. But ultimately the world's got to centre round Kyle, and when it doesn't, well, he can be a bit of a wanker.'

Meg pursed her lips together and her eyes welled up, she didn't like Suzie talking about Kyle like that, but she didn't argue. Suzie repeated her trick with the brandy and tried to soften her words. 'Maybe it's just how I see it. It's a weird world we live in, Meg. I mean, look at me — twenty-eight and all I do is lounge around swimming pools and occasionally buy the band a few shirts.'

'Does it bother you?'

'It beats working,' Suzie said with a shrug.

'What did you want to be when you were a kid?' Meg asked as she rewound her own mind back to the days before she met Kyle.

Suzie laughed. 'You're beginning to sound like Kyle,' she said sipping her brandy. 'I suppose I wanted to be a nurse. And hey, maybe that's what I am, administering drugs and fluffing up Zed's pillows.' She sat back into the cushions of the chair and laughed again at her own joke.

Meg remained serious. 'What do you think you'll do when this is all over?'

'Good God, Meg. Now you need to spit three times and spin around. I hope you've never asked Kyle that — he'd go ape.'

'It's a legitimate question.'

'But you don't say it. It'll bring bad luck.'

'Kyle knows that it'll come to an end soon, even with all his planning. Nobody lasts more than five years, and this tour, well, it seems like they've already hit their high point.'

Suzie swirled her drink around watching it coat the sides and ooze back down the glass while she considered her answer. 'You're being a bit fatalistic. I suppose I just want to enjoy the ride and worry about tomorrow when it comes.'

'That's how I ended up pregnant.' Meg said. Then she was quiet for a long time.

Suzie interrupted her thoughts. 'What happened that night between you two? After you left the party? What made you go to the airport? Did you have a fight?'

Meg realised that she had to face an ugly truth. 'Clare came back.'

'Yeah, I saw her at the gig, but…' Suzie sat back in her chair and looked straight at Meg, 'it doesn't mean anything.'

Meg rubbed up the bridge of her nose and onto her forehead with her index finger, as she tried to ease away the start of a headache. 'I suppose I was just keeping him warm for her, that's what they all thought. They're back together, you know that, right?'

Suzie looked genuinely shocked. 'Zed never said.'

'He wouldn't, would he? They've got that stupid honour code. He thinks I don't know. He tries to sound normal when he phones, but I know she's there.'

'Kyle wouldn't do that, I mean maybe one night for old time sakes, but he loves you.'

'I phoned her agency — she's got bookings in Tokyo and Osaka. The dates match.'

Suzie shook her head. ‘I really thought it was over with Clare this time. What did he say?’

Meg shrugged, she hadn’t had the energy to directly confront him with what she knew, finding it easier to listen to his lies. ‘Maybe it was just as well about the baby,’ Meg said and for a moment she allowed herself the vision of arriving at Glasgow airport with a baby wrapped in pink. Heard her mother call her a stupid eejit and let herself look down at the baby’s face. Suzie took her hand and squeezed it, and let her cry ever so quietly.

The next few days Suzie kept Meg busy with pedicures and seaweed wraps, late lunches and evening strolls through the glimmering lights of the city. The geriatric pace suited them both, letting them relax and take time with each other. But Suzie talked more and more about Zed; about how his drug use was beginning to change him; about how much she worried, and by Saturday afternoon Meg was happy to wave her off to the airport.

Suzie hugged her tightly before she left. ‘I’ll speak to Todd the minute I get over there, okay? It doesn’t matter about Kyle, the band needs you. But I’ll speak to Kyle too. He really is a bastard if he’s gone back to her.’

Meg nodded, willing to let Suzie think she could fix things. But as she walked back through the airport alone, she spotted Kyle and Clare reunited on the cover of a magazine facing out from the newsagents. It was not one she would add to the archive.

With Suzie gone, Meg cancelled her reiki session and went to bed. She lay in the white Egyptian cotton sheets and stared out the window, watching as the blue sky dimmed and darkened, then brightened again. She heard a noise in the lounge and got up to find a waiter laying out breakfast and a porter delivering a vase of deep pink roses. She read the card and it made her smile.

'You've come this far, now just keep going,
– Love Suzie and Zed.'

'Shall I pour your coffee ma'am?'

'Thanks.'

As she chewed her toast she let her hands caress the petals of the flowers. The scent and the colour gave her a slim pleasure she couldn't fight against, but it also made her even sadder about Kyle's white lilies.

When she had finished breakfast she lifted the phone and waited patiently for an answer. 'Hi. It's Meg. I'm at the Four Seasons in Miami. Can you come, Cerise? I really need you.'

And in Entertainment news today, the shock engagement of super-model Clare Driscoll to MindSet's lead singer Mac Marchmount. Clare previously dated Kyle Watt, the band's drummer and in an exclusive interview to ABC Clare shared the happy news. "Even when I was with Kyle, I always felt a strong connection with

> Mac. When Kyle and I broke up, Mac was a great support, and our love just grew and grew."

Kyle hadn't phoned for four days since the news broke, and Meg wasn't sure what to think. Many times she had asked for reassurance that things were totally finished with Clare, but she knew that all those feelings wouldn't just disappear now he was engaged to someone else, and for that someone else to be Mac… he would be raging. A few times she excused herself from Cerise and went up to her hotel room to sit on the bed, phone in hand, trying to summon up the courage to call him. But every time she kept coming back to the fact that he hadn't phoned her. Was she just some daft girl who had fallen for a rock star, and now, sitting with her hands poised over the numbers she felt like a stalker. All her life she had heard her mum talk about the stupid groupies who expected something from the band. Had she really been that pathetic? Val was different, she knew what she was getting and that was fine by her. '*They're better quality than anything you'd pick up at the dancing,*' she would say on the nights she felt like sharing her wisdom. '*Their gear's better too.*' That was until the gear turned bad, and she'd ended up in hospital. Meg sat beside her for days; made up palatable stories for the teachers about appendicitis; kept it together enough to stop the nurses from phoning social work. When she got better, Meg got her clean, locking her in the flat while she went to school, getting Tam to let her cover her mum's shifts. After that they worked together, Val vowing never to touch anything worse than a joint, Meg keeping a watchful eye. She had always been so careful, but now everything was crumbling. She thought about Val, working away without her, making a go of it at the new place. Meg knew she didn't belong there anymore, so she sat on the edge of the bed gently rocking back and forwards, wishing for someone to hold her and tell her everything was going to be all right.

The tour of Japan had another week to run when Meg told Todd she felt able to travel again, but he didn't see any point in her joining them for such a short time. 'Why don't you head straight for London?' he said. 'We could do with another push when the live LP comes out, sorry CD — I don't think I'm ever going to get used to saying that. Liaise with the record company and see what needs sorting. But get them to do the hard work and then catch up with your folks?'

All the Things I've Left Behind

1 set of fingerprints
2 lovers
35 T-shirts
2 suitcases – lost/stolen
1 virginity
1 integrity
6 notebooks
1 baby
1 camera
2 Sony Walkmans
6 miles of tangled tape
2 broken Dictaphones

December: London

It took a while for Meg to find Kyle at the venue. He wasn't at the food table; checking through the wardrobes or playing pinball with Wayne. She finally spotted him in the wings, just making out his silhouette in the darkness as he peered out through the drapes. She stood beside him for a few minutes watching the audience come in, before he acknowledged her.

'When did you get back?' he asked without turning his head

'About 5,' she said. 'I've been catching up with Todd.' They both knew she had been given a separate room, but it was no more than Meg expected.

'You okay?' Kyle asked.

'Yeah.'

He pulled back the curtain a little further increasing the number of visible fans without being seen himself. She had never seen him do this and wondered what it was he was hoping to see.

'I heard about Mac and Clare,' Meg said.

'Yeah.'

'Tough on you.'

'I really couldn't care less,' he said, but he dropped the curtain back into place and walked away.

'You're back then,' Dave said, as he appeared from behind a pillar of amps. 'Sorry about the kid,' he said and slapped her on the back.

She was getting in the roadies' way, so she went to the dressing room to see if she could be used. A TV crew were set up and the band lined up for an interview. A couple of blonde girls worked between the band and the interviewer, brushing powder on their faces, and adjusting their clothing by millimetres. Mac stood next to the interviewer, messing his hair every time someone tried to tame it, then Zed, Wayne, and on the end, Kyle looking miserable. Within minutes the cameras rolled and the guys turned on their *happy to be here* faces.

The interviewer did a piece to camera in German, then turned to the band and said in perfect English, 'So Mac, how does it feel to be nearing the end of the tour? It's been mammoth, yeah?'

'Absolutely. We're been on the road for nearly two years so we're looking forward to a break, but I think the European fans will keep us rocking until the end.'

'And do we hear wedding bells after that?'

Mac gave a coy smile and shrugged while Kyle turned his face away from the camera. He needn't have bothered, Meg thought as she watched the monitor — only Mac was in shot.

'So Mac, this video for *Alibi* — you shot it in Japan, right?'

Mac nodded, and Meg realised how much she'd missed.

'We loved all the neon in Tokyo,' Mac told the interviewer, 'and it really captured the feeling behind the song, so it was cool to make.'

'Let's see it then. Thank you, MindSet.' The red light on top of the camera went out and the band moved as far away from each other as they could. Wayne became immediately engrossed in a book; Zed turned to graze at the food table, the strict anti-drug laws in Japan having cleaned him up; Mac went into the corner to use the phone; and Kyle went out the door.

'Can you take me as far as London?' Meg remembered the words she had used over a year before. She'd taken a long route to get here, but maybe now it was time to fade away. She had been foolish to think she could just fit back in with the band. *'I could see if the streets really are paved with gold.'* But she hadn't stopped in London last time around, because something, someone made her think she could find more if she just knew where to look for it. She stepped out into the corridor and shouted, 'Kyle.'

Kyle stood at the other end, drumming the wall with his sticks. 'Can we go somewhere and talk?' she asked.

'We can talk here,' Kyle said without interrupting his rhythm.

Meg moved closer to him, and leant against the wall, forcing him to stop and listen to her. She spoke quietly, hoping that no one who walked by would be able to hear enough of their conversation to make sense of it. 'Why the separate rooms? Is this because of Mac and Clare?' she asked, trying to keep the quiver from her voice.

Kyle tapped his drumsticks in his hands a couple of times then without looking at her said, 'No. Of course not. This has got nothing to do with her.'

'What then Kyle? You've abandoned me?'

'You're here aren't you?'

‘But why, Kyle?’ she said, ‘Why have you brought me back only to push me away.’

‘Todd brought you back.’

Meg gasped.

‘No, look sorry, I really didn’t mean that. She felt his fingers brush against hers, then briefly stroked the back of her hand. ‘I feel like I’ve corrupted you,’ Kyle snapped, more at himself than at her, then he took a deep breath and lowered his voice again. ‘You were so innocent when we met, Meg. You said it yourself, not old enough to have sex in half of America.’

‘I was hardly innocent,’ Meg replied.

‘You were. You were so lovely, so unfazed by all of this,’ he swept his hands in a large circle. ‘You didn’t treat us like stars and it rocked. But you’re young Meg,’ he said, looking deep into her eyes, ‘too young for everything that’s happened.’

Meg put out her hand to touch his hand again, but he pulled back and started to walk away. ‘I can’t Meg, I’m sorry, I need more time.’

Glasgow

While Todd gave Meg time to get back on her feet again; Meg gave Kyle time. Not even Suzie mentioned the separate keys, when the rooms were assigned in Birmingham, Manchester and Liverpool. At least when they got to Glasgow Meg was spared some humiliation. When the coach parked at the front of The Grosvenor, there was Val, holding up a cardboard sign with *Maggie Burns: Welcum Home* written on it. Meg went straight to her, hugged her, and moved the sign out of sight in one swift move.

'Hi, Mum, wow, you look well.'

Val did a little spin — with a new pixie haircut, her Susi Quatro look had morphed into Madonna — and then whispered, 'Kyle still giving you the stony treatment?'

Meg nodded and watched as Val glared over at Kyle's back. But it became a smile when Kyle turned around, and came over to embrace her. 'Hey Val, how are you? Are you stealing Meg?'

'Just for a couple of hours,' Meg said, 'I'll be at the sound check.'

'It's okay, spend the day with your mum if you like — come back tomorrow.'

Meg considered his words and tried to find added meaning in the contours of his face, but not for the first time recently, she was at a loss as to what she read in it. Val pulled at her arm, so Meg just gave Kyle a weak smile, and retrieved her suitcases.

'Graham's parked along here,' Val said, taking one of the cases, 'I told you I was set, Meg, you cannae go wrong with a man wi a motor.'

When they reached the car Val introduced Meg to its owner. He wasn't the worst Meg had seen her mum with, and as they drove along Great Western Road she had to admit he seemed like quite a nice guy.

'So where is it you stay?' Meg asked after she had established that he was a van driver by day and barman by night.

'Oh,' Val said before Graham could answer, 'well, you see, Graham had a few hassles wi his last flat, so he's staying wi me for a wee while.' Val giggled and squeezed Graham's knee.

Meg had bought the flat and everything in it, even called it *Val's new house,* never really thinking that it mattered. Now suddenly, she was confronted with the realisation that it did. Val had cleared a drawer for her, even bought a bed-couch for the spare room. 'A bit of a change eh?' Val said. 'You've done me proud. And there will always be a bed here for you.' Val said, her beaming smile beginning to rub off a bit onto Meg. She really shouldn't begrudge her mum this pleasure — her own roof, no landlord, and heat, but she'd hoped that this could be her place too, not just somewhere for her boxes of mementoes to get shoved at the back of a cupboard.

'You want a cup of tea girls?' Graham asked and Meg tried not to mind that he knew where everything was.

But as Graham clattered about Meg leaned close to her mum and whispered, 'Will we get a chance to catch up on our own?'

'Tonight,' Val said, 'after the concert.' And Meg knew that meant '*no.*'

There was so much she wanted to say — all the things she found it so hard to talk about over the phone while she stared at mass produced prints on hotel walls. She wanted her mum's face in front of her so she could confide her fears. As the tour had drawn closer to Glasgow, the old worries that she's never shared began to re-emerge. When she was awake she could convince herself that the police had moved on. But at night, horror filled her dreams and she woke screaming, feeling she was being smothered, feeling she was being drowned.

Barrowlands was smaller than the Apollo and despite the mirror ball and the polished hard wood floor, it lacked the romance. The venues in the States had been getting bigger, with talk of stadiums next time round, but record sales had slumped in the UK after *Drums in the Distance* and there wasn't really any other choice.

Meg wandered around the empty hall while the band did their sound check, and when they were finished Kyle jumped down from the stage and came over to her. 'Good to be home?' Kyle asked. It was a question Meg couldn't answer — *home* implied things that Glasgow didn't, like love and safety and belonging.

'Listen kiddo,' he said squeezing her shoulders, 'will you show me round the city. We've not spent much time together recently, and I need a day out.'

'There's not much to see,' she shrugged, but at least he wanted to be with her, it was a start, and she was willing to see where it took her.

The taxi stopped where Argyle Street meets St Enoch's Square and Kyle climbed out. Meg hesitated, the smell of diesel fumes and chips unwelcome in her nostrils, but he reached in and took her hand. Easy contact, it had started like this before, their flesh pressing together accidentally and then deliberately. The move and counter move, the coy dance around each other. She had loved the excitement of it all. The first kiss. She wanted it all over again, to feel her body fizz when he touched her, but he'd left her and made her spend all those long nights with her pain.

'Man, these buildings are incredible,' Kyle said, breaking into her thoughts. 'Look at the entrance to that store. Wow.' Kyle pointed over to Frasers, where the shop doorway was topped by two stone colossuses, arms bent above their heads, straining their forms to hold the weight of the building. People noticed him as he stood in the middle of the pavement. Some tutted, annoyed that he was getting in the way; others looked over to see what held his attention and gave an appreciative nod in memory of the stonemason; while keen-eyed women saw a man taller, more tanned and more handsome than was usual in these streets, and stared. Meg only looked at the statues for a moment then continued scanning the faces around her. She could see two police helmets walking up Buchanan

St, but she'd changed enough, she reckoned. She wouldn't match any description they had of her now.

'My god, Maggie Burns, is that you? Where have you been hiding yourself?' A voice and a shove came from behind Meg, and made her jump.

'Oh hi,' Meg said to the two girls who had accosted her.

'Are you kidding? *"Oh hi."* Is she kidding? We thought you wur deid. Oh my God, is that him from MindSet? Are you him from MindSet?'

Kyle stretched out his hand and turned on the charm. 'Hi, I'm Kyle — the drummer.' He raised his brows in a self-deprecating way.

One of the girls blushed purple, while the other, Tracy, took his hand and gave it a chivalrous kiss. Then she turned to Meg. 'So what's this about?'

'We're in Glasgow for a gig,' she explained.

'I'm coming,' the purple Karen said, once she found her voice. 'I'm a big fan.' She jumped up and down on her heels. 'I've got all your albums. I'm coming.'

Kyle laughed, 'Well, it's your lucky day then. If you're a friend of Meg's we could get you back stage to meet the rest of the guys.'

'Even Mac?' Karen said, her voicing pitching higher and higher.

'Especially Mac,' Kyle said. 'Ask for Meg tonight when you come.'

‘That’s me, by the way,’ Meg said, as she could see the girls hadn’t made the connection.

They giggled to each other. ‘Get you. Meg.’

‘Well, bye girls, we’ll see you tonight,’ Kyle said, giving them the hint to walk away. He turned to Meg, ‘That was nice bumping into friends like that,’ he said, but Meg’s face told a different story.

‘Why did you say they could come back stage?’ Meg spat. ‘They made my life hell at school, and now I’ve got to spend another night with them.’

‘I’m sorry Meg, I didn’t realise.’

Meg shook her head, trying not to let memories take root. Cerise said that time only flowed in one direction and you had to flow with it — forwards to the future. They didn’t matter anymore. Nothing in this place did. *Leave it in the past,* she thought, *I’m just passing through* .‘Come on, then,’ she said with a more mellowed tone, ‘I’ll take you to my favourite shop.’

Although they hadn’t long left the States, Meg knew that the Americana in the front half of Flip would keep Kyle busy while she rifled in the second-hand section at the back. She ignored the 50s prom dresses so beloved of the rockabilly girls and went instead to the rows of men’s jackets. She felt the fabric and looked for signs of too much wear at the elbows or ripped lining. She could afford a better quality now, not needing to make do with £1 jackets that she had to patch and mend, so took her time, mustard and green tweeds, grey and black suits, stroking them, finding comfort in this familiarity.

Kyle had some baseball trousers and a few pairs of Converse in his arms when he came through to the back. 'Are you ready thrift-shop girl? My god it stinks back here.'

Meg winced — the memory of Karen and Tracy too fresh in her mind. The taunts of '*Tinker*' and '*Someone's been to Paddy's Market*' coming back to her. 'Not yet,' she said, turning from him so he couldn't see the hurt in her face, and continuing her rummage through dead men's clothes. She finally picked a grey cord jacket and a black tuxedo.

'I'll get these,' Kyle said, but Meg thrust a tenner at the assistant and left Kyle to count out ten times that for his own things. She'd let him own her, flashes of his wallet buying a little bit more of her each time it appeared. A chill ran through her — what had she become?

'God, Meg, it's only ten pounds, don't make a deal out of it.'

When they got out into the sun again Meg flagged down a distant taxi. 'You better go and rest,' she said.

'I don't need to rest,' Kyle said, refusing to be dismissed.

'Look Kyle, you don't seem to realise how hard it is to be back here. There's stuff happened here that you've got no idea about and now you're inviting bitches backstage and insulting me.' Meg was aware that her voice was getting louder, but there was nothing she could do to hold back the anger she felt. 'I can't afford all your fancy shops and designer labels, this is how I live, making do with things other people have thrown away. It's who I am.'

'It's not who you are,' Kyle said, taking hold of her arms, 'not anymore. You've made yourself into something.'

The taxi tooted waiting for them to get in, but when neither of them moved, it drove off.

'You think I've got money on the crappy wages I get from Todd?' she said, all the pain she had ever felt coming through her words. 'And then there's my mum who doesn't seem to think that paying her mortgage is enough. Look.' Meg dug into her pocket and pulled out a shopping list. 'Duvet covers, a new kettle, a bloody wok.' When she looked up from the list, Kyle was laughing.

'Why are you getting so upset?'

'Because that's all my life is to you, to any of you, a list of things you want from me. No one ever asks me what I want.'

'Oh, now you're just being crazy.' He turned away from her momentarily to hail another taxi. 'You never tell people what you want. You never tell people anything. You couldn't even tell me you were pregnant until it was too late. Have you ever asked yourself why I don't know anything about your past? You've never fucking told me.' And he got in to the taxi and slammed the door before she had a chance to decide if she was going with him.

Meg watched as the taxi disappeared. *Fuck it.* She turned and strode off down Queen St, took a left and carried on along Trongate and The Gallowgate to the east of the city. With each step she continued a silent argument with Kyle. *Why on earth would I have had a kid with him? What sort of a bastard is he that suddenly wants to talk about the baby in the middle of the street? Who does he think he is? "Be my tour guide, Meg. Now bugger off Meg."* Her steps took her closer to the venue, but when she reached it she kept going, turning up side streets, not caring where they led. *How can I see him every day if it's going to be like this?*

'Meg?'

She turned and saw Zed standing outside a tattoo parlour. She'd walked passed him without even noticing. 'Hey,' she said, 'What are you up to?'

Zed pointed to a design in the window, 'I want to get a surprise for Suzie. What do you think, oh *Meg the Wise*?'

Meg looked at the Celtic knot work and nodded. 'Do you have room?'

'There's always room for one more,' Zed said. 'My left shoulder blade's blank,' he tapped it, 'or is it my right?'

'So are you going in then?' she asked.

'Just need to get a little something to take the edge off first.' He pulled a scrap of paper out of his pocket with a map scribbled on it.

'I thought you were trying to get clean,' Meg said, hoping that Zed would hear the disappointment she felt in her voice.

'I'm clean enough,' Zed said, and signalled for Meg to walk with him. 'It was more the drink and those stupid fucking painkillers they gave me in the States for my wrist than anything I took to party, that did my head in. Well,' he said winking, 'that and Suzie. She's got everyone warned not to run for me, so now I've got to get my own gear.'

'Or stop,' Meg said.

'You're funny Meg, I like you.' They walked for a bit in silence, passing blackened buildings that the sandblasters would never reach, until Zed stopped at a post box a few feet after a junction.

'What are we doing?' Meg asked only to be shushed by Zed, who nodded at two guys in pastel-coloured shell suits, blowing into their hands to keep warm, who sat on a nearby wall. They got up and came towards Meg and Zed, their shoulders punching the air with each stride.

'You ah right man?' One of the guys said to the space just above Zed's head.

'I'm good,' Zed said, 'but I could be better.'

'Jellies are good, man.'

'Speed you up?' Zed asked.

'No man. Slow you right doon. Sort you out wi both if you got the readies.'

Zed nodded and took a couple of steps away from Meg leaving her with the dealer's pal. She kept her eyes down, '*if you didnae see nothin, yi cannae say nothin*,' but she could feel eyes drilling into her. The dealer's pal took a step forward and put his hands on the red post box, hemming her in.

'You one of they Aussies too?'

Aftershave caught at the back of her throat — Kuros — she'd sniffed samples at the airport, done her research until she was sure she had the right one. She didn't know until now why it had mattered. He breathed on her again, fried onions and Kuros used instead of soap, an unmistakable combination slamming her back in time.

There was something therapeutic, after the noise and chaos of a concert, to go out into the cold night air; feel the drizzle cool your cheeks; hear the slosh of the paste brush against the wall. And stop. Smooth out the poster; feel the texture of the bricks beneath it; get all the air bubbles out without ripping the sodden paper. She loved this, she felt free, the silence, no one telling her what to do, just Maggie and the wall and the brush and the paste.

But she is pushed; falls to the ground; feels gravel puncture her cheek. He pulls at her clothes; squeezing her breasts until she yelped with pain; forcing his hands inside her jeans; pulling them down just far enough to accommodate and restrain. She tries to shake him off; thinks of stray dogs when they try to kill a rat; thinks of Billy McPherson when he had that fit.

But hand over mouth; can't bite.

Legs forced apart; can't push them closed.

Fingers into groin; can't get them away.

Cock tearing and pulling and straining against the dryness.

Pain ripping through her; you stupid bitch.

Then his body relaxes.

Her hand reaches out, finds something solid to hold. He crumbles as the rock crashes into his skull. It hits again as he falls from her. His body folds foetal as she kicks — back and front — kidneys and face. She doesn't stop, even when he says 'no', even when he cries, even when he pleads, she doesn't stop.

'No,' she said, looking him in the eye, 'I'm not an Aussie.'

'A Yank then?' He leered at her, rank breath in her face, little bits of spit spurting out of his mouth as he talked. 'I've never had a Yank.'

Then she saw it — the written confirmation on his knuckles. 'For fuck's sake will you hurry up,' she shouted at Zed.

Zed turned round, looking annoyed, but something in her face registered with him and he quickly shook hands, swapping money for pills, and walked away from the dealer. Meg felt aware of the wind as it whipped around her neck, the rain as it fell on her face, the pavement stabbing at her feet. She kept her eyes front, quickened her pace, made Zed rush to keep up with her.

When they were a couple of streets away Zed stopped suddenly. 'What gives, Meg? You look like you've seen a ghost.'

Meg turned to look at him, tears pricking at her eyes. 'I have.'

'Shit, Meg, you're shaking.' Zed pulled her in tight; holding her as her knees weakened, her arms limp by her side. He found a café and sat her down at the least dirty table, shouting an order for tea. Then very quietly he asked, 'Was it him?'

Meg clasped at her jacket, crossed her arms around her, sank into herself, but she managed a nod.

'I fucking knew this would happen,' Zed said sounding more sober than he had in months. 'I saw you go off with Kyle and I thought you'd be okay. God, how could he leave you alone when he knows how much you hate this place?'

'Not hate,' Meg said very quietly.

'Fear then? Is that what you're afraid of Meg — of that guy? Was he the one who hurt you?' He sugared her tea and held it up to her. 'Drink,' he said, and put his arm around her again as he lifted the cup to her lips. 'You shouldn't be afraid — you're not that little mouse anymore and besides, I heard you gave as good as you got.'

'What?' Meg said pulling away from him, 'what I did to him doesn't come close to what he did to me.'

'Oh come on Meg,' Zed said, almost amused by the drama, 'Kyle told me all about it, said you nearly killed him.'

Meg felt her face blanch. So many times she had thought about telling Kyle. All the times when even his most gentle touch was wrong and his face pleaded for an explanation; or when she woke up in the middle of the night, screaming and fighting invisible hands that crawled over her skin, and he held her and stroked her hair and she wanted so much to let it all out. But she held on to it tight.

'Kyle doesn't know,' she whispered. Zed didn't say anything for a minute, so Meg repeated it. 'He doesn't know, Zed, neither does Suzie, so how can you?'

Zed picked at his blackened thumb nail and sighed. 'You're right. I'm sorry Meg, I've known for a long time — I heard you on the phone once, way back. You must have been talking to Val I think.'

'Shit.' Tears welled in Meg's eyes but she rubbed them away before they could fall. 'All that time?'

Zed nodded. 'I'm really sorry, Meg, I didn't really know you then so I kind of turned it into a joke in my mind. Shit, that was crass. I've not been much of a friend have I?'

She'd never expected him to be. She couldn't imagine how they could have ever had that conversation, but now the words just poured from her. 'You know the worst of it?' Meg said, 'I blamed myself. I get so angry when people say that women ask for it, like who in their right mind would ask for that to happen, but I still wonder if I could have done something different.'

'He would just have found someone else,' Zed said without any emotion wrapped around the words and Meg realised it was true. If she had seen him coming, turned to face him, he would have walked on, raped the next girl he came across and she would never have left.

'Maybe I should have told you I knew, but…I don't know…it's not really the type of thing you can just drop in. I always hoped you'd told Kyle — you shouldn't have to deal with this on your own.'

Meg sat quietly, and everything fell away again, she was on her own. The way she was that night, the way she had been in Miami when she lost the baby, and now the stupid fight with Kyle had taken away any hope she had.

Zed drained his tea before he said, 'Are you sure it was him?'

It took Meg a moment to realise Zed was talking about her attacker. She ran her finger over her knuckles, 'T.O.M.O.,' she said, 'I saw it.' Then she sat, sick and furious and glad. Zed knew. Maybe that was all she needed — someone to know and not try to convince her that it was just part of the shit life threw at you.

She went to the toilet, washed her face, looked straight into her own eyes in the mirror. *Not that timid little mouse*. By the time she returned to the table Zed had ordered all-day breakfasts and she realised that she was ravenously hungry. They sat side by side eating their fry and drinking their tea without speaking. Meg knew Zed was giving her time to open up; people had done it before — her guidance teacher, Jacqueline McBride's mum. But she had always out-silenced them, trumping awkwardness with resistance.

'How come you're here, Zed?'

He turned to her with a smile — he was a master at avoidance too. 'In this café or on this planet?'

'In a scabby café with that crap?' She tapped his pocket.

'I told you, it's for my tattoo.' He offered as a suggestion.

'An aspirin would do that,' she said.

'Suzie wanted me clean, so I got clean,' he said, 'but apparently I'm not that much fun anymore.'

'She hasn't said that,' Meg said, but she'd heard them through the walls, shouting, crying.

'All the meetings say you've got to be ready to stop, to really want it, but I think you've both got to want it. She still wants to look after me; buy things for me; decide what I'm going to wear. She treats me like a kid — does the same with you. Maybe life would be easier if I let things go back to how they were.'

'You using isn't what she wants,' Meg said, knowing it would kill her if Val ever went near drugs again.

'It'll stop me caring.'

Meg thought back to the leaflets she'd got at Al-Anon when she was a kid. 'Maybe you're both dependent — just on different things?'

Zed nodded slowly. 'And what about you Meg, what are you dependent on?'

'Nothing I couldn't leave behind,' she said without thinking.

'That's sad,' he said, and looked like he meant it.

'It's just how it is.'

The waitress came over and cleared away their dirty plates, waving their bill at them as she wiped the table with an old cloth. Zed paid and signalled to Meg it was time to leave. The rain had stopped but the grey clouds were no less oppressive.

‘What now?’ Zed asked.

‘Tattoo?’ Meg said, screwing up her face.

‘What about Tomo? Does he get away with it? We could go to the cops.’’

‘No,’ Meg said instinctively. She had imagined every scenario in her head, but she never thought she’d get the chance to act on any of them. ‘You know he didn’t even recognise me,’ she said, looking back up the street. ‘The minute I saw him I knew something was up, even before I realised what it was. But you would have thought he would have remembered my face. Would you not Zed? At least he should have remembered my face?’

Zed put his arms around her again and she let the tears stream down. ‘You’ll be okay,’ he said, but he kept holding her until gradually her crying stopped and her gasping subsided.

A loud noise came from Meg’s bag and made them break apart. It took a couple of seconds for Meg to realise that it was her new cellular phone. She fished it out and said, ‘Hello, yes? Shit.’ She hung up, pushed down the aerial and turned to Zed. ‘I need to get back — something’s kicked off at the venue.’

Zed sighed, ‘Mac and Kyle will be at it again.’

Meg looked at him quizzically.

‘Japan was a nightmare, Meg. You were well off out. Apparently Kyle’s too disruptive of Mac’s energy or some bull.’

‘That doesn’t sound like Mac,’ Meg said.

‘Mac channelling Clare, she’d been in California, kept coming out with New Age shit.’

‘I might have known she’d be involved,’ Meg said.

‘You shouldn’t be too hard on her, Meg, I mean she did have a point about you and Kyle,’ Zed replied. He was right. How could she have spent so much energy on Clare when Tomo was still wandering the streets? Stupid, stupid, stupid. But MindSet got her through; got her away.

‘It’ll be fine though won’t it?’ she asked, not stupid, a survivor. ‘A holiday, then the next album?’

‘Who knows?’ he said and Meg realised he didn’t seem that bothered.

‘I’d better go and sort it out,’ Meg said, but she was annoyed Kyle hadn’t mentioned how bad things were with Mac. ‘Are you not coming?’

Zed shook his head, ‘Why bother?’ he said. ‘Just leave it to Todd — they’ll not listen to you and if it comes to blows again you’re better off out of it.’

‘No, I’d better go,’ Meg said, even though she didn’t have a clue what she was going to do.

Zed touched her face, ‘You need to get cleaned up first; you look like shit with all that crying.’ Meg rubbed under her eyes, and made her fingers black with smudged mascara. ‘That’s better,’ Zed said and he caught a wisp of her hair and tucked it behind her ear. ‘You’re fit to be seen now.’

While she was trying to persuade Mac that there wouldn't be anyone in Glasgow who could massage his chakra, her phone rang and for the second time that day the caller said, 'I need you, can you come?'

The urgency in his voice transmitted immediately to her feet and Meg left Mac and ran out of the Barrowlands, past the café where she had left Zed and on into the street where they had met the dealers earlier. Her phone rang again. 'Up here, can you see me? To your left, got me.'

Meg squeezed through the gap in the boarded up doorway and took the stairs two at a time. Syringes and condoms littered the close, but she barely registered then, instead she kept the phone to her ear, and listened to Zed's quiet pleading.

'I'm coming, Zed, just hold on.' She pushed the metal door to the flat and walked in. The smell of shit and vomit assaulted her, but she kept going until she found them. Tomo on the bare floor, a badly tattooed skull and crossbones in the crook of his elbow and in the middle an empty needle sticking out. *His arm around her neck.* On the fingers of his right hand T O M O. *His hand shielding his face.* Scars under his skinhead. *Rock smashing into his head.*

Zed knelt on the floor beside him.

'What have you done?'

'Some people don't know when they've had enough,' Zed said rather sadly, then he bent forward, put two fingers to Tomo's carotid artery and bowed his head as though in prayer. Finally he looked up. 'Turns out he did remember you Meg. He was waiting for me at the tattooists. He said he wanted to meet you again, made me phone you.'

'What the fuck do you mean? He made you phone me. Was this meant to be some sort of trap?'

'He had a knife. So I phoned you.' He looked down again at Tomo's motionless body. 'He gave me something, took it himself. I don't know Meg. Just, it just, he was bragging and calling you an easy lay, and it just happened.'

'Where's his pal?' Meg asked quickly checking around her. Hyper-alert.

'Not about,'

Meg stood for a minute. Her lungs inhaled deeply, and a feeling of relief swayed through her body. For nearly two years she'd worried that the police would find her. Worried that Tomo would somehow find out who she was and come after her. But he was gone. It was over.

'Fuck.' Zed said suddenly, as though he had just sobered up. 'Shit, Meg, Fuck. We should go.

But Meg wasn't ready to leave. She opened her bag and pulled out her camera.

'Don't Meg.'

She didn't listen, but stood beside Zed, loaded her film and quickly fired off the whole roll. On the twenty-fourth click she unloaded and tucked the film into her jeans pocket. 'Now it's done.'

But as Zed tried to stand up he stumbled forward, and Meg noticed a purple stain coming through the black cotton of his Thin Lizzy t-shirt.

'Shit.'

'He didn't go without a fight,' Zed said as he gripped on to Meg's arm and pulled himself up. A glint of light came through a crack in the boarded up window and reflected off Tomo's blade, illuminating blood on the tip of it. Without thinking she bent down and prised it out of his hand.

She wanted to get as much distance between them and the body as possible, but progress was slow with Zed leaning on her as heavily as she had leaned on him earlier. She saw her old tower block in the distance and used it as a beacon to guide her to the river. When they were a street away Meg sat Zed on a low wall and calmly walked towards the water. She pulled the knife and the scarf it was wrapped in out of her bag. She knew it was Zed's blood, but they didn't need any complications at what she was trying to think of as the overdose scene. As she tossed them into the river she felt the film in her pocket dig into her groin. It was enough that she had taken the photos, violated his dead body. She didn't need to see them to confirm he was gone. *Finally, thank God, it was over.* She pulled the film from its plastic housing, exposing it to the light and threw it into the river as well. She watched as the ripples dispersed — *It's over* — then hurried back to Zed.

Zed slumped against her for a few minutes, neither of them to speak. Beads of sweat formed along his brow and he grimaced as he tried to get more comfortable. Meg knew they had to move before they attracted attention, so when she saw a private hire she flagged it down.

The driver didn't glance round, but threw a roll of kitchen towel back to them. 'That's a tenner extra.'

Meg squeaked into the plastic covered seat. 'Aye fine, just drive.' She gave the address she had memorised as a child and hoped he was still there. '*If anything bad happens, Tam will help*.' She should have gone there the night of the attack. Filed a police report, got the bastard locked up. But she hadn't gone, and the next day Kyle had appeared and made her believe that she could escape from all of this. Zed groaned again.

Yvonne made them tea while Tam dabbed Zed with TCP. 'Fairly superficial,' he said as he took some gauze out of a Fox's biscuit tin and taped it down across the wound. 'I've seen worse. I've got worse.' He turned round and lifted his shirt to show a two inch white scar between his shoulder blades. 'Stabbed in the back, eh?' He laughed.

Yvonne came in with a tray and gave him a scowl, 'Will you put that away.' She put down the tea cups and looked long and hard at Meg.

'I worked with Tam at the Apollo,' Meg said answering the unasked question.

'Oh, I remember you now — the wee lassie that ran away. Had your poor mother demented.'

Tam cut over his wife's clucking, 'I knew you'd make good pet, certainly whenever I see Val she's always bragging about her new flat and how well you've done.' Meg gave a weak smile. 'But what's all this about?' He looked over at Zed.

'Just stuff… from before…you know…unfinished business,' Meg said. 'But it's done now.'

'You sure? Nothing going come back to bite you?'

'Nothing, I'm sure.'

Zed took a couple of jellies and Meg left him as he sank into the couch with his feet tucked beneath a tartan travelling rug. She went into the kitchen with Tam. The Apollo had been closed down and Tam was concentrating on other business activities which he remained vague about. She listened to his reminiscences while Yvonne clattered around the kitchen wiping already clean surfaces and interjecting with details when Tam forgot —she must have heard these stories a hundred times or more. She wondered how he would tell her story — if he would airbrush out the slightly illegal bits or embellish them with lies like jewels.

At 6 o'clock she woke Zed, checking to see if the bleeding had stopped. Tam watched as she carefully lifted Zed's t-shirt.

'Leave it Meg,' Tam said as her fingers moved towards the dressing. 'How's the pain, son?'

'Not great.'

'Will you be able to play?' Meg asked beginning to turn her mind back to more mundane concerns. He moved his arm and winced.

Tam went out of the room and they heard his heavy footsteps above them then the thudding back down the stairs. He handed a bottle of pills to Zed. 'Take a couple of these and you'll be fine.'

'Cheers,' Zed said, popping some into his mouth and swallowing them down with whisky Tam had thrust in his hand. Meg perched on the couch as Zed finished his whisky and accepted a refill.

'He needs to play tonight. He can't be comatose.'

Tam gave her a look that made her feel fourteen again, he was experienced at this it said, he knew what to give and when to stop. Wasn't that why she had come? She'd closed her eyes to so much of this, known when to make herself scarce, but she always knew what was going on. Now Tam took the bottle of pills and put it directly in her hand

'Give him another couple before the show and he'll be fine. Just don't let him mix it.'

She nodded and took Zed back to The Barraowlands and straight into Suzie.

'Where have you two been?' she screamed. 'I've been out of my mind.'

'Zed wanted to see the sights,' Meg said, keeping her hand firmly on Zed's elbow to support him. 'Then we had a drink with an old friend.'

Suzie looked disgusted. 'Well you could have told me. I've been stuck here on my own all day with nothing to do,' Suzie said, directing her anger at Zed, 'Mac and Kyle have both gone and Todd's away to find them, he was going crazy trying to get you. And Meg, your mum's here. I've had to keep her company. '

'So not on your own then,' Zed said, ramping up the effects of the drink and drugs for Suzie's benefit.

'You shit, are you using again?' Suzie said as she whacked Zed and made him yelp in pain. Then she turned her anger on Meg. 'How could you let him get high? For Christ's sake, Meg, I excepted better from you. You know how hard I've worked to get him clean.'

'He worked hard to get himself clean, and he got himself high, Suzie, I didn't have anything to do with that.' She knew how hard it would have been to get Zed straight, but she needed to keep Suzie angry. 'He's a grown up, Suzie, he can make his own decisions.'

'Screw you,' Suzie shouted and left.

'Result,' Zed said with a more sober smile. 'She doesn't need to know this.' Then he turned to Meg, 'will you help me get changed?'

There was no sign of the rest of the band when they got to the dressing room, but Meg locked the door anyway. Zed poured himself a large measure of Glenfiddich and topped it up with coke.

'Want one?'

'Just the whisky,' Meg said.

‘I meant the coke,’ Zed said trying to poke humour into the grim situation, but he poured her a measure. She downed it in one, shaking her whole body as the alcohol burned down her throat and nipped her eyes.

‘Shit.’

‘You want another?’

Meg nodded, but took the next glass over to the couch and sat there with it nestled in her hands. ‘I’m sorry I got you involved in all of this,’ Meg said finally. ‘I should have sorted it out myself.’ She paused for a moment. ‘Thank you Zed.’

Zed examined the dressing in the mirror. ‘We’re the same, you and me — fighters.’

Meg swirled her drink, ‘I’m fed up fighting. All my life it’s all I’ve done, I don’t have the strength for it anymore.’

Zed came and sat next to her. ‘It’s peaceful here without the others,’ he said, and Meg nodded, surprised that he was right. *Peaceful* wasn’t something she experienced very often, especially not in venues.

‘You know what would make it perfect,’ Zed said. He lent down and pulled a joint from his sock, lit it with his Zippo, took a long draw and held it out to Meg. She took it tentatively. ‘For your nerves.’

She emptied her lungs with a long exhale before she put the joint in her mouth. She always swore that she wouldn’t touch drugs, but then she’d never been an accomplice to murder before. She inhaled and immediately felt like she was going to faint. She crumbled forward, stuck her head between her knees and stayed there until the blood flowed back to her head. When she became aware of her belt buckle sticking into her stomach she knew the fuzz had gone and she pulled herself up again. She took another draw before handing the joint back to Zed.

'You feel good?' Zed asked.

'Not really. A bit hazy,' she said.

'A bit hazy's good,' he said as he brought his mouth close to hers.

She turned her face away from him and took another sip of whisky. She leaned forward and put the glass down. 'We've fucked things up a bit today, eh?'

Zed feigned indifference, as though he killed people every day, but Meg could see from his eyes that the shock hadn't quite left him. 'And now everyone's breaking up,' he said, resigned to the worst day of their lives.

Meg turned her face towards him. 'The band's not finished,' she said. 'I've lost too much already — I can't bear to lose anymore.'

'It can't go on forever Meg, none of it can. One minute you're here, the next,' he clicked his fingers.

'Don't Zed,' she said.

'Look at us — I'm the only one here, and I don't even know if I can play.' He raised his t-shirt to examine the wound again. 'I'm not sorry I did it, Meg. I mean…I know I should be sorry, fuck, really sorry, but I couldn't let him get away with it.'

'Don't,' she whispered. She looked into his dark eyes but didn't see the pity for her that she expected to find, instead there was understanding, understanding of her whole life. The sinews in his hand strained across his dressing and pulled at the bloodied fringes of it. She put her hand on top of his and held it tight. He relaxed his hand and slipped it out from under hers.

'You're so pretty, Meg,' he said as he began to stroke her cheek. She didn't care that it wasn't true, she just liked that he wouldn't be comparing to Clare. Her fingers traced around the white fringes of the gauze and onto Zed's warm stomach. She felt it clench, imagined the slash of the blade, and ran her hands over the Fender guitar tattooed on his chest, telling herself that she was checking for injury. 'Don't,' she breathed as he kissed her neck, her lips, teased his tongue into her mouth, pulled her to sit on top of him. 'Don't,' he whispered as she undid his buckle. 'Don't,' as they both came.

Meg buried her head in his shoulder and closed her eyes, willing him not to be Zed, hoping that somehow the joint had got her muddled, but it was definitely Zed who pushed her off gently and with a grimace went towards the toilet.

'No one can know about this,' he said turning to her, but he averted his eyes as she buttoned her 501s. Meg nodded. 'Don't ever tell Suzie, even if you feel guilty, even if I'm not still about. Don't ever tell her.'

'Of course,' Meg said, and she downed the last of the whisky.

You want pumped up?

You want some rock?

You want — MindSet.

Paphos

Meg wasn't sure how Todd had pulled it off, but he'd got an assistant to book a villa in Paphos and since he'd added it onto the tour schedule he could insist that everyone came. In a couple of days they would go off in separate directions for Christmas but for now they could relax and party. Zed had steered clear of her, and since Suzie was stuck to his side, it meant she had avoided her too. So she headed for the beach ready to form new alliances, or at least have a beer and a laugh without being too conspicuous. She hated to admit it, but maybe she should have taken Clare's advice and stuck with the crew, just shagged a roadie like a normal person.

She followed the lights by the pool and down a long path to where a bonfire burned in a pit. The sun was low in the sky and a cool breeze blew off the sea, wisping sand over her legs as she got closer to the crowd. Her eyes, like those around her, were protected by sunglasses, but as the sun dipped she lifted them onto the top of her head and took in the view.

It looked like a set-up from a fashion shoot and she was tempted to go back and get the camera she hadn't dare touch since she'd photographed Tomo. But she hadn't felt the same need to put the lens between herself and the world. She took her place in the circle of blankets by the fire. Zed strummed on an acoustic, accompanied by one of the roadies on bongo drums, while Mac encouraged everyone to sing Delilah. Her eyes lingered for a moment on Zed, and while she was grateful to him for getting rid of

Tomo, she detected no desire. Kyle was far more handsome, even if his strong features and angular nose sometimes made him look a bit stuck-up. Oh but those glorious blue eyes — eyes that you could dive into and lose yourself. But Zed had let her glimpse the vulnerability in his chocolate brown eyes. *Stop it.* Whisky, pot, or the adrenaline of what they had done had coursed through her body that night and overwhelmed any impulse to stop. An animalistic urge which disappeared as suddenly as it had appeared and left her with a feeling of unreality. Val would have said that all is fair in love and war. But it wasn't love she felt for Zed — maybe it was the final act of war.

Zed was absorbed in the music and oblivious to her. But Suzie wasn't, Suzie was watching. The fire licked shadows onto her face making her look like a demon. Surely he hadn't told her. But at the very least Suzie must be blaming Meg for the state Zed was in at the Barrowlands, and probably she featured in whatever excuse he had come up with for the stab wound. Meg smiled at Suzie as casually as she could, trying to brazen it. *It was only sex.* She thought it, even though she knew it was no excuse. She looked over to Suzie again, hoping she would signal an invite to come over, but when none came she turned to watch as some of the girls attempted to dance. The music was too calm — a tempo for winding down and making up — and gradually they gave up. Meg stepped forward to pull a beer out of the cool box and when she sat down again, Kyle came over.

'We haven't had a chance to talk since last week in Glasgow,' he said quietly, 'I'm so sorry I upset you. I was having a really shitty day.'

'Yeah, me too,' Meg said, their fight just a flicker in the distance.

'I suppose we haven't talked properly since Miami,' Kyle said after a few minutes. He made a little mound of sand beside him while he spoke and didn't look at her until he had finished.

'There's not much to say.'

Kyle seemed to disagree and he stood up, stretched out his hand and pulled her up. 'Let's go for a walk.'

She lifted her sandals and fastened her black cardigan as they walked down to the shore. If she was brave she would just keep walking, let the water lap her feet, then her legs, let the night pull her under.

'I'm sorry I wasn't there for you, Meg,' Kyle said, disturbing her trance. 'I tried to be, and I know I shouldn't have been so easily put off, but that woman in Miami said you didn't want to speak to me.'

'What woman?' Meg asked surprised that his reason was one she hadn't even considered. 'You never phoned,' she said accusingly, 'not after Mac got engaged.'

'I did — I spoke to some American, she told me not to phone back — she sounded so sure.'

'Bitch,' Meg said. Miami, London, Glasgow she had been furious with him, tension clenching her shoulders and making her snap at every attempt at communication. Now it scared her that none of her actions were justified any more.

'Who was she?' Kyle asked.

Meg wanted to say a friend, but what sort of a friend was Cerise when she was bad-mouthing Kyle for not phoning when she knew all along that he was.

'Nobody — just someone who kept me company after Suzie left.'

'Would you have talked to me?' Kyle stopped and turned to her.

'Of course. I was so empty, but then those pictures of you and Clare — they said she was in Japan with you. I was devastated Kyle. It felt like you'd abandoned me.'

'I should have come back to get you, but mum thought I should give you some space, just let you get over things in your own time. And I needed to clear my head of all that.' He signalled back to where Mac and Clare sat entwined, but it was Zed's gaze that Meg caught, he was watching her after all. Kyle took her hand and led her along the shore, far away from the others.

'Your mum?' Meg said, bringing her attention back to Kyle. She had never really given Kyle's mum much thought before. She knew they spoke occasionally, and Kyle liked to send her expensive silk scarves, but she never saw her as an advisor, particularly not about their relationship.

'Why did you go to the airport that night?' Kyle asked.

Darkness had fallen quickly, but the light from the full moon illuminated a tenderness in Kyle's face that had been missing for a while.

'You were with Clare,' Meg said, surprised she had to explain.

Kyle looked at her with disbelief. 'I wasn't, Meg, God, is that what you thought? No wonder you left.'

It hit her like a slap — she hadn't waited around for an explanation, and had started a chain of events that led to here. She was a fool, but then she realised something more important, 'You weren't with me though, were you?'

'No,' he said, 'I wasn't, and then, you know, you losing the baby, it really shook me up. Mum was the only person I could talk to. I felt so guilty. I kept thinking that if I'd gone back to our room that night instead of going to the bar. It was just seeing Clare with Mac,' he shrugged, 'if I'd been there I could have helped sooner. We should have talked about the baby before then.' He stopped, but Meg sensed he wasn't finished. 'I wasn't sure if I could cope,' he said finally.

'And you thought I could?' Meg said, suddenly lifting her head and looking straight into his eyes. Eyes you could lose yourself in. She had thought a million times that he might not want the baby, but him not being able to cope, that had never occurred to her.

'I couldn't figure out why you hadn't told me — I tried to encourage you, and then, well, it was too late.' His voice shook a little as he spoke and she could see tears catching the moonlight. She led him over to a dune, and they sat with their backs against it, buried their toes in the sand, and looked out to the sea, black but for a broad band of silver reflected moonlight. *When did he try to encourage me to talk?* Shouts and cheers went up from the beach party making them turn towards the noise, but they turned back to each other.

'Every time I tried to tell you about the baby I chickened out. I didn't know how you'd react and I felt so stupid for getting pregnant. I can't tell you how many times Val warned me.'

'A baby would have been good though,' Kyle said tenderly.

'Yeah,' Meg felt her own tears now, but Kyle held her hand and kissed them away, first one cheek, then the other.

'I'm sorry I screwed up,' Kyle said and then he held her for a long time. Meg wanted to sit there forever just listening to the waves, breathing in time with him, never have to move again and break the fragile connection, but the sand was cold and uncomfortable and she gave an unintentional shiver. Kyle gently tapped and they both stood up and straightened their clothes.

'You want to go back to the others?' Kyle asked, but Meg shook her head. If she'd been wrong about Kyle being with Clare; wrong about him not phoning; maybe she should give him another chance.

'Let's go to bed.'

1987

February: Milson's Point, Sydney

Visa Approved

Margaret Burns

'Here we are, home sweet home,' Kyle said as they entered the cubist apartment next to the Harbour Bridge.

When Kyle talked about his apartment Meg had never imagined this. The lounge area was enormous, bigger, Meg thought, than four Val-sized apartments, with hard wood flooring and floor-to-ceiling windows where the fourth wall should be. The furniture was sleek and looked brand new, black ash and glass, and proper art on the walls. Meg looked at a huge painting of a conch which hung over, and was as big as, the six-seater sofa. 'I had a friend once who took photos like that,' she said, and the thought that went with it stopped her commenting on the photos of Kyle and Clare covering ever surface.

Meg heard a shuffling sound as a door to the left of the lounge opened and a small Asian-looking woman walked through.

'Welcome home, Mr Kyle,' she said. 'Was your flight pleasant?'

'Yes, very pleasant. This is Miss Meg,' Kyle said, and Meg nodded to the woman. 'Bring us some drinks to the balcony, Lili,' Kyle said, then to Meg, 'She's been with us for years, well with

Mum. I've just borrowed her until we can find someone more permanent.'

'We need a maid?' Meg said, but Kyle answered by sliding the glass open and leading Meg out to the balcony. They stood for a minute and watched the boats, cars and little people eight floors below. 'It's magnificent,' Meg said above the roar from the bridge that had seemed so silent inside. 'Like something out of a dream.'

'You should see it when it gets dark,' Kyle said and he kissed the back of her neck. She closed her eyes, leant back into the kiss, but he was already leaving and when she turned around she saw him putting some of the photos into a drawer. He realised she was watching. 'I'm sorry,' he said. 'That's Herb Ritts,' and he pointed to a large canvas 'You wouldn't expect me to take that down.'

It hung in the air — the Australian intonation of a question that didn't need an answer. It wasn't the photographer she objected to, but the image of their naked forms.

'It was her house too,' Meg said, deciding on conciliation rather than confrontation. She'd get rid of it later.

'We can buy somewhere new if you like,' he said, and Meg was amazed at his casualness. You couldn't just buy and sell houses like that, certainly not ones as beautiful as this.

Lili put some ice tea on the wrought iron table outside and asked if they would like something to eat. Meg felt really tired, and if they had been alone she would have told Kyle she just wanted to lie down, but since Lili had gone to the trouble of making ice tea she felt obliged to drink it. 'Thank you so much,' she said.

'Just something light,' Kyle said, answering the maid's question, 'then you can go back to Mum's.'

Meg tried to ignore the lack of please and thanks in his words, and hoped it was jetlag.

'I've arranged to see Mum tonight,' Kyle said, turning his attention to Meg again, 'so once we've eaten we can have a quick nap then out.'

Meg nodded. Even though she had slept for a good bit of the flight she felt exhausted, so she was glad when the maid finally left and they could go up the spiral staircase to Kyle's room. His bed was enormous, like the ones in America when two doubles had been put side by side. And in front of it was a huge window with the same amazing view to the Bridge. 'Don't worry, it's special glass,' Kyle said almost reading her thoughts, 'no one can see in.' Then he pulled back a white gloss panel and revealed a spa bath and double sized shower. 'En suite here and your clothes should be here.' He opened another panel to show her clothes already neatly arranged on the rack.

'Great,' Meg said. She had left her nightshirt at the top of her case, but where it might be now she didn't know, and didn't have the energy to care. 'The maid's away, right?'

'Right,' Kyle said.

'Good,' she said and slipped off her trousers, pulled her bra out from under her t-shirt and flopped on the bed, 'then I'm ready to sleep.'

'Fair enough,' Kyle said, and he stripped and joined her on top of the bed. 'Mum's going to love you.'

Meg's mind pinged awake, *Kyle's mum,* but it was a momentary panic as the heaviness of her body dragged her to sleep.

'Shit, Meg, wake up, we're late,' Meg heard his voice and felt his hands on her shoulders shaking her with more vigour the more conscious she became. 'We'll never get there in time,' he said as he dashed into the en-suite and turned on the shower.

'Can we not just meet your mum tomorrow instead?' Meg pleaded, cosying under the sheets, but Kyle came back into the room pulled them off her and offered her a hand to get up.

'I'll order a taxi — you can shower first while I shave.'

He pushed her slightly towards the en suite, but she stopped and stared at the lights on the Bridge and across the Harbour. It made her think of Christmas and the shop windows and all the hope that came with twinkling lights, even though it was always dashed by a stocking that contained only a Mars Bar and a fiver. He had given her that feeling again, the tingling hope of *I do believe in fairies,* and she loved him for it. 'Thank you Kyle,' she said, 'for bringing me here.'

When they got to the Opera House Kyle had a word with the usher and finally, with a note or two pressed into hands, they were allowed in to the hall. They were told very firmly that they should not move away from where they were placed at the back of the hall, but Meg was happy that at least she had something to lean against.

Kyle whispered in Meg's ear about this being Mahler, and after a few notes Meg was happy they were late. The music scratched in her ears, with too many instruments competing for her attention. After a couple of minutes the irritation turned to boredom, so Meg watched the orchestra more than actively listening to them. It wasn't like any concert she had ever seen before. The women, elegant in long black gowns and gathered up hair, and the men, so smart in their tuxedos that Meg couldn't imagine anyone snorting coke or having sex in a toilet cubicle. And there, at the front, conducting them all was Kyle's mum. Her back held straight, her hand swaying and pointing, watched by all.

Meg nudged Kyle to ask him what the tune was called, but he put his finger to his lips and shook his head. In front of them everyone sat totally still, as though they had all fallen asleep. Wasn't music meant to make people want to dance or at least sway in time? There were no woops, or feet stamping, but when the music finished a wild applause went up. *Just shows you.*

Eleanor took a bow, then the orchestra stood and bowed to the audience, and to Meg's surprise the orchestra clapped Eleanor and she very graciously acknowledged their applause. *Mac would love that,* she thought, *if the rest of MindSet clapped him.*

Before the hall began to empty, Kyle led her backstage where they waited for a few minutes until they were given the nod to make their way to the dressing rooms. The smell of stale sweat and the sound of laughter backstage weren't so different after all, but what amazed Meg was the large number of people who performed the symphony compared with the relatively small number of hangers on. With MindSet it was reversed. Kyle knocked on the door they had been directed to and waited.

'Enter.'

Meg had never heard anyone say '*Enter*' without irony and it made her suddenly very nervous. The sight of Kyle's mother unnerved her even more. Eleanor Watt stood in the middle of her dressing room tying the sash of a black and silver kimono. She stepped forward when they came in and embraced her son. She was almost as tall as Kyle, even without shoes and matched his poise point for point. But she was older than Meg had imagined — fifty at least, with lines around her eyes and her perfectly shaped mouth.

'I want you to meet Meg. Meg, this is Eleanor.'

Despite her new dress and the fact that Eleanor was only in a robe, Meg felt decidedly shabby as she shook Eleanor's hand. No wonder Kyle was frightened about being late, this was like being up in front of the head mistress.

'Kyle tells me you are Scottish. Is that correct?' Eleanor said. It sounded more like an accusation than a question and when Meg opened her mouth she realised that her smoothed out accent had deserted her.

'Aye, that's right. I'm from Glasgow.'

'Kyle's paternal great-grandfather was from Inverness, I think, or some such place, which is why he is a Watt. Would you know where the Watt clan hail from?'

'I wouldn't, no,' Meg said as she felt perspiration beginning to win the battle against her deodorant. Kyle had disappeared from Meg's side and now sat at his mother's dressing table like a little boy, alternately fingering the items on it and preening himself in the mirror.

'It was a great concert,' Kyle said, forcing his mother to break her forensic examination of Meg.

'Did you enjoy it Meg?' she asked, lifting a suit bag from a peg on the door and disappearing behind a screen.

'It's the first classical concert I've ever been to,' Meg said. 'But what a great venue — I'd always imagined it would be more space-agey inside. I didn't think there would be as much wood.'

'It's for the acoustics,' Eleanor said. She might as well have added '*stupid*' for how it made Meg feel.

Kyle jumped off his seat. 'Can I take you two ladies for something to eat? Performance always makes me hungry, even when I'm not doing the work.'

'Of course,' Eleanor said, 'There's a table booked.'

A launch took them across the Harbour to Kirribilli where a taxi drove them to a waterfront restaurant, so close they could have walked.

‘Are there many female conductresses?’ Meg asked when they had been shown to their seat, her esses going on forever.

‘I prefer conductor,’ Eleanor said.

‘Or maestro,’ Kyle added, which made his mother laugh but made Meg feel small.

‘So what are your plans for Australia?’ Eleanor asked, as she focused her bright blue eyes on Meg with the same intensity Kyle had.

‘I’m not really sure. A rest would be nice,’ Meg said and when that didn’t seem to meet with Eleanor’s approval she continued, ‘we’ve been working pretty hard for the past couple of years.’

‘Hmm,’ Kyle’s mother said before she turned to Kyle, ‘Was Lili there for you when you arrived today?’

‘Yes,’ Kyle said, ‘thank you.’

Meg ate her pink snapper as Kyle and Eleanor discussed the evening’s music. It reminded her of the first meal she had with Kyle when he and Zed had done the same and she had listened and been enthralled. She had understood more about that first conversation than she did now, but tonight she didn’t feel like she might be uncovered as an intruder and kicked out at any moment. She let the night wash over her, listening to the chink of glasses behind them and the muted shouts from the kitchen. The more they talked, the more Meg realised that Eleanor had never once asked Kyle about his tour, or his music, it was all about her and her fights with critics and with musicians. She had been worried about meeting Eleanor, but now she realised she was just like every other mother, only interested in herself. Meg would be different. She sat back and soon their words became a gentle hum in the background.

Somewhere in the distance Meg heard the scrapping of chairs and a woman's deep voice said, 'I think your little friend is bored of all this talk.'

Meg shook her head in an attempt to wake up and used her napkin to cover her mouth in case she had been dribbling. 'I'm so sorry,' Meg said.

Kyle laughed and squeezed her knee. 'You must excuse Meg, Mum, it was wrong of me to pull her out tonight after such a long flight. But I didn't want to miss your Mahler. Still, we should be off.' Kyle waved the waiter for the bill, but his mother was dismissive.

'Don't be silly, Kyle, this is my treat,' Eleanor said, and Meg was amazed when Kyle agreed so readily.

Kyle kissed his mother at the door of the restaurant and held her hand as she eased herself into a taxi. 'We can just walk from here,' Kyle said, and Meg was glad of a bit of air after the climate control of the restaurant. The night was balmy but with enough coolness in the air for it to be pleasant. As they walked Meg apologised again for falling asleep, but Kyle seemed to find it less endearing than he had in the restaurant.

'It was really rude, Meg, I can't believe you did that.'

'I know, I'm sorry, but I'm shattered.' Kyle merely shrugged, so Meg decided to get him to talk rather than let him sulk. 'You've never really told me about when you were a kid — it must have been really exciting growing up with musicians.'

'Well, you've met my mum and she's about as dull as it gets. Pouring over scores for hours then rest, rehearse, perform, that's about it.'

'And what about your dad?' Meg asked.

'What about yours?' Kyle snapped back without missing a beat.

'That's not fair, Kyle,' Meg said, surprised that his annoyance had turned so quickly into something nastier, 'you know I didn't know him.'

'Well, I didn't know mine either,' and he ended their conversation and quickened his pace.

For the next couple of weeks Meg and Kyle hung around the apartment, sleeping and watching soaps on TV, and as their bodies adjusted to the new time zone they eased into comfort. A new maid appeared but Meg decided she'd wait until she felt better before she would ask to get rid of her. She didn't want an outsider getting in the way, but for now it was good to let someone else make the meals and clean the flat. She had never been happier than when they sat on the leather sofa together with the blinds closed and the air conditioning on, Kyle's hand on Meg's hardening belly. *Things will be different this time around.* She hadn't had a period since Manchester, two weeks before Glasgow, three before Ibiza, but she was stronger now, they were stronger. A memory kept emerging, though of Kyle worrying he wouldn't be able to cope with a baby. It was such a strange thing to say, particularly when men didn't seem to have much to do with the whole thing. But she began wonder if it was connected to his dad and why he refused to talk about him. One day when Kyle said he was going to see Todd about a compilation album, she took a taxi to the Central Library and found the floor where the newspaper archive was housed.

'I'm looking for an old article,' she told the woman on the desk, 'about a musician who died. Suicide possibly?' She wasn't sure where that had come from, but it was the best explanation Meg had come up with for Kyle's silence.

'What year?'

'Oh,' Meg said, she didn't even have the basic information. She had always assumed that Kyle must have been quite young when his dad died, as he didn't feature in any of his childhood stories.

'Have you got a name then?' the librarian asked, as she approached a large cabinet with dozens of tiny drawers.

'My name?' Meg asked.

'No, the name of the person you're looking for,' the woman said, irritation seeping through her professional tone.

Meg gave an immediate response. 'Kenneth Watt.'

'The violinist?' The librarian questioned her the way Miss Boyle, her chemistry teacher used to, and it made Meg doubt herself for a moment.

‘Yes, that makes sense,’ Meg said, ‘Kenneth Watt the violinist.’

‘Well, it’s not an article you’re looking for, it’s an archive,’ the librarian said, as she moved away from her catalogue and came out from behind the counter. She seemed to warm to the subject. ‘He was one of Australia’s greatest musicians, a true talent. His son’s in some band or other, MindSense is it?’ She stopped and pierced Meg with her look. Meg tried to keep her face from betraying anything, but she had obviously failed.

‘You look surprised,’ the librarian said.

‘I’m not from here,’ Meg said. *One of Australia’s finest musicians?* ‘Obviously I’ve heard of MindSet,’ Meg stuttered, ‘but it’s the violinist I’m interested in.’

The librarian led her to where the shelves ran on rails and had to be controlled by a large wheel. She shunted one rack after the next until she made an aisle she was happy with. ‘Wait here,’ she said and she pulled a cord on the ceiling to illuminate her way.

Meg sat down at an empty table and waited until the woman placed a couple of document boxes in front of her. ‘There will be more on the microfiche, but this will get you started.’

Dead Violist Found

Mystery still surrounds the death of Kenneth Watt, whose remains were recovered today after an eighth day of searching. Kenneth Watt was last seen walking across Sydney Harbour Bridge on Tuesday night, but never returned home. His pregnant wife, cellist Eleanor Watt, was devastated when the news broke that her husband’s body had been found. ‘I cannot believe he took his own life and urge the police to investigate the matter further,' she said. The police are not looking for anyone else in their inquiries and have refused to comment on whether the body was weighed down.

Meg read her way through the eight days that preceded Kenneth's body being dragged out of the harbour by a fisherman. Obituaries described him as a kind man whose whole life had been devoted to music. They noted that he was survived by Eleanor, but only a couple mentioned the pregnancy. If his father had killed himself, then it made sense that Kyle was frightened. Meg knew what it was like to be abandoned, and while she had been prepared to go through the last pregnancy alone, this baby, conceived in a frenzy to put right so many wrongs, needed a father.

She put the newspapers carefully back into the archive box, thanked the librarian and headed to the apartment. She tried to frame the questions she had for Kyle, but wondered how she could do it without it sounding like she was spying.

He was already home when she got back and he buzzed about the place with more vigour than she had seen since they had arrived in Australia. It didn't seem right to break the mood by asking why he lived in an apartment that overlooked the scene of his father's death. And when Kyle kissed her passionately and said, 'Right, I think we need a holiday,' the opportunity was lost.

Meg laughed, 'I thought we were on holiday.'

'No,' Kyle said, 'a proper holiday, a few days away, see Australia.'

Kyle's eyes sparkled brightly and while the thought of packing and travelling again was the last thing she wanted to do, she desired more than anything to keep him happy. 'Great,' she said, 'where are we going?'

Meg tried not to get too excited, but when she had tried to mention it casually, Val had screamed down the phone at her.

'When are you going? Are you going to say yes?'

'He might not even ask me.'

'He'll ask you.'

Uluru

A couple of days later they flew to Alice Springs, moved quickly through the airport and found their chauffeur casually holding a card at his side with *Watt* written on it. He took the luggage from Kyle and led them to a 4x4 where he opened the door and gave Meg his hand to help her climb in. Kyle put his arm around her once they were settled and she snuggled into his chest, not daring to say anything that might make him change his mind.

The engine on, the air conditioning kicked in as they began their journey through the red desert to *Longitude 131°.* The tented bungalows gave an unimpeded view of the Rock so while the porter explained to Kyle how to use the sound system, Meg just stared at the monolith as cloud shadows danced across it.

'Good, eh?' Kyle said as he tipped and dismissed the porter.

'Incredible. The sky looks so big.'

The pop of a champagne cork made Meg turn back to the room and as Kyle handed her a flute, she held her breath.

He raised his glass. 'Here's to an unforgettable weekend,' Kyle said, and they chinked glasses and kissed. 'Now what shall we do until sunset?' he said, leading her over to the canopied bed.

Each time Kyle paused to change his rhythm or hold a beat Meg expected the question. Each time she moved, or stopped for a sip of champagne she willed it. Each pant held an *ask me, ask me, ask me.* But all she got was *'I love you'*.

She drifted off to sleep and woke to see Kyle fully clothed again, sitting on the veranda nibbling from a plate of antipasto. She had got used to many things, like having to pour sugar from a canister, or ordering coffee when you really wanted tea, but she never experienced the invisible hands of maids and butlers, without a shiver.

'Come on sleepyhead — the sun's beginning to dip.'

Meg pulled her satin robe around her and got up. Her suitcase had been emptied while she slept and her camera had been placed on the side table as though it was an ornament.

She looked between Ayers Rock, the Olympus and Kyle and decided the photographs could wait. As she kissed him, he slipped his hand under her robe, but the sound of voices from the next bungalow made Meg brush him away to go inside to dress.

She quickly pulled on lacy knickers, a long navy silk shift dress, and clasped her diamond pendant around her neck. More champagne cooled in a copper bath next to the table and Meg could see a cream jacketed waiter a discreet distance away. 'This is such a beautiful place, Kyle. Absolutely perfect.'

He smiled and she saw his hand shake. He was so gorgeous when he was nervous. 'Meg, I…I…oh bugger it.' He got up from his chair and came around to her side of the table. He took her hand and knelt down in front of her. 'Meg, listen. I know things were a bit rough after, well, after Miami, but since we've been back here everything's been really great between us, hasn't it? And I don't want anything or anyone to get between us again. And, shit, what I'm trying to say, Meg, is will you marry me?'

'Yes. Yes of course I will.' She let out a sob.

'You don't need time to think?'

'No, no. Of course I'll marry you Kyle. Of course I will.'

Tears ran down her face and they kissed and smiled and hugged. And as they watched the setting sun blaze Uluru red and orange and yellow Meg said quietly, 'I'm pregnant Kyle. I hope that doesn't change anything,' and Kyle squeezed her and said 'I know babe, I know.'

Darkness fell and a million stars came out.

They married quickly and quietly with Meg in vintage Balenciaga 60s style satin with a high waist to skim her bump and a beaded neckline to draw the eye. Kyle wore a white suit with a bright blue shirt to match his eyes and the bouquet of irises Meg carried. Zed and Suzie acted as witnesses with Eleanor, Wayne and Todd the only other guests. Val couldn't make the wedding. When Meg told her about the proposal and the pregnancy, she'd laughed and said, 'Me too. Can you believe it — Graham's going to make an honest woman of me? And the babies are due just a couple of weeks apart, they'll be like twins.'

Something that felt like vomit turned in Meg's stomach.

‘I’m not even the oldest at the clinic, there’s a woman here who’s forty-one. Mind you that’s a bit old, don’t you think?’ Val continued.

Meg thought her mum was too old at thirty-five, but she didn’t say it. Instead she listened to her mum’s frantic babble about her Lady Di inspired dress and the thrill of pregnancy and Meg tried to move into her mum’s world where it was the first baby for them both.

1988

March: Vaucluse, Sydney

When Ruby was six months old they left the Harbour and moved to an art deco villa in Vaucluse, but they were barely settled when Kyle broke the news one morning that MindSet was getting together again.

‘Great,’ Meg said, glad that Kyle would have a purpose other than monitoring Ruby’s fluid intake and output.

‘I thought everyone could move in here, so we can write new material. It would be really organic, just hanging out and playing like back in the day. You can always tell when bands just meet in studios — the music sounds forced.’

‘Are you mental?’ Meg said as she abandoned her search for something to wear and turned towards him. ‘We’ve got a baby.

‘No, it’ll be great Meg, just like old times,’ Kyle said, kissing her on the forehead and pulling out a dress she hated to hold in front of her.

‘But it’s not old times. I can’t have you lot making a racket with Ruby trying to sleep.’

‘It’ll be peachy,’ Kyle said, ignoring her pleas, ‘I’ve got a guy coming this afternoon to do some soundproofing.’

‘So it’s all arranged.’

‘Yeah,’ Kyle said as he moved to the dressing table and rubbed some of Meg’s face cream onto his hands. ‘It’ll be good for you too, having Suzie about. You've hardly been out since you've had Ruby.'

'I've been busy,' Meg said, 'and I don't really have much in common with Suzie these days.' She pulled the dress over her head and lifted Ruby from the floor and began to unpop Ruby's babygrow and change her nappy to emphasize the point. She could barely admit it, but motherhood left her ripped apart and empty. She hadn't realised how much she would miss the feeling of Ruby kicking inside her, a feeling that the squalling baby couldn't replace. One day she whispered to Val on the phone, 'It's really boring, all this baby stuff, isn't it?'

'I don't know, hen, I'm quite enjoying it this time round. I couldn't be arsed when you were a baby but then you were a narky wee thing, always crying for something.'

She didn't know why she even bothered to speak to Val when she always made her feel so bad, out of habit she supposed. Her mum had always failed her when she looked for support. '*And besides,*' Val would say, '*you've your nanny*'. She did have her nanny, but part of her couldn't bear to hand Ruby over, while the other part worried she might never want her back.

'Well, let the nanny be busy,' Kyle said, pulling her back to the present, 'that's why I employed her. You chill out a bit with the girls.'

'The girls?' Meg said. 'Do not tell me Clare is coming here. I won't have it.' But Kyle wasn't listening.

Zed and Suzie arrived first and at Meg's insistence were put at the far end of the house, well away from Meg and Kyle's suite. Wayne pitched up, with a van load of basses and a small bag of clothes but Mac and Clare declined the invitation, and rented a house nearby so they could have their own space.

Kyle was invigorated with the band getting together again, but Meg felt uneasy to be living at such close quarters, particularly since she hadn't had a chance to make the place into a home yet. Suzie fussed around Ruby even more than Kyle and was constantly questioning her, '*Do you think a soother is good for her? I've heard kids end up with crook teeth.*' '*Are you sure she needs a nap, she seems to be sleeping half the day?*' '*Why don't we head out and see if we can get her some cute things to wear?*'

But at least while Suzie lay on the floor building endless towers for Ruby to knock down, Meg could sneak out of the playroom and go to bed. She was only beginning to acknowledge how worn out she was, particularly since Ruby and Kyle never coordinated their sleeping, and both demanded her attention.

One night when Meg had barely been asleep for an hour she woke to the sound of Kyle crawling around their bedroom. 'What on earth are you doing?' she asked.

'I'm making a recording of the pipes. The bath clicks and burps for about five minutes after you wash your hands, so I've been running the taps and flushing at the same time and I'm getting all these amazing sounds.'

'I know, the plumbers coming in the morning.'

‘I think I could programme them into the drum machine. It’ll be spectacular.’

‘You know that sounds mad, it’s 4am,’ Meg said.

‘Not mad,’ he said, giving her a cheeky smile, ‘genius.’

‘Just don’t wake the baby,’ Meg said as she eased herself up on one elbow.

‘You really need to move her cot into the nursery, Meg, that’s what it’s there for.’

She wasn’t having this conversation again. She needed to see Ruby when she woke up in the night panicking that the baby might have stopped breathing. And she’d realised that as long as she didn’t confront him she could pretty much carry on with things as she wanted. ‘Do you promise to stop crawling around if I say you’re a genius?’ Distraction her best weapon.

‘Almost finished,’ Kyle whispered.

‘Oh come on Kyle, come back to bed, I need a cuddle.’

In the evenings, with Ruby settled, Meg would sit on the deck with the others and sip cocktails and sing songs. She listened as new tunes were picked out, and lyrics penned from initial hums and tried to believe that the idyllic picture they presented to the world wasn’t more complicated than it looked. Mac and Clare were still in the kissy-kissy phase of their relationship which everyone else snided about it behind their backs. Meg said the least, maybe because she was affected the most. Wanting to reach out and be touched, but she feared rejection from Kyle, who would accuse her of trying to compete with Clare. She needed to reach out and be touched, and she feared acceptance from Zed, who still occasionally gave her that look that said, *I remember, Meg. I know who you really are.*

The recording studio had always been barred to Meg, but when it was in her house, the band seemed less precious about shooing her away. She popped in a few times, leant against the padded back wall and watched Kyle's intense concentration as he drummed the start of the song — focusing on his snare and high hat, then as the song built, his body would open out to mid and low toms, and all the time, his foot hitting the bass to dictate the beat. But when Meg looked around the room, she realised that Mac and Wayne's eyes were firmly on Zed. His head nodded to Kyle's beat but as watched him she was drawn to the dexterity of his fingers as they slide up and down the fret, contorting his hands into arthritic shapes. He acknowledged the attention of the others with an occasional smile then would stop suddenly, leaving Mac singing without any music.

'It's not working,' Zed said. 'Can you keep with a straight beat a little longer Kyle, and Mac, it's too wordy, you're going to have to pare it down man.'

Meg thought she had better slink away as there was bound to be a fight, but Mac apologised and said he'd work on the lyrics, and Kyle, 'Sure. More like this?'

'Got it. Ok,' Zed continued, 'sweet, let's try something else. How about *Cuckoo?'*

Kyle clicked his sticks on the side of his snare, *'two, three,'* and off they go.

One afternoon when Meg was in the kitchen discussing the evening meal with the cook she heard hoots of laughter coming from the lounge. It had been the right idea to invite them here, she need to give Kyle credit for knowing that, otherwise they might both have been driven mad with torpor. Zed popped his head around the door and said, 'Hey Meg, you need to come and see this. There's some chick on the news says she was your lover.'

The boys hooted again from the next room, and more laughter. Mac saying something indistinguishable to Kyle. Zed shouting for Suzie to come and watch. The phone rang. The cook lifted it, but Meg hit the cradle and hung up. It rang again. She unplugged it at the wall. Her mobile rang; she switched it off; told the cook to go home. Kyle came into the room laughing but Meg turned her back on him, walked to the fridge and pulled out a beer.

'I mean Cerise, is that even a name?'

Meg turned to look at him and watched the colour drain from his face.

'Meg?'

She felt as though she was about to throw up, but instead she whispered, 'I can't explain.'

'You can't explain? You'd better fucking explain. There's some arsehole photographer outside and now it's on the news there'll be more.'

'No,' Meg said, shaking her head. Cerise was so far in the past she couldn't believe that she was hearing her name again.

Kyle's mobile rang and he threw it against the wall, smashing it into pieces but it didn't silence the buzzing at the garden gate or the rings coming from the rest of the band's phones. 'For Christ's sake Meg — I can't have a wife who bats for the other side.'

She rushed by him, but he grabbed her arm and wouldn't let go. 'Meg!'

'I'll sort it,' she said, trying to wrestle her arm free. 'You're hurting me.'

'You said you were a virgin when we got together.'

'I never said that,' Meg shouted, no longer caring if the others heard. 'Is that why you care? Have I fucked up your record for corrupting innocents?'

Kyle looked at her with sheer hatred in his eyes, causing her to cower away from the hit she expected, but Zed came into the room. 'Hey,' he said, as he held out a whisky for Kyle, and when Kyle didn't let Meg go, Zed stepped between them. 'Take it.'

Kyle finally relaxed his grip and as Meg rubbed at the red fingerprints, he downed the whisky, took Zed's and downed that as well.

'She's no lezzer. You know that mate. It's just the press making stuff up again,' Zed said, trying to get Meg to agree.

'Why am I not laughing then? Why is she not laughing?' Kyle stormed out to the garden, and Meg heard a splash as he jumped into the pool. She stood staring at the door, until Zed interrupted her trance.

'Shit Meg, you're full of surprises. But don't worry, it'll blow over,' he said in a calm voice. 'What does it matter if you slept with her?'

'If it's on the news it obviously matters to somebody.'

'It's just because he was named as Australia's sexiest dad in that magazine.'

'Shit,' Meg said. 'Doesn't do much for Kyle's reputation, does it? Is that why he's so angry?'

'Who needs a reputation?' Zed said, but when he reached out, she pulled back and ran up the stairs ignoring Mac and Wayne who continued to watch Cerise on the TV. She closed the door of her bedroom, standing behind it to stop any intruders. *Shit, shit, shit.* When her breathing eased she went over to the window and saw Kyle still ploughing through the water like he was trying to escape. She had to fix this. She dug through her drawers, found her abandoned Filofax and dialled the gallery in San Francisco where an assistant happily gave out Cerise's mobile number. She took a couple of deep breaths while the phone rang, but they didn't calm her.

'You were meant to be my friend and you've betrayed me,' she screamed by way of an introduction. 'I turned a blind eye to the fact that you've been selling my prints, but this, this is despicable. Why on earth are you raking all this up?'

'Because you forgot me,' Cerise said coldly. 'I made you Meg, yet you've never once credited me. I've read all the profiles of you as rock-wife-photographer, yet I was the one who saved you, I was the one who came to you when you needed me. Me Meg, not him.'

Meg couldn't believe what she was hearing, *saved her?*

But Cerise went on, 'I'm meant to be happy with a Christmas card while you're living in luxury. You can't grudge me making a few bucks, can you?'

Meg grudged it all right, but she couldn't find words in her brain to reply.

'I'm in Melbourne just now,' Cerise continued in a more conciliatory tone, 'we could meet up for a photo shoot — they'll pay good money for that.'

Meg struggled to keep up with Cerise's words as her mind kept going back to what hurt the most. 'You made me? Are you kidding? You got me a haircut for God's sake. Do you have any idea the trouble you've caused here? It's all over the news.'

'I'm doing an exhibition for Mardi Gras and the journalist asked me if I knew anyone here. Your name must have slipped out. You shouldn't be ashamed, Meg, it's who you are.'

'Don't dare tell me who I am,' Meg shouted as she slammed down the phone, and when that didn't help, she kicked over the table, and screamed. 'Fuck it.'

Her mind spun. This was nothing compared with all the shit she had put up with before now, but it cut her deeper. She had thought that her life was sorted. Ruby, Kyle, the new house, the prospect of making new friends as Ruby got older. But now, Cerise had crashed into her present, ready to destroy her out of pettiness. But why should she be destroyed? It wasn't as though she was standing to be pope or prime minister. She was just an ordinary person who had made a mistake. No, not a mistake. San Francisco wasn't a mistake. Neither was Cerise. No matter the bother she was causing now, she couldn't imagine what would have happened to her if Cerise hadn't welcomed her into her gallery. Maybe she would have lasted on her own for another week, maybe two, but how long before she had cracked and given up all hope? How long before she had taken the bus to the airport and headed home to a job in Fine Fair?

She was aware of voices downstairs and Suzie's heels moving about in Ruby's room. Ruby. She would never have had her if Cerise hadn't come to Miami. She was so lonely, so lost. A bottle of pills washed down with vodka would have done the trick, but she phoned Cerise instead, and Cerise came.

She got thirsty so made do with water from the tap while she watched the twenty-four hour news. She quietly hoped for a natural disaster or a good murder to displace the coverage, but her wedding photo, followed by a video of Cerise, sometimes with her voice, other times with the newsreader reporting the story, kept appearing on a loop. The worst was the vox pox, teenage girls filmed at the local mall saying: *If she doesn't want Kyle, I'll have him.*

Meg lay on her bed and curled into a tight ball. She'd never seen Kyle so angry, never imagined that her reaching for a friend in her worst moments would bring such a reaction. It was outrageous for him to think that there was anything going on between her and Cerise. Pol was her partner now and she had made it clear that she had only come to Miami to tend to Meg's emotional needs.

There was a tentative tap on her door.

'Yeah,' she said, pulling herself up, ready to accept Kyle's apology. But instead Ruby's little body appeared with a ventriloquist's voice saying, 'Hello Mummy.'

Zed poked his head around the door. 'Can we come in?'

'Yes, of course,' Meg said, stretching out her arms to take Ruby onto the bed beside her.

'I thought you might need some company.'

Meg ran her hands over Ruby's dark baby hair then held her tight as Zed stood awkwardly by the bed.

'Thanks Zed,' Meg said then she kissed Ruby lightly on the forehead and expected Zed to take the opportunity to leave. But instead he sat down.

'You right?' he asked.

She shrugged. She didn't think she was, but she hoped, she prayed.

'Looks like you fell short of Kyle's code of conduct,' Zed said, his voice more serious than Meg had ever heard it, before his face broke into a smile and he held his hand up for a high five. 'Welcome to the club.'

Meg slapped his hand and patted Ruby's against it too.

'No Ruby,' Zed said with a theatrical wag of the finger. 'You can't be in our club — you're too perfect.'

'She puked on Kyle's favourite shirt yesterday.'

'Well, welcome Miss Ruby. You can be our president.'

Meg laughed for a moment, but her thoughts were immediately drawn back to Kyle. 'I've never seen him react like that before. You'd think I'd murdered someone.'

'No. That was me,' Zed said flatly.

'Don't Zed. You promised.'

Zed stood up and headed for the door. 'You'll sort it out,' he said, but he hesitated before he left. 'He can be a bit of a prick sometimes, but you guys love each other, things will be okay.'

You guys love each other. The words reverberated around the room. *You love each other. Love. Each. Other.*

When Ruby was asleep and the house finally became silent Meg was ready to look for Kyle. She found him lying on a spare bed in the East Room pretending to sleep. She stood at the door for a moment, letting her eyes adjust to the inky black. When Kyle didn't move, she went across and sat on the bed.

'Are you awake?' she asked, although she knew from his breathing he was.

He grunted.

'Will you let me explain? Please Kyle. You're not being fair — it was before we were even together.'

Kyle turned on the lamp, threw the duvet off and got up. 'I'm not being fair?' He hissed. 'This will ruin my image, Meg, you know that. I'm a laughing stock.'

'You're not,' she said, pleading, 'I'll make a statement. People will understand. Please will you just listen?'

He pulled back the curtains and looked out into the night with such intensity that Meg wondered if there was any way she could fix this.

'Can you turn off the light?' she asked.

He came back over to the bed and did as she requested. She sat perched on the bed facing away from him, but it still wasn't dark enough so she closed her eyes and began. 'You have to understand Kyle what a shit year I'd had. I'd left home and had been travelling with you guys and then I got up one morning and you'd all disappeared. Todd had forgotten I needed a visa and I was left in limbo until you came back. And you were talking about taking a year off. I thought I might never see you again.'

Neither of them spoke for a few minutes then Kyle said, 'She said on the TV that she's licensed to sell your photos. That she's your agent or something. I've never seen any money coming through the accounts. Where's the money?'

'The point is,' Meg said, ignoring his last comments, 'I was left in San Francisco. I couldn't go back to Glasgow, and I didn't know what to do. Cerise took care of me. Can you not understand? She was the first person who ever did that. But that doesn't make me a lesbian.'

'Did you sleep with her?'

'What does it matter?'

'Of course it matters. Did you sleep with her?'

Meg nodded, and there was just enough light for her to turn and see Kyle's look of disdain.

PRESS RELEASE

Meg Watt is returning to Scotland to visit her mother and new half-brother. She will return to Australia later in the year. No further statements will be issued.

Whitecraigs, near Glasgow

Val had found her a house by the time her plane had touched down.

'You'll love it, hen. Dead posh. Galleried hall and ah things.'

'Brilliant,' Meg said, not knowing how or when they had become familiar with such terms.

Within a month Meg had moved in, hired a designer, a gardener and a nanny, and set them to work, over-seeing them the way she had with the band. She discussed colour schemes and decorators' schedules, and unpacked the treasures she had bought on her month-long honeymoon which had lain in a storage unit since — glass from Murano, marquetry from Sorrento, textiles from Marrakech. When she had bought them she couldn't have imagined that she would be separated from Kyle within a year. She pushed the thought from her mind. Not separated, just a break. It would be madness to try and tour with Ruby in tow, so it made sense for her to come back to Glasgow.

When windows started being replaced, and plastic sheeting covered the top floor, she found ways of keeping Ruby amused. She was a bit more fun now that she was crawling about the place and babbling away, so Meg would leave the nanny ironing tiny outfits and go to:

Monday: Mums and Toddlers
Tuesday: Pushchair parade
Wednesday: Tippy and Tumble

Thursday: Mini Movers and Shakers

Friday : Bash and bang.

Meg even persuaded Val to go with her. 'It's meant to help their development.'

'You made do with a rusk.'

'Ah,' Meg said, 'nothing better than a Farley's Rusk dunked in milk. I had one the other morning when I was trying them out on Ruby.'

'All that mushy goo,' Val said, admitting that she had tried them too. 'But listen, don't tell these wummen that I'm yur mammy. I'm yur cousin, right? I don't want them thinking I'm ancient.'

Meg laughed. 'There's no danger of that, some of them are older than you. They don't know how I managed to make it into their wee circle, they just know my house is the biggest in the area and it pisses them off.'

'So what day yi tell them? That yur a gangster's moll?'

'I don't really tell them anything.'

'Ur yu kidding? You can make anything up now. You don't even sound like yur from round here — we'll need to start calling you Lulu wi that accent.'

'Aye well,' Meg said, making herself sound more Glaswegian than she had in months, 'yu'll need to try talking proper or you'll get papped right out.'

But around 6 o'clock each evening, when Val had left to make Big Graham and Wee Graham their tea, she became more aware of noise in the lane; of cars revving up driveways; of squeals as daddies with ties and briefcases were welcomed home. Each noise made her conscious of the hollow where her heart should be. She gave the nanny more evenings off than was stipulated in the contract just so she had something to do. But the doing of it didn't satisfy her either — sitting for an hour while Ruby ate her dinner atom by atom; sitting while she splashed in the bath; sitting on the rocking chair until Ruby finished her feed and a mechanical lullaby eased her to sleep.

When she couldn't pretend that she was being of any more use, she would pull down the side of the cot and place Ruby gently between the sheets. Another couple of minutes could legitimately be spent checking that the movement hadn't wakened her, then she would blow a kiss and make her way out of the room by the light of luminous stars scattered across the ceiling.

It became a habit to wander around the upstairs of the house. She would open each door and stand for a minute in the doorway of the unused guest bedroom next to unused guest bedroom, pretend that she was looking at the swatches pinned to the walls, or try to visualise the furniture that had been photographed for the mood board. At the end of the corridor, stairs led up to the stores, the nanny's suite and the darkroom she had put in, even though her cameras were still in Australia. She would stand at the bottom for as long as she dared, waiting for some noise to prove she wasn't alone.

She would distract herself by looking at the photos which adorned the walls of Ruby and of Wee Graham, a child so pale he was almost translucent. She had commissioned them from a local photographer, keen that their childhoods would not be undocumented like her own. But the wind would creak the rafters or a dog would bark outside and Meg would feel self-conscious, frightened that the nanny would catch her standing there in her own house, and she would make her way back along the landing.

More and more she felt herself drawn to her bedroom, but she knew that if she napped at 7 p.m. she'd wake at 4 a.m. and spend the rest of the night in limbo. Lying on the bed she would want to speak to someone, but friends her own age were hard to come by. Some of the women from the groups she attended, who were on their sixth or seventh child would talk about a teenage daughter going off to university, but Meg could never find a way to make a connection with these mythical girls who gave their mothers no end of worry. Once or twice, after she had passed her driving test, Meg had taken the car down to the Gorbals and cruised around. She told herself it was to get Ruby off to sleep, but it was also take stock. The glaikit expressions she saw on the faces of the girls trudging back from the shops with their messages hanging off buggies, made her thank Kyle for taking her from what her life was destined to be. But that was immediately followed by growing anger that he had cast her aside with a reaction so severe it made her wonder if he ever had been the caring man she once loved or if it just suited her to imagine him that way. In May, when their first wedding anniversary came around she answered the door to flowers, though not roses, and diamond earrings to match the pedant she never wore in case Ruby pulled it off.

Her heart beat faster than it had in weeks as she picked up the phone and dialled the number of Kyle's latest hotel.

'Thank you for the earrings. They're beautiful.'

'Well, I thought I should get you something.'

'I feel guilty now I never sent you anything.'

'The card arrived.'

'I'll get you something,' she said about to add *when,* but she didn't know when.

'It's fine. I don't want anything.'

'I was thinking about the wedding earlier. Do you remember...'

'Look Meg, I'm glad you like the studs, but I've got to get going.'

'Oh, what are you up to?'

'You know what it's like Meg. This, That. Anyway, give Ruby a kiss from me. Bye.'

After that their conversations rarely moved beyond the functional.

'Is Ruby sleeping?'

'Did the roofer come?'

'How is the housekeeper working out?'

So she called Suzie, even though they were separated now by more than miles. '*Why don't we meet for New York Fashion Week?*'

Suzie would say, or '*Fly out and we'll have a blast.*' But when Meg tried to explain that she just couldn't turn up, Suzie would turn cold, as if she refused to believe that Kyle had thrown her out. 'That baby's pulling you down, Meg, I told you, you shouldn't have had her.'

She preferred it when Zed answered. He was never too busy or preoccupied to talk and recently there was a new vigour in his voice which convinced Meg that he really was clean this time.

'How's Ruby doing? Has that tooth come in yet?' he would ask. He even took time to talk to Meg about non-Ruby matters, 'Is your mum still driving you crazy?'

'Yip, she wants us to take up callanetics,' Meg said.

'I always thought your handwriting was really neat.'

'Not calligraphy, callanetics — it's for our bums,' Meg said trying to sound indignant.

'Now writing with your bums, that is a talent. I think we've got the wrong Watt on the stage. Maybe we should get you here as a support act.'

They would laugh together and then Meg would hear the door in the background and he would say, 'You're in luck, that's Suzie back now,' and Suzie would come to the phone.

'Hey babe, you right? Can't talk I'm afraid — I'm meeting Clare for cocktails.'

So she would talk to Zed some more, often phoning back after Suzie had left the room, not really intending to go behind Suzie's back, but just enjoying Zed's easy banter rather than having to listen to how fabulous Clare was, and what a time they were all having.

In July, not long before Ruby's first birthday and two weeks after she knew the band had finished promoting in America, Meg got a phone call from Suzie. 'Hey Meg, listen, Zed and I have rented a place in Italy for the summer. Why don't you come over and hang for a while?'

It wasn't the most enthusiastic offer Meg had ever heard — Suzie and Meg struggled to find things to talk about, maybe because of all the things that went unsaid. *Oh, by the way I slept with your boyfriend. And do you know it makes me feel awkward when you send Ruby so many clothes and keep asking for photos with her in them.* But Kyle was lined up to produce some tracks with a new band from Seattle and he was vague about his plans after that. Certainly he didn't seem to be rushing to see either her or Ruby. Val and the Grahams were going to Majorca for a few weeks and even the toddlers group was stopping for the summer. Besides Zed had already asked her to come and she felt she owed it to him. She put her reservations to one side and said *yes.*

In the early days of touring Meg had found it difficult to keep a grip on fashion. The fact that men kept their ponytails in Germany and America didn't mean they weren't years out-of-date in the UK. She stressed about it until one day she realised that MindSet *was* fashion, and it gave her the confidence to shop more eclectically and with a ballsy attitude — harem trousers from Morocco, T-shirts from

The Village, fluorescent Ibiza or Gap college. She moved, she changed, and other girls copied her style from magazine photos. But since her pregnancy and Ruby's birth she felt out-of-touch. The women in the neighbourhood were too *Dynasty* for her taste, so she riffed on Lisa Bonet and Melanie Mayron and never quite felt herself.

Now the thought of sunshine gave her a new purpose so she went straight to the Italian Centre and bought summer clothes to fit her lighter mood. Then she went to Jessops and got kitted out with camera equipment again.

July: Tuscany

Ruby pulled herself onto her feet and walked round the sun loungers. Her chubby fingers curled around the frames as she eased herself along.

'Oh Meg, look, how darling. That's it Ruby, that's a good girl,' Suzie said.

Meg absent-mindedly held out her hand to be a staging post in case she was needed, but she was too hot to join in the pleasure Suzie was getting.

'Careful babe, oh, that's it,' Suzie clapped her hands then opened them out, welcoming Ruby to walk across. 'Do you think she can make it? Come on Ruby.'

Ruby turned her head to Suzie, but the action unbalanced her and she plopped to the ground. Suzie jumped forward to pick her up, but Meg had already taken her hand and re-attached it to the handhold.

'She's well padded,' Meg said patting Ruby's nappy to illustrate, 'they don't hurt themselves when they fall.'

'Poor baby,' Suzie said and she screwed up her face and made Ruby's lip start to quiver.

Meg turned her head towards the swimming pool. The water looked so lovely, but she couldn't summon the energy to leave her seat.

Suzie seemed to read her thoughts, 'You should get Zed to teach you,' she said, causing Meg to turn back to see Suzie and Ruby engaged in a game of peek-a-boo. 'He used to be a life guard, you know.'

Meg laughed at the thought of Zed sitting on a giant's highchair with a white stripe down his nose, but the idea had been bubbling under ever since she had Ruby, swimming would be good for them both. 'Could you not do it?' Meg asked.

'Me, oh no,' Suzie replied, as if it was the most outrageous thing she'd ever heard, 'I've no patience for that. Anyway I can look after Ruby — I'll take her down to the town and do some shopping.'

'You've changed your tune,' Meg said.

'About what?'

'Kids. I thought you hated them.'

'Well, she's cute,' Suzie said kissing Ruby, 'and I get to hand her back when she starts fretting.'

'Ok, just don't let her get dehydrated.'

Meg hadn't considered the practical aspects of her swimwear when she had packed, and she felt very bare in her bikini and conscious of the white veined stretch marks on her stomach and thighs as Zed coached her into the water.

'It's good of you to give this a go,' Zed said, 'I've never forgiven myself for nearly drowning you.'

'Don't remind me,' she said tensing and pausing with her foot on the second step of the ladder, her hands gripped tight to the rail. The water was chilly as it lapped against her calf, like ice flakes should be forming on it, but her shoulders burned and despite herself she could feel some refreshment moving up from the soles of her feet.

'Just ease yourself in. I'm right behind you,' Zed said, breathing on to her back.

'I don't think I should be doing this,' Meg said.

'You're fine,' he said as he put his hands onto her hips. 'Come on, I've got you.'

'Zed, I really don't think I should be doing this.' She stopped her slow descent and twisted her head to face him. 'It doesn't feel right'.

'It's just swimming,' Zed said in such an innocent way that Meg wondered for a minute whether she was reading too much into the gentle pressure he had used on her hips before. 'I can't teach you without touching you.'

'It just feels a bit funny.'

'It's not,' he said, and she realised it didn't have to be. 'Now come on. Suzie will wonder what we've been doing if you're not even in the pool by the time she gets back.' He gave her a friendly smack on the bum. 'Pool, now.'

She took a deep breath and stepped down into the water. He took her hand like a chivalrous knight. 'Just walk across the pool. Not swimming, just walking.' She felt the water slosh between her thighs and bubble in the hand she trailed on top of the water, hoping it would steady her.

'Just one step at a time — there's no rush.'

The sun glared off the water, and Meg screwed up her eyes, but she kept walking, clenching Zed's hand in little pulses with each step. They made it to the other side, and Meg wanted to cheer, but Zed didn't seem satisfied.

'Keep your back to the wall and we'll walk up the way — we'll stop when it gets too deep.' It was already too deep, the water edging up above her waist, wetting her bikini top, 'Shoulders in and you'll be fine.' Meg obeyed, gasping slightly, but Zed held out both hands and smiled reassuringly. 'Now we just bob for a while.'

They bobbed until Meg felt the tension release from her shoulders and she managed a small smile. They walked some more, then stopped, bounced up and down and looked out over the vineyards and cypress trees that bordered the property, and off across the hills to where the sun was finally beginning to drop from its zenith.

'So, Lesson One: Happy in the Water? Tick'

Meg looked around. She was happy and cooler than she had been all day and she was also amazed by the silence. No baby crying, no nanny or housekeeper asking for instructions, no Val and her endless chatter.

'I'm glad you came,' Zed said.

'It's good to have some company,' she replied.

'What about Kyle, is he still in the States?'

Meg nodded. 'He's still pissed off with me.'

'What, about that lesbian bloke?'

'That lesbian bloke? Honestly,' Meg faked disgust, but couldn't help laughing, 'That lesbian bloke has practically destroyed us. Kyle wanted us both out of Australia until the furore died down, but he didn't want me to go to America with him.'

'And Glasgow's a safe place to be?' Zed said, absent-mindedly rubbing the patch on his back where his tattoo had been planned.

'Yeah,' Meg said. 'I checked through the newspaper archives when I got back. It didn't even get a mention. Why would it? He overdosed, right?'

'Yeah,' Zed said. 'Now hey,' he put his hand under her chin and pushed it up. 'We're not murderers. I can believe that if the cops do'

'No, you're right. You gave me back my home. I'm not afraid there anymore,' she said and managed to give him a smile, *just lonely*. 'Did you ever tell Suzie?' Meg asked.

'Course not. We agreed we'd never talk about it,' Zed said, 'and besides I was so wasted, it's all a bit blurred.'

Meg wished that day wasn't still so clear to her. She had thought that getting rid of Tomo would end all her problems, but instead it had brought new ones, with bigger secrets.

'What about Kyle? Did you tell him?'

'No. I didn't tell him anything.' She looked into Zed's eyes. How much of a blur was that day for him? She broke the silence. 'Can I ask one more favour?' Meg said.

'As long as it doesn't involve psychos.'

‘You know when Suzie lies in the water with her arms on the floats.’

Zed nodded.

‘It looks amazing. I’d love to be able to do that.’

‘Sure, it’s just like being in the bath,’ Zed said.

‘I’m more of a shower girl.’

‘OK,’ Zed said. He jumped out of the water and grabbed the floats that were kept at the side of the pool. ‘So one under each elbow, lean back and lift up your feet.’

‘Oh,’ Meg was horrified, lift up her feet? She knew it would come to this point but now it was here she just couldn’t. The memory of trying to run and there being nothing beneath her; of trying to stand and instead sinking deeper, came back clearer than ever.

‘Come on, we’ll try this,’ Zed said, picking up on her reluctance. He put his hands around her waist. ‘I’m not going to let you go, you just need to lean back and trust me.’

Meg tipped her head back slightly and felt the sun sharp on her face. She crinkled her eyes until they were almost closed and felt Zed’s hands move up under her arms. ‘You can do it.’

She leant back, let her feet slip and lift from the solid bottom of the pool, felt Zed take her weight. She couldn’t believe it, but she felt safe.

‘Good girl,’ he whispered in her ear, but his reassurance broke the trust and she kicked her legs frantically and tried to fight her way out of his arms. ‘Don’t panic,’ he said. ‘That’s how accidents happen.' Meg's heart pounded in her chest, but Zed was calm, so she smiled and leaned back again.

'I thought you'd be doing laps by the time I got back,' Suzie said as she parked a sleeping Ruby in the shade of a tree.

'Suzie, this is wonderful,' Meg said as she pulled her head forward, and gently eased her legs to the floor. 'Even if I don't learn to swim at least I'll be able to get in the water and cool down.'

'Another couple of lessons and you'll be swimming no worries,' Zed said as he moved away from Meg, jumped out of the pool and started to towel the beads of water off his body. Meg watched, admiring the artistry in the swirls and lines that inked his body, but pulled her eyes away from the Fender and the scar which had added another string. She took a couple of steps on her own to the ladder and got out of the water too.

'Look at what I bought Ruby,' Suzie said as she pulled a white linen dress embroidered with tiny lemon daisies out of a paper carrier. 'Isn't it adorable? I just had to have it.'

'She doesn't need any more dresses Suzie,' Meg said. 'They get tangled round her knees when she's crawling.'

'I thought about that. I know she's nearly walking, so I bought her the next size up in this one, and it's got a matching hat.' Suzie took an almost identical dress out of the bag, and modelled the hat. Meg had to concede. 'Thanks, they are cute.'

Then Suzie lifted the poolside phone and called for cocktails, took off her t-shirt and bra and sat on a lounger between Zed and

Meg. A little pot belly hung over her knickers and her boobs drooped in a way that Val had been told Meg hers would if she breastfed. And the pox scars on Suzie's face turned a brighter red than her cheeks, while Meg's pale skin took on a caramel shade. For the first time ever Meg felt as though she compared well with another woman's body.

'You know, it was so funny,' Suzie said, 'all the women kept saying "*Italian baby, you have an Italian baby*". 'Isn't that sweet? I kept saying "*not mine, not mine*." But that sounded like I'd stolen her.' But while her mouth was smiling, her eyes weren't, they were boring into Meg's soul. 'You've got Italian blood in you, haven't you Zed?'

'No, babe,' Zed said quickly, 'Greek. Europe's not all the same country you know.'

Meg looked across at the sleeping Ruby. Babies are born with blue eyes, everyone knew that, but from the moment Ruby was born it was clear that she would prove them wrong. When she flashed open her lids for her first look at the world she revealed eyes the colour of bottled ink. Maybe just, if pushed, you might agree there was a hint of indigo, but within a couple of days that hint had gone and what remained were orbs the colour of the darkest chocolate. Everyone remarked on how they had never seen eyes so dark, how they were almost black, then they would look at Meg's pale blue eyes and Kyle's, like the sky on a perfect day, and thankfully they would say no more.

It became their routine to have a lesson before breakfast, while Suzie was still sleeping off the previous night's excesses, and Ruby was content to sit with her toys in a playpen. After the first couple of days Meg could get into the water and walk about in the shallows without panicking. She got more used to Zed holding her firmly around the waist as he calmly spoke his instructions, *'push your arms out and then sweep them back, that's it, legs too. That's my girl.'* And every day he explained a different tattoo to her — the MindSet logo and the *Dark Side of the Moon* prism spoke for themselves, but he gave her the tour of the rest. A swan's neck inside a red V for his team; the Chinese symbol of life; a straight lines bracelet around his upper arm clasped with concentric circles, the Aboriginal symbol for travelling with resting places. The day he told her about the shield on his heart, studded with two red stones was the day she swam her first breadth. She squealed as she reached Zed and he scooped her up and gave her a quick kiss on the lips. As soon as he'd done it he let go, and they stood looking at each other for a moment before Meg took a step back. 'Sorry,' she said.

'No, it was me.'

But she wasn't sure if it had been. She got out of the pool and dried herself.

'I've ordered breakfast.' It was Suzie's voice, and it made Meg spin round so fast she nearly toppled into the pool.

'Great, I'm starving,' Zed said as he swam across to where the bale of towels was and pulled himself out.

Italy suited him, she thought, being away from temptations and out in the sun. Swimming for hours every day had made him lean, tanned and muscled. She watched as he wiped the droplets off his back. Then Ruby shouted and bounced up and down from the playpen, her signal that she wanted some attention. Meg went to her and gave her a long cuddle, trying to hide in the embrace her thoughts of Zed's kiss and Suzie's appearance moments after it.

'I've got a great idea,' Suzie said as she lifted her tequila sunrise off the tray, 'why don't we take a day trip to Florence tomorrow? It would be mad for you to go home without seeing it.'

The word *home* drove into Meg's stomach. She felt peaceful here, enjoying Zed's company, and managing to push aside worries that Suzie was mentioning Ruby's dark eyes too often.

'We've been to Florence before, right?' Meg said, pitching her voice to the usual Australian intonation. But she had left too long a gap after the question, while she weighed up whether or not she wanted to spend a whole day with Suzie, and Suzie had now drained her drink and settled down to sunbathe. 'It would be an awful faff with Ruby,' Meg said, hopeful that Suzie hadn't drifted off, and might start listening, 'I don't know if I could be bothered traipsing her around the city.'

'Leave her with Zed,' Suzie said as she flapped her arm in Zed's general direction. 'He's worse than Ruby going round the shops.'

Zed shrugged his shoulders, 'Yeah, why not? Go and see the Uffizi, get your arses pinched.'

Their day trip to Pisa the previous week hadn't been a resounding success. The sky was grey and thousands of tourists jostled for the exact spot where you could take a photo holding up the Leaning Tower. Thunder had rolled in the sky so they had taken refuge in the Baptistery. Suzie plopped herself onto a bench at the door and said she would mind Ruby leaving Zed and Meg to wander.

Instinctively they had started off in opposite directions and it was only after ten minutes that they met up again on the balcony.

'What you snapping?' Zed asked.

'The window,' Meg replied as she took her camera down from her eye and changed the lens. Zed looked up to two stained glass windows — one showed some saint or other while the other consisted of just feet, a head and plain glass in between where the body should have been.

'Don't tell me, you were taking the damaged guy?'

'I took photos of them both,' she said. 'You appreciate more the less there is to see though.'

Zed shrugged and went back to Suzie, but Meg was determined to take her time. She stopped every couple of steps to photograph the columns or the crowds. Then a sharp clap of hands made her jump to attention.

'Silenco. Silenco por favour.' His tone was brusque, but the guard's walk to the centre of the Baptistery was casual.

Everyone in the whole place turned to face him. Was he going to throw them out for being sacrilegious? He cupped his hands to his mouth and turned his face upwards. One clear note came from him and spiralled towards the dome, followed by another and another until he had formed a chord reverberating around them.

He paused, let the sound dissipate then he started again. This time a minor chord, pure and true. And again, and again. He took a mini bow when he was finished but the crowd waited, breath held, until the last echo sounded and they dared to applause.

Meg didn't clap — she was too busy trying to stop the tears which were streaming down her face. She was glad it too her a few minutes to walk back to the stairs and down the stone spiral back to Zed and Suzie. Ruby had been released from her pushchair so Meg was able to lift her and hold her should any more tears come while Zed talked about the experience.

'That was amazing, eh? As though God was answering that bloke's call.'

'For fuck's sake Zed,' Suzie said, 'you're an atheist who knows about acoustics, you don't need to over-dramatize. Now come on, if I don't get out of this church I might kill someone.'

The taxi arrived at the villa at 8 a.m. the next morning, announced discreetly by the maid who came in to clear away their breakfast dishes. Suzie draped a black linen jacket round her shoulders while Meg went through Ruby's routine again.

'Make sure she keeps her hat on,' she said, unconvinced that leaving Ruby was a good idea.

'I will.'

'And don't leave her outside on her own. She moves that quickly now, you can't take your eyes off her, even for a second.'

Zed bent down and picked the crawling Ruby off the floor. 'I know Meg, now will you go and enjoy yourself, you can trust me.' He lifted Ruby's hand and waved it as Meg finally went over to the taxi. 'See you mum,' he said and Meg was overwhelmed by how like her dad Ruby looked.

Meg looked across at Suzie to see if she had noticed too, but Suzie was backing into the taxi, straightening her skirt and tucking in her legs.

They started at the Accademia Gallery, Suzie map in hand, marching between one religious icon and the next. Meg tried to take her time, paying attention to composition and light, but Suzie didn't hide her impatience, tapping the map against her thigh if Meg paused too long. She had little more than a glance at Michelangelo's Peita with its anguished Mary before Suzie pulled her towards David and stopped. Throngs of people filled the gallery — tour guides speaking in Italian, Japanese, broken English. It was only when they moved on that Meg and Suzie edged forward and started the slow walk around the statue.

'Do you miss Kyle?' Suzie asked as they considered the perfection of the boy David's buttocks.

Meg spluttered a laugh, which caused some large Americans to tut, but her eyes were drawn to the stone David held in his hand, ready to slay the giant. 'I suppose,' Meg said, finally answering Suzie's question. 'Things have been awkward, you know.'

Suzie ran her hand around the marble plinth. 'Zed's getting restless,' Suzie said with sadness in her voice, 'and when he gets restless he starts doing stupid things.'

'Is he?' Meg said, hoping that she wasn't one of the stupid things Suzie was referring to. 'I thought he seemed quite chilled.'

'That's just since you got here. I've been worried he's so bored he might start using again, that's why I decided to get people out here, take his mind of things.' She took a step back and examined the statue from head to toe, then looked down again at her guidebook. 'The piece of marble was called Goliath. Michelangelo said that the statue was already inside it and all he had to do was get it out.'

Meg smiled. 'My god, they're all the same, aren't they? Kyle says things like that, *"you just have to listen to the world and hear its beat before you can make it into a song"*.'

'*Yeah man*,' Suzie said imitating Zed, '*it's like it just emerges when we're jamming man.*'

The girls laughed together for the first time in ages and Meg said, 'Thank you for inviting us over. I wasn't looking forward to the summer.'

'Yeah?' Suzie sounded a bit surprised, 'I thought you enjoyed being back in Glasgow, and having a baby always seemed to be what you wanted.'

'More than you could know,' Meg said sighing, 'But I didn't expect to be doing it on my own. I'd forgotten what it was like to be on lonely, you know?'

'So get Kyle back. Just let him know you need him.' Suzie said a matter-of-fact way.

'It's not as simple as that,' Meg said, knowing that it was getting more complicated the more time she and Ruby spent with Zed.

But Suzie looked straight at her. 'I think it would be good for all of us,' she said, and turned towards the exit.

They had lunch near the Duomo but Suzie complained that the shops had closed for siesta, and they'd wasted the morning looking at art. Throughout lunch she criticised the service and gave a loud swingeing commentary on the passers-by making Meg wonder if Suzie's brandy after their bottle of wine was such a good idea. But they soon joined the tourists again and walked round to the square where the Duomo and Campanile stood. Meg took her camera out of her bag, attached the wide angle lens and drifted away from Suzie to get some pictures and some peace. Every step brought a new focal point: carvings of angels and Saints; mosaics of religious scenes; and intricate work that made stone columns look like lace. She changed lens again, putting on a macro and started to photograph the inlaid marble panels. She was jealous of the art and the craft of it, trying to capture some of the beauty on film, but worrying that she lacked the skill.

She'd been to a gallery in Glasgow, and while the owner had been kind, he'd been unimpressed by her work. '*I don't know. People don't really want pictures of someone else's kid on their walls. Maybe if you had some of your husband...they would sell. No. I suppose you've got a good eye for composition and they might be good enough to get you into the Art School, if you expanded your portfolio a bit, but I couldn't sell them here,*' he'd said. She'd managed to thank him, and get back to the car before she'd started to cry — if she didn't have photography what did she have? But by the time she'd got home she was rational enough to phone the Art School and ask for a prospectus. If she was honest she had never felt like a photographer, it was Kyle who had pushed her into it and Cerise who had encouraged it, but now she wanted to take ownership. So she concentrated, thought how each shot would fit into her portfolio. It was only when Suzie hit her on the arm that she remembered she was not alone.

'Sorry Suzie, isn't this place amazing? Do you want to go in?'

'Not really, but there's nothing else to do.'

They made their way up to the little Italian woman at the church door whose job it was to stop those in shorts or vests and point at the sign which required visitors to dress appropriately. 'Shows you how much they know about respectability if they let us in?' Suzie said loudly as they went in unhindered, their long straight skirts and oversized t-shirts meeting with approval.

The bright, cool of the interior was a welcome relief after the wilting heat, and Meg thought for a moment that she should be more grateful for the Glasgow weather. Small Italian women knelt at the altar saying their rosary, black mantillas covering their heads. She itched to get closer to inspect the lace but she knew it was an intrusion too far. Instead she watched their lips, mouthed the words she remembered from school and said a little prayer that Ruby would never be afraid. They moved on and Meg stopped occasionally to point her camera down to the mosaic floor, or up to the magnificent frescos in the dome. Suzie stood close to her shoulder, impeding Meg's movements, and limiting the number of shots she took.

'What's next?' Suzie asked when they came into the sunshine again.

'Would you mind if we go back?' Meg said, 'I've had a great day, but I don't want Ruby to start missing me.'

'She'll be fine,' Suzie said in a tone that wouldn't be argued with, 'you've had your fun, now it's my turn. The shops will surely be open now.'

'OK,' Meg said, but she found a pay phone and called Zed before she went on.

There was a Porsche 911 and a large silver Mercedes parked outside the villa when the taxi drew up. 'Are you expecting visitors?' Meg said turning to Suzie who didn't seem in the least surprised. Instead she shrugged, leant forward, counted out thousands of lire and tipped the driver when he lifted out their shopping bags and placed them on the doorstep.

As they walked towards the house Meg could hear music coming over and through the house. And Australian voices. She turned to Suzie who was grinning behind her. 'Surprise!' Suzie said.

Meg rushed through the house and out to the courtyard and the pool beyond.

'Here they are,' Zed said and as he turned he revealed Wayne and Mac behind him.

'Hey girls,' Mac said, coming over to embrace them.

Then Meg heard a woman say 'Hello', and as she feared it was Clare. But as Meg turned, Clare came towards her with open arms. She'd changed in the past few months since Meg had last seen her, less perfect but better somehow, like she'd just had a really good massage and all the tension had floated away.

'Oh hi,' Meg said, accepting the unexpectedly warm hug.

'You look amazing,' Clare said without any sarcasm in her voice. Meg felt hot and sticky, but she didn't care what Clare thought of her anymore. *If Mac and Wayne were here then...*

'Did you know these guys were coming?' Zed asked Suzie as Meg continued to exchange hellos.

'Of course,' Suzie said, 'Aren't I just full of surprises?'

'And Kyle?' Meg asked, barely daring to speak his name.

Ruby's cries from an open window made Suzie look up, 'Sounds like someone needs you,' Suzie said with a cocked eyebrow.

Meg hurried to her bedroom, her heart beating quickly, and then she heard it, under Ruby's increased cries, the familiar tones. 'It's okay Ruby, Daddy's here.'

'Kyle?' Meg pushed open the bedroom door to see Kyle crouched next to the cot trying to soothe a scarlet-faced Ruby.

'Just lift her,' Meg said, walking towards them, excited to see Kyle again, but concerned at her daughter's distress.

'She keeps hitting me away,' Kyle said, looking almost as upset as Ruby.

Meg bent, but when Kyle didn't present his lips to her she lifted Ruby out of the cot and gave her the reassuring kiss. 'No wonder she's screaming, she's soaked through.'

Kyle didn't move to stand up, so Meg set about stripping Ruby while she tried to gauge the mood. She looked at her watch and decided she might as well give Ruby a bath, so she went into the adjacent bathroom, put Ruby on the tiled floor and turned the taps before speaking to Kyle again. 'I can't believe you're here. Suzie hadn't said anything about you coming.'

'No, Zed didn't know either. Looks like she's been scheming again.' Kyle moved over to a chair by the window and sat down, looking more uneasy than Meg had ever seen him.

'I missed you, Kyle,' she said. It was certainly true when she was in Glasgow, but with Zed and Suzie for company she'd hardly thought about him. She tentatively put her arms around him. *Zed and Suzie, when had their names switched places in her head? She really needed to get a grip on reality.* 'I'm really glad you're here.'

Kyle squeezed her slightly, but his attention was focused on Ruby who had reappeared in the bedroom and was slide-crawling over the floor.

'She's scared of me Meg. I was watching her nap and she woke up, saw me and started screaming.'

'She was wet, that's all. And five months is a long time for her.' She didn't add that it was a long time for her too.

'I know. I can't believe how she's grown. She looks bigger than in the photos you sent.'

'Nearly walking,' Meg said and they looked at her together for a few moments before Meg continued. 'Why didn't you say you were coming? It's so fabulous, but…' Meg jumped to stop Ruby pulling a lamp down on top of herself, then lifted her chubby body and went to check on the bath.

Kyle came and stood in the doorway. 'According to Suzie, Zed thought we should get back together and finish the album we'd started. Since everyone was in Europe here seemed like the best place to meet.'

Meg turned off the taps with more force than she meant. He had come back for MindSet, not her. And what did her mean *everyone was in Europe? Had he not been in America?* She plopped Ruby in the bath, persuaded her to put on the visor Suzie had bought to prevent shampoo getting into her eyes and started to drizzle water over Ruby's head.

'How was LA?' Meg asked as casually as she could. 'I never managed to catch you at home.'

'Yeah, good,' Kyle said.

'Did the sessions go well?'

'Think so. Squander's management seemed happy, and most of the band were too. A lot of fighting for a first album but they can always bump the troublemaker — that's what I'd do.'

Meg scooped more water over Ruby's hair and began to massage in some strawberry scented shampoo. 'So do you reckon you guys can make an album without fighting? The last time you were together you didn't produce much.' Meg said, knowing that after she had left for Scotland all talk of a new album had evaporated.

'I was distracted then,' Kyle said, 'It's done with — we can move on.' Meg wondered if he was talking about them or MindSet but didn't know if she was strong enough to hear the answer.

The gong in the hall sounded for dinner, so Meg fished Ruby out, dried her and put her into a nappy and sleepsuit. She was in a much better mood after her bath so Meg handed her over to Kyle without a fuss, while she put on a clean top and changed the sheets in the cot.

As Kyle and Meg took their seats Suzie told the assembled company about the wonderful platter of antipasto they'd had for lunch and poked fun at Meg for taking photos of it.

'The textures were good,' Meg said, 'and the colours.' Meg knew no one was remotely interested, so turned the conversation to the wonders of Michelangelo, but before she could talk about the amazing sculpture Suzie butted in.

'You should have seen her Kyle,' Suzie said, 'she's been so starved of love she was almost ready to hump the statue.'

Meg frowned at Suzie who was draining another goblet of wine. She'd felt a low-grumbling resentment since she had arrived, and even when Suzie was being friendly it felt less genuine, like she knew And now that Suzie had an audience it looked like she was about to erupt. Clare came to Meg's rescue.

'I'd like to see David, if you wouldn't be bored going back. You know all these months we've been in Venice and yet we've never travelled to see one of the most wonderful works of art man has ever produced.'

'Hey, what about my art?' Mac said, giving her a playful swipe on the arm, she cooed her lips and they kissed before Kyle broke in.

'You'd hardly call what we do art? Rock should be the antithesis of art. Hunger — not beauty.'

'When have you ever been hungry?' Mac snarled, but Clare butted in, extending her role of peacemaker.

'He's not talking about music,' she said, rolling her eyes at Kyle. 'He's talking about his painting. He's becoming quite accomplished. That's why we moved to Venice, for the mood.'

'Now moods he is good at,' Kyle said under his breath.

'I'll never be as good a painter as you,' Mac said keeping his attention on Clare, he lifted her hand to kiss it and Meg watched as the chivalry subtly turned to something more sexual, his tongue nipping out to lick between her fingers. He moved his lips along her index finger, and took it into his mouth. Clare sighed, her eyes fixed on Mac with an intensity matched by the rest of the table.

'I didn't know you could paint,' Kyle said to the tiny space between Clare and Mac.

'There's a lot you don't know, Kyle,' Clare said dismissively. Meg prayed for someone to break the awkwardness. She looked over to Suzie who usually had so much to say, but Suzie's eyes were on Ruby who sat quietly in her buggy, sucking a cloth book. A breeze came through the open window and gently moved the black curls on her forehead and she gave a little giggle as though the angels were tickling her. But there was a look of sadness on Suzie's face which concerned Meg.

'So, you liking the slide guitar of *Texas?'* Zed asked anyone who would listen, and within seconds there was a full blown discussion about what people were listening to, and how there was a more soulful feel to music than there had been even a few months before. Thankfully Zed said nothing about how he had become an expert on new Scottish bands and Meg decided it was safer to let the boys talk without interruption from her.

Clare smiled across at Meg. 'I think I could live here, couldn't you?'

Meg nodded. It was the first normal thing Clare had ever said to her and it took her a moment to think how to respond. Questions were always good. 'So, tell me about Venice.'

Clare and Meg chatted through the primo and secondo courses, but by the time dessert was served Suzie had managed to draw Clare on what she thought of Versace's collection and was it true that she had turned down an offer to model for him.

'I should get Ruby to bed,' Meg said when she realised that the grizzles of the last few minutes were beginning to get louder. She wiped her mouth and put her crumpled napkin on the table.

'I'll take her,' Suzie said and moved over to the buggy, jerked the brake off and spun Ruby round but Meg kept walking towards them and kept her voice calm. 'It's fine — I've hardly seen her all day.' Suzie didn't take her hands off the handles, so Meg reached down, unbuckled Ruby and lifted her out.

Kyle stood up and nodded a goodnight to the table. 'I'll come with you,' he said.

While Ruby was settled, Kyle went out to the balcony overlooking the gravel driveway at the front of the house. It was dark except for the small glow from the carriage lights on either side of the front door, and if the moon hadn't been full, Kyle would have disappeared. As it was, his white linen trousers and gauze top looked blue in the moonlight. Meg stayed next to Ruby's cot for a few minutes longer and thought about her conversation with Suzie earlier and her swimming lessons. *It was a kiss of congratulations*, she thought, she'd swum a breadth and Zed was just saying *well done.* But the pressure of his lips, his hands, his body, had made an indelible imprint. She closed her eyes, thought of Suzie and Kyle. Opened them, and thought of Ruby. She went out to Kyle, closing the French windows behind her with a gentle click, causing Kyle to turn towards her. He looked gorgeous sitting there, and if that was all that matter she could be happy forever.

'Will she sleep 'til morning?' Kyle asked.

'I hope so. I forgot to ask Zed when he put her down.'

'Four.'

'I didn't realise you were here that early.'

'Have you left Ruby with *him* much?' Kyle asked.

She answered quickly, 'No, just today. Looks like Suzie hatched a plot so that I'd get a surprise to come back and find you here.'

'Not too much of a shock I hope,' Kyle said, continuing to speak quietly as he looked down at his hands.

Meg leant across and took his hands in hers, 'No. Of course not.'

But he took his hands away and sat back into his chair. 'I met your friend in LA,' he said with more force.

'I didn't know I had a friend in LA.'

'Magenta, or whatever the fuck she's called.'

Meg cringed at the thought of her. 'Hardly a friend after all that's happened.' Meg stopped and considered how much of it really was Cerise's fault, and how much was Kyle's over-reaction. 'How on earth did you meet her?' she asked when she realised Kyle wasn't going to go on unprompted. 'I wouldn't have thought you moved in the same circles.'

'Her friend cut my hair. I'm not sure if it was a set up or what, but Squander told me about this fantastic girl he knew and when I got there, Magenta was there too.'

'Cerise,' Meg said in a whisper, 'Cerise and Pol.'

'That's right, a colour and a bloke's name — bloody weird. She's pretty though. You've got good taste.'

Meg got up and walked to the balustrade, she wasn't going to discuss her ex-girlfriend with her husband. San Francisco seemed, was, so long ago and yet it continued to drive a wedge between them. She fixed her eyes on the brightest star in the sky, watched it blur and wobble, listened to the rising noise of the cicadas. She clenched her hands around the railing, needing something solid to anchor her.

'She wanted to apologise,' Kyle said after a while.

'What?' Meg turned to face him.

'She said she was sorry that she'd caused so much trouble between us. She's trying to make amends.'

'Why?' Meg asked with all the cynicism she felt. 'Twelve Step Programme or something?'

'Cancer.'

'Shit.' Meg turned from him again. 'Shit.'

Kyle came and stood beside her. 'She'd tried to contact you, but she heard I was in town and decided to meet me. She thought I needed to hear the apology as much as you. So nothing happened in Miami,' Kyle continued, 'only San Francisco?' His voice trailed off.

'I should never have asked her,' Meg said, 'but Miami was horrible.' She'd tried to forget about what had happened, and the despair she felt afterwards. Now the tension returned, the feelings of loss, of thinking Kyle had abandoned her for Clare, of losing the only thing that had been truly hers. 'I'd no one else to turn to.'

'You should have told me.' He placed his hand over hers and rested it there.

'You never gave me the chance. Okay, so in San Francisco Cerise and I were lovers, but you were with Clare then. It's not fair that you're still blaming me.'

'You should have told me.'

'I thought you didn't want to hear about my past, and you've never talked about yours.'

'Well maybe that's our problem,' Kyle said, 'too many secrets. I could have sorted out this licensing problem sooner if you'd told me.'

Meg pulled her hand away and took a step back from him. 'Is that all you're worried about? Business?'

'Not any more. It's sweet. I got my lawyer to draw up a contract — she continues to sell your work, but we get a cut.'

Meg closed her eyes. Rationally she knew he was just looking out for her, but it hurt like hell. 'Is that all that matters, not that we're not being truthful to one another?' she said finally when she thought she could speak without screaming.

'We'll be truthful from here on in,' Kyle said, 'if you're willing to give it another go.'

Meg thought for a moment and looked out again at the starry sky. There must be art schools in Australia, she thought, and even though he hadn't exactly given a persuasive argument, Kyle seemed prepared to put the past behind them, so maybe she owed it to Ruby to make it beyond her first birthday still married.

'So is that it?' Zed asked as Meg poured a coffee the next morning. 'All forgiven?' He stood close to her and she could smell the chlorine from the morning swim she had missed. He reached across her for a mug, gently brushing the back of his hand against her breast.

'Don't Zed,' she said firmly. A couple of days ago, even the day before, she would have reacted differently, let his hand linger, return, add to the dozens of little intimacies they had sneaked passed Suzie, but she had committed to Kyle again.

'Me and Suzie,' he said, 'it's just out of habit, you know. Neither of us have the courage to end it.'

'Then don't,' Meg said. 'She stuck with you, Zed. She should be allowed to reap the rewards.' She didn't say the words *now you're clean,* knowing how destructive it was always splitting your life into *clean* and *unclean* compartments. 'You need to enjoy life now. You've got the money and nothing to tie you down.'

'I've been enjoying life more with you around.' He touched her cheek this time, and she couldn't resist letting her lips meet his fingers as they brushed over her mouth.

'I don't know why you're doing this to me Zed. You know Kyle's the best chance I've got.'

'For what?' Zed asked, looking intently into her eyes.

'Security…and…'

'He left you after the miscarriage. Threw you off when all that stuff came out about Cerise, and now you're just going to forgive all that.

'It was me who needed forgiving.'

'If you really think that Meg, then I'm truly worried for you.'

Before Meg could respond Ruby flew through the door, 'Whoosh,' high in the air at the end of Kyle's long arms. 'Aeroplane Ruby coming down to land.'

Ruby squealed with excitement as Kyle dropped her into the high chair and fastened her in. 'Right Ruby Tuesday, what we having for brekkie?'

As they ate, Meg looked at the men across from her — one tall and blonde, proud and inscrutable; the other nearer her own height and colouring, tender, vulnerable — both capable of breaking her heart in different ways.

Kyle poured attention on Ruby, complimenting every mouthful of cereal she managed to get into her mouth. 'What a good girl. Hasn't mama taught you well?' He was trying hard to impress her too.

Zed attacked his poached egg, slashing his knife across it so that the yolk bled onto his toast. 'I don't know if Mac's back on board,' Zed said. For a minute Meg thought he had said her name instead of biting out Mac's. 'He's pretty settled here you know with all his painting and stuff.'

'Nah,' Kyle said, dismissing Zed's concerns with a wave, 'we need to get back to work. He'll find out soon enough how expensive Clare is to keep. And Daddy needs to make some cents for his precious girls too.'

Meg coughed. Last night she'd been sure that sleeping with Kyle was the right thing to do. It had certainly felt right as they caressed each other's bodies. It was hardly a hardship to give Ruby back a father, but it was a father who peppered every sentence with another woman's name. *Would it ever stop?*

'Why does it always come back to bloody Clare?' she said when she couldn't keep it in any longer.

'I'm sorry babe, I didn't mean to.'

'You never do mean to, but you always do. Clare this, and Clare that. And if you'd bothered to talk to her last night rather than just bitch, you would know that she's gone all hippy. "*Material goods are of no interest to me now,*" "*All I need is enough for bread and vino rosso.*' Meg said in a mocking voice.

'Meg,' Kyle snapped, before he pulled his emotions back under control. 'Not in front of Ruby, or Zed.'

‘Forget it,’ Meg said throwing her napkin into the centre of the table. *Not in front of Zed?* Zed was the only one who had cared about her over the past few months, but it was too dangerous a thing to say, so she locked the words away and went to pack. She wouldn’t stay at the villa any longer.

1990

February: Vaucluse, Sydney

Out of Your Mind – MindSet

For those who thought they could do no wrong just listen to the much-delayed new offering by MindSet. After a long break, singer/songwriter Mac Marchmount takes a long journey into his subconscious where no serious music fan would dare to follow. Referencing Dali and Duchamp might go down well with the Europeans he's been hanging with, but the rest of the band seem to be at a loss — not knowing what music to throw at these ramblings. The resulting mess draws on too wide a range of styles and influences. The only bright point in the collection is the track Cuckoo, which makes us yearn for simpler times. We don't want art-house from these guys we want great solid rock.

Out of Your Mind — we think so.

'Everyone goes through this,' Kyle said as he threw the review to one side. 'It doesn't mean we're finished. We weren't spending enough time together and the lack of cohesion shows.'

Meg stood up to stretch her back, aching from pregnancy, and looked around the collected faces in the room. Zed bit his nails until she could see blood on his fingers; Wayne stared at Kyle's bottom lip and Mac wandered around the room, picking up ornaments and weighing them in his hand. Suzie and Clare pushed back on the sofa with identical looks of anticipation on their faces.

Kyle went on. 'I shouldn't have pushed for this one, and I'm sorry that I did, Italy was wrong for us, we didn't get the right flow of ideas. Maybe if we hadn't moved out of the villa…damn, I blame myself. But we need to put this into perspective — there isn't a band in history that didn't make one duff album, so this is ours. It's done, now we move forward.'

Mac turned around and sprang across the room, stopping just in front of Kyle. 'Duff album? It's the best thing I've ever written. Italy speaks to my soul. Why should we even care what the critics think?'

'Because if the critics don't like it, the fans won't buy it,' Kyle said.

'The fans will always buy it. If they're too stupid to understand the subtleties of our music then we can do without them,' Mac said punctuating with a pointed finger which got closer to Kyle's chest with every word.

'They pay our wages.' Kyle said, his voice getting louder.

'You've never needed wages, trust-fund boy,' Mac said, his voice taunting like a school yard bully.

'You're no different, Maclean,' Kyle said.

'Don't be a cock.'

Kyle threw the first punch. Mac swung the glass paperweight he had lifted from the piano and hit Kyle in the temple. Suzie grabbed for Mac. Meg leapt up to stop Kyle from retaliating and took Mac's spit in the face.

'Bastard!' Kyle shouted.

Mac struggled away from Suzie and left the room and then the house slamming both doors as he went. Clare gathered up her Birkin and ran out after him.

'So what do we do now?' Suzie asked, once the reverberation had stopped.

Meg wiped the spit off her face with her knuckles and said, 'Todd's meant to be confirming the US dates, but we need to be realistic and book smaller venues — the American reviews aren't any better.'

'I fired Todd this morning,' Kyle said.

Everyone looked at him in horror, but it took Meg to speak, 'You did what?'

'We don't need him anymore. Things aren't as big as they were, we all know that and we can do without his expenses.'

'Kyle, we've not even discussed this,' Zed said. 'You can't take a decision like this on your own, man.'

'I'm the leader of this band. It's my decision.'

Zed got to his feet, 'Just because you had the van when we were eighteen doesn't make you the leader of this band.'

'So who is? Tell me. I've made every decision for years. Me — not Todd. He was just there for the logistics.'

Zed sat quietly considering his response. 'I'm not happy about this,' was all he said before he took Suzie's hand and left too.

'This is crazy Kyle, you can't take on the management of the band, it's too much,' Meg said as she wrapped some ice in a napkin and held it up for him to put on the growing lump on his head.

'You can help, and Dave. We need to slim down a bit, get back to what really matters.'

'I can't help,' Meg said, 'I'm having a baby in a few weeks, I haven't even decided if I'm coming on tour with you and even if I do I'll be looking after the kids. And,' she said, thinking of even more reasons why it was crazy, 'Dave's loyal to Todd.' She didn't tell him that she'd heard rumours that Todd had been touting round other bands, obviously realising that his days with MindSet were numbered.

'Did I not say?' Wayne said from his position on the easy chair, 'but I've given up touring. I've got a gig as a TV gardener.'

'You?' Meg said.

'Sure. My roses won prizes at the Royal Adelaide Show and the producers reckon having a rock star presenter will bring the appeal of gardening to a new generation. I'm getting married too, a beautiful girl, she's a botanist.'

'Oh for fuck sake,' Kyle said, and left.

When Wayne finally stopped talking about his TV show and went home, Kyle emerged from his den, took Meg by the hand and led her to the bedroom. She sat on the bed and took a slug of heartburn medicine for the acid that was rising in her throat. Kyle closed the door with a flourish, and threw himself down beside her. 'It's going to be alright,' he said finally sitting up, 'we can set up a studio, help young kids get started. If MindSet's finished then we move on.'

'Is that it? MindSet finished?'

'I think getting your head smashed in counts as splitting up due to artistic differences,' Kyle said touching the large red mark on his head.

'So I write my last press release tomorrow?'

'We can always watch Wayne on TV,' he said laughing as pushed Meg's shoulders down and tried to negotiate his way over her bump. 'I'm excited about this, I really am,' Kyle said.

'Really?' Meg asked. 'MindSet's been your life.' It had been her life too, but she couldn't let this become about her even though she felt the impact. She'd grown up with them, become a woman and a wife, become a mother. And what about Zed and Suzie? She couldn't imagine a time when they weren't all mucking about together. But they wouldn't have any reason to now.

'We move on,' Kyle said, as if he could read her thoughts. 'What else can we do — it's finished.' He kissed her hungrily, his arms quivering to keep his weight from pressing down too hard

'Maybe we should switch round,' Meg said and she slipped out from under him, took off her pregnancy support pants and dimmed the lights. She couldn't believe he was taking the death of the group so calmly. She knelt on the bed not willing to uncover her stretched skin as she watched Kyle strip. She wondered how his toned body would change when he wasn't drumming every day. And how would it affect him? He'd been in a state of low level anger for the last few weeks since the album was finally completed and the reviews had started dripping in. But now he seemed excited that he could make plans for something totally new, something he didn't have to share with three other men.

Naked, Kyle lay on the bed again and she climbed on top of him. She was uncomfortable and ugly, a pregnancy mask dappling her face, indigestion burning in her chest.

'That's it,' Kyle said encouraging her manoeuvres as his hands roamed over her body.

'Shit.'

'What?'

Meg stopped moving. 'Sorry, it's just the baby's kicking really hard. It's moving too much now. Sorry.' She ended the conversation with a slow kiss, and tried to get going again. The baby kicked again, this time rippling through to Kyle's stomach.

'That hurt,' he said.

'Tell me about it — I'm cushioning the blows here. The baby's always really active at this time of night. Just ignore it.'

But Kyle put his hands on her shoulders again, pushed her off and walked naked to the bathroom and closed the door. 'Forget it.'

Perfect. She was tired and fat, and really just wanted some antacid and a hot bath, but duty drove her to the bathroom door. She knocked. 'Why don't you run the bath? There's room enough for all three of us in there.'

Kyle opened the door and squeezed passed her. 'I'm going to grab a beer and pull some figures together. I don't think I could sleep just now but you look shattered. Get some sleep.'

Meg stood in the doorway, her mind switching off to protect it from the rebuke. Then she ran the bath, poured in more bubbles than she needed and sat and cried.

Kyle and Meg Watt (née Burns) are delighted to announce the birth of Joseph Kenneth Watt on 8th of March 1990, a brother for Ruby. Another little rocker.

When the baby arrived Kyle shone out of him like the sun. His blonde curls, bright blue eyes and, within weeks, smiles that quickly turned to giggles. He had been called Joseph for the few days Meg stayed in hospital, but one kangaroo soft toy followed another and when she held him close he became her Joey. Motherhood was so much easier second time around. She had been frightened every time she lifted Ruby that she might break, but Meg was more confident with Joey, not worrying that any wrong move might screw up his whole life. Ruby was even allowed to sit in the corner of a chair and rest his head on the cushions and she would smile down at him, but otherwise she paid little attention to her new brother.

Meg had grown more used to being in charge too. Her nanny from Glasgow had been let go, with a phone call and a cheque, and now a matronly woman called Jane ruled over the children, with strict ideas about when they could be stimulated and when they had to rest. But Meg didn't feel she had to explain herself if she disagreed with their schedule.

'I'm taking the kids to the beach now. They can nap in their buggy after they've had a play.'

She bumped into Zed once or twice after she had mentioned on the phone how she liked to walk around Neilsen Park after lunch.

'How's Suzie?'

'Fine. And Kyle?'

'Yeah, the same.'

They'd walk for a while, talking about nothing in particular then Zed would splash about in the shallows with Ruby before they would all seek shelter from the sun in a café and have ice creams. Meg never asked him how he spent his days, not wanting the void of no MindSet reflected in his eyes.

Occasionally on a Sunday afternoon Eleanor would swan over to see them, or more usually command that she wanted a visit and they would put on their best clothes for the presentation.

'That girl's hair is getting rather unruly,' she said one day. 'I hope they are just baby curls. You don't want her growing up with hair like that.'

Meg did her best not to rise to the bait, and she kept her counsel after they'd left. She had learned early on that only Kyle was allowed to criticize his mother, and her mother, and her.

She took snips of the children's curls, put them in her memory box, in case they would straighten with age, and for the first time in her life she began to wonder if the curls were a legacy from her father.

Miss Newton stretched out her hand and silenced the metronome. 'You're not paying attention to the rhythm Mrs Watt,' she said, and Meg realised her mind was miles away.

'You need to listen, tick, tick, tick — follow it — tick, tick, tick.'

'I was just bringing my own interpretation to the music. You're allowed to do that, right?' Meg said, in the hope that it would fool the teacher.

'Only when it is by choice — not because your fingers can't keep up,' Miss Newton said with a shrill tone. 'If you'll allow me, I'm surprised it's taking you so long to pick up the basics. Ruby is progressing faster than you, and she's barely three.

'I suppose her talent comes from her dad. He's the musician in the family.'

Kyle thought it would be good for them, although Meg had argued that Ruby was far too you to appreciate it. '*Nonsense.*' Kyle had said, '*I was playing the piano and violin at her age,*' and that was the end of the conversation.

'You need to up the practice then Mrs Watt, don't you?' Miss Newton said, making Meg feel like a child again. 'Your hands are less supple than Ruby's so you have to work harder. After all, wouldn't it be magnificent to have this beautiful piano sing again?'

The teacher stroked the baby grand and Meg wondered if she should just give her the bloody piano and be done with it, since Meg's abuse of it offended her so much. Maybe a cheap upright like her granny's old one would have lowered Miss Newton's expectations.

Learning to play fell into the same category as joining the tennis club and the riding lessons — things to do while Kyle got WattAge up and running. But the queasy feeling she had from the moment she opened her eyes every Tuesday morning made her wonder if music really was for her. She could feel its effects alright through the vibrations that entered her eardrums and soles; the lyrics that wormed their way unchecked into her memory and the melody that made her cry for no reason. But she was kidding herself that it was her life-force.

She'd had chances enough in the past, when Tam would prod her. '*Their backing singer has gone AWOL/got a sore throat/passed out backstage. They're desperate pet, you go for it.*' But she hadn't gone for it. She hadn't felt the compulsion to shoobedoowap or bapbapbap babababababa into a microphone. She had never even felt the need to sing in the shower like you were supposed to. So why the hell was she putting herself through this torture?

Miss Newton tapped her pencil on the top of the music book. 'Let's take it from the top again.'

June: Vaucluse, Sydney

'I've been speaking to an editor about getting my diaries published,' Zed said rather sheepishly when the four of them were having dinner at the surf club one cool July night.

Meg looked at him in horror, 'You're kidding, right?'

'God, Meg you should see your face. Are you worried he's stealing your thunder?' Suzie said in a snide tone that was becoming habitual. 'Meg — the great documenter of MindSet's history.'

Meg shook her head, not recognising the picture Suzie painted, but Suzie continued, 'Zed needs to raise his profile, and I think it's a great idea.' She raised a glass of champagne to it, but wasn't joined in the toast.

'It's just, you always said your diaries were private,' Meg said, ignoring Suzie now and looking into Zed's eyes, feeling slightly sick. Why had he never mentioned this when they were out walking together?

'My God, Meg,' Kyle said forcing her to acknowledge his presence in the room, 'you would think he'd something to hide.'

'Other than the drug-taking and larceny,' Suzie laughed.

Zed addressed Meg's fear straight on, 'They'll be edited of course.'

'But not too much or no one will want to buy them,' Suzie cut in.

'Do you really think it's a good idea? I know you wrote them, but they're not just about you — other people will be affected too,' Meg said.

'That's why you're here,' Suzie said and Zed gave a little nod of agreement.

'Well it's fine by me,' Kyle said. 'It'll be good to remember some of the old times.'

'Surely anything you've forgotten isn't worth remembering,' Meg said trying desperately to pour cold water on the idea.

'It's for the fans, Meg, and let's face it, we could do with the money,' Suzie said.

'I know Todd's court case took its toll on the finances but if you'd invested like I told you…' Kyle said obviously irritated his advice hadn't been taken. Zed shrugged. And Meg wondered if Kyle would ever see life as anything other than business.

'There's a bit put away — trust funds and stuff,' Zed said.

'Yes,' Suzie said, 'well these blind funds are all very well, but we've got expenses now, and the book would help cover them. Everyone else has agreed.'

'You've spoken to the others?' Kyle asked, and when Zed nodded he said, 'Sure, go for it,' Kyle said.

Meg shifted in her seat. She wanted to ask if her opinion counted for anything, but Zed, and particularly Suzie, seemed so hell bent on the whole thing that she was worried the answer would be *no.* Zed picked up on her anxiety again, and her annoyance that this was the first she'd heard of it.

‘I meet the editor once a week and we go through the bits of the diaries that I think are relevant. We only copy those pages — no one gets to see the rest.’

‘Not even me,’ Suzie said, ‘it annoys the hell out of me, but then,’ she paused and called for another bottle of champagne, ‘I suppose everyone needs some privacy.’

Meg thought she didn’t sound that convinced.

As they got ready for bed Kyle began to needle Meg about what had happened in the restaurant.

‘Why did you have such a downer on Zed’s book? It’s obvious Suzie’s spending money faster than it’s being made. You need to butt out of their plans.’

‘I can’t butt out, not when it affects me, us,’ Meg said correcting herself and angry that Kyle had taken their side over hers.

Kyle came and stood right in front of her, towering over her as she sat at her dressing table. ‘What are you so frightened that he’ll reveal Meg? What secrets does he know?’

There was only one secret that Meg was certain of, the one that used to terrify her the most, but now it seemed the easiest one of all to tell. ‘You’ve got no idea have you?’ she said, the anger inside her rising. ‘All these years together and you’ve still got no idea. Do you really think I left Glasgow because you guys were the best band I’d ever seen? Are you really that arrogant? I needed to get away. I put a man in hospital the night before I left and it was only a matter of time before the police tracked me down or someone grassed me up.'

Kyle took a step back and looked at her with an expression of disbelief Meg had never seen before. 'You put a man in hospital?'

So Zed never did tell him. 'He attacked me.' Meg spoke very slowly. The vision of that night had been in her mind often over the years, but she had only twice put the words together to explain what had happened. 'I was fly-posting. Val was meant to be with me, but she had gone off with Mac. I went on my own. You're always on the look-out for the cops — making sure you don't get caught. But this guy, he came up so suddenly that I didn't see him. I couldn't stop him.'

She stopped, felt the fear again. 'He pulled me down this lane. There were people there, prostitutes, who gave my description to the police, but no one came to help. I managed to get hold of a rock and I whacked him. I must have caught his eye or something because he started bleeding really badly.'

'And you didn't go to the police?'

'I just wanted to go home. I thought if my mum was back she would know what to do, but she wasn't. So I went to school the next day like normal and I met you that night.'

Kyle was quiet for a long time then he said quietly, 'Did you ever tell your mum?'

'Not then,' Meg said, 'but a few weeks later. The police were looking for me — I had to tell her why.'

'What did she say?' he asked.

'She said I shouldn't have gone out alone? I don't know, maybe she was right.'

'You know she's not right. This is horrendous. You have to phone the police. Can you remember what he looked like? You could still get him prosecuted.'

Meg shook her head. 'He's dead.'

Kyle came over and held her, but it didn't feel like how she had imagined it would. Then Kyle pulled back from her again. 'I still don't see what this has got to do with Zed?'

'He knew about it,' Meg said, getting into bed and trying to sound as casual as she could.

'But you didn't tell me?'

'He found out. You remember him joking that I was some sort of assassin, well, that was why. I just don't want him to put it in his book.'

'I suppose I understand that,' Kyle said, 'I'll phone the lawyer in the morning, put an injunction on him.'

'No, it's fine,' Meg said. 'I'll speak to Zed.'

'Whatever you think is best,' Kyle said getting into bed turning on the TV to watch the replay of The Swans game while Meg closed her eyes tightly.

Kyle's low voice in another room, and she's tossing and turning, pushing out her arms and legs in the empty bed, then Zed standing with a bloody knife in his hands, a girl in a fisherman's cap with a bloodied stone, a needle, a river. 2:02 she closes her eyes and this time her camera spools out guts that wrap around her legs and pull tight. She falls. Hits the bottom. Awake. She sits up, gasping.

The housekeeper said that Kyle had left the house just as she had arrived at 8am, and no, he hadn't said when he would be home. Meg went into the den and tried to call him, but his cell was switched off, and there was no reply at the recording studio. She left a casual message, trying to keep out of her voice the question of how he could just get up and leave after all she had told him.

Then it struck her, he had gone to see Zed. She lifted the phone again and dialled. 'Hi Zed, is Kyle there?'

'No,' Zed replied, 'should he be?'

'No, I don't suppose so.'

'Are you okay? You sound a bit stressed.' Zed said, and the question immediately brought up a bubble of emotion that had been tight in her stomach since she had woken.

'It's just the diary thing,' she said. 'I had to tell him.'

'You told him what we did?' Zed asked.

'We didn't do anything.' Without thinking she had stressed the first word, and Zed immediately picked up on it.

'Ok, what I did.'

'I didn't mean that,' she said quickly. 'I'm sorry Zed. I mean I told him about the attacker, just the start of it, nothing else. I'll never tell him anything else. I've promised you that. But all this talk about the diaries, it's brought it all up again. You can't write about it Zed, it's too dangerous.'

'I won't Meg. I've promised you that. I'm not going to jeopardise what we have.'

Meg wondered for a moment what they did have. Listening to his reassurance she could almost feel him next to her; holding her head up out of the water; not letting her drown; teaching her to swim; spinning Ruby above his head at the beach; Joey smiling in his sleep as though an angel was whispering in his ear. And Zed, Zed kissing her on both cheeks when they said goodbye; holding her just long enough for it not to feel casual.

'Do you want to meet Meg? Bring the kids to the beach and I'll tell you exactly what's going to be published.'

'No, it's fine,' she said. She had made her decision in Tuscany — she wasn't going to change her mind. 'I trust you. I've just got to find Kyle now. I'm going to wander down to WattAge and see if I can catch him there.'

She had only been to the studio a couple of times, but she knew the way without needing her map. When Kyle came up with his grand plan to give something back to the city, Meg insisted that he should base the studio in one of the poorer areas. '*You might only get the middle class kids coming down,*' she had said, '*but at least they'll be able to see what places like this look like.*'

When she got there the grill was pulled across the entrance to the building, but it wasn't padlocked. The lights were out in the entrance hallway, but the doors were unlocked, so Meg checked the rehearsal rooms before coming into the studio. The engineer jumped to his feet in the mixing booth when he saw her, but Paul, the project manager, didn't stir from his morning nap.

Meg waved through to the sound engineer then knocked Paul's feet off the amp.

'What the fuck? Oh, Mrs Watt. Sorry I didn't realise you were coming today.'

'Obviously,' Meg said, looking around the place at the discarded Coke bottles and old copies of the *Daily Telegraph.* 'I'm just looking for Kyle. I thought he said he was working with some new band, Candy Cane, is it?'

'Mmm,' Paul said.

Meg pulled up a tall stool and sat down, giving herself a height advantage. She didn't like the vibe she was getting. 'So, how many people have you got using the studio?'

'Don't know, not many,' Paul replied.

Meg stared at him, Kyle had been so keen to set up the studio and had been working so hard at it, but it didn't seem to have taken off. She looked down at her hands and felt the heaviness of the diamonds on her fingers. She had made it out of an area like this, but she remembered how cynical she had been when anyone tried to help her. 'What are you doing about it then? Have you been round the schools?' she asked, looking him directly in the eyes, 'I'm sure there are loads of kids crying out for a place like this.'

Paul pulled out a cigarette. 'Outreach work isn't in our job description.' He lit up.

His arrogance flicked a switch inside her, 'Are you kidding me? You're meant to be running this place. You're not getting paid to be sitting here on your arse smoking. You're meant to be helping kids — is that not what you signed up for?'

He shrugged.

'We're funding this out of our own pockets, you know,' Meg said, getting angrier. 'Now I need you to get out there and make this place work. Consider it part of your job.'

'Look Mrs Watt,' he said, 'I know you guys are new to all of this but I've been working in projects all my days and if it's not in the job description then I'm not obliged. And anyway, Kyle's in charge.'

'We're both in charge. And,' she said, deciding on the spot, 'I'm going to be more involved now. You're right I'm new to bureaucracy and job descriptions, but I've worked in this industry all my days and you get stuck in and get things sorted. Okay? Otherwise it's going to be difficult for us to work together. Now where did you say Kyle was?'

'Sorry Mrs Watt,' Paul said, 'lunch break.' He knocked the glass to the sound booth, and signalled for the sound engineer to come with him, but he shook his head and carried on rewinding cables.

When Paul had gone Brian spoke through the intercom. 'Don't mind him, he's a bit of a waster, I'll help you. I'm fed up listening to the clock tick.'

'Thanks,' Meg said and she didn't ask where Kyle was again.

2nd of Nov 1990

Over the next few months Meg and Brian put up posters and handed fliers into the high schools. The phone started ringing and young guys began to pop in to check out the space and see what studio time was on offer. Meg carried on working quietly, building the organisation and relishing having something other than the kids to keep her busy. Even Paul's mood lifted when they started a beginners' guitar class and local bands came to lay down tracks and ask for his advice. Zed did a couple of masterclasses and even Wayne popped down, although it was middle-aged women who swarmed the place with withered plants in their hands when he came.

At 5 p.m. Meg made her way back home. They had been living parallel lives for weeks, Meg eating with the kids, Kyle never needing more than a midnight snack when he came home. So she was surprised to see Kyle's car parked outside the house so early. She pulled her Mercedes in next to his and looked through the window of the family room to see Ruby dancing in front of the TV. She loved the fact that Ruby was so carefree, twirling around in her pink tutu, waving her magic wand at a collection of soft toys watching TV with her, but Meg wondered why the nanny's car wasn't parked in her usual spot when she obviously wasn't out with the Ruby and Joey.

Meg opened the front door and followed the sound of piano music to the lounge. When she got there she saw a blonde teenage girl sitting on the stool next to Kyle playing the most sublime music she'd ever heard. He looked enchanted and for a moment she was captivated too, but the girl stopped suddenly and turned to face her, breaking the spell. She gave Meg a weak smile and nudged Kyle, in a way so familiar that Meg felt like an intruder.

'Hey Meg,' he said, as if it was the most natural thing in the world to find a beautiful girl sitting so close to your husband. Meg gave him a quizzical look so he said, 'This is Candy.'

The girl stood up and held out her hand, 'Candy Cane,' the girl said in a voice that suited the sticky sweet name, but Meg didn't shake her hand, instead she addressed Kyle, knowing that the best way to hurt the young girl was to pretend she didn't matter. 'Why are Loretta and Jane not here? Their cars aren't outside.'

'Jane's gone home,' Kyle said, 'and I thought we could get take-out so I gave Loretta the night off. Candy just dropped by so I could hear this song.' The way he looked at Candy suddenly brought back words she had heard Clare say *then he moves on to his next project.* She'd known for weeks, she supposed, and had ignored it. She had let Joey sleep between them in the bed so she didn't have to confront her feelings, but deep down she knew that she'd been kidding herself into believing that Candy Cane were a band, it didn't surprise her for a moment that they were one young, pretty blonde.

Had they been like this, she wondered, casually building a relationship under Clare's nose, with '*Meg can join us for dinner',* and *'I just need to speak to Kyle about this.'* She'd asked the lawyer to draw up contracts for WattAge so that the bands would have to give something back, making the studios less dependent on Kyle's goodwill. And for a couple of weeks she'd carried the paperwork in her bag waiting for a good time to broach it with Kyle and get his signature. But then she would have to admit that she'd taken his place at WattAge, and finally question where he had been when he had pretended to be there. Now the answer was before her, and another question jumped to the front of her mind.

'If Jane's gone home where's Joey?'

Kyle pointed towards the next room. 'With Ruby.'

'Is he?' Meg said, her mind immediately replaying the scene she had watched through the window, and finding him missing. Without registering that her feet were moving she was in the family room. 'Ruby, where's Joey?'

Ruby twirled round and shrugged her shoulders.

Meg ran out into the hallway, 'Joey?' she shouted, 'Joey?'

Kyle came into the hallway from the lounge and casually walked towards her. 'He can't have gone far — he was with her a minute ago.' But Meg felt sick, *he's not there now.* Her nerves bristled, she saw her old mustard door in front of her, felt the fear she used to have coming home from school and having to open it. At the end of the hallway she saw a curtain sway in the draught.

The door to the garden should not be open.

Her mind processed the facts.

The gate to the pool should not be open.

She felt bile rise.

A small body should not be in the pool.

Bobbing.

For a split second an invisible force held her back, like all of nature was telling her not to go on, but she pushed through it, jumped into the pool and let out a primal roar.

She flipped Joey over. Snatched him into her arms. The gardener jumped over the fence on one side of the pool, and Kyle appeared on the other. 'Phone an ambulance,' Kyle screamed. 'Give him to me, Meg.' She waded to the side, lifted her arms and felt Kyle take the limp body from her. Heard Kyle beg as he pumped his lungs, 'Joey, come on Joey mate, can you hear me? Breathe for daddy.' Watched Kyle try to breathe life back into him. Saw Candy put down the phone. Heard her pray. 'Oh my God, Oh my God.' A tiny fragment of her brain registered a bikini discarded by the pool. But her attention focused again on the nightmare in front of her, Joey lying blue on the tiles. Kyle sobbing.

9th of Nov 1990

Meg had taken the tranquillisers the doctor had left and a couple extra, courtesy of Zed, so as she sat in the limo following the hearse all she knew was that her left shoe was rubbing her toe. She could feel the start of a corn and knew that if only she could be bothered, she should take the shoes off and throw them out the window.

But her shoes were still on when she got to the church and she and Kyle stood behind the little white coffin. It didn't need six strong men to carry it, only one, and she watched as he bent his knees and lifted it into his arms. She walked behind, felt the hands of Val and Eleanor on her elbows as they took her weight and guided her to the front pew. It had been a long time since Meg had been in a church, but she knew all the rituals and complied. The high ceiling was meant to provide a sanctuary from the soaring outside temperatures, but it felt cold and unwelcoming. She pulled her jacket more tightly round her and squirmed along the pew to steal some body heat from Val.

People sang and the priest talked, with words like *tragedy* and *grief* spiking through the muffled sound. Meg kept her eyes fixed on the coffin. She looked at the twirl of the handles; the carving of angels on the panels; the blue kangaroo which Ruby had insisted go on top. But she couldn't think about her baby's body inside nestling in the satin. He always had a sheen of sweat on his little head. Maybe he'd gone to the pool to cool off. Was he cold now, she wondered.

She thought she might throw up.

Ruby pulled her hair and Meg turned and lifted her away from Suzie. Then she sat with Ruby in her arms, holding on tight, rocking her to the music while everyone else stood. Kyle's black suit remained in her peripheral vision, she could see he was crumpled but she couldn't begin care.

A crowd of onlookers had gathered outside, but stayed on the other side of the churchyard railings and kept their cameras unobtrusively low. TV crews filmed, but only Wayne provided them with a comment.

They lowered Joey into the ground in a graveyard next to the ocean on a day far too beautiful for a funeral. Meg looked out across the rows of headstones and monuments and wished that the sky would turn grey and that the heavens would open and nature would match the misery she felt. There was movement in front of her. Val let out a strangled sob and was steadied by Kyle as she stepped up to the grave to say her final farewell. Then she thrust out her hand, found Meg's and led her daughter forward to drop her rose on top. Meg wobbled and Val put her arm around her and held her back so she couldn't fall into the grave with him. One by one the mourners stepped forward with a flower or a poem or a sod of earth, until the undertaker gently moved them back to their waiting cars.

At the house Meg ignored Eleanor's insistence that the guests had to be acknowledged and went to lie down. She was vaguely aware of her door opening and a figure standing in it, once Val, another time Suzie, but when she finally woke the house was quiet.

She looked at the clock, 8 p.m., hopefully everyone would be gone, but as she walked down the stairs she heard voices.

'I knew she was trouble from the moment I saw her,' she heard Eleanor say, then Kyle's low tones which she couldn't decipher. She opened the door to the formal lounge. The curtains and windows were closed despite the heat and if the air conditioning was on it didn't stop Meg feeling suddenly very hot as everyone in the room turned to stare at her.

'Well, here she is now,' Eleanor said, and Meg couldn't figure out why her tone had changed so dramatically from sympathy to vitriol.

Meg looked around the room — only those closest remained, but the atmosphere was less than friendly — Suzie, Zed, Val, Eleanor and pacing the room, Kyle.

'What's wrong?' Meg asked, hoping for a minute that someone would tell her there had been a mistake and Joey wasn't really dead. Maybe a neighbour's child had fallen.

'We're keeping Ruby,' Suzie said in a matter-of-fact way that brought with it a terrible chill.

'Ruby?' Meg remembered the nanny quietly taking her from Meg in the church, whispering that a graveyard was no place for a child. She'd let her go without a fuss, let her take her child, let them take her children. 'Where is she?' Meg screamed. 'Where's Ruby?'

‘At our house,’ Suzie said, dismissing Meg’s anxiety. ‘I sent them there earlier, when you were in your bed.’ It sounded accusatory, like Meg was having an indulgent nap. ‘We’re having papers drawn up.’

Meg closed her eyes and wondered for a minute if she was still asleep and this was the continuation of a week-long nightmare. None of what Suzie said made any sense, so she looked at Zed for an explanation.

‘I thought Kyle would look after her better than me,’ Zed said after a long pause, ‘that’s why I’ve never made an issue of it before. But now, maybe it’s better she’s with us.’

‘Oh God,’ Meg said sinking to her knees.

Kyle came and stood in front of her and when she looked in his face she saw a murderous rage. ‘You got to be so sanctimonious today, didn’t you? Blaming me for what happened to Joey, poor little Meg, and all this time there’s been a cuckoo in the nest.’

Meg felt her world disintegrate, ‘No Kyle, honestly,’ she said.

‘“*Honestly*”, do you hear her?’ Suzie said. ‘It’s all here in black and white.’ Suzie lifted the large notebook that had been lying on her knee — one of an ever-changing series that Zed used as his journals.

Meg heard Zed say ‘I’m sorry Meg,’ and he began to cry and pull at his hair.

‘Just because he’s written something down doesn’t make it true,’ Meg said, beginning to see a way out. ‘My God, Zed was so smacked up that you can't believe anything he wrote. Tell them Zed.'

But it was Suzie who continued, 'you know when Ruby was born everyone said she looked so like Kyle, but do you know, I never thought that.' Meg looked at her, trying to face her down, but Suzie was more determined. 'I've got pictures of Zed as a baby. I could show them to you — the family resemblance is remarkable.'

Meg brushed away a tear before it fell onto the floor and whispered, 'You're wrong.'

Suzie got to her feet and put some distance between herself and Meg. Then she walked over to the window and pulled back the curtains giving an opportunity for the press pack below to get a photo. 'I'm not wrong. I've always known. I can't believe I ever felt sorry for you, but you know for such a scrawny little thing, you really know how to cause trouble.' She looked directly at Meg.

'Trust me, Ruby is Kyle's daughter.' Meg looked between Kyle and Suzie in the vain hope that one of them would believe her.

'Prove it,' Kyle said.

'You can't ask me to do that. Please just trust me.'

'Okay,' Kyle said, 'so tell me you weren't shagging Zed nine months before you had Ruby.'

'Leave her alone,' Zed snapped. 'I've done a test — Ruby's mine. You don't need to know anything else.'

'So what?' Kyle said, 'I bury my son and now you want to take my daughter?'

'It shouldn't be too hard to prove that Meg's an unsuitable mother,' Suzie said, 'There are enough witnesses here for a start.'

'Now wait a minute, you,' Val said, as she jumped forward and squared up to Suzie. 'No one says that about my girl. She's been a brilliant mum.'

'What would you know?' Suzie said. 'You're hardly an expert.'

But Zed pulled Suzie away, 'Come on, leave it to the lawyers,' he said.

'You can't take my baby,' Meg sobbed.

'Well you're in no fit state to look after her,' Suzie said. She pointed an accusing finger at Kyle, 'and he doesn't want her. Now come on Zed.'

The last modicum of energy oozed from Meg, but Val screamed after the slammed door. 'Ruby's our wean and nobody is taking her.'

Kyle turned to Meg again. 'Has my world not fallen apart enough this week without this shit resurfacing?'

Meg shuddered. 'Resurfacing?' she said.

Kyle looked at her with sheer hatred. 'Do you really think that Zed never bragged about how he got you into bed? Do you think he never winked at me every time he played with Ruby? He knew she was his, and so did I. I knew it from the minute you were pregnant.'

'What?' She had lied to herself about for years, but now Kyle was saying that he always knew. 'Why did you never say?' she said very quietly, still not wanting to admit it was true.

'I suppose I tried to believe she was mine, even though it was obvious she wasn't.'

'You've known all this time?'

'You know the stupid bit? I dreaded you telling me. I thought that if we both kept quiet then it would be fine. I felt so guilty about you losing the baby — thought that if I'd been with you that night instead of drinking myself stupid, you wouldn't have run off and none of this would have happened. I thought you deserved another chance, and Ruby deserved a father.'

'She still does,' Meg said, but she was no longer sure which one would be best for her.

'Get up Maggie,' Val said as she jerked Meg onto her feet 'those bastards aren't keeping her.' She guided Meg to the door and out to her hire car, pushing her head down and into the passenger seat.

Meg knew her mum had been drinking since breakfast but she didn't care if the journey was to end with a rock-n-roll tree. But before Val could get into the car Graham appeared and took the keys from her.

'You, intae the back. Meg, where we going hen?'

As he revved the engine Meg focused. She gave Zed's address and whispered, 'Please God let her be there.' She felt Val's hand lightly on her shoulder.

Graham followed the signs as much as he could, but had to stop a couple of times to ask for directions and look at the map. He had barely pulled up when Val sprang out of the car and ran up to Zed's door banging furiously on it.

The door was opened cautiously by Jane, who tried to shut it again the minute she saw Val, but despite being a fraction of her height, Val was a she-wolf. She pushed the nanny aside and ran into the house.

A few minutes later she walked back out shaking her head just as a taxi stopped outside the house and Suzie and Zed got out.

Meg stepped out of her car and raced towards them. 'Where is she?'

'Do you really think we would be so stupid as to bring her here?' Suzie sneered.

'You bitch,' Meg screamed and she flew at her, arms and legs flaying, grabbing for hair, scratching for eyes. 'Where's my baby, you bitch. Where's Joey?'

But Zed grabbed her before she could inflict serious damage on Suzie.

'That's why we took R-U-B-Y, not Joey, you mad cow,' Suzie said, getting in Meg's face, 'to keep her safe. You've already killed one kid — you're not killing Zed's too.'

'Tell them it wasn't my fault, Mum. Tell them,' Meg pleaded.

'Ruby's not here, pet. I checked. She's not here,' Val said quietly, taking Meg from Zed's arms and into her own. She led her towards the car again and watched as Graham helped her inside. Then Val turned back to Zed and Suzie. 'We're going to the polis, do you hear me. This is kidnap. We'll git you two put in the jail.'

'Just try it.' Suzie said, but Zed kept his eyes firmly on Meg.

ALL THE PAIN I'VE EVER FELT !!!!!!!!!!!!!!

Meg didn't know where Kyle spent the night, but he was nowhere to be seen when she got up at 10am. The women who ran the house, — Loretta, and since she had arrived from Glasgow, Val — busied about the ground floor, but there was no Jane, no Ruby.

She picked at a croissant for breakfast and every time she looked up Val's face was set with more determination. 'We'll get her back. They can't take her, Meg, you can't let them.'

But Meg was too exhausted to even think about trying to find her lawyer's number. She went back upstairs without responding, opened the window wide in the en suite and pulled down the blind, letting it flap in the breeze. She turned the taps on full and took some bath oil she had had made in Grasse from the cabinet and poured it into the bath. The porcelain hugged her shoulders but despite the soothing colours and textures of the natural stone her head churned.

She leaned forward, pulled up her knees, and looked at herself reflected in the large chrome overflow cover. She'd made such a mess of her life. She hunched more, feeling a physical pain in her chest before she pulled herself out of the bath, wrapped herself in a towel and went to dig out her camera. It was all she knew how to do. The only thing she had never mucked up. She eased herself back into the warm water and picked the camera off the floor. She positioned her body so she was reflected back, keeping her nipples covered and her face and camera out of the frame. She moved again, rising up so that only an image of her stretched marked stomach appeared dotted with water from the chrome. Finally she put the camera on the ledge at the side of the bath, adjusted its position with some towels and set the self-timer. This time she appeared in the sequence letting her face display the grief she felt. When she was finished she ducked under the water and held her breath.

By the time she had dried herself and put on a cotton robe she felt clammy again, so she opened the blind, stuck her head out of the window and listened to the birds.

Zed was sitting on the edge of her bed when she opened the en suite's door. 'Shit.'

'Sorry,' he said, 'I didn't mean to startle you, but your mum said you were up here.' Meg pulled her robe tight around her. 'You've been in there for ages. I was starting to worry in case…' his voice trailed off.

Meg went over to her chest of drawers and pulled some knickers on under her robe. She could hear voices in the garden, workmen to fill in the pool, so she put her back to the window and faced Zed. He sat watching her, his eyes locked with hers, then down to her body, imploring. She grabbed a dress and went into the en suite, locking the door behind her. She took her time, pulling her hair into a loose knot, rubbing at the puffiness around her eyes, but he was still there when she came out.

'Kyle will kill you if he finds you here,' Meg said, wondering if he actually would.

'I wanted to apologise for yesterday,' Zed said, hands clasped between his knees. 'I didn't know what Suzie had planned.'

Meg sat down on a pale blue winged chair at the window and watched as Val set out a teddy bears' picnic for little Graham in the garden below. She twisted to look at Zed. 'You can't have her,' she said plainly.

'It's complicated Meg,' he said sadly, 'more than you know.'

'How could it possibly be more complicated?' Meg asked.

'Suzie can't have kids.'

'I thought she didn't want them?'

'We didn't. She even said I shouldn't see Ruby after she saw how attached I was becoming to her in Italy. But then well, Suzie had had some abortions, and I don't know if it was that or, they say maybe chlamydia, but one way or another she's knackered. She wants a kid now, and she can't have her own, so she thinks mine will do. She wants someone to look after.'

'Ruby's not a doll she can dress up,' Meg said, remembering all the stupid outfits Suzie had bought her. 'Ruby's mine.'

'Ours,' Zed said.

Meg tried to process her conflicting thoughts before she spoke. Maybe Ruby would be better off without her. She'd had her chances with three children and she had ended up with none. Tears ran down her cheeks unchecked. Everything had seemed so perfect when she married Kyle. She had been so happy to give Ruby a father, but maybe, she thought, she had neglected to be a mother. She let out a sob. Kyle hadn't spoken to her for weeks before she had got pregnant and she might never have gone back to him if she hadn't slept with Zed. She had constructed a man who would protect them, but she had closed her mind to the fact that he had never loved her. She looked over at Zed. He'd been there for her when Kyle wasn't; he was here now. She nodded, 'our child.'

'I want to be part of her life,' Zed said after a few minutes in silence.

'You always have been,' Meg replied, 'you always will be.'

'More,' he said.

'Did you really do a test?' Meg asked.

Zed nodded, 'She's mine.'

'Why now, Zed? Why did you never say before?'

'Do you know why they call me Zed?' he asked.

'What's that got to do with it?' Meg asked. All she wanted to do was sit and think about Joey. All she wanted to do was hold Ruby in her arms.

'Pretty much everything,' Zed said.

'Suzie said it was because you were at her centre.'

'Did she?' Zed laughed as though it was the most pathetic thing he'd ever heard. 'I was called Zed before I met her. No,' he said, his voice serious and quiet, 'it was because of the accident.'

‘What accident?’ Meg asked, but he didn’t reply immediately and Meg saw that he was trying to compose himself.

‘I used to be a lifeguard,’ he said pointing to the red and yellow swimming cap tattooed on his forearm, ‘but I fell asleep. Kyle thought it was some big joke, Zzzs, you know. But a girl nearly died.’

‘What’s this got to do with Ruby?’ Meg asked.

‘We’d been playing the pubs at night, driving home in the early hours and then I’d be on duty the next day, when I really shouldn’t have been. I was normally hungover and in the heat I sometimes dozed off. Normally it was okay, but this day I heard people shouting and I saw that there was someone too far out and they were really struggling. I should have called for help first, but I just ran down the beach and started swimming.’

‘Did you get to her in time?’ Meg asked.

‘No, that’s the thing, Kyle got to her first. He was in a motor launch he’d rented that summer, and he saved her. He was the one with the resources to get to her. Don’t you see — he’s held it over me ever since.’

‘That was so long ago,’ Meg said as she moved over to the bed and sat beside him. ‘Why should it matter now?’

‘I knew I was her dad Meg, but I thought Kyle would keep her safe. He was always so much more together than me.’ Meg rubbed his back as he slumped forward. ‘But I can’t trust him with her now.’

‘You know the worst of it, Zed,’ Meg said, ‘every time I close my eyes I can feel the panic Joey felt. I know how much he would have struggled and…’

‘It wasn’t your fault Meg.’

‘My mum keeps ranting about how Kyle’s to blame, but none of that matters — my baby’s dead.’ Meg said the words, but couldn’t really believe them. She still hoped that Joey would prove her wrong and crawl into the room being chased by a squealing Ruby. ‘Maybe we’re being punished.’

‘God’s not that cruel,’ Zed said, but he jerked his head around, responding to a creak in the hall.

Meg followed his gaze, and saw Kyle in the doorway.

‘What the fuck is he doing here?’ Kyle said, anger seething out of every pore.

‘I’m just leaving,’ Zed said.

‘You’re not wrong.’

Zed squeezed Meg’s knee, and went towards the door. ‘I’ll look after her,’ Zed said to Kyle, but Kyle ignored him, and let him leave.

Kyle didn’t speak, and Meg listened as Zed closed the front door, started his car engine and drove off. Meg looked at her husband. There was bitterness tucked in his face lined with grief, and Meg knew there was no way back.

‘Just go,’ he said eventually. All the words he needed to end a marriage.

'He was here to talk about Ruby,' Meg said, feeling she had to defend Zed.

'Do you think I care?'

'No, Kyle,' Meg said, 'I don't think you ever did.'

Meg took an overnight bag out of her wardrobe, threw in some underwear and a couple of clean T-shirts and checked in to the Sydney Hilton. Val stayed for a while, but as days turned into weeks she went home.

'Come back with me,' she said, but she didn't argue when Meg said, 'I can't desert her.'

Without Val and little Graham to cajole her she rarely left the suite, simply lying on the bed staring at the folds in the curtains, she was no better than Val, no better than her own father. But three times a day there would be a knock at the door, and a waiter would unbidden lay out a meal, and she would rouse herself enough, for her children, to eat it.

On the Tuesday before Christmas the phone rang. It took a while before Meg converted the sound into a need for action, but it was persistent and she finally lifted it.

'Hey Meg — it's Jay.'

'Who?' Meg said, although the voice seemed so familiar.

'My real name's Jay,' Zed said. 'I've decided to go back to it. I'm not going to be defined by them anymore, not by Suzie, or Kyle.'

'Oh,' Meg said. She felt Maggie rise up suddenly from within her, but she was so diluted now that she was easily put away. 'How's Ruby?' she asked, her voice croaked through lack of use.

'That's why I'm calling,' Jay said. Meg gasped, but he continued, 'she's missing you. She cries for you every day. She's only sleeping because she's too exhausted to stay awake.'

'I know how she feels,' Meg said very quietly.

'Suzie can't cope. She's drinking again,' Jay said, very definitely. 'Ruby won't calm down for her, and she's blaming me for not taking her sooner.'

'I don't know what you want me to do,' Meg said, already exhausted by the conversation. 'I've got nothing to give her. Kyle's filed for divorce, cut Ruby off without a penny.'

'You've got everything she needs,' Jay said.

Sorrow engulfed Meg. 'Except a father,' she said.

'I've thought about that Meg, that's why I'm at the airport with her.'

'What airport?' Meg said, suddenly alert, her feet hitting the floor. 'Don't take her from me.'

'God Meg, no, I'm not.' His voice was calm, soothing. 'I want you to come — for it to be just the three of us. I've left Suzie — I can't let the past dictate what happens next.'

'And what does happen next?' Meg asked, feeling, in the question, her sorrow replaced by a freedom she'd never known.

'We leave.'

'Go somewhere we've never been?'

‘I don’t care Meg,’ he said. ‘Will you come?’

Meg nodded, ‘Yes,’ she said. She looked down at the creased, dirty clothes she had slept in, and none of it mattered. All that mattered was Ruby and Zed. ‘I’ll be there as soon as I can.’

‘Take your time,’ he said with relief in his voice, ‘We’ll wait.’

Acknowledgements

I would very much like to thank all the people who help me get to a point where this book was ready to publish. To my family, especially Gerry, Tony, Helen and Liam for supporting me along the way with chocolate, coffee and 'is that book not finished yet?' To Janice Galloway and the wonderful Glasgow Faber Academicals who helped enormously with Meg's birth. To the G2 Writers for their continued support. To all the readers of early drafts, too numerous to name, but including my book group and other friends, who gave me really useful feedback.

My research was also helped by Stevie, Jamie and the rest of Rebel 69 who let me watch their rehearsals, Stan at the Barrowlands who gave me a guided tour (including the roof) and answered all my questions. To Eddie from the late great Glasgow Apollo. And to Gabby Hancock for final draft advice. And of course to all the handsome drummers, bassists, guitarists, keyboard and singers who inspired me to write this novel.

About The Author

Colette Coen is from Glasgow where she still lives with her husband and three kids. She graduated from Glasgow University with an Honours Degree in English Literature and worked as a librarian and lecturer before giving it all up to work in a supermarket and concentrate on writing. She has been published widely in print and online and won the Waterstones Crime in the City Writing Competition in 2012. In 2010 she completed a Novel Writing Course with the Faber Academy and this is her first novel. She still receives great support from fellow Faber Academy writers and others at the

G2 Writers' Group and wishes to thank them publicly along with Faber tutor Janice Galloway.

Colette's loves: chocolate; red wine; Muriel Spark; Margaret Atwood; Barbara Kingsolver; Umberto Eco (although she only understands about half); binge watching; Mad Men and Grayson Perry.

From the Author

I hope you enjoyed All the Places I've Ever Been. If you did I'd be grateful if you could post a rating and/or review (here or at Good Reads) and tell your friends, family and all the random folk you know on Facebook as, despite what people would have you believe, writers need to eat too.

To find out about my writing, and the life that conspires to get in the way of it, you can follow my blog at http://colettecoen.wordpress.com My short story collections The Chocolate Refuge and Five a Day are available as eBooks.

12964837R00205

Printed in Poland
by Amazon Fulfillment
Poland Sp. z o.o., Wrocław